SACRIFICE

Also by Sarah Singleton

CENTURY

Winner of the Booktrust Teenage Book Award
Highly Commended for the Branford Boase First Novel Award
Winner of the Dracula Society's Children of the Night Award

HERETIC

Sacrifice

Sarah Singleton

SIMON AND SCHUSTER

For Poppy

SIMON AND SCHUSTER
First published in Great Britain in 2005 by Simon & Schuster UK Ltd
A CBS COMPANY

Copyright © 2007 Sarah Singleton
Cover photograph © 2007 Simon Mardsen, www.marsdenarchive.com

The right of Sarah Singleton to be identified as the author of this
work has been asserted by her in accordance with sections 77 and 78
of the Copyright, Designs and Patents Act, 1988.

1 3 5 7 9 10 8 6 4 2

Simon & Schuster UK Ltd
Africa House
64-78 Kingsway
London WC2B 6AH

A CIP catalogue record for this book is available from the British Library

ISBN-10: 1-416-91708-X
ISBN-13: 978 1 416 91708 3

Printed and bound in Great Britain by Cox & Wyman, Reading, Berkshire

www.simonsays.co.uk

CONTENTS

Prologue

North Africa, 1890

Halls of stone. Endless days in the desert's furnace, long nights of aching cold.

The years, like waves, have beaten over my head, have lulled, choked and drowned me. But still I breathe. Still I endure. I'm not a man anymore, but a bag of broken bones, a web of clogged arteries and torn hide. I linger in forgotten places, a substantial ghost from a lost past. Now, at last, the tide of time is falling away.

Seven hundred years have passed. Seven centuries ago I was a young man caught in the fire of war and death. Hear, then, my confession. I stretched out my hand and acted without thought, conscience or compassion. And I have been punished – with life. This life is an excruciation. Each day, another barb in my skin.

Soon now. Soon you will know everything. The three will come.

1

Avondale
London, 1890

The carriage trundled through darkening London streets. It wended its way from the heart of the old city, from the black river, the docks, the accumulated centuries of stone. It rumbled over cobbled, airless soil, where generations of bones had powdered and the long-buried privies of the Jacobeans seeped. A veil of smoke covered the city. Above the rooftops, a last streak of burnt orange, and the night soaking down among the houses.

Miranda and her mother's maid, Marianne, were sitting side by side. Miranda gripped a cardboard case. The motion of the carriage had numbed her body, all the stopping and starting in the jostle of cabs and carts, the bumping on uneven roads. From time to time Marianne pursed her lips and tutted.

At last the hectic traffic began to thin, and the city streets joined wider suburban roads lined with red-brick villas, punctuated with trees.

'Make sure you're well behaved, Miss Miranda,' Marianne said. 'I know it'll come hard to you, seeing as you're so used to your mother's free and easy ways.' She sniffed, disapproving. Miranda didn't reply. She turned away from the maid, and stared into the distance, cold as a piece of ice. She sensed Marianne was eager to be rid of her now. This one last task, escorting her across London, was an irritating final duty. A new post awaited Marianne, in a big house, with a reliable wage.

Miranda sighed, and gazed through the window. Here the houses were stout and solid, three and four storeys, with stained glass and iron railings. These were the homes of prosperous bankers and businessmen. An aura of comfort and respectability pervaded. Marianne glanced out, and nodded approvingly.

'Don't forget to put your gloves on,' she said. 'Remember your manners, Miss Miranda. Don't speak unless you're spoken to. Things will be very different, in a place like this.'

The maid's voice and her litany of advice pricked like so many needles. Indeed, beneath the apparent concern, Miranda thought Marianne was positively gleeful at the prospect of her spoiled charge finally getting her comeuppance. As if she hadn't suffered enough. Following hard on the heels of this thought came an image of her mother shouting out, calling her name. Miranda closed her eyes and threw her head back. She drummed her heels against the wooden seat.

'Shut up,' she said abruptly, without looking at the maid. 'Shut up, Marianne.'

Marianne was stunned into silence. Miranda had always been quiet. Wayward yes, indulged and brought up with a loose hand – but never forthright or aggressive. Miranda felt a fleeting pleasure at the maid's response, at her power to shock.

More seemingly identical streets passed the window, now illuminated by street lights. At last the carriage drew up in front of a villa with a powder blue door and a fanlight bordered with red stained glass. The path from the gate to the door was paved with red and cream tiles, and a lavender bush grew in the narrow front garden. Miranda was pleased with the place. It looked inviting, after all. The name, carved on the stone gatepost, was Avondale.

'Here it is,' Marianne said. Miranda glanced at the maid, and nodded.

'This is it, then,' Marianne added. 'Time to say goodbye.'

Miranda swallowed hard, an impediment like a lump of dough lodged in her throat.

'We've been part of each other's lives a long time,' Marianne said. 'I've watched you growing up, Miss Miranda. Don't think I won't miss you.' Her voice wavered, as though she were close to tears.

Miranda squeezed her eyes shut. She hadn't cried before, and she didn't want to cry now. Perhaps, she thought, it would satisfy Marianne if she did. She imagined Marianne telling her new employer, smugly, how much she was loved, how the daughter at her old place had wept to see her go. But if Marianne truly loved her, why was she letting them take her away? So many excuses had been offered, but if she was like a daughter to her, why hadn't Marianne found a way?

Miranda bit her lip and quelled the urge to cry. She climbed out of the carriage, still clutching her case. Marianne stepped out behind her, and fussed as the driver unloaded Miranda's box. Then she led Miranda up the tiled pathway and knocked on the door.

Above the house, a sickle moon was rising. Miranda leaned back on her heels, tipped her head back to look up at the stars. The door opened, but Miranda didn't look to see who had answered. Instead she swivelled on her heels and contemplated the sky, the darkness putting out the final embers of the day. What did it matter? There was nothing she could do now. When her mother had gone, unknown people exchanged telegraphs and it was settled she should stay with her grandparents – people she had never met before. Like a bundle of old clothes, like rubbish, dropped on the doorstep of strangers. She was unwanted, certainly, and probably unwelcome.

'Miranda. Miranda!' Marianne hissed. With a sigh Miranda

turned around. A servant stood in the doorway, a short, round woman in the uniform black dress and white pinafore. She glanced at Miranda, gave her a quick smile.

'Come in,' she said. Miranda crossed the threshold, looking at her feet. The driver stepped forward with the box, and dropped it in the tiled hallway at the bottom of the stairs.

'Won't you come in and have a drink before you go?' the servant said to Marianne. On the doorstep, Marianne gave a little wriggle. Perhaps she was tempted.

'No, thank you,' she said. 'I must be off. I have a new position, you see. Another journey.'

The servant nodded kindly. 'Very well.'

From the corner of her eye, Miranda saw Marianne beckon, and the two women put their heads together. She couldn't hear what was said, except at the end as Marianne drew away:

'She's a cold child. Very cold. Not a tear for her mother, and none for me either. And I've been like a mother to her.' This was issued in a whisper she was, perhaps, intended to hear.

'Goodbye, Miss Miranda,' Marianne called brightly, over the servant's head. 'Good luck, my dear. Be a credit to me, and to your poor mother.'

Miranda squeezed her mouth shut, and refused to look at the maid. They had been friends once, so she thought. But everything was different now.

Marianne hurried away, and the servant pushed the door to. For a moment they stood together, the two of them. When Miranda raised her eyes she saw the woman was still smiling kindly.

'Miss Miranda,' she said. 'My name is Mrs Norton, and I'm the housekeeper here. I'll show you to your room. Have you eaten? I'll bring you some supper on a tray. Your grandparents want to meet you, of course. When you've washed and changed, I'll take you to the parlour. Don't worry about the trunk now, Smith will bring it up later.'

Miranda nodded numbly and followed the housekeeper upstairs. She was escorted to a plain bedroom with a single bed. Mrs Norton lit the gas light on the wall and a warm, yellow glow fell upon an embroidered picture above the headboard. It said: The Lord is My Shepherd. This statement seemed more a threat than a comfort, because the embroidery was decorated with iron-grey crooks, interwoven like a prison gate.

'I'll leave you to settle in,' Mrs Norton said. She looked at Miranda a moment or two longer.

'It may not be as bad as you think,' she said, stretching out her hand to touch Miranda's arm. She closed the door gently, and Miranda was left standing on her own, still gripping the handle of her suitcase. She closed her eyes, and took three deep breaths. Sometimes, these last days, she found it hard to breathe. She had to force herself, stretching ribs tight as barrel bands. At last she unfurled her fingers, and placed the case on the bed. The quilt caught her eye. In the plain room, it was a riot of colour. Patches of so many sizes and shapes, scraps of luscious velvet and shiny silk, crimson, emerald, antique gold, and embellished with bits of ribbon, diamonds of patterned fabric, beads and mirrors. Miranda stretched out her fingers to touch it. How beautiful it was! Her mother would have loved it.

This sobering thought drew her up short. Miranda turned her regard from the quilt and opened the suitcase. There was little enough inside. A shawl, her journal, a silver-backed hairbrush and comb, a nightgown and three blouses, all of them a little small for her now. And right at the bottom, wrapped in a black silk scarf, a pack of tarot cards. These Miranda stroked, before she stuffed them, along with the journal, under the mattress. She would find a better hiding place soon enough. This would have to do for now. Finally, at the bottom of the case and tucked in a tear in the lining, a single black and white photograph. Slowly Miranda drew it out. Contained in a silver frame, it was a picture of her mother. She forced herself to look at it.

Julia Maysfield. Her shoulders and throat were bare, except for a string of pearls. Her lush, black hair was pinned up and decorated with a jewelled comb. She had a warm, brilliant smile. And she was beautiful. Miranda ran a fingertip over her mother's face, and raised the picture to her lips.

Someone rapped on the door, and Miranda instantly dropped the picture onto the bed. Mrs Norton stepped in, manoeuvring a tray.

'Some soup,' she said. 'There's a little bread and a slice of Dundee cake for you too, and a cup of tea with plenty of sugar. You look as though you need lots to eat.'

The housekeeper placed the tray on a table beside Miranda's bed. Her eyes fell upon the picture, lying face up on the bed. Miranda, with a pang, wanted to grab it and hide it away, but it was too late now. Mrs Norton gestured.

'May I?' she said. Miranda gritted her teeth, but she nodded. What else could she do? Mrs Norton picked up the precious picture.

'She's a beautiful woman,' she observed. 'And you look a little like her. Though there's something of your father about you too. In your eyes especially.'

Mrs Norton gazed at the picture a little longer.

'I think it might be wise to keep it in your drawer,' she said gravely. 'Out of consideration for your grandparents. Keep it to yourself.'

Miranda didn't answer. Instead she unpinned her hat and placed it on the bed beside her gloves. Mrs Norton took the picture to a chest of drawers and dropped it in the top drawer. Then she picked up the three small blouses and put them over the picture.

'Eat up,' she said. 'Your grandparents want to see you in ten minutes.'

They were sitting bolt upright, side by side on a red velvet couch beside the fire. John Kingsley had a newspaper in his hand. Eliza Kingsley held a piece of embroidery – perhaps a companion piece to the one on Miranda's wall. The room was overwhelmingly red, with patterned wallpaper and enormous plaster cornices, and a ceiling rose the size of a cartwheel, from which an elaborate golden gas lamp depended. The walls were covered with paintings and mirrors. A forest of framed photographs crowded the lid of a baby grand piano in the corner.

Miranda stepped into the centre of the room, her hands folded in front of her, and they regarded each other. The unwanted granddaughter. The unknown and obligated grandparents. Despite herself, Miranda had to suppress a mad urge to giggle. How preposterous they were, these two, so stiff and hidebound.

Mrs Kingsley spoke first, tucking her needle away and laying the embroidery to one side.

'Miranda,' she said, studying her granddaughter all the while, summing her up. 'How old are you?'

'I'm just fourteen,' Miranda said.

'Fourteen!' Mrs Kingsley repeated. 'You don't look as old as that. You're not very well grown. Twelve, I would have guessed.' She turned to her husband. 'She is very small for her age. Very thin too. And I don't like her complexion. Sickly-looking, I think.'

Mr Kingsley cleared his throat. He looked Miranda up and down.

'I can't see anything of David in her at all,' he said. 'Such pale hair she has. Colourless. Like a dead fish! Still,' he added more gently, perhaps remembering she was listening to his analysis, 'something might be made of her yet. She's young, Eliza. You know how these girls are. It's a difficult age.'

Miranda lowered her eyes and dug her fingernails into the soft skin of her palm. Mrs Kingsley sighed. She was dressed in a tight black dress with large drops of jet hanging from her ears. David, her son, and Miranda's father, had been killed in

North Africa three years before and Mrs Kingsley was still in mourning.

Unfortunately for Miranda and her grandparents, David and Julia had never married. Miranda, for so long unacknowledged by the Kingsleys, was a disfiguring stain on their precious family virtue. She was the shameful secret they had ignored for fourteen long years. Now here she was, in the heart of the profoundly respectable home, and they could turn a blind eye no longer. Circumstances had thrust her upon them. No wonder they hated her. Despite the blazing fire, Miranda's hands were cold. She squeezed her nails deeper into her palm. She had nowhere else to go. She could only endure, and wait till her mother came back again.

Miranda's bed was cold, despite the heavy blankets. She had tried to pray, on her knees, before climbing between the smooth, white sheets, but the words wouldn't come. Instead her thoughts wandered to her mother, where she might be, what they were doing to her. Father in Heaven, her prayer began. But she didn't know how to continue. Surely God, who was all-knowing, would understand what her constricted heart was trying to articulate?

Then she lay in bed, stiff as a board, willing her cold limbs to warm. Distantly she could hear her grandparents moving around, preparing to go to bed. From time to time, the sound of horses' hooves clopping in the road and, far away, the shriek of a train whistle. Later, in the attic room above, she heard the muted voices of the two housemaids as they settled down for the night. Despite her exhaustion, sleep was elusive. Her mind wouldn't let go. She was taut as a wire. The night stretched out, a vast, black space, inhabited by countless tiny, isolated souls. She had no one to turn to.

Eventually she must have drifted off, into a shallow, fitful sleep. She dreamed, how sweetly, she was back at her aunt's country house. Miranda and her mother had spent a great deal of time at the house when she was young. Her aunt Mary was an intellectual, a free thinker, who supported Julia when many others had turned their faces from her. Such long, golden summers they spent at the country house. And it was the summer of her eighth birthday Miranda half dreamed, half remembered, as she lay in her cold bed in her grandparents' house.

The sun was declining behind a dusty hawthorn hedge. A little girl walked along the lane, kicking at the pale stones with the worn tips of her boots. The scuff and scuttle broke the evening's heated silence. Ahead, upon the hill, the air shimmered above the white road.

Under her arm Miranda carried a fat parcel of muslin. Passing a gateway, the sun flashed in her face. She stopped, lifting her hand to shade her eyes. A full-bellied yew tree almost obscured the grey church, rearing beyond the graveyard. Amid billows of hogweed, briar stems and yellow grass, headstones emerged, broken like driftwood. Two figures stood in the lake of shade beneath the yew tree. The little girl stepped up to the gate, and stared.

The gentleman wore a faded black frockcoat. His hands were thrust in the high pockets of his trousers, brass buttons blinking on his waistcoat. Beneath a top hat, bald at the seams, thick locks of dark grey hair reached to the top of a winged shirt collar. A lady, sitting quietly upon a listing sarcophagus, turned the pages of a little book upon her lap. She was curiously colourless. A white dress, a straw bonnet, a shawl of delicate pink.

Miranda climbed upon the gate's lowest bar to afford herself a better view of the strangers. The gentleman looked up. He called out.

'Excuse me, would you help?'

Miranda frowned.

11

'Do you know how far it is to the village?' the gentleman asked abruptly. He paced up and down. The sun caught a silver pin, bright like an eye in his cravat.

'Two miles, sir.'

The gentleman stamped in agitation. Upon the ground, beyond the sarcophagus, half a dozen boxes were heaped.

'The coach, it dropped us off too soon. How am I going to transport my equipment? Is this All Saints?' He waved the cane at the church.

'Yes, sir. But the village is further on. The old village was here, but a long time ago the water turned bad. They knocked it down. This is All Saints church. You should've said All Saints village.'

The gentleman turned away, and cursed. The girl continued to stare.

The lady smiled again.

'Would you send someone from the village, to collect us?' she said.

'Yes. Yes please,' the gentleman said. 'We're visiting the Maysfields. I'm a photographer and I have a commission. Do you know the family?'

Miranda put her hand to her mouth, suppressing a laugh.

'Yes I do,' she said. 'They live in the village.'

'Quickly then,' the man said. 'Can you run? Tell them to send a cart, for my equipment.' He gestured grandly to the pile of boxes.

Miranda clambered over the gate and ran along the white road, up the hill, and down again, towards the village. Powdery chalk rose in her wake, settling slowly. The thick heat pressed down. The road was silent again.

The next time Miranda saw the curious couple she had discarded her harum-scarum outdoor outfit and wore instead her best dress of bottle green velvet, with the wide silk sash. Her pale hair was neatly brushed and tied with a ribbon. Miranda

12

stepped into the room holding her mother's hand. The photographer was taken aback to see her. His wife laughed. In the drawing room the boxes had been opened, and a complex camera assembled. A large screen had been unfolded, bearing a painted scene, a view of exotic hills and forests. A cardboard pillar, like something from a Roman ruin, was posed as a prop.

'We meet again,' the photographer said gruffly. 'Why didn't you say who you were?' Perhaps he regretted his abrupt orders, now he realised she was a client.

It was a wonderful adventure. The photographer and his wife spent a day and night with them, setting up photographs of Julia, Miranda and her aunt. It was a painstaking process and boring at times, keeping still for the picture to be taken, trying not to jump when the light flashed. But they dressed in different outfits, posed and preened. The photographer took many shots – individual and group portraits, inside the house and out in the garden. Later, Mary invited the couple to dine with them and the photographer regaled them with tales of a travelling life and anecdotes about the famous people he had photographed, including, he boasted, the noted engineer Isambard Kingdom Brunel.

The photographs came in the post several weeks later. The postman delivered the large, sturdy parcel wrapped with brown paper and tied with string, bearing a Bristol postmark. Miranda, barefoot, dashed into the house calling for her mother.

'The pictures! They've come, they've come!'

Julia was still in her dressing gown, her hair tumbling over her shoulder, her skin perfumed with sleep and rosewater. Excitedly they sat at the table in the kitchen and began to tear open the packaging.

There were five photographs, including the stunning picture of Julia with a bare throat and string of pearls. Julia picked it up, thrilled to bits. Beneath it, they saw a fine picture of Julia and her sister Mary, and one of Mary standing before the painted screen, beside the Roman column. But where were the pictures of Miranda? They hunted through the pictures again, turning them over, sifting through the packaging.

'Perhaps they're sending them separately,' Julia reassured. 'Don't worry darling. Maybe they'll come tomorrow.'

But Miranda had a bad feeling. Something wasn't right. Eventually, beneath the card and paper, Julia unearthed a letter in an envelope. She pulled out a bill and an apologetic note from the photographer. She frowned as she read.

'What is it?' Miranda asked. 'Where are my photographs?'

'He says they didn't develop properly,' Julia said, scanning the words for a second time. 'I don't understand – how can that be? He says none of the photographs of you worked out.' She gave an abrupt sigh and dropped the letter on the table. 'He says he hasn't charged me for the photographs of you, but what good is that? I wanted a picture, Miranda. I wanted a picture of you to send to your father.'

Julia stretched out her hand, and placed the palm against her daughter's cheek. David was often away, travelling across Europe and North Africa, on business her mother said vaguely. But they both missed him dreadfully.

'I'm sorry,' Julia said. 'We'll try someone else.'

Miranda sighed and tears filled her eyes. She had longed to see the photographs. She picked up the envelope and one small picture fell out onto the table. It was a portrait of Miranda and her mother. Julia was sitting upon a chair and her daughter was leaning against her. The picture was perfect. Julia looked beautiful and wistful, staring into the distance. Her loose, dark hair contrasted against Miranda's pale locks. The photograph was crisp and cunningly composed – except for one curious feature.

Miranda's face was entirely blank.

Instead of portraying features, the oval of her face was an even grey blur. According to the letter this had happened in every single exposure. For some inexplicable reason, the camera entirely failed to register Miranda's face.

An empty space. A smooth grey nothing.
A void.

Miranda awoke with a start, gasping for air, as though a huge
weight were pressing on her chest, pinning her down. She
fought with the blankets, struggling to be free, kicking her legs
in a panic. The bedclothes slumped onto the floor, and Miranda
lay on the bed, burning hot and out of breath.

How late was it now? Hard to tell. Had she been asleep for
hours or minutes? The house was silent, but outside the ceaseless city noises continued, the trains and faraway factories.
Impossible to try and sleep now. She was often troubled by bad
dreams and was afraid to fall asleep again so soon, in case the
dream resumed. Instead Miranda climbed out of bed and pulled
out the silk-wrapped deck of cards she had hidden under the
mattress. She drew the curtain, so the dusty light from the
streetlamp fell upon the floorboards. Sitting cross-legged on the
floor, in the puddle of light, she peeled the black scarf from the
cards and began to shuffle them.

They were tarot cards, long and slim, with bold pictures in
red, blue and yellow. A summer ago, caught up in the craze for
Madame Blavatsky and the Theosophical Society and all things
arcane and magical, Julia and Mary had bought the cards and
spent a week or two constantly consulting them with great
enthusiasm but very little result. They were Miranda's cards now.

Her flush of heat had ebbed away, so Miranda pulled a blanket over her shoulders, and continued to shuffle. She closed her
eyes and let her thoughts spill away, shuffling the cards all the
while. It was a knack she had learned, emptying her mind, so a
dark space formed in her head as the train of thoughts faded.
The dark space expanded, becoming a long tunnel, and far
away at its end a bright light shone. The light beckoned, inten-
sifying as it drew near. Radiant, pearl white, the speck became
a jewel. The shape shifted constantly, casting a glitter all around

it, burning in Miranda's mind. In a trance, barely aware of her surroundings, she laid out ten cards in a circle on the floor. Her eyes still closed, she put the rest of the deck to one side.

The light receded, the tunnel pulling away. Quickly a flow of thoughts jostled in her mind, assaulting the empty space she had cleared for such a short space of time. Room, night, house, Marianne, grandparents, mother. Thoughts and worries swarmed. Miranda's eyes flicked open and she shivered, pulling the blanket closer. Then she studied the cards.

Her eyes skipped from one to another. It was a knack she had, a knack neither her mother or aunt possessed, to see the cards and the pattern in which they lay, to understand the relationship between them and knit together their vague, individual messages into some kind of whole. Still, it was an inexact ability. She couldn't predict the weather or answer a specific question about the future. Instead, the web of cards gave her a glimpse, now and then, of events still to come. It was as though a curtain were briefly drawn aside, so she could break away from the borders of her own mind and the present time, to see into the minds, and times, of others.

Miranda scanned the cards again, making connections. The Queen of Cups. The Tower, blasted by lightning. The Ten of Swords and the Knave of Rods. The Hierophant, a stern old man with his hands raised. Cataclysm and ruin. Sorrow and travel. A young man and a loving woman. The threads of the story wove together, creating a whole. Images rose up in Miranda's mind, vivid and bright with colour, but as random as a dream.

A woman in a dark suit on a train, smoking a cigarette.

Julia, all alone in a plain white room, tugging at her hair and whispering to herself.

A gawky boy walking upon a field of broken stone, by the sea. A man standing in the desert, his head shrouded in a black turban.

And last, a vision she feared, the back of a girl with long, tangled hair. The girl was sitting in a dark place, full of dust, and held a mirror in her hand.

Miranda gasped, tearing her eyes from the cards. Quickly she pushed them all together, wrapped them up, and stowed the cards beneath the mattress. She had seen nothing comforting, and her mother was as bad as could be.

2

Blackberries
The West of Ireland, 1890

A cluster of fat blackberries dangled on the whip of bramble stem just out of reach. Jack edged forwards, stamping down fierce, dusty nettles and the blades of dry grass, hand outstretched to grab them. Thorns scratched the skin beneath his wrist as he strained to reach. But it was no good. They were too far away.

The palm of his hand was sticky with blackberry juice, congealing in the creases. He looked at the forest of brambles and the jewels of berries on the barbed, iron tendrils. Plenty more, he thought. Enough to make a vat of jam, if only he could reach them.

Beyond the billows of bramble were the walls of the broken house. From his lowly position Jack could see a segment of wall, an empty window and a slide of roof where tiles gaped, letting in birds and weather. But he didn't want to see the house, not at all. Even these little glimpses made him shiver. The problem was, he needed blackberries and on the remote, inaccessible house side of the bramble mountain he suspected the fruit would be thick and ripe. For miles around, the hedgerows had been plundered by the village children, but none of them dared step into the shadow of the house. From their earliest days they were warned away. It was home to the village's store of ghosts, banshees, goblins, witches. If you're naughty the Old Man will get you, the mothers said. Or the bloodsucker, or the elf hag, or the servants of the devil himself, depending on the enthusiasms of the mother in question. At fourteen, Jack was too old for his mother to threaten anymore, and his belief in banshees was fading fast – but years of stories had laid deep foundations in the mind. Even grown men kept away from the old house.

It was late August, the air hot and oppressive. It had been a good year for blackberries, with all the rain in July making them good and fat, but Jack didn't have much time to collect them anymore. His father had left Ireland to work in London, and the running of the farm and the business had fallen to Jack. His little sister wasn't very well, and in the dark, fruitless winter months his ma loved blackberry jam so much, he couldn't let the season pass without getting a good lot. So he set off every evening, after tea. Probably his mother didn't know how far he walked, how many miles, how much he wanted to help and please her.

This was the fourth evening he had gone out with his basket, and now the pickings were sparse. If he could just get one more load, it would be enough. If he could just work up enough courage to go inside – if he could find an easy way into the grounds of the old house. He pictured the basket piled with fruit, the pleasure lighting up his mother's face. Then he stood up straight and drew his shoulders back. There was nothing else to be done.

The old house was about a mile outside the village, and close to the sea, above an island with a cairn on top. It was sur-rounded by a stone wall overwhelmed by trees, brambles and ivy. The iron gates at the front were locked, rust flaking from fancy curves and coils. Jack walked around the wall. The gate was his best chance for climbing, he thought, because the walls were defended by spiky brambles and slippery ivy. He would have to be careful of the spikes along the top. Jack wasn't tall for his age, but he was slim and wiry, his muscles strong from years of hard, physical work. And he was naturally dextrous, able to walk on his hands, to somersault and tumble, just like a circus performer. This climbing of a gate should not prove a problem in itself. Only fear would hold him back.

Jack stared through the gate. At the end of a short drive the house loomed. It was a big place, compared to the cottages in the village, but not as large as the houses he'd seen in the town. The old house was built of pale, sandy-coloured stone, stained with long violet shadows cast by the declining sun, with small mullioned windows, mostly broken. It had two floors, with steps leading to a big front door and the huge hole in the roof.

Jack tugged at the gate, making the loops of chain rattle. Beyond, swallowing the drive, the grass was thigh deep. Inside the garden a blackbird was singing. Another band of cloud covered the sun, and Jack reminded himself the gate would not be hard to climb, and wondered why he hadn't done so yet – and what he was waiting for.

But Jack had set himself the challenge and he wasn't going to back down. He took a deep breath, stepped back, and tossed the basket lightly over the gate, where it lodged in a bush. Thus committed, Jack told himself he had no alternative but to follow. Quick and limber, he climbed upon the gate and carefully hoisted himself over the spikes at the top. Then he jumped all the way down, landing lightly on his feet. Then he looked back the way he had come, the village just visible in a cleft of the hills. It was odd to be on the other side of the gate, looking out. Jack didn't give himself the chance to think about this too long. He grabbed the basket and headed for the hitherto hidden side of the blackberry bush.

The pickings were rich in the shadow of the old house. The blackberries were ripe and luscious, plentiful, easy to gather. Jack fancied the brambles leaned to his hand, eager to be plucked from the bush. Now he was a hero from one of his grandmother's stories, the likely lad stealing the forbidden fruit from the witch's garden. He enjoyed the sense of adventure. Within ten minutes or so the basket was piled high, and there were still plenty of blackberries left. It wasn't so bad here. Perhaps he would come again.

Now the job was done Jack didn't want to leave. The excitement of the adventure gripped him. The colours in the garden were curiously bright, his senses acute. Why not explore a bit, now he was here? Jack dropped the basket of fruit by the front gate, and skirted the house, beating a path through the overgrown garden. Here and there the more sturdy garden plants endured. He saw a huge, bent plum tree covered in bloated fruit, and marigolds, splashes of orange. A rambling rose had swallowed up a wooden summer house at the back of the garden.

As he walked, Jack was aware of the old house crouching beside him, the black eye-spaces of the windows. He bided his time, waiting for the right moment to make his approach.

The back door was skewed open on one rusty hinge. A faint draft emerged, cool and sweet, as though the house was breathing. Jack edged closer. He saw a tiled hallway, covered in dust and fallen plaster.

A pigeon flew out, in a mad clatter, and Jack jumped back in a panic. But he stepped closer again, lured by the hallway, wanting to see where the house might take him – what might be inside. He slipped through the angled door, rubble and plaster crunching underfoot. The house swallowed him up.

His eyes adjusted to the dim light. He tasted dust on his tongue. The tiled hallway ran right through to the front door, rooms leading off to left and right, and a staircase curved up to the first floor. Jack explored one room and the next. No furniture left, no paintings on the walls. Here and there fragments of the painted plaster mouldings on the ceilings survived, cherubs

21

and clusters of fruit. Dead leaves had accumulated in piles. Beetles and woodlice scurried from the dirt and rubble Jack disturbed with his feet. The place was too broken, too filthy and derelict to scare him anymore.

He glanced around the kitchen, and then made his way upstairs. At the top of the staircase he glimpsed the sky through the breach in the ceiling where the rain had poured in. The floorboards didn't lie straight, all warped and buckled by the damp. Jack trod a careful path to bedrooms beyond, but they were bare too, stripped of any furnishing, falling into ruin. The last room, at the end of the corridor, was the lightest, sunlight shining through an intact pane of glass.

Here stood an old iron bedstead, and beside it on a low cupboard, a ewer and basin. A huge cobweb, strands thick with dust, filled the loop of the jug handle. A stinking pile of mouldering clothes and blankets lay upon the mattress. He poked the unappetising heap. Tiny insects scuttled and a foul pocket of air puffed out. Then a clump of blankets fell to the floor with a damp thud – revealing a dead man.

A dead man.

Jack backed away, pressing his back against the wall. He couldn't believe it. A dead man.

The silence was oppressive now – as though the attention of the house was focused entirely upon the body on the bed. Jack looked around him in a panic, sensing a watcher, alert for a threat. All he could hear was the thunder of his own heart, and his breath, both intolerably loud to him, as though everyone could hear, all the ghosts and demons in the house.

The moments passed. The body remained where it was. No one jumped out to catch him and Jack struggled to overcome his sense of shock. Perhaps a vagrant had hidden out in the house and died here. It was nothing to be afraid of, a dead body. He'd seen them before, his grandmother laid out in a coffin before the funeral, the baby brother who hadn't made it to his third birthday. In the midst of life, death was all about them.

Jack crept back to the side of the bed, and steeled himself to look properly at the dead man. It wasn't such a surprise he hadn't noticed him at once. The man looked a part of the pile of hideous blankets, only his upper body and right arm visible among the mishmash of cloth. Probably the man had been dead for a long time, though for some reason, he hadn't decayed so much as dried out. The white skin on his face had shrunk against the skull. The eyes had fallen back into their sockets. The lips stretched back to reveal strong white teeth. The one visible hand was a tight glove of bones, skin thin as paper, revealing the complex puzzle of joints.

Jack leaned over and sniffed. The body didn't smell. He considered rifling in the man's pockets for some clue to his identity but could not quite brave himself to do it. He would have to tell someone. The body should be taken out and buried properly. Someone must know who the dead man was.

Jack wondered how old the man had been. The skin was so parched and strange it was very hard to tell. And he looked peaceful. There was no sign of violence, no indication how he had died. Unable to resist the temptation, Jack gingerly lifted the blanket from the corpse and folded it back. Tiny mites scurried, and the dust rose.

Not a tramp, no. The mystery was ever more intriguing. The clothes were grimy, but they once had been fine, fit for a gentleman. Beyond the window the leaves shifted, and the sunlight fell briefly upon the body. Something glistened at the throat. Jack stretched out his hand. It was a piece of gold, he thought. Could he take it without touching the skin of the dead man? Closer he drew, till his hand was hovering just above the chest. His fingers fluttered uneasily. The air seemed to shift in the room, as though the house was sighing. His fingers, a bare inch from the body, waited to do his bidding. Then Jack grasped the bead of gold.

In the same instant, a hand seized Jack by the wrist. The dead man – a grip like iron. Jack screeched and pulled away, his cry echoing around the empty house, sending the dust spinning. He struggled with every ounce of strength, trying to break away from the vice of the dead man's fingers, in a horrible panic. He couldn't see, couldn't think, threshing about in horror. How strong it was – even Jack's wildest struggles didn't shift the body on the bed.

The grip didn't yield and finally Jack exhausted himself. He was sat on the floor, his wrist in the air still encircled by the corpse's dry bony fingers. Jack gasped for breath. Shaking with terror he clambered to his knees and peered into the dead face.

The dark, hollow eyes were open. Bright blue eyes turned and fixed on Jack. In the decayed face, the shining eyes were hideous, monstrous. The old stories flashed in Jack's mind, the old man who drank the blood of children in the night, the devils on the roof, the elf hag.

'Let me go,' he said. His throat was dry. 'Let me go.' He tugged away again, stretched out his free hand for something to use, some kind of weapon.

The dead man still stared. Then the face convulsed horribly. The lips moved, the dry tongue shifting behind the teeth. Was it trying to speak?

'Let me go,' Jack said again, trying to be fierce.

The eyes blinked. A cough escaped the white lips. The man's chest began to rise and fall. The mouth flexed again. A tinge of colour rose into the face.

The man swallowed and swallowed again. He kept his eyes fixed on Jack, clinging on to him, as though he were drowning.

'Let me go,' Jack said, more gently now. 'I'll help you. I will. But let me go. Please. You're hurting me.'

The man opened his mouth.

'Who are you?' he whispered. The voice was stale and dry, hard to hear.

'Who are you?' the man repeated. His voice was stronger this time. 'A little thief. Come to steal from me.' The blue eyes flashed.

'I'm not a thief,' Jack said. 'I thought you were dead.'

The man half closed his eyes, and grinned, so the parchment skin became a web of creases. His body shuddered, and his mouth gave out a desiccated croak. Jack realised the creature on the bed was laughing.

'Dead,' the man echoed. 'You thought I was dead. If only I were dead.'

He continued his ugly, painful laugh and let his fingers slip, at last, from Jack's wrist and its bracelet of purple bruises.

Jack was angry now, after the panic and the old man's laughter.

'You looked dead,' he said. 'Shall I go then? Shall I leave you? You're not supposed to be in here. It's not your house.'

'And you're not supposed to be here,' the man replied. 'This house is haunted, don't you know? A vampire lives here. Or a witch. One or the other. I forget.' He lapsed into a kind of vacant dream for a moment or two, and then his attention latched on to Jack again.

'What's your name?' he said.

Jack scowled, furrowing his brow. A lock of his thick, brown hair fell over his forehead.

'Jack Elliott,' he said.

'From the village?'

Jack nodded. The man brooded, trying to remember something.

'The Elliotts are farmers and horse traders,' the man said. 'Good ones. Are you good with horses, Jack?'

Jack straightened up and nodded, proud the man knew about his family and their talent with horses. The man began to cough, gently at first, a rasping in the throat. But the coughing grew louder, as though he had a bag of dust in his belly. Then he began to laugh again, the miserable dried out laugh Jack had heard before. He sounded like a lunatic. Jack backed away.

'Are you going?' the man said, looking up at Jack. 'Will you come again?'

'I don't know,' Jack said.

'Come back. Come back tomorrow. Bring me something to drink, will you? My name is James Maslin and, contrary to your earlier assertion, this is my house.'

The effort of so much speaking seemed to exhaust the man, Mr Maslin. His head rested on the old bed and his eyes closed, sinking back into his head as they had done when Jack had supposed he was dead. But it wasn't quite the same. Maslin's face had a hint of colour now and the lips were closed over his teeth. Jack could see the shallow movement of his breathing. Had he been in a faint before? Some kind of profound fit? The man's mind was addled. Maybe it wouldn't be safe to come back, or he should fetch the doctor, someone who could help? At the very least, he could fetch him some blackberries to eat. Jack backed away, out of the room and down the splintered stairs. He slipped through the back door into the garden and grabbed the basket, returning with a handful of fruit for Maslin. He left them on the table, beside the dusty jug.

It was getting late. The sun was sinking into the tops of the trees. Outside, the air was moist and fresh. Jack hurried to the iron gates and carefully climbed out.

Then he looked back, to the old house, the forbidden place. Everything had changed. Strangely he felt a pang of disappointment. The house had yielded its secrets. The old man had frightened him, but in the end, there was no ghost or vampire. Simply the ruined house, and the mad man. Staring at the house, where no one dared to tread, Jack felt a slice of magic had slipped from his life.

3

The Tower
Bohemia, 1890

Jacinth was sitting in the dark, with a mirror in her hand. Long, tangled hair fell behind her shoulders, the ragged ends brushing the dirt floor. Feathers were caught in her hair, and tiny twigs and broken cobwebs.

She had been sitting a long time. The tower's lower chamber was never bright, with one barred window to the east, but now in the hour before sunset the light was almost extinguished. The mirror was dark too, offering no reflection. Jacinth put it face down on a low table and stood up. Barefoot, she walked across the small, square room and up a flight of rough wooden stairs to the first floor, with its books and desk, and then to the second floor, where she had a bed. From here she climbed a steep ladder and through a hatch to the tower roof.

A chilly breeze pulled at her hair, black tendrils fluttering. The sun had buried itself on the horizon, beyond dark trees that stretched as far as the eye could see. The tower stood in a small clearing, a narrow track leading away. But the track was soon swallowed up by the mass of gloomy trees. The tower was a small island in an ocean of fir and larch. And often the forest sounded like the sea, when the wind soughed through the trees.

Jacinth waited. Frayed ribbons of crimson and fiery orange flared at the rim of trees. Dusk gathered and the wind dropped away. This was her favourite time, when night drew on. She rubbed her arms, cold despite her warm, woollen dress.

The first star blinked. He would come tonight, she knew it. She sensed his approach, the faraway thud of hooves on the path, the heat and energy of the horse pounding its way towards the tower. In the distance, a startled pigeon flew up from the trees. In the peace of the forest, animals shifted, retreated or hid themselves away. The rider sent out a ripple of disturbance.

There he was! All of a sudden, the rider broke the cover of the forest, the horse pulled roughly to a halt. Jacinth stared down from her height, curtains of dirty hair falling around her. She imagined herself from the rider's view, looking down, indistinct in the twilight, her face masked with shadows. The horse wheeled, still excited from the long gallop, and the rider tugged the reins.

'Good day!' he called out, in bad French. His greeting was a formality, containing no warmth. 'Unlock the door, Jacinth. I don't have much time.'

Jacinth waited, however, still staring down. It was her one small power, to keep the Englishman waiting for a little while.

The man swung a leg over the horse's quarters and dropped lightly to the ground. He had a leather bag over one shoulder and a whip in his hand. The horse barged and fretted as the rider wrapped the reins over a post by the tower. Jacinth waited a moment more, until the Englishman was standing outside the door, and then she climbed back through the hatch into the body of the tower. From her bed she picked up a felt hat. She put it on, and drew the long, black veil over her face and shoulders. Thus apparelled she stepped slowly down the two flights of stairs to the tower door and turned the huge iron key to unlock it.

The Englishman stepped in immediately, almost knocking her over. With a brief glance around he made his way to the stairs and Jacinth followed him up to the room of books. He sat on the wooden chair, pushing it back so he could stretch out his legs and rest his dusty, booted feet on the table, upon a heap of Jacinth's papers. He took his hat off, and rubbed his head. Then he stared at Jacinth, peering as though to see through her veil, though he insisted she wear it whenever he visited.

The Englishman's name was Nicholas Tremayne and in many ways Jacinth owed him a great deal. He had provided her with a sanctuary and protection. He made sure she was fed, and furnished her with all the books, quills, papers she required. He had enabled her to hide away and for this she was grateful. However, despite her appreciation of his guardianship, Jacinth did not much like Nicholas Tremayne because he so obviously didn't like her. He accommodated her in order to use her. The hidden home and its modest comforts were provided in much the same way a farmer would provide a stall and hay for his cattle – creatures he would faithfully tend until the day he cut their throats, to eat them.

'How are you, Jacinth? Have the peasants troubled you?'

Tremayne's French accent was excruciating. It was three years, now, since he had brought her from Paris to Prague on the train, and then in a locked carriage to this forest in Bohemia. Despite their many conversations his French had not improved. Tremayne was staying in Prague. He travelled widely, however, and during the times he was absent, paid a servant to make a weekly trip to the tower with supplies for his prisoner-guest. The servant never spoke to nor saw Jacinth. He simply deposited his load outside the door, picked up a list with her requirements and hurried away. Tremayne was the only person she had spoken to in those three years.

'I am well,' she said. 'And no, the peasants haven't troubled me at all. They stay away now.'

'Good.' Tremayne nodded. They stared at each other in silence for a while. Tremayne was in his late thirties, with rather long, curling dark brown hair. With bright blue eyes and strong, masculine features he was good-looking, she supposed. His clothes were expensive, if well worn, a long riding coat trimmed with fur and twinkling cufflinks with fat Bohemian garnets.

'It's getting dark,' Tremayne observed. 'I can't stay long. Light a candle, will you?' He opened his fat leather bag and took out two old books and a handwritten manuscript on aged, yellow paper.

'They may be of interest,' he said. 'And I've brought you more ink and quills. The rest of the stuff is in the saddlebags downstairs.'

Tremayne stared again, narrowing his eyes. 'You've seen something,' he said.

Jacinth nodded. 'I have.'

Tremayne took his feet from the table and leaned forward, propping his elbows on the desk instead, suddenly engaged in the conversation. He broke into English for a moment, and she struggled to understand him – some exclamation.

'What is it?' he said in French again. 'Tell me, what is it?'

'I've found one,' she said.

'Found one? Another one – like you?'

'Yes. Like me. A girl.'

'Where? Who is she?' Tremayne babbled in English again. Jacinth, who was struggling to master this alien language, made out one or two excited words but he spoke too quickly for her to understand. She could read it well enough, after her studies, but spoken English was a different matter. She didn't have enough practice. Tremayne calmed himself, and addressed Jacinth intently.

'What have you seen? Slowly now, so I can understand everything,' he said.

'I've seen her,' she said. 'I can tell you where she is, Monsieur Tremayne. After all this time.' A small, cold space opened inside her. The clutch of loneliness. The flavour of betrayal. She pushed these away, having no room for them.

'In the morning two days ago,' she said. 'I travelled away, looking, always looking, and I found her.'

'Where? Where is she?' Tremayne was insistent, reaching out to seize her arm, pulling back at the last moment.

'In London,' she said. 'In your own country. She's living in London.'

'Where exactly?'

Jacinth had been lying in bed, just after dawn. No curtain hung in the window, and no glass kept out the cold and wind. She had only a rough wooden shutter which was bolted across, to keep out the rain. Now a pale, grey light poked its way around the ragged edges, as Jacinth huddled under her blankets. Even in early September the tower was cold. She had awoken after what seemed like hours of dreaming, and just before waking the dreams had become lucid, so Jacinth could direct them as she pleased. This was a great delight. She was walking through the streets of Paris, with her father, among the hustle and bustle of happy people who didn't stare at her.

When she woke, some of the glamour of the dream remained. Her mind felt a little detached from the waking world, a part still wandering the streets of Paris. She let this state persist, poised between waking and sleeping. And slowly, moment by moment, she let her mind unhook itself from her body. Much practised in the art now, she let go the bag of flesh and bone, the web of nerves, the stew of veins and arteries. Bit by bit she plucked at the threads stitching her into a physical self.

She rose up, hovering just above the bed for a moment or two, and then rising higher to the ceiling. Looking back, Jacinth saw her body lying under the blankets. The body's eyes were open but entirely empty. She floated through the top of the tower, then drifted in the air above it. Filled with a surge of energy, she shot up, like an arrow, into the sky and through billows of rain clouds that would have chilled and wetted her, had

31

she possessed a body. The flight exhilarated, filling her with a sense of power and freedom. She lingered for a moment, high in the atmosphere, hundreds of feet up, the face of the earth obscured by white and silver cloud. Then she dived down again, through the bed of clouds, to pass above the crown of the forest.

Unlike Tremayne, her passage did not disturb the forest animals. She saw a fox slinking along the fringe of the dirt path to the tower, and a huge grass snake, like a thick rope, and roosting pigeons beginning to stir in the early light. A couple of miles away, she saw the village right at the edge of the forest. The villagers thought she was a witch and stayed away from the tower, though now and then a youngster with something to prove would dare himself to approach.

But Jacinth had no time to think of them now, the petty, parochial villagers scratching out a living from the land. This was her moment of power. She soared over the huddle of buildings and continued onward, searching, always searching, for a light as bright as her own.

It was hard to measure how long her journeys lasted. Time stretched, as she flew above towns and cities and long, winding rivers. Perhaps, for her body waiting in the tower on the bed, her absence was no longer than the space between one breath and the next. A body could not survive without its animating spirit for very long, after all. This astral travelling took place in another stream of time, the many hours she spent floating above the roofs of city slums perhaps lasting the length of a heartbeat. The patchwork of fields unfolded, the hillsides embroidered with vineyards, the spires of mountains and at last, the line of the seashore, white waves breaking on cliffs and the scoops of beaches.

Jacinth flew above the sea, exchanging the green landscape for the hills and valleys of waves. She passed over a steamship, and a herd of fishing boats, and then a range of white cliffs rose up before her, and the roll of the South Downs. How did she know which way to go? It was hard to say. She was drawn by invisible threads here and there, searching and searching.

Then London unrolled beneath her, the capital of the world. She recognised the signature shape of the River Thames with its jam of vessels and bridges. Sinking low above the houses, she peered through rooftops and caught snatches of lives, a servant resting in an attic room, a child playing with a nurse, a woman in a slum dwelling singing as she prepared a pan of porridge for her multitude of children. Jacinth felt something tugging her now. The sense of purpose increased. Although the pace of her long journey had slowed, the strength of the call grew stronger and stronger. Jacinth felt a mixture of excitement and apprehension.

She sank lower in the street, passing above the heads of horses and pedestrians, hearing odd words of their conversations. No one could see her, but perhaps the more sensitive might have shivered when she drew near, or felt a moment's unease. But Jacinth had no thought for them. She could see the light now, a bright shining like a mirror reflecting the sun. It flashed towards her, flashed again. Helpless, Jacinth was pulled towards it. The call was insistent.

Everything happened at once, a peculiar heaping of images and words filling her mind. A girl with pale blonde hair walking along a pavement, looking up as Jacinth spiralled down to meet her. The girl's face – very white and strained with cold blue eyes and shadows around her eyes. And the girl saw her, for a moment. *Saw Jacinth.* A crowd of people around them, and a barrage of voices. *Miranda,* a voice said. *Miranda Maysfield.* Then a jumble of pictures looming up, one after another. A house with a blue door, and the name, Avondale. A pile of tarot cards strewn over floorboards. A woman in a locked room pacing up and down, her face, suddenly, rising up to fill Jacinth's field of vision.

'Go away!' the woman screamed. 'Go away! Do not torment me!'

It was too much, all too much. In a panic Jacinth wanted to pull back. For a moment there was terrible struggle, a fight to break free. Everything went black, the ordered world breaking up into pieces. This had never happened before –

– and then she was free again, shooting up over London, flying faster than thought over downs and sea, over mountains and forests and cities, over the mass of spruce and fir to the tower. Then down, like a shot, through the ceiling and landing in her body with a veritable thump. She gasped for breath, as though she were drowning, sucking in air to bursting lungs. She gripped the sheets with both hands, hanging on to the bed, drenched in sweat, and her heart pounded, fit to burst her ribs.

Slowly the panic ebbed away. Jacinth sat up in bed, and pushed her hair from her face. She took another deep breath, and laughed out loud. Success at last! She had done it – she had found another one, like herself. Miranda Maysfield, living in London, England. After so many fruitless months, and despite Tremayne's increasing impatience, she had finally made the connection.

Tremayne listened to her account with increasing excitement. He interjected with questions and demanded extra details. Did she have an address? Did she know the road? What exactly did the girl look like? Jacinth told him everything she knew. She didn't stint with the details, but neither did she embellish the tale. Tremayne wrote everything down. His eyes were shining.

'Look again,' he said, at the end, overcoming distaste in his enthusiasm and touching her arm. 'Find another one, Jacinth. Another one. There are many more. Keep looking. Perhaps now you've found one it will be easier.'

Jacinth gave a cool, modest smile, tipping her head forward. 'Yes,' she said. 'Yes I will.'

It was almost entirely dark now. Tremayne picked up the candle to light his way back down the stairs and out of the tower, leaving Jacinth in the dark. She heard him draw the door shut, and mount his horse. Then the thud of hooves as he urged the animal into a canter and wove his way through the trees, and out of the forest. Presumably he trusted his horse to be sure-footed in the darkness, to find the way back to the village, and in the morning, to the city.

Jacinth remained where she was for some time, waiting for peace to settle over the forest. Of course this peace was an illusion. Under cover of night countless animals were hunting and feeding and dying. Jacinth sighed. She removed the hat and veil from her head and placed it on the table. Fumbling with the matches, she lit another candle so a pool of light fell over papers soiled by Tremayne's boots. She pushed them into some kind of order, her long and complex genealogies, family trees dating back hundreds of years. These genealogies were patchy and incomplete, however. Not so much a connecting chain as a haphazard collection of broken links. Somehow her own parentage was connected with this web of dead ancestors. So was Tremayne. And so was Miranda Maysfield.

Jacinth stood up and moved to the window. An oval moon had risen above the forest, casting a faint radiance on the fringes of treetops. She blew out the candle and found her way down the stairs in the dark. Outside the tower door she found the bag of provisions Tremayne had left, so she took it inside. Then she stepped out into the night.

The air was fresh and cold, faintly scented with the dusty, resinous perfume of the larches. The wind sighed through the trees, a low, mournful sound she was used to. Jacinth turned her face to the sky, glad to be alone and unseen. Here, in the dark she could be free. The peasants would be huddled up around their fires, telling stories, but none would dare stray near the tower at night. She was the witch, the fairy-tale monster. They had rarely glimpsed her – and once, when a youth spied her in the sunlight on the roof of the tower, he had cried out, and run away. Jacinth was not overly perturbed. She had learned to soothe and mask the ache of loneliness. Over these last three years she had made up a new story for herself. She adopted the identity they had given her. She was a witch. Her powers were indisputable, her far-sight. The exhilaration of her flight was consolation. The blight on her face was the price she had to pay for the extraordinary ability she possessed. Jacinth wasn't ordinary. She wasn't like the peasants grubbing out their lives from the soil. She was the cursed princess from a folk tale – a visionary. The sorceress in a tower. A witch. Yes, a witch.

Despite her self-sufficiency, it gave Jacinth a vague sense of comfort, to think she was related to Miranda. The relationship might be very distant, but it was there nonetheless. She did not want to meet her, of course. Jacinth didn't ever want to meet anyone. This was her life, here in the tower on her own. Tremayne was a necessary irritation.

A shadow moved beneath the trees at the edge of the clearing. Jacinth spied the seemingly disconnected forms – the sweep of a tail, a pointed snout. For a moment, moonlight reflected in depths of a pair of eyes. Jacinth sank to her knees. Her hair fell over her shoulders, covering her. The fox stepped into the clearing, ducking its head, cautious to be out in the open. Proud too, in the bearing of its body. It was a young male, Jacinth thought, burning with vitality. The fox stepped forward, aware of his watcher but not alarmed. She didn't move, and her scent was familiar, so the fox stepped closer.

'Fox,' she said. 'Fox.' He pricked his ears, still raising and lowering his head, testing the air. Then he walked towards her on silent feet. Like a young prince, he graciously lifted his face towards hers, and sniffed. Jacinth felt his breath upon her cheek, and she could smell him too, the acrid, smoky scent of fox. He wouldn't allow himself to be petted, his pride too high, and perhaps he wasn't far enough from being the cub his mother had petted to accept it now. But they exchanged a greeting, fox and girl, witch and prince. He raised a paw, and briefly rested it upon Jacinth's thigh, before turning away and continuing his quest in the forest. He disappeared among the trees, intent on his adventure, and Jacinth was alone again.

4

The Hospital of Our Lady of Sorrows
London, 1890

On the third day, Miranda received through the post a letter from the maid, Marianne. As soon as she saw the handwriting on the envelope, Miranda felt a pang of guilt for her bad thoughts about Marianne. She remembered how coldly she had treated the maid, how cross she had been that Marianne could simply hand her over like a piece of unwanted furniture.

Mrs Norton had propped the letter against an empty vase on the breakfast table in the dining room. Mr and Mrs Kingsley – neither she nor they were prepared for a less formal address – were sitting on the other side of the table. Breakfast was a sizeable feast at Avondale. The table was laden with cold game pie, steaming mutton chops and spicy kedgeree in a blue and white china bowl. Mr Kingsley always said a dour grace before they tucked in, the grandparents consuming vast quantities of food while Miranda struggled to stomach half a piece of toast and butter. Each day, so far, they had admonished her to eat more. They seemed to regard Miranda's lack of appetite as a weakness of character.

She didn't open the letter at once. She couldn't bear to, under the disapproving eyes of her grandparents. After breakfast Mr Kingsley would travel on the underground to the city, where he was a director in a bank, and Miranda would begin her first day at an obscure day school, twenty minutes' walk away. She was overwhelmed by a weighty sense of foreboding. Living required so much effort. She imagined the horde of unknown girls, the regiment of expectant teachers. She didn't want to have to deal with them. Instead, she yearned to lie in her bed with the covers pulled over her face so she could sleep and sleep, and never wake up again.

'Who's the letter from, Miranda?' Mrs Kingsley asked sharply.

'Oh,' Miranda said. 'It's from Marianne. My mother's maid. The woman who brought me here.'

Mrs Kingsley gave an imperious sniff. 'Aren't you going to open it?'

'I'll open it later,' Miranda said, picking up the envelope and stuffing it into her pocket. She had been furnished with a brand new uniform for the school, a scratchy grey pinafore dress and a white shirt, with long black woollen stockings and a straw hat. She had clumpy black shoes for her feet, and felt utterly grace-less, like a clown. Oddly, her grandmother seemed to expect gratitude for the provision of this horrible outfit. It didn't make Miranda look older. It made her look more like a child, like an eight-year-old. She had told them she didn't want to go to school. The Kingsleys would have none of it. Doubtless they wanted her out of the house as much as possible. She suspected they were looking for a suitable boarding school.

Miranda dropped her half-eaten toast on the plate and took a mouthful of scalding tea.

'May I be excused?' she said. 'I want to leave in good time, on my first day. It wouldn't do to be late.'

If the grandparents suspected any note of sarcasm in her voice, they made no sign of it. They stared at her, two pairs of gimlet eyes, mouths still chewing on mutton chop. Mr Kingsley swallowed first.

'You may go,' he said, flicking her away with his napkin. As she left the room, Miranda heard her grandmother muttering:

'She doesn't stand up straight. She *slouches* so.'

Miranda ran upstairs to pick up the stiff new school bag, crammed the straw hat on her head, and hurried out of the house. The front door shut with a satisfying bang.

It was chilly outside but the September sky was a brilliant blue. The great trees lining the street were still green, just the first hints of auburn heralding the autumn to come. It was such a relief to be out of the house. She had spent the first two days hiding in her room and avoiding her grandparents – except for obligatory attendance at meals. Her grandfather had tried to make conversation once or twice but since the topic of her parentage was clearly not to be touched, she thought they had little to talk about.

She ran to the end of the road and across a little park. On the far side, beneath a cherry tree with leaves like flames, she sat on a park bench and took out Marianne's letter. Miranda turned it over and over in her hands. She sniffed the envelope, delighting in the maid's rather childish handwriting. The postmark said Streatham – presumably where Marianne had her new post. Finally Miranda opened it.

My dear Miss Miranda, the letter began. *It seems a very long time since I left you with your grandparents and I hope you're behaving yourself, and doing your mother and myself proud. I am worried it will come hard, living with such respectable people after the kind of life you had with Miss Julia. But I know you are a clever girl, and you'll do what you have to.*

You're not the only one to have a change of circumstances, Miss Miranda. My new place is very formal and proper, and I have a uniform and have to say yes ma'am and no ma'am to the house-keeper, who is as stiff a little body as you are likely to see. I don't mind telling you, I think of you and your mother when I go to bed, and I've shed a few tears for us all. I remember the times we had, when your mother was well, and all the laughs and the visitors coming to the flat, and the happy parties that went on till the sun came up. And the summers at your aunt's house. I liked them best of all I think, though it seems a long time ago and very far away now. Listen to me going on. I can feel the tears coming again, so I'll sign off, Miss Miranda. Write and tell me you are well. Say your prayers, and don't forget one for your mother. Keep your chin up. Respectfully yours, Marianne Porter.

Miranda dropped her hand into her lap, and stared across the park. Her eyes filled. The tableau of trees and neatly mown grass blurred and a fat tear plopped onto her cheek. A lump rose in her throat, and a sob escaped her, though she balled her hands into fists and held them tight. She squeezed her eyes shut, more tears escaping, and willed the world to disappear so she could abandon herself in the overwhelming sense of anguish.

No such luck.

'Miss? Are you all right, miss?' Miranda closed her eyes tighter, wishing whoever it was would leave her alone.

'Miss? I say, miss?' The man's voice persisted. Miranda waved it away, but there was no quashing his desire to come to her assistance.

'Have you got a handkerchief, miss? Here, have mine, will you?'

A hanky was thrust into her hand. It smelled of lavender, and, faintly, of tobacco, from the man's pocket. Blindly she pressed it to her eyes, mopping up tears. She could see him now, blurrily, a little man dressed in tweed with a bowler hat and a battered leather bag.

'What's up?' he said cheerily. 'It can't be so bad.'

Miranda shook her head, struggling to speak. She tucked the letter back in her pocket and stood up.

'I'm fine,' she reassured, ashamed she had exposed her feelings like this to a stranger. 'It's my first day at a new school, that's all. Just nerves.'

She wiped her eyes again and blew her nose.

'St Hilda's?' the man asked. 'My daughter used to go there.

It's a nice school, don't you worry. Lots of lovely girls there. You won't have any trouble.' His good humour was almost irritating, but Miranda struggled to be grateful for his help. He escorted her through the park gates and down the next road, before pointing out the street she should take to the school gates. By the time she had arrived, her tears were properly folded away in the hanky, and she prayed no one would guess she had been crying.

The day did not turn out as badly as she had expected. Miranda did as she was told, kept her head down, and made every effort to blend into the background. She was neither sufficiently pretty to attract attention nor vulnerable enough to draw any kind of trouble from the dominant girls. The school was small and possessed an air of genteel impoverishment. The pupils were mainly the children of ambitious shopkeepers and accountants. Some were ex-colonials, children who had grown up in India or North Africa with parents who had served the British Empire. They were all a collection of misfits in one way or another, and while they studied Latin and Greek, and read Shakespeare, the books were old, broken and falling apart.

Miranda had never been to school before – she had been randomly tutored by her mother and aunt – but she survived her first day well enough. She understood it was better to keep her opinions to herself. She had every hope this was simply a stage in her life – a number of weeks she would have to endure as best she could. Her mother would be better soon, and her real life would begin again.

Lessons ended at four o'clock. After languishing in a tedious French lesson, the girls ran out into the playground, laughing and shouting out to each other. Miranda picked up her school bag with its weight of homework and walked past the crowd of happy girls, through the school gates and onto the open street. A moment of freedom. She tipped back her head and breathed a deep draught of cool, sunny air. She had no idea when her grandparents expected her home, but she had no intention of returning yet. Instead she stuffed the straw hat into her bag with her books and sauntered along the streets, taking random turns, enjoying the opportunity to walk where she pleased and the pleasure of physical activity after several days cooped up in the suffocating house.

She passed through many respectable streets, full of red-brick houses with tiled paths and stained glass in the doors, through little parks hemmed in with iron railings, and passed a brace of tennis courts where half a dozen bright young things were playing a haphazard game. She stood and watched them for a while, remembering how many people like these had come to her mother's flat for parties, how they drank and smoked and chatted all night long. The tennis players didn't notice her, the dowdy schoolgirl in her grey pinafore on the other side of the fence. She was a world away.

Time passed in a blur. Miranda was in such a strained state of mind, so profoundly tired and yet so tense and worried, nothing quite seemed normal. Hours passed without her realising. Now and then objects and scenes shone out with curious significance, like the peacock butterfly with ragged wings on a brick wall, or a splash of sulphur yellow on the leaves of a maple tree, or the sun blinking on the white face of a little girl with a skipping rope. Then she heard someone calling her name. Where? Who was it? The voice was blown on the wind. Miranda wheeled around, trying to find its source. She tipped back her head, making herself dizzy. The voice came again, and Miranda was suddenly cold all over, as though someone had tipped a pail of water over her head. Someone was looking for her – she sensed it, the alien presence. The image of the girl in the dark flashed into her head, and she started to run. The endless London streets unravelled. Her mind was coming apart at the seams.

It was getting dark when she finally came back to herself.

She was very tired and the bag cut into her shoulder, the heavy new shoes were pinching. She asked a man for directions. It wasn't so far, thankfully. She had walked a path like a large horseshoe, but it was gone seven and night had fallen by the time she reached the house. Mrs Norton ushered her in through the back door.

'Where've you been?' she asked. 'Your grandmother is in a proper state, Miss Miranda. We'd all thought you'd run off. School finished hours ago, and you've missed your dinner.'

'I went for a walk. I got lost,' Miranda said. Mrs Norton looked into her pale, exhausted face and couldn't resist squeezing her shoulder.

'They were worried about you, the master and mistress. Don't take it too hard if they scold you.'

'Worried about me?' Miranda said. She dropped her bag and swapped her blistering shoes for a pair of soft, silky slippers she had brought from her mother's house.

'Yes, they were worried. A young girl, out on her own in the night.' Mrs Norton smiled. 'And you have a visitor,' she whispered.

Miranda stood bolt upright. 'What?' she said.

'You have a visitor.'

'Who? Who?' Hope, like a bird, fluttered in her chest.

'Brush your hair,' Mrs Norton admonished. 'Come on now. Make yourself presentable. Your face is all red from the cold.'

Miranda fretted while Mrs Norton fussed over her. Her thoughts tumbled over each other. Who could it be? Of course one small voice in her head suggested it might be her mother, that Julia had made a miraculous recovery and wanted to take her home again, away from all these weary trials.

'Come along,' Mrs Norton said. 'Your grandparents are in the parlour taking tea with your visitor. She's been waiting an hour or more to see you.'

Hurrying along the corridor Miranda imagined her grand-parents trying to explain her absence, excusing their incompetence at allowing her to disappear. No wonder they were cross.

Mrs Norton opened the door and ushered Miranda inside. The grandparents were sitting side by side on the sofa in the red parlour, looking very uncomfortable. And there, at the side of the fire, her legs stretched out and scandalously smoking a cigarette, was her aunt Mary.

'Mary!' Miranda cried out, unable to control herself. 'Mary!' She dropped to her knees in front of her aunt and threw her arms around her waist, pressing her face into her lap. Mary laughed, simultaneously trying to hug her and extinguish the cigarette.

Miranda was beside herself. 'Mary, where've you been? They've taken mother away and I didn't know where you were and I've had to stay here and go to school.'

Mary stroked her hair. 'We thought you'd run away,' she said. 'Your grandparents have been worrying about you. It was very thoughtless, to go tripping off without telling anybody.'

Miranda recalled the presence of her grandparents and drew away from her aunt, trying to regain her dignity. They were staring at her, and at Mary, with expressions of intense disapproval.

'Get up off the floor, Miranda,' Mrs Kingsley said. She looked furious. 'Behave with some decorum.' She turned to Mary. 'I am most sorry for this outburst, Miss Maysfield. I wouldn't have expected it. She's usually a most cold and unaffectionate child.'

Mary raised her eyebrows. 'Is that so?' she said. Mary looked admirably out of place in the stiff, red room and doubtless her clothes as well as her informal manners and cigarettes had scandalised the Kingsleys. Mary was dressed in loose-fitting black trousers, leather boots and a long tailored jacket from which a plum-coloured silk shirt frothed. She had long chestnut brown hair, casually pinned up so long tendrils brushed against her cheeks and over her neck, and several strings of beads. Mary was a radical supporter of dress reform and didn't approve of corsets that squashed the waist to a circular and very uncomfortable fifteen inches. She was also a member of a group promoting a woman's right to vote. Miranda didn't know how much of this outrageous behaviour her grandparents knew about – but her appearance, her relaxed manners and casual way of speaking were quite enough to have them prickling all over like a pair of alarmed hedgehogs. Miranda laughed suddenly to think of it.

She had so much to ask her aunt, so many questions. There would be time, later, when they were alone.

'How was your first day at school?' Mr Kingsley asked gruffly.

'Fine,' she said, careless and offhand now rescue was in sight. She wouldn't have to worry about the school any longer.

'Shall I pack?' she said to Mary. 'It won't take long. Are we going to the country?'

The room fell silent, and for a moment nobody moved. Miranda looked at her aunt, and then at her grandparents. Still nobody spoke.

'You are taking me with you,' she said. 'That's why you've come.'

Behind her, the Kingsleys shuffled on the sofa. Mary regarded her niece but she didn't speak.

'It isn't gratifying to hear how eager she is to leave us,' Mrs Kingsley said. Her voice grated. With some perverse satisfaction (for surely she wanted to be rid of the illegitimate grandchild?) Mrs Kingsley added: 'You will remain with us, Miranda. Your aunt isn't in a position to take you.'

A dark door seemed to open under Miranda's feet, and she fell, down and down. She couldn't breathe, couldn't hear what her grandmother said next. There was nothing to hold on to. Mary reached out to hold her hand and steady her.

'Miranda,' Mary said. 'Miranda, I'm sorry.' Miranda drew back, away from her aunt. Her feelings had got the better of her and now she tried to get a hold of them, to stuff them all back inside. The room was very hot, with the fire blazing. Miranda rubbed her face. Her dress itched.

'I've nowhere to stay at the moment,' Mary explained. 'I've just returned from Greece. I arrived in London this morning, you see. I went to see your mother and then I came to see you.'

Miranda winced at the mention of her mother. Perhaps the old people did too, though for a different reason. She was surprised they had allowed Mary into the house at all. What had Mary offered then, if it wasn't to relieve them of their unwanted burden?

'Stay with your grandparents, Miranda. They'll take good care of you, and they've agreed to let me see you. It's good you have a school to go to. It'll help you keep your mind off things.'

Miranda nodded but she didn't speak. Mary stood up to leave, and the grandparents escorted her to the front door. Distantly, Miranda heard Mary make an arrangement to see her on Saturday. The door was closed and Miranda heard her aunt's footsteps on the garden path, and then more faintly on the footpath along the road. She ached all over.

Mrs Kingsley retired to her room, leaving the business of Miranda's trial and punishment to her husband. He wasn't as severe as she had expected.

'In future you must come straight home from school,' he said. 'Your grandmother had no idea where you were. It isn't right for you to be wandering on your own around the streets.' Mr Kingsley was standing in front of the gas lamp, so his face was shadowed. When he had finished speaking, he stood for a moment or two, as though he had something more to say. Stiff and uneasy, he seemed to struggle for words. Then he coughed abruptly.

'Run along to bed,' he said, as though she were a child. 'Mrs

Norton will bring you something on a tray. I expect you're hungry.' And he turned away from her, shuffling over to the baby grand, where he clumsily adjusted the photographs.

Later, in her room, Miranda tried to read the tarot cards but she was too tired to concentrate. She fell asleep with the long, sleek pictures scattered over her pillow and woke at dawn, before Mrs Norton called in, with a card stuck to her cheek and others caught in her colourless hair.

On Saturday the golden September weather gave way to grey skies and pouring rain. Miranda stood at the window in the parlour watching out for her aunt. She was still smarting over Mary's refusal to take her from the Kingsleys, but her disappointment hadn't entirely overcome her desire to find out what was happening and to ask again if Mary could take her away from Avondale.

Just five minutes after the appointed hour, a hansom cab drew up outside the house. The driver, cape dripping, jumped down from his box with an umbrella to knock on the door and escort Miranda down the garden path. The poor horse between the shafts stood patiently in the rain. Mary opened the cab door.

'Hop in,' she said. 'Quick quick. It's a filthy day.'

They sat side by side. Beyond the window, the streets passed in a grey blur. The wheels splashed noisily through puddles, and water seeped in through the wooden floor.

'Now then,' Mary said. 'How are you? You look very pale. It must be a nightmare living with those ghouls.' She gave a little shudder.

'My grandparents?' Unexpectedly, Miranda felt indignant at Mary's description, though she hated them too. Was this some native family loyalty rising in her after all? Despite everything, the Kingsleys had taken her in.

'They're just the kind of people I hate,' Mary said. 'They

stand in opposition to everything I fight for. Socialism. Women's emancipation. Education reform.' She curled her lip, as though the very thought of the Kingsleys brought on a need to write letters of protest.

She looked very dapper today, in a neat brown skirt and close-fitted jacket with mutton chop sleeves, a huge black umbrella rolled up by her side. Miranda didn't think Mary was as beautiful as her mother. She was altogether more boyish. More practical too – able to travel abroad unaccompanied, to take charge and make things happen. Both Miranda and her mother had always been a little in awe of Mary, the accomplished and competent elder sister.

The cab took them into central London, and drew up outside a hotel. Mary unfurled her umbrella and they hurried inside, splashing over the pavement. The tea room was quiet, only two or three of the fifty white tables occupied by diners. A vast glass roof stretched over the heads, pattered by the rain.

'This is where I'm staying,' Mary said. 'It's a nice place, but not like being at home. A new central heating system though, and entirely electrified. It does have its comforts.'

As she spoke, Mary lit a cigarette. Then she peered at the menu.

'What do you fancy?' she said. 'Have whatever you like. You deserve a treat.'

Miranda couldn't imagine eating anything, but out of politeness she opted for watercress sandwiches and iced cakes. Mary chatted on, inconsequential observations about the hotel, while the tea was served. Then, at last, she looked directly at Miranda.

'I've been to see your mother again,' she said. 'Do you know where she is? You must have a good idea.'

Miranda shook her head. 'A hospital. That's all I know. The man who took her, they wouldn't tell me where she was going.' Her lip trembled.

'That man was Dr James Roe. He's an eminent doctor. She's

staying at the Hospital of Our Lady of Sorrows. They have a private wing for people suffering a mental disturbance.'

'You mean a madhouse – an asylum,' Miranda said bitterly.

Mary shook her head. 'It's not as you think,' she said softly. 'There have been many advances in the treatment of cases like Julia's. They're not like the barbaric places of the past.'

Miranda swallowed. The evil day rose in her memory. Her mother had grown more and more unstable, forgetting who she was, sometimes screaming at people no one else could see. From time to time she would wander off barefoot and return, hours later, with bleeding feet and mud all over her clothes. Marianne and Miranda had struggled to take care of her when these moods took over. Mary had been far away in Europe, impossible to contact. At last, one afternoon, two strong women and the man, Dr Roe, had called at the house. They pushed their way into the house, brooking no refusal by Marianne, and forcibly escorted Julia into the carriage.

Julia was screaming at the top of her voice: 'No, no, no!' On and on it went, till Miranda's skull was fit to burst. She fought tooth and nail, hanging on to the door, kicking out and spitting, but the women were imperturbable. Probably they had seen it all before.

The watercress sandwich remained on Miranda's plate, untouched.

'Who committed her?' she asked. 'Had someone made a complaint? One of our neighbours?'

Mary looked hard at her niece. 'Miranda,' she said. 'Your mother committed herself.'

Miranda's mouth fell open. 'She can't have,' she said quickly. 'You're lying. You didn't see how she fought them, you didn't hear her scream.'

'She committed herself,' Mary said. 'Think about it. You were there, you know what she's been like this last six months.'

'While you were away, in Europe,' she answered bitterly.

'Julia has always been troubled,' Mary said, ignoring the dig. 'Even when she was a child she had curious ways. It seemed whimsical then – her depressions, her wandering off and losing track of time. Our parents put it down to artistic temperament. It does seem, however, this kind of mental instability is common in our family. Looking at the records, we have a number of relatives who were committed to institutions.'

Miranda stared at the table. She thought about the walk after school, when her thoughts had drifted and she lost track of time, when the voice from nowhere called her name. Was she losing her mind too? Would she end up, like her mother and these relatives, mad and locked in an institution?

'Tell me what you mean, that she committed herself,' she said, struggling to keep her voice level.

Julia sighed. She reached into her pocket and drew out an envelope. Miranda took it from her. The envelope was much soiled and creased. It was addressed to Mary, care of a hotel in Greece, and the handwriting was clearly her mother's.

'Read it,' Mary urged. The letter was dated some two months back, and contained only a few paragraphs. Julia stated her moments of sanity were becoming fewer, and in the interests of her daughter's welfare and her own health, she intended to commit herself to the Hospital of Our Lady of Sorrows. She said she was entrusting Miranda to the care of her paternal grandparents, who had a duty, if not the desire, to take care of her. Finally she urged Mary to come home as soon as possible.

I don't know where you are, or how long it will be until you read this letter. I pray it is soon. My mind is like a dark forest, where I am swallowed up and pursued by terrors, and the moments of clarity and sunshine are growing few and far between. Please watch out for Miranda. She is everything to me. I can't bear to think I have to let her go.

Miranda placed the letter on the table. The room was very

quiet, except for the patter of rain and the occasional clink of cutlery on china. She squeezed her hands together.

'Why didn't she tell me what she intended to do?' Miranda said, in a small voice. 'It would have been easier, if I had known.'

'Perhaps she meant to. Or maybe she didn't know how to say it, or her lucid moments were too few for her to explain what was happening,' Mary said. 'To be honest, I don't know why she didn't tell you.'

'Can I see her? I want to see her.'

Mary shook her head. 'She's in a bad way, and Dr Roe thinks it best you stay away for the time being.'

'But she will get better.'

'There is every hope,' Mary nodded. 'They say she needs rest and quiet, and a complete lack of stimulation. She'd been drinking a great deal, and taking laudanum in the hope of suppressing the condition. I have to tell you she's developed an addiction which is complicating her treatment. Give her time, Miranda. This is her battle.'

'I want to see her,' Miranda repeated lamely, like a child of six.

Mary sighed. 'This is hard for me too,' she said. 'Be patient. Come on now, eat something. Don't worry about the sandwich – have a cake. Treat yourself.' Mary took the silver tongs and lifted an elaborately decorated iced cake onto Miranda's plate. Without enthusiasm, Miranda lifted it up and took a bite.

After tea, Mary suggested they visit a gallery, but Miranda wasn't in the mood for sightseeing. Instead they went to Mary's centrally heated room and chatted for a while. At least, Mary did the chatting, trying to lighten the afternoon with talk about her latest travels, and a play she'd seen here in London.

'I'll take you out soon,' she said. 'Somewhere your grandparents won't approve of. And in the summer my tenants will be moving out from the house at All Saints so we could stay for a while. Would you like that?'

Miranda nodded politely, but her thoughts were miles away. Eventually Mary summoned another cab to take her back to Avondale. It was dark when she returned. Her grandparents were out, visiting friends. The house seemed cold and empty. Miranda, alone in the parlour, could hear Mrs Norton and the two housemaids laughing in the kitchen but they seemed a world away. She mulled over the afternoon with her aunt and thought about her mother locked away in the hospital. With a convulsive little shiver she stood up and wandered to the window. There in the rain, beneath a street lamp, a woman was standing. She was young and blonde, smart and fashionably dressed, though she must have been soaked through, without an umbrella. She was peering at a soggy piece of paper, and then at the house. Curious, Miranda moved closer, so her face was against the glass. Was this woman a friend of her grandparents? She thought not. The young woman turned to the house again, and this time spotted Miranda at the window. Their eyes met. Miranda didn't look away. She held the woman's gaze and the moment stretched. Then a commotion in the hall, and the elder housemaid entered with a scuttle of coal.

'Oh,' she said. 'I didn't see you there, miss, in the dark. Would you like the light on?'

'No.' Miranda shook her head. 'No. I'm going to bed now.'

When she looked back, the woman beneath the street lamp had gone.

5

Inheritance
The West of Ireland, 1890

Two riders picked their way across the stony ground. They were caught between the flat, grey web of cloud pressing down from the sky and the similarly grey pavement of broken limestone beneath them, making up the Burren.

There were no trees or shrubs. Long cracks and gullies riddled the surface of the rock, where a little soil gathered and a few tough strands of grass eked out a life. The horses trod carefully, one behind the other, on a weaving path. It was silent, except now and then for the echoing bleat of a faraway goat, and the desolate clink of its bell.

James Maslin began humming to himself. Jack, riding at the rear, could hear his quiet, discordant tune. They had been riding for three hours now, Maslin on an Elliott horse he had hired for the duration of his stay.

'I'll not be here long,' he had warned, without specifying how many days or weeks or months this 'not long' might be. The Elliotts had only half a dozen horses now, and two of those were long in the tooth and another was a mare in foal. Times were hard. Jack's father had a job in London as an ostler at a coaching inn and sent money home when he could, with long, lively letters about life with the English in the big city and how much he missed them all.

Maslin had their best horse, Tam, a tall bay whose grandfather had won races in Limerick. Even Tam was past his prime but his coat was soft as silk from Jack's lavish grooming, and he was a well-mannered ride. Jack thought the brittle-looking old man needed a reliable mount. Kicking on his own shorter and less amenable pony, Jack studied Maslin as they wandered over the Burren.

Jack had returned to the house the day after he had discovered Maslin, apparently dead in the upstairs room. He had brought a flask of beer, cold meat and potatoes folded in a piece of cloth for the old man to eat. Going over the events of the previous day, Jack concluded Maslin must have been deeply asleep. He pushed aside his clear recollection of the man's dry skin and sunken eyes, the stiffness of his body. What other explanation could there be? Today Jack climbed over the locked gate without a second thought and made his way through the back door into the derelict house. He called out: 'Mr Maslin? Mr Maslin, sir? It's Jack Elliott.' And then a clear voice replied:

'Jack! My dear boy, you've come back.' Maslin came clattering down the stairs, looking remarkably lively for a man who just the day before Jack would have committed to the ground. He spoke and looked like a gentleman, and suddenly Jack was shy. He licked his lips.

'You're looking a lot better today, sir,' he said respectfully. Then he handed over the food, suddenly conscious how basic the fare was, how faded the cloth in which his mother had wrapped the cold potatoes.

'You'll be wanting something to eat,' Jack said. 'I'm sorry we haven't anything more fancy.'

But Maslin shook his head dismissively, and seized the food. 'Come and sit down,' he said. 'I've lit a fire. And we'll have tea, Jack. I never go anywhere without it. Though we have no milk. Did you bring any milk?' Maslin looked hopeful, but Jack shook his head.

'I didn't think of it,' he said.

Maslin scuttled around the house, skipping over fallen plaster, to the front room where a fire was chewing over pieces of broken furniture. A black pot was balanced precariously over the flames on an arrangement of stones. Maslin squatted beside the hearth, unfolded the cloth and hungrily began to eat a potato. Jack took the opportunity to stare. Maslin looked very old. As old as his grandfather perhaps, and he was over eighty. But his grandfather didn't move much now. He had become heavy and clumsy, troubled by his hip. He spent most of the day in a chair by the fire, at home. Maslin, however, was thin and limber. His movements were quick, his fingers still nimble, and though his hair was white, it was long and thick. His clothes were soiled and dusty, but, as Jack had observed the previous day, it was not the outfit of a poor man.

Maslin raised his bright blue eyes. 'I'm sorry,' he said. 'Where are my manners? Are you hungry, Jack?'

Jack shook his head. 'You'll be needing food more than I,' he said.

Maslin's accent was hard to place. There was Irish there, certainly, but other places too. 'If you don't mind me asking, how long have you been here?' Jack said.

Maslin shrugged. 'Not long. I'm not sure. A day or two, I think. I fell asleep you see. Ah, I have bad dreams, Jack. Terrible dreams. I'm glad you woke me.'

Jack considered. 'But you say this is your house?'

'It is indeed. It's been in the family for generations. The Maslins. We must be known here still. Does your mother remember the name? Your grandfather perhaps? Long, long ago your family sold us the land to build this house, and the beach and the island too – that's why it's still called Elliott's Island.

'The Maslins were an important family, many years ago. And I lived here until I was ten. I've come back from time to time, just to see the place. Not for a few years now though.' He thought for a moment. 'Don't you know the name, Jack? Maslin?'

Jack shook his head. 'No,' he said. 'It's not a name I've seen in the graveyard either. I could ask my grandpa. He might remember. The house's been empty for a long time.'

Maslin surveyed the wreckage of a once-beautiful house. Perhaps he could still see in his mind's eye the home of his childhood, perhaps seventy years before.

That night, back at home, Jack asked his grandpa about the Maslins. It was after supper. Jack's little sister was already in bed, and his mother was locking up the chickens in the barn behind the house.

'The Maslins?' the old man said, sitting up straight. He'd been the finest horseman in the county sixty years before. There wasn't a horse he couldn't ride and the family had prospered. Then came the great famine, and so many dying of hunger, and many others leaving the country altogether. The village had never recovered, and neither had the fortunes of the horse traders.

'The Maslins,' the old man repeated, taking the pipe from his mouth. 'That's a name I haven't heard in a while. They had the big house by the sea, the old place. Bad people, though. The stories we heard – the goings-on. This was when I was a child, mind. They abandoned the place.'

He looked at Jack. 'Where did you hear the name?'

Jack frowned. 'They've come back,' he said. 'James Maslin. He's an old man, Grandda – as old as you. He's staying in the house.'

Maslin and Jack rode across the Burren. They passed a dolmen, a huge slab of rock lying flat on the backs of several supporting slabs, like a table. Maslin raised his hand, pointing at it. Further on, an old woman was praying at the ruins of a holy well, a crone in black, in the middle of the limestone wilderness. She curtsied to Maslin as they rode past, and he tipped his head in reply.

Jack had no idea where Maslin was going. This was the third day he had ridden out with him. Maslin had plenty of money. He had inherited estates in England and France as well as the land in Ireland. Agents collected rents and deposited them in his bank accounts and he had an ancient family fortune now invested in stocks and shares. This he briefly explained to Jack when they rode into town, to the bank. Jack wondered why such a wealthy man should be hiding out in a ruin, instead of living it up in a big house with servants, but he didn't dare ask the question. He sensed Maslin was running from something – hiding out in the old house. In any case, he paid Jack handsomely for the hire of the horses and his services as groom and servant. After monotonous months managing the farm and taking care of his family, Maslin's employment proved a welcome distraction. And Jack was utterly intrigued by the strange old man. He had a hundred questions, but Maslin only gave a tantalising little handful of his story, every now and then.

'Where are we riding?' Jack had asked the first day. Maslin said he wanted to reacquaint himself with the home of his childhood. So they rode, along the coast away from the house, riding on the beach, or plodding over the Burren through tumbled villages where no one had lived since the famine. Most of the time, Maslin didn't speak at all. He stared across the landscape, as though he were searching for something. Sometimes he hummed to himself. And day by day he seemed to grow taller and stronger. Jack saw he had nothing to worry about as far as horsemanship went – Maslin was like a centaur, entirely at one with his mount. But he still looked like a scarecrow – an aristocratic scarecrow – with his wild hair and dirty clothes.

After a long ride, they returned to the old house through the iron gates, which Maslin had opened with one of a huge bunch of keys. He jumped from Tam's saddle and tossed the reins to Jack, who unsaddled the horses in a roofless stable, where pigeons perched on the bare rafters. Afterwards he cooked dinner for himself and Maslin, in the old range in the kitchen. The place was barely habitable, but Maslin had refused an invitation to stay at the farm, or the village inn.

'This is my home,' he insisted. 'This is where I'll stay.'

Outside, evening was drawing near and it was getting cold. Jack had brought supplies from the village for Maslin, and tonight cooked mutton, peas and potatoes which he served up on wooden bowls. Doubtless Maslin had enjoyed more refined dining, but he made no complaint. They ate together before the fire in the living room, which Jack had swept clear of old leaves and broken plaster. With the ruins of a chair and a makeshift bench, the room was almost homely. After the meal Maslin took out from his pocket a small glass bottle and, as he did every night, poured a few drops of its liquid contents into a cup of brandy. He always carried a hip flask in his pocket. Jack wrinkled his nose.

'You're frowning at me,' Maslin said.

'It's laudanum, isn't it, sir?' Jack said.

And Maslin, whose hands were beginning to shake by the evening, shrugged and said: 'I'm old, Jack. My body aches. It takes away the pain, and the bad dreams.'

Maslin stared into the fire, his hands clasped. His blue eyes glittered. Jack wondered if Maslin's death trance had been some laudanum-induced stupor. He bided his time, eager to ask questions again, wondering how much the old man might reveal this time. He had recently come from England, crossing to Ireland from Liverpool, Jack had learned. He had no fixed home, no occupation. He paid other men to take care of his fortune, and had spent most of his life travelling and living abroad. He imagined James Maslin as a young man, tall and imposing, roaming around the world and living among other idle, moneyed people.

To Jack it seemed an empty life. There were no children, no Mrs Maslin. He was the last of the line.

'So, Mr Maslin, why have you come here, if you don't mind me asking?' Jack asked.

Maslin sighed. 'Why have I come here?' he echoed. 'This is my home, Jack, I've told you. The only home I had.'

'But why now?'

Maslin shrugged. 'Circumstances.' The firelight cast deep shadows in the runnels of his aged face and the crow's feet at the corners of his eyes. But something caught his attention. He sat up straight.

'What is it?' Jack said.

Alert now, Maslin looked directly at Jack. 'Have you told anyone I'm here?' he said.

Jack shook his head. 'Only my grandda, and my ma, sir. You know that much.'

Maslin rose from his chair and walked to the broken window.

'Put out the fire,' he said. 'Quick, put it out.'

'What is it, sir? Have you heard something?' Jack quenched the fire with his tea, and stamped his boot on the ashes. The room was immersed in gloom. Maslin shushed him angrily. Jack strained to hear. Was it just the wind, whining through the empty house? No, there was something. Horses. He could hear horses and the rumbling of a heavy carriage. Jack peered through the smashed glass. Up the road, coming from the village, a carriage pushing its way through the gloomy evening.

'I didn't lock the gates!' Maslin hissed. 'Stupid! Stupid man.' He balled his fist and banged it down on the windowsill.

'Who are they? Who is it?' Jack whispered. Maslin was tense – possibly afraid. Was he hiding out, then? Were there pursuers? Was he, dread the thought, a fugitive from the law? Jack remembered his grandfather telling him the Maslins were a bad lot. James Maslin turned to him.

'Go home, Jack,' he said. 'Go home now and don't look back. There'll be trouble.'

'Who are they?' Jack repeated. 'I don't want to leave you.'

'There's no time! I thought I'd be safe here. Go home. Do as I tell you!'

Still Jack lingered. The carriage was accompanied by four or five outriders who called out to each other as they clattered through the iron gates and down the driveway to the house.

'We could hide,' Jack said impulsively. 'Hide somewhere. They won't know we're here.'

Maslin curled his lip. 'Too late for that. They'll see the horses in the stable, and the warm ash in the fireplace. This is my trouble. Get away from here. Take Tam and ride home. They won't stop you – it's me they want.'

Jack hesitated, torn between his fear of the intruders and his loyalty to the old man. But what did he know of Maslin, really? What terrible thing had he done? Suddenly the men were all around the house, noisily forcing their way through the broken doors. Maslin didn't even try to escape. He stood in the middle of the room, waiting for them. Jack waited beside him, his heart thundering. The men strode in, wearing dark coats and hats, strong men with unshaven faces. They gathered in a circle around Maslin and Jack, shoulder to shoulder, without saying a word. Their attitudes were threatening. One had a thick stick, which he whacked into the palm of his hand. Jack stepped closer to Maslin, so he was pressing against him. Despite his outward calm, Maslin was shaking.

Outside, another man climbed out of the carriage and, at a leisurely pace, followed the others into the house. He was smartly dressed, this leader of thugs, scented with Cologne and wearing a grey bowler hat. His own stick was covered in black leather and topped with silver.

'Maslin, how delightful to see you again,' he said. Maslin's hunter was an Englishman. 'You've gone to ground,' he said. 'But here I am with my hounds, come to dig you out.'

Maslin gave a high, nervous laugh. The men squared up all around him.

'I had no idea you would be coming,' Maslin said. 'As you see,' he gestured to the house, 'I haven't prepared for visitors.'

Without warning, the Englishman drew back his right arm and belted Maslin across the face with his stick. The sound of the impact was sickening. Jack flinched in horrible shock. Maslin was knocked back, gave a shudder and moan, and almost instantly bright blood welled up on his forehead where the skin was split. Maslin leaned forward, stunned, and raised his hand to his head. He touched the wound, and his hand was covered with blood. Maslin moaned again. The Englishman grinned. He raised his stick to strike again . . .

'No!' Jack shouted out. Without thinking, he launched himself against Maslin's assailant, knocking him back. Fists flailing, Jack pummelled and punched the Englishman in a fury. Jack was lean, but he was fit and strong after years working on the farm and tending the horses. The Englishman roared, and his men stepped forward to pull Jack away – but his blood was up. He'd lost control of himself, furious with the Englishman for his violent and unprovoked attack on an old man. It took three to subdue him. A punch was landed on the back of his head, a boot on his shin, but he felt nothing, in the storm of his rage. Even as the men held him, Jack heard himself swearing and cursing the Englishman, still struggling in the hold of his captors. The Englishman grinned coldly.

'Bravely done, boy,' he said, pushing back his hat with the end of his stick and wiping his face with a handkerchief. Then he turned to Maslin again. The old man was standing up straight, but his face was covered with blood.

'You have a disciple,' the Englishman said, gesturing to Jack.

'What do you want?' Maslin answered weakly. 'There is nothing I can tell you.'

'But how do I know that? When we last spoke, for instance, you didn't tell me you still had a country house in Ireland, did you?'

'Such as it is,' Maslin said. 'It's a ruin. There's nothing here, Tremayne.'

'But if you've lied to me once, how do I know you haven't lied to me again?' He nodded to his men, and two of them seized Maslin under the arms and pushed him back against the wall. Jack's head began to throb. He realised he was shaking all over, like a leaf. What would they do to Maslin? It was too horrible. He felt sick to death.

'No!' he shouted out. 'Don't hurt him. What's he done?'

The Englishman turned his head over his shoulder and regarded Jack with some surprise.

'I thought we'd heard enough,' he said. 'Be quiet. This business has nothing to do with you.' He stepped closer, stretched out a gloved hand, and pressed it against Maslin's cheek, a gesture which combined a show of tenderness with a frightening menace. Maslin was breathing heavily. He looked very frail and vulnerable, as though his elderly bones would snap like twigs.

'My dear cousin,' the Englishman said softly. 'For so we are, in some distant fashion. I only want to know the truth.' He twitched his head to his men. 'Let him go. Look around. See if you can find anything.'

Maslin slumped against the wall as they dropped him, and four of the six stormed around the wrecked house.

'What about the boy?' said one, who still held Jack. His accent was Irish, from the north. The Englishman had gathered his roughs en route to the Burren. He sighed and scowled. Obviously Jack was a nuisance.

'Tie his hands,' he said abruptly. Then, with a pretence of concern, he handed Maslin his handkerchief and escorted him to the old chair by the fire, so he could sit down. Jack could hear upstairs the clatter of the men tearing apart what remained of the furniture, searching for he knew not what. Surely it wouldn't take them long to realise there was nothing here. The house had been empty for decades. The Englishman sat beside Maslin on Jack's bench.

'James,' he said. 'Why did you run away from me if there was nothing to hide? I only want you to share a little of our inheritance. That, surely, is my right.'

Maslin, still breathing heavily, curled his lip in a sneer.

'Our inheritance?' he said. 'What do you want?'

The Englishman narrowed his eyes. Something caught his attention, glittering on Maslin's chest. It was the piece of gold Jack had spotted that first time in the house, when Maslin was a corpse lying on the bed. And like Jack, the Englishman stretched out his hand to seize the gold. Maslin didn't stop him.

'What about this?' the Englishman said. Maslin stared. Their faces were only inches apart now, held together by the chain around Maslin's neck, the pendant in the Englishman's hand.

'The lily,' he said quietly. With a sudden jerk he broke the chain, taking the pendant away from Maslin. The Englishman was intent on his find but Jack saw the flash of grief on the old man's face. The necklace was precious.

The Englishman leaned back, staring at the pendant as though he wanted to eat it up with his eyes. Greedily he closed his fingers over it.

'My brother will be very interested to see this,' he said. 'But it isn't enough, cousin. I want more.'

Curiously the loss of his piece of gold seemed to revitalise Maslin. He was sitting up straight now, looking the Englishman in the eye.

'You're chasing fairy tales,' Maslin said. 'I have nothing to tell you. Beat me as much as you like, and the total of my knowledge will still amount to nothing. Let the boy go, will you? This is nothing to do with him, Tremayne. Untie him. Send him home.'

The Englishman shook his head. 'Not yet,' he said. 'There is only one thing I want to know.' He held up the pendant on its chain, in front of his face, so the sunlight caught it again as the heavy gold twisted back and forth. Old gold, dark and deeply coloured, the surface worn smooth, shaped like the symbol Jack had seen on a coat of arms in the church. A fleur-de-lis.

'Where is it, cousin?' the Englishman asked. 'Where is it now? Your family guarded the lily for centuries. You must know where it is.'

'I've told you before. There is no lily. It's an old story, Tremayne. A fantasy. Give it up. There's nothing for you to find.'

The Englishman sighed, and dropped the golden fleur-de-lis in his coat pocket. He fiddled with his stick impatiently.

'I know a great deal about you, cousin,' he said. 'You've done nothing with your life. Your mother died in a lunatic asylum in England, and your father killed himself in a riding accident. You have a fortune but you do nothing with it. Instead of using your talents, you have wandered round the world consorting with people of the lowest sort. You're an alcoholic and a laudanum addict. All in all, a very sad case.' He said these last three words very slowly, and with great relish.

Jack was stunned by the catalogue of Maslin's misfortunes, and Maslin himself flinched.

'So why do you still torment me?' Maslin said. 'Surely my record speaks for itself. If the story was true, wouldn't I have used the lily to my own advantage? For God's sake! I've nothing to tell you.'

'It is a puzzle,' the Englishman admitted. He rose to his feet as the men came back into room.

'There's nothing,' one said. 'It looks as though nobody's lived here for years. No books, no papers. Just rubbish.' They all looked expectantly at the Englishman, waiting for further instructions. The Englishman considered.

'No,' he said. 'I don't think he knows anything. He's a wreck. Like the house. The last of a noble line. And look at him.' The Englishman laughed, and kicked over the makeshift bench. The sunlight ebbed from the window. Soon it would be night. The Englishman took a watch from his pocket.

'Burn the house,' he said, turning away from Maslin. 'I want nothing left behind.'

'No!' Maslin shouted out. 'No, no!'

But the Englishman was already walking away. Two men heaved Jack and a struggling Maslin out of the house and into the garden, while the rest strode around the house, dousing rags in oil and setting the place alight. The flames rose quickly, feeding hungrily on bare rafters, floorboards, the dried up rubbish still littering the house.

'No, no!' Maslin was still shouting. He and Jack were dumped unceremoniously on the ground. Jack could see the Englishman climbing back into his carriage, as the last of his thugs left the burning house and clambered on their horses. The driver cracked the whip and wheeled the carriage in a circle. And they were off, the horses leaping into a canter, straining at their harness, while the entourage of riders whooped and yelled, spurring their mounts, galloping away from the gathering inferno.

Maslin hurried to his feet.

'Jack! Quick – we have to put out the fire!' He jumped up and down like a skinny goblin.

'It's too late, sir. It's too late!' Jack said. 'Look at the place. We'll never stop it.' Already flames were leaping out from the windows. Maslin fumbled to untie Jack's hands. His face was agonised.

'This was my home, Jack. My home!' he cried. When Jack's hands were free, Maslin ran to the house, helplessly stepping back and forth, powerless to halt the destruction. Jack ran to the stables and chased the horses outside. Alarmed by the noise and flames, the animals stampeded away from the house, towards the sea. Maslin was harder to deal with.

'Come away! Come away!' Jack tugged Maslin's arm, trying to drag him from the shadow of the burning house. The heat scorched his face, and the roar of the flames was deafening as they leaped higher and higher. They would see it from the village, Jack thought, but no one would come and help. They were all afraid of the house. Maybe they would be glad to see it destroyed. But Maslin wasn't glad. He pulled free of Jack, apparently impervious to the blast of heat and the rain of burning sparks that flew from windows. Somewhere a glass pane exploded.

Jack watched from a distance. Maslin wouldn't be helped and there was nothing he could do. The fire engulfed the house, consuming the roof, great flames stretching up into the gathering darkness. Soon the broken roof collapsed, and then, with a great crash, the first floor caved in, throwing huge coils of black smoke into the air. The firelight sent long shadows racing across the garden, and on the nearest trees, the autumn leaves crisped black and dropped to the ground, and the branches were scorched.

The fire burned right through the night, but its destructive power began to falter once the first floor had fallen. Slowly, starved of nourishment, the flames diminished. Jack curled up by the garden wall, out of harm's way, but his face was coated with soot and grit from the fire. He must have slept for a time, because when he opened his eyes it was just before dawn, the sky a low grey over the blackened, smoking remains of the house. His head ached, and gingerly touching his scalp with his fingers, he found a lump, from the blow to his skull. A large red and purple bruise had risen on his shin. Stiffly Jack climbed to his feet. Where was Maslin? It was beginning to rain. Jack wandered to what little remained of the house. Just four black walls, and inside, a heap of charred wood and ashes, still smoking.

'Mr Maslin!' he called. 'Mr Maslin, sir, where are you?' He walked around the house, searching for the old man, shouting out his name. He found him curled up asleep beneath an overgrown apple tree, his face smudged with soot and holes burned into his coat.

'Mr Maslin,' Jack said, shaking him awake. The old man opened his eyes. They were red-rimmed in the mess of soot and blood blackening his face. For a moment, Maslin seemed unaware of where he was and what had happened. He sat up, in a state of confusion, recoiling from Jack. His hand reached impulsively to his chest, searching for the stolen pendant. Then his eyes flew to the wreckage of the house. He shut his eyes again and groaned.

'They've gone,' Jack reassured. 'You're safe now, Mr Maslin. And the house was already a ruin.'

Maslin didn't seem comforted. He put his hand to his head, testing his wound. His hands were shaking. Slowly, he reached for the hip flask in his pocket and sipped from the brandy inside. Then he offered it to Jack. But Jack shook his head.

'What was it all about?' Jack asked, squatting down beside him. 'What did he want? The Englishman – what was he talking about, Mr Maslin?'

Maslin looked away, into the distance. He took another sip from the silver flask.

'You may find it hard to believe,' he said. 'There is a story in my family, improbable though it may seem, that at the time of the time of the first crusades, an angel of God gave its blessing to their campaign and handed a lily to the bravest of knights.

'This lily bestowed strength and courage on the knights who received it, helping them achieve an illustrious victory. After the crusades, they set up an order, with strongholds all over Europe and in North Africa. They adorned their shields and banners with the symbol of the fleur-de-lis, and became powerful, gathering lands and wealth, and influence.

'But they became too powerful. At first both church and princes courted them, wanting the order as an ally. Eventually they wanted to be rid of them. Charges were brought – treason, heresy. The leaders were tortured and executed. Their treasures and garrisons were confiscated. That was the end.'

Jack absorbed the story, trying to make sense of it. He gestured to his own chest. 'And the pendant?'

Maslin nodded. 'It was my link with them, my ancestors, members of the Order of the Lily. There are people who think the story of the angel and the lily was an allegory – a story of symbols, the lily representing their faith in God and purity of intention. There are some, still, who think the lily was real – an unearthly object conferring a great power. These people believe the order preserved the lily in a box of glass and gold, and that the knights hid it away when the leaders were arrested. The knights underwent terrible tortures and never broke their silence. There are legends the order went underground, continued in secret for years after the trials and the public dissolution. It is rumoured the secret society broke up two centuries ago. If there was a lily, I have no idea where it is.'

'And what do you believe?' Jack whispered. 'The Englishman thinks it's real – and he thought you knew where it was.'

Maslin turned to Jack, and gave him an unsettling smile. 'I don't know,' he said. 'There were stories my family possessed the secret. They were, for generations, guardians of the lily's hiding place. If so, that secret was never passed to me. You must know, Jack, my family also has a history of insanity and suicide. It isn't an inheritance I could take any pleasure in.'

'But,' Jack interrupted. 'But the Englishman called you cousin. Is he part of your family too?'

'In a manner of speaking, yes. Edmund Tremayne and his

brother have uncovered documentation, some other piece of evidence, suggesting the lily is real – and they want it. They came after me, thinking I knew more. The brother, Nicholas, wrote to me and tried to enrol me in their campaign. When I refused, Edmund resorted to threats. That is why I came here, Jack. And Edmund followed too. I suppose it would not have been too hard for him to find out the Maslins had a property in Ireland.'

'But do you believe it?' Jack repeated. 'Do you believe the lily is real?'

Maslin looked at him gravely, through a mask of soot and blood now spotted with rain. 'I don't know,' he said. 'I have undertaken researches on my own account, over the years. I had lost my parents, and I wanted answers. I have to confess, I found very little. So I think not. It is an unlikely story, isn't it?'

Maslin rose to his feet, very unsteady. Jack jumped up, offering a shoulder for support. Maslin pointed at the house.

'One last look,' he said. 'Then we had better find the horses.'

Maslin hobbled to the yawning doorway and stepped inside. He picked his way over heaps of hot ash and the last charred remains of the interior. Blobs of melted glass had dripped from the windows. Coils of smoke spiralled. Jack kicked at the ash, sending dust spinning in the air. He wandered about, feeling the heat of the ground beneath his feet. When he turned back to Maslin, he saw the old man was crying. Tears were leaking from his eyes, leaving trails in the filth on his face. Jack felt a pang of compassion. Perhaps those first ten years of his life, growing up with his parents in the house by the sea, were the only truly happy ones Maslin could remember.

Jack pushed with the toe of his boot one bright, glowing ember, like a jewel in the soft ash. His foot hit something hard. He pushed again. It didn't feel, or sound, like wood. Something metal perhaps – coming through the fire unscathed. Carefully, not eager to be burned, he dug away the ash with his foot. He uncovered a narrow metal box, maybe a foot long and wide, and the depth of two hands. The box was black from the fire, and still hot to the touch. He called out to Maslin.

'I've found something. Is this yours? What is it?'

Maslin hurried over. His eyes widened. 'I've no idea,' he said. 'It isn't mine. I've never seen it before.'

'Perhaps it was hidden away – nailed under the floorboards or in the roof space or something. Maybe the fire has uncovered it.'

They looked at each other, the boy and the old man. A spark of excitement ignited. Jack swallowed. 'Could it be?' he said.

'I don't know.' Maslin's hands were still shaking. He reached out to touch the box, but exclaimed when he burned his hands. It was too hot to touch.

6

Witch
Bohemia, 1890

The train powered through the night and rain. The railway track was strapped on the back of fields and moors like a harness. Behind the train spread its long banner of smoke. The iron sides of the engine glistened. Briefly, a glimpse of the furnace door and the red-hot interior.

Jacinth rose up, away from the train, and the line of carriages snaked away. The windows were bright like a chain of beads where tiny people sat in warmth and light. She followed as best she could.

The trail had begun with a blazing fire, in a house by the sea on the west of Ireland, beyond a broken pavement of stone. Huge flames leaped up, a forest of fire. Men rode away whooping and shouting. Jacinth floated above the flames, untouched by the heat and smoke. She was drawn by another kind of light, though it was dim and flickering. Somewhere, amid the noise and confusion of the fire, there was someone with a gift like herself.

Jacinth had reported this to Nicholas Tremayne several days ago – but he knew what had happened already and his face clouded with anger. He balled his fist and banged it on the table with a curse.

'My brother!' he said, in a voice thick with rage. 'I got a

telegram – this morning. He bungled it! Burning the house – what possessed him?'

Jacinth looked at Tremayne, waiting for an explanation. Usually he didn't provide her with details of the bigger picture, only passing on what details he thought Jacinth needed to hear. But she knew about Edmund Tremayne, the hot-headed younger brother. He was a partner in the endeavour – and while his impulsive behaviour was useful on occasion it could evidently cause problems too.

'He found nothing,' Tremayne said. 'He said Maslin was insane and useless.'

'Maslin,' Jacinth echoed. This was the source of the dim light. She knew his name from the genealogies. The Maslins were direct descendants of the leader of the knights of the lily – and as far as she knew, this so-called insane old man was the last of them. Jacinth's own ancestors were related to another of the knights, but a family tree of such antiquity was huge and complex, a giant mesh of branches growing wider and wider with each generation. Now only very rarely did the weakened line throw up the powers the lily had bestowed – like her gift of farsight. The brothers Tremayne were also a part of this sprawling web of descendants, though it hadn't blessed them with any ability she was aware of. And did Maslin have a gift? Maybe not, because his light was dim. Tremayne, however, was convinced Maslin knew where the lily had been hidden away.

'Find him again,' Tremayne ordered. 'See where he goes.'

So here she was, drifting over the fields of France, following the steam train. It was easier to find Maslin, a second time. He had ridden across Ireland to Cork. For an old man, Maslin had a great deal of energy and determination. It was a difficult journey lasting several days, and he didn't rest at the end of it. When Jacinth searched for him again, she found Maslin on a steamer crossing from Ireland to Roscoff in France. Then the long train journey, day and night, to Paris and eastwards again. Tireless, the train thundered past villages and market towns, through newly ploughed fields, by the glistening ribbons of canals and rivers, past forests turned gold and chestnut with the season.

'I think he's coming to Prague,' Jacinth said. Tremayne had returned to hear her latest report. It was morning, and outside the tower, rain pattered on the dying leaves.

'What makes you think so?' Tremayne said.

'He's heading east. Prague is the obvious destination for the hunter of the fleur-de-lis, isn't it? The order had its headquarters here after the crusades. That's why you're here,' she said.

'You think he does know something?' Tremayne said. 'Maybe that's why he's coming – to check we haven't found it. To protect it.'

'I have no idea,' Jacinth said. 'Unfortunately I don't know what he's thinking. I only have glimpses of where he is.'

Tremayne compressed his face, lost in thought. 'Keep following him,' he said. 'Don't lose Maslin. He must know where the lily is. Why else would he be coming here?' He chewed his lip. 'I told Edmund. I told him! Maslin has to know something and Edmund missed his chance.'

He jumped to his feet. 'My brother's travelling to Bohemia. And the English girl – I shall be taking her too.' Tremayne was thinking aloud, but at the mention of the English girl he turned to Jacinth.

'Shall I bring her to you? Would you like a friend, Jacinth? Or would you frighten her?'

Jacinth gave a cold shiver. She couldn't help it. Tremayne's words were needles digging into her skin.

'No. You don't have friends anymore,' he persisted, pushing the needles deeper. 'Except for me, of course. I'm your only friend.'

Jacinth was glad of the veil, which obscured the tremble of her lips. She didn't give an answer. The thought of the English girl had been a comfort. In her fantasies, the English girl wasn't

74

horrified by Jacinth's face and, both having gifts, they loved each other like sisters. In this private dream, they lived together in the tower. Conveniently Jacinth overlooked her own less than admirable role in Tremayne's scheme, to help him kidnap and make use of any of the few remaining lily-gifted descendants in the hope of exploiting their talents to find his treasure.

Tremayne put his hat on and picked up his whip.

'Keep looking for others,' he said. 'And follow Maslin too. I want to know where he goes.'

Tremayne was about to leave, but he seemed to think of something.

'I have a photograph of Maslin,' he said. 'My brother stole it from Maslin's lodgings in London.' He reached inside his jacket, and took an envelope from a pocket. 'Perhaps you can use it to hurt him. See what you can do.'

Jacinth swallowed. 'What you're asking – it's not in my power,' she said slowly. The very prospect opened a deep sense of dread.

'Try it,' he said shortly, slapping the side of his boot with his whip. 'Perhaps we can slow him down. Better, stop him. Then Edmund can get hold of him again. I don't want Maslin dead – but if you can wound him, trip him up – that would be help-ful.' He turned away. 'Remember who your friends are,' he called over his shoulder, as he disappeared down the stairs.

Tremayne rode away. Jacinth picked up the envelope and slowly drew out a small black and white photograph. On the back, in faded black ink, it said: James Maslin. Jacinth flipped the picture over. The picture was very odd. James Maslin didn't have a face. There he was, standing outside a grand doorway, lean and tall with a thatch of wild-looking hair. And beneath the hair, no face – only a blurred oval – no features at all. It was profoundly unsettling. Without thinking, Jacinth raised her hand to her own ruined face. What was it about him the camera failed to record?

Now, though, Tremayne wanted her to try and damage Maslin, through the agency of the photograph. His own research into the earliest days of the knights had revealed they had the power to inflict wounds from a distance. This very potent skill had proved devastating in battle, if the stories were true. Legend told how enemy soldiers had fallen from their horses, skulls shattered, before the battle lines had even drawn together. In their tents, miles from battle, heathen commanders had been found dead, their hearts stopped, because the Knights of the Lily had used their magic through the agency of a stolen lock of hair, or letter, or piece of clothing, belonging to the victim.

Jacinth, however, was entirely doubtful about her ability to undertake this kind of distant attack – and she had no wish to harm Maslin. It would be evil to try and hurt him – her heart cried out against the idea. But she was already complicit in the brothers' crimes. She was helping them and now they had burned down Maslin's ancestral home. What else could she do? Tremayne protected her. She had absolutely no one else to turn to.

Jacinth spent the rest of the day lying in bed, in a pit of despair. Tremayne was right, of course. She had no chance of a life, outside of the tower. No one could bear to look at her. Even the English girl, Miranda, would be afraid and horrified. Nothing could be done. She had no choice – none at all – except to hide herself away, to live a life on her own. The four walls of the tower and the narrow space of the clearing in the trees was the extent of her physical world. Only in the measureless realms of her imagination, and the real gift of far-sight, could she leave the confines of the tower. That was the truth of it.

A wave of grief crashed over her, lying in the bed, while outside the rain poured down. Jacinth covered her face with her hands and cried.

She woke suddenly. Darkness filled the empty space of her

window. Night had fallen while she slept. After hours of crying and sleeping, she felt wrung out and hollow inside. And cold too. She pulled up the covers, with a shiver.

She heard a sound from outside, the breaking of a branch and a voice calling. It had happened before, the village boys daring themselves to touch the witch's tower. Would they break in? Would they breach her place of safety? She cowered beneath the covers, hardly daring to breathe. Voices again, calling to each other. And the sound of movement in the trees around the clearing. How many people were there? She heard a woman's voice, loud and clear, chanting. Was she cursing the tower and its inhabitant? Jacinth didn't know what to do. If she appeared at the window, or climbed to the roof of the tower, the people might be scared away. Then again, they might not. This might incite them further, to acts of violence.

So she lay on her own, heart thundering, remembering she hadn't locked the door when Tremayne departed. They could come inside, oh so easily, they could creep up the stairs to find her. She squeezed her eyes shut and willed them to go away.

The woman outside called out again. She uttered a long string of words in a high voice. Her language was incomprehensible but the meaning was clear to Jacinth. They feared and hated the witch in the tower. They wanted to be rid of her. Jacinth was shaking like a leaf and her teeth started to chatter. She was frozen with fear, just waiting to hear the opening of the door, the hammering of feet upon the wooden stair.

Minutes passed. The sounds died away and the door remained shut. Had the villagers gone? Jacinth didn't move for a long time, her limbs heavy as stone. Dread chilled her, clouding her ability to think. Images rose in her mind, the crowd of angry people assembled all around the tower with hate in their hearts for the witch living in the forest – hate for her. How could she live with it? How was it possible to carry on, for the heart to beat, to draw breath, when everyone reviled you? Tears leaked from Jacinth's eyes, running over her cheeks to the pillow. She considered using her far-sight, to see if a crowd was standing around the tower, but she was too distraught to reach the necessary state of mind. Time passed, an agony of minutes and hours. Gradually the night spent itself, and the pallor of dawn filled the tower window. There were no more sounds and Jacinth was convinced the villagers had gone away. With a blanket wrapped around her, she peeped out of the window, and then climbed down the stairs to the ground floor and slowly opened the door.

Barefoot, she crept over the cold, dewy grass. The forest glittered with the rain of the previous day. She breathed the scent of wet soil and the tangy perfume of spruce and larch. Then she saw something odd – a white trail in the grass. What was it? Jacinth edged closer. The white line continued in a large circle around the tower. She crouched and stretched out a hand, to touch the substance with the tip of a finger. A few grains clung to her skin, and she dabbed them on her tongue. Salt. Of course, a circle of salt. The superstitious villagers thought they could contain her within a barrier of salt. It was almost comical. Defiant, she stepped across the white line and walked to the trees. Something else had caught her eye. A splash of colour amid the tree trunks, something dangling from a branch. Jacinth didn't want to see what this might be, nor could she resist the curiosity driving her on.

It was a doll, cunningly sewn from scraps of material. Clearly it was a representation of Jacinth. Its brown hair, probably cut from the tail of a horse, reached the doll's knees. And the face – oh the face. She couldn't look. She should ignore it, leave it alone. Again, she was compelled by curiosity, driven to know the worse. She stretched up her hand and tugged at the doll, breaking the string that tethered it to a branch. The poppet was about two hands in length, and the white cloth face was stitched all over with crude red thread. No eyes, no nose or mouth – just the random zigzag of angry scarlet stitches, dozens of them, their cruel representation of her scarred, spoiled face. Jacinth stared, soaking it up, the spectacle of the poppet, the embodiment of their fear. She turned it over again – and the doll bit her. With a cry, she dropped it. A bead of blood swelled on her palm. Cautiously Jacinth rolled the doll with her foot. Beneath the neatly stitched dress, she saw with horror the body of the poppet was speared through and through with giant thorns. It was utterly shocking. For a moment, she felt them in her own body, the spears of the villagers' malice, through her heart and belly and bowels.

'Pick it up,' she told herself. 'Pick it up.' Her body obeyed.

'Pull out the thorns,' she said. From a distance, her fingers obeyed. They tugged out the evil wooden needles and dropped them on the floor, so the poppet was left with a dozen holes.

'Now what shall you do?' she said to herself. 'Shall you burn it?' The idea was appealing.

'You could tuck it away somewhere safe,' she advised herself. 'Somewhere you'll never see it, and then you can forget about it.'

For the moment this seemed the best course of action. Jacinth crossed the circle of salt, with the poppet in her hand. In the tower, she wrapped it in a piece of cloth and hid it beneath a loose floorboard, under her bed.

For the rest of the day, she sat in a daze at her desk, thinking about the poppet and the depths of the villagers' hostility. She couldn't work, couldn't focus on reading or writing. An imaginary Tremayne rose up in front of her, nodding his head.

'You see, I'm right,' he said, this Tremayne of her mind. 'You have no one, except me. Worse than no one. Everyone else hates and fears you.'

Jacinth's bruised heart began to freeze.

'They only fear me because you told them I was a witch,' Jacinth said.

'But, Jacinth,' the phantom Tremayne answered, a cruel voice inside her head. 'You are a witch. Think what you can do.'

'Then I shall stop doing it,' she said to herself. 'Then I won't be a witch.'

And if she abandoned her far-sight? Her one true escape from the tower prison? What would she be then? Without family, without friends, without a face – then she would be nothing. Surely it was better to be a witch, than to be nothing. Her gift was power. It was all she had.

Jacinth drew out the photograph of Maslin, and stared at the blur where his features should be. She thought of the villagers' poppet, and she took from her desk a felt bag of sewing things.

'If Tremayne finds the lily, he tells me my gifts will be multiplied,' she said to the picture of Maslin. 'What power I have now is just a whisper of what will come to me once the lily is unearthed and I can hold it. My power is all I have, you see,' she said, in a low, serious voice. 'And I'm afraid you want to stop me, James Maslin. You want to keep the secret buried. Isn't that selfish of you?' She sighed.

'We're all selfish,' she mused. 'I'm selfish too.' Jacinth tipped a dozen pins from her felt bag. She picked one up, and carefully stuck it into the photograph, and back through again.

'It's not personal,' she said to Maslin. 'I don't hate you. I have to do it, you see. We have to find the lily.' Jacinth picked up a second pin and stuck it through the picture. When the sixth pin was in place, Jacinth held up the photograph. The black-and-white Maslin now had a halo of pins around his head. Jacinth shuddered. It looked appalling. Would this piece of clumsy magic hurt him? She didn't know, for certain. It was horrible, all the same – an image of evil.

She dropped the mutilated photograph on the desk, and went up to the second floor, and her bed, unseeing, groping her way with her hands on the stairs. The walls of the tower seemed to close in. The very walls of her skull pressed against her brain, squeezing out the light of her mind. She fell upon the bed, pulling the blankets around her, burying her face into the pillow, desperate to escape the treadmill of her own thoughts. Fingers of guilt poked, but she steeled herself against them. Probably the pins would have no effect on the real Maslin, as the thorns in the villagers' poppet had not affected her. But as she lay, curled up tight, limbs tense, pulse thundering in her body, she felt the thorns of the villagers' malice pierce her through and through. Heart, belly and brain, she was wracked by the needles of loneliness and fear.

7

Kefalonia, Greece, 1755

A tawny island, in a glittering turquoise sea. Mountains jostled, forested with pines. In a rocky harbour a ship was tethered, sails bound up, waiting for the voyage to come.

Two men dined together in a white house, on a feast of cheese, tomatoes, newly baked bread and olives. Six salty sardines, fresh from the sea, lay on a plate. The window gave a view of the sea, and the ship fretting at its anchor.

The house was a grand affair, surrounded by orange and lemon trees, encircled by a tall wall. The sun-baked air was spiced with the perfume of rosemary and mint. The two men ate hungrily, eying each other as they dined. They didn't speak.

One was fair, his face and neck sunburned, pale hair tied behind his head. The other was dark, with long black hair over his shoulders, a thick beard and coffee-brown skin. Both wore pendants – the golden fleur-de-lis glinting on the white shirt of the fair man, and on the thick chest hair visible at the open neck of the dark man's jacket. He called for wine, and an elderly woman appeared from the kitchen with a clay pitcher. She poured the cool, amber liquid into the two glasses on the table, and disappeared again.

'We leave tomorrow,' said George Maslin, the dark man. His companion frowned.

'If you're certain this is the right course of action,' Jacob answered. The men were half-brothers, having the same father and different mothers. George's mother was Greek. She had died of a fever shortly after his birth. His father had married again within a year, to a delicate young Englishwoman. Jacob was the fruit of this second union. The brothers were now in their forties. George had inherited the estates and the substantial family fortune.

'We have discussed this over and over,' George said. He glared at his brother. 'We decided.'

'You were swayed by the others,' Jacob said. 'You gave in to them – submitted to their decision. But we're the guardians, George. We are the closest in line. We don't have to do as they say.

'Everything we have,' he gestured to the house, their surrounding, 'is thanks to the lily. It gave us power, and wealth. It is our good fortune.'

George put down his knife and balled his fist in frustration. Must he put up with Jacob's arguments time and time again? A decision had been made, and it was the right one. They would take the lily from the island and hide it far away. Perhaps if it remained hidden deep enough, and for long enough, its influence would die. Then, he hoped, the many, many descendants of the knights of the lily would finally be free. The lily's gifts were increasingly rare now, but its blight had grown more common with each generation. And then the worst tragedy of all. Two years ago his father had succumbed to a crushing malady of the mind. In the end, raving and insane, he had killed his second wife, before shooting himself with a pistol. This horrible tragedy had finally decided the Council of the Lily. Its time was over.

'How can you think this way?' George said, in a tight, frustrated voice. 'You know what happened to our father and your mother. If you had found them – if it had been you, Jacob, maybe you'd think differently.'

'We are strong men, George. It won't happen to us,' Jacob argued. The brothers stared at each other, the air between them thick with animosity.

'A decision has been made,' George said. 'We aren't the only ones involved in this. The council agreed what has to be done – and it's up to us to carry out the order. I don't want to talk about it again.'

Jacob pushed back his chair, knocking over his glass of wine. He jumped to his feet, and strode out of the room. The wine pooled over the table and dripped onto the stone-flagged floor.

George sighed. He picked up his own glass and drained it. He possessed a gift of foresight himself, though he rarely chose to use it. Even now, without trying, odd flashes opened, like windows in his mind, offering fleeting glimpses of what was yet to be. His childhood dreams had been haunted with images of his father's death – but this dubious gift of seeing into the future had not enabled him to change the terrible path of events. Now he was troubled by further images of violence. He didn't trust Jacob – and he didn't know what to do about him either.

The next morning, very early, George saddled his horse and rode away from the white house. The roads were quiet and dusty, lined with silver-grey olive trees and dark cypresses. Already the sun was fierce, beating on his head. The horse tossed its head, irritated by flies. George Maslin rode over the headland. A bright blue sky, and below, the sea in swathes of cobalt and azure, and the white lines of waves unfurling on the long, empty beach. He rode for an hour, the horse plodding steadily, the reins long and loose. George had grown up here, on the island. Later he and Jacob were sent to school and university in England, but it was a damp, dreary place. The sun was never strong. George was glad to come back to his father's house. This was where he belonged. A breeze from the sea picked at his hair, blowing it across his face. Far away, a fishing boat perched on the horizon.

He took a road winding inland, beginning the ascent into the mountains. The forest closed in, groves of fragrant myrtle, giving way to columns of pine. George shut his eyes and took a deep, satisfying breath. It was good to be in the shade. A bridge carried the road across a stream, where half a dozen gypsies had set up an encampment, but George turned into the trees instead, following a narrow pathway through the pines. From time to time he stooped to avoid branches. The horse picked its way carefully around rocks, hooves muffled by the litter of fallen pine needles. The path took them further up the mountain. Another hour passed, and the horse's neck was slick with sweat. George was hot too, his shirt clinging to his back. Finally, among the trees, a wall of rock rose up. George dismounted, crossed his stirrups over the saddle, and tied the reins to a tree in the shade. He patted the horse, and continued on foot to the rocks, though his legs were stiff after the long ride. Like the bones of the mountain, the wall of rock had burst through the thin skin of soil. Familiar with its nooks and crannies, George made his way through pillars and humps of stone to a narrow cave opening, just wide enough for a man to pass. A gate of thick bars blocked the way, but George had a key in his pocket – an ornate piece of iron as thick as a child's finger. He slipped it into the lock.

Below him, a horse whinnied. George froze. Had he been followed? His brother knew the path, of course. Was Jacob planning to stop him? Uncertain how best to proceed, George waited beside the gate. A minute passed. There could be no hiding, of course. Whoever had come would have seen his horse already. If it was Jacob, would it come to a fight, in the end? They were evenly matched, the brothers. Jacob was taller, but George was heavier. And what if Jacob was armed? George had a knife in his belt but he didn't fancy his chances if Jacob had a pistol. He was a good shot.

George waited. His horse whinnied again, and finally a man appeared, making his way through the rocks.

'George!' the man called out. George waved a cautious greeting. Jacob stepped up to the gate, his face red from the heat. He smiled at his elder brother and extended his hand. George shook it warily.

'I've come to help you,' Jacob said. 'I've been thinking about this all night long. The council's right. You're right. I've been selfish and stubborn. I haven't been thinking straight. I'll come with you, big brother. The council will be broken up and dispersed. We'll hide the lily where no one will ever find it again.'

George stared at his brother. He longed to believe him – to have his company on the voyage. Jacob looked sincere enough, but it was impossible to tell for certain if he was telling the truth.

'Good,' he said at last. 'Come along then.' George pushed open the iron gate and led the way into the dark interior of the long, narrow cave. He used a tinderbox to light a lantern stowed just inside the gate and proceeded to walk along the corridor into the mountain. Jacob hurried behind him. After a matter of yards they came up against a second door, this an arched wooden doorway carved with leaves and flowers. George unlocked this with a second key.

He had visited the chapel of the lily many times, but it never failed to astonish. He raised the lantern aloft, and the yellow light glinted off walls of gold. It was stunning, like a hidden treasure box, like the mountain's golden heart. An altar stood at the far end, and behind it, a triptych – a three-panelled picture as tall as a man. In the central section a painting of the Virgin Mary and an angel, with a white lily in its hand. To the left and right, knights clad in armour kneeling before the holy twosome, the fleur-de-lis painted on their shields. It was a highly stylised painting, like the icons of ancient Byzantium. The faces of the Virgin and the angel were ivory-white ovals, lacking in perspective, and the entire altarpiece was glittering with the richest colour and plastered with gold. George genuflected before the altar and crossed himself. How calm the Virgin's face was, how noble and grave the angel with the lily. He couldn't understand how the lily, a gift from God, had come to cause so much suffering. Why had the angel's blessing brought them madness and murder? It was a matter the council had debated for months, before making their decision. The council was made up of twelve men, all descendants of the twelve knights who received the lily in the desert. In the order's heyday, this Council of the Order of the Lily had governed an empire of lesser knights, administrators, soldiers and servants. Now the council was all that remained of the order, and its existence was a carefully guarded secret.

A mass of secret documents had been consulted and argued over before the council met in Kefalonia and reached their conclusion. Clearly the lily was perfect, coming from God, but mankind was fatally flawed. The lily was given to the knights to empower them during the crusades in the Holy Land, but successive generations had used it for more selfish and worldly purposes, to generate power and wealth, to give them high standing amongst men. The descendants had become infected with arrogance and pride, and this had corrupted the pure gifts of the lily. They agreed, the twelve men of the council, it was only by giving up the lily – by sacrificing its powers – they could atone for their sins, and the curse would be lifted. Perhaps in years to come, when the need was great and their motives were pure again, the lily could be brought back into the light.

George sighed. The order had many secrets, and one of them was Matthias, the eldest of the council, who had wandered out into the world and disappeared. There were rumours Matthias was as old as the lily itself, but where he had gone, nobody knew. George suspected he was long dead, but others claimed that he had been locked up for years or else had hidden out in the desert, the origin of the lily. Perhaps Matthias would know how best they should deal with the problem.

George rose to his feet, placed the lantern in the altar, and wandered around the chapel, feasting his eyes on the wooden panels patterned with gold leaf, the ornate candlesticks, the elaborate mosaics on the walls depicting the first twelve knights of the lily, dotted with gems, mother-of-pearl, deep blue lapis lazuli and red carnelians. Mosaic also on the floor and the ceiling, carvings on the narrow pews – not an inch of the tiny chapel was unadorned. It was overwhelming, almost claustrophobic – as though he had been swallowed by a golden mouth. George swayed on his feet, overcome. Then he closed his eyes, to regain his balance and still his thoughts. They had met one last time, the Council of the Lily, here in the chapel. The other councillors had come from all around the world to pray together and touch the lily for the last time. After today, the chapel would be locked and he would set an explosion at the entrance to seal up the gateway with a mountain's weight of stone, ensuring its existence remained a secret forever, that no one would ever find it.

George opened his eyes. Jacob was sitting patiently on a wooden chair to the left of the altar.

'It's time,' George said. He walked to the altar, folded back the wings of the triptych and took out a third and final key. Behind the altarpiece there was a thick iron door in a wall of rock. George turned the key, opened the door, and lifted out a gold and glass box. For a moment the lily glimmered through the thick, occluded glass. George hesitated before handing it to Jacob so he could lock the door again and reposition the triptych. George picked up the lantern, and the two men walked from the chapel together. George turned once, to see the golden, glowing colours and the ivory face of the angel.

The ship flew across the water. The crew of the *Dove* were in high spirits, singing as they manned the sails. Soon the tawny island was lost in the distance. The sun glittered on the bright water, and four shiny dolphins ran alongside them, leaping from the water. The clean, salt perfume of the sea filled the air.

George Maslin had commissioned the English ship to take them far away from Kefalonia. The voyage would take several weeks, and they were stopping en route at Palermo in Sicily, then Algiers, and on to Malaga in southern Spain before heading into the Atlantic Ocean, and then north into the cold, dark waters of Scandinavia. The ship's crew had been told they were carrying passengers and cargo on a trading expedition, and to this end the brothers had loaded the hold with sealed bottles of olive oil and honey, and wooden crates packed with valuable spices. George had the lily wrapped in a cloth, locked in a heavy chest, in his cabin. He still distrusted Jacob, and slept with his door barred shut every night. George wasn't a man to be idle and every day he worked hard, hoisting the sails with the crew, or plotting a course with the stout, jolly captain, on his vast, creased maps. He spent the first days stripped to the waist, his dark skin soaking up the heat, his hair tangling with the wind and salt till he started to plait it as the sailors did. His hands and muscles hardened, and he was happy, gloriously happy, to feel his body infused with power, and his mind keen as a blade. Jacob, in comparison, spent the first week of the voyage locked away in his cabin, out of the sun. He passed his time smoking large quantities of tobacco and lying on his bunk. Presumably he sneaked out at night for food. George tried to engage him in the life of the ship, but Jacob was not to be enticed from his lair.

At night, after dining on the captain's rough fare, George lingered on the deck with the sailors. One was a fiddle player and the crew entertained themselves at the end of the day listening to his tunes, and singing sea shanties and folk songs from the West Country they had left behind. Despite his higher social standing, the sailors welcomed George, shared their songs and stories. When it was time to sleep, George returned to his cabin, locked the door, and took out the lily in its glass case to inspire him as he prayed.

The case was as long as his forearm, as wide and deep as his hand. It was a mosaic of glass pieces, held together in a strong web of gold. Some of the glass was coloured – amber, blood red, sapphire blue – and even the clear pieces were dense and cloudy. The case had been sealed shut long ago, so it was hard to see the lily clearly – just fragments and glimpses. But it glowed constantly, the flower imbued with some eternal, heavenly radiance. It cast a faint light through the clear and coloured glass pieces onto the bed, where it rested, so the white sheets appeared to be stained. Peering through the glass, George could just make out five curling petals and the stout, pale stalk. On his knees, George touched the case with his fingertips. The glass was warm, and inside, the lily seemed to glow brighter in response to the contact of his hands. He felt the heat rise through his arms and into his chest, a delicious enlivening balm filling his body with power. All night long he worshipped the lily, till the pale dawn stole through the porthole and he folded the glass case back into its cloth and locked it in the chest again. He didn't need to sleep. The lily fed him strength and sharpened his brain.

The days passed. The captain marvelled at George's ability to calculate and memorise. The crew laughed when he could sing back a song, only once heard. Soon he had learned a hundred tunes, all the fiddler knew, and he could clamber up a mast faster than any of the seasoned sailors. The crew were soon in his thrall, adoring this heroic lord who could work with the best of them, who had the common touch as well as the presence and burning charisma of a king. Soon George forgot to worry about Jacob. What did he have to fear from anyone? He had the world in his hand. He was untouchable.

After Malaga, sailing up the coast of Portugal, the weeks of sunshine gave way to days of cloud and rain, rough weather and waves that tossed the ship. The sailors grew more serious, moods dampened by the challenge of the sea. At night, in his cabin, George brooded over the lily and marvelled at the power it was giving him. From time to time, premonitions of the future disturbed him, images of blood and violence connected to Jacob and the lily, but George refused to explore them. These shadows cast by the future he set aside, failing to heed them. Instead he braved the foul weather, rejoiced when the sea threw up waves as tall as the mast, when the sailors feared they would be overwhelmed by the shining walls of water looming over the ship. Nothing could touch him – not the might of the sea, and certainly not his younger brother, growing soft and addled with tobacco in his cabin.

Finally the storms blew themselves out and the winds died away. Sailing along the west coast of Scotland the sea levelled, though the sky was still draped with flags of cloud and mist. But the sailors refused to be cheered. A rumour had started among them of a ghost haunting the ship.

George told the captain the fears of the men, but the captain laughed them off. The sailors were a superstitious bunch, he confided. Never a voyage passed without some rumour or other of mermaids, or sea monsters or other figures of evil omen. Probably they liked it, the thrill of supernatural fear, to pepper up the boredom of a long sea voyage. He told George not to worry.

The ship passed the scatter of Scottish islands and broke into the North Sea, when unexpectedly the wind died away. Clouds hung low, as though the mast itself was holding them aloft. Veils of cold fog drifted over them, choking the lungs and throat. Seabirds, invisible in the cloud, flew overhead and unsettled the sailors with their long, melancholy screeches. The ship drifted.

Oddly, George felt a strange relief. Their destination was drawing nearer and he had come to dread the prospect of hiding the lily away. Each day's delay was a blessing now – he didn't want to relinquish the power it had given him. Another day, he wished. Give me another day. But the men weren't happy at all. The stories of the ghost hadn't faded. Indeed the tale had been embellished. It wasn't a ghost but a terrible monster haunting the ship in the long hours of darkness. They had seen it, creeping over the deck and shinning up the mast, to stand high up in the crow's nest in the middle of the night, its arms outstretched. The captain, who was also unsettled now, ordered a thorough search of the ship but nothing was found. George called on his brother. He hadn't seen Jacob in days and he feared – what did he fear? Deep down he had a nagging suspicion the sailors' monster was Jacob himself. George had seen his father's descent into madness. He remembered the wandering at night, the mindless vacancy in his father's eyes. Had his brother succumbed to the family curse? Was he losing his mind?

George knocked gently on the cabin door. There was no answer for a minute or two and he was just about to knock again when a lazy voice called out: 'Come in. It isn't locked.' Slowly George opened the door and stepped inside, dreading what he might see. To go through that again – it wasn't to be countenanced. Once was bad enough.

Jacob was lying on his bed. He looked bad – very pale and dirty, his hair untended, his clothes in disarray. His eyes were too big for his face, and very bright, the pupils widely dilated. The cabin was saturated with the reek of cheap rum and tobacco smoke. Jacob made no attempt to sit up.

'Big brother,' he said. 'What brings you here? Have you come to ask me to guard the lily now?' Jacob's voice was empty and languorous. It was hard to imagine him having the energy to climb a mast.

'No,' George said shortly. 'I've come to find out how you are. The sailors are telling stories of a monster roaming the ship at night.'

Jacob laughed. 'And you think it might be me? How charming. Clearly you've come to cheer me up. This interminable journey has been a descent into hell. I've been miserable every moment of it.'

'You didn't have to come.'

Jacob didn't answer. He eyed his brother, taking in his appearance.

'You look well,' he said finally. 'Very well.' Then Jacob frowned. 'Have you kept the lily locked up in the chest?'

'Yes,' George said smoothly. Why did he lie? He didn't want to talk about the lily.

'How long till the journey ends?' Jacob asked. He was still studying George, his expression concerned.

'With a good wind – maybe another week. But the wind has died away to nothing. We're making no progress at all. Tomorrow, perhaps, it'll pick up again. Clear away the damn cloud.'

Jacob shrugged. 'The sooner the better,' he said, lighting up his pipe again. George backed out, repelled by the smoke. Was Jacob truly the monster frightening the sailors? It was best to take no chances. It was possible his brother was waiting for the right moment to steal the lily. George went to his cabin, checked the lock on the chest, and took out a pistol from his luggage. He tucked it into his belt. The atmosphere on the ship was strung tight. He should trust no one.

That night the captain was murdered. George knew nothing about it until dawn, when he heard the first mate screaming and yelling. He thrust the lily into the chest, locked it, and ran out onto the deck. At first he could see nothing – except the sailor leaping and shouting, his face blanched, pointing at something high up.

'What is it? What is it?' George demanded. 'Pull yourself together, man. Speak. What is it?' By now the rest of the crew were all gathered round, and the first mate was still pointing up, at the main mast.

'Look, in the crow's nest,' one said. A murmur rose, getting louder, as they realised what they were looking at. George tipped his head back to see. There, high above the ship, the dark shape lodged in the crow's nest, arms and legs dangling, and long streaks of blood dripping down the mast and staining the white sails. Like children, the crew all gazed at George and then they began moaning and crying. One was beating his head.

'The monster,' he said. 'It'll kill us all.'

George drew back his jacket to reveal the pistol. He stepped forward.

'I'll take over the ship,' he said. 'We'll keep a watch every night. Don't forget, we are many and the monster, whatever it is, is only one. We shall be armed.' The men weren't comforted, instead staring at George in alarm. He ordered the first mate to climb the main mast to recover the body of the captain. The sailor lashed a piece of rope around the dead man's middle and lowered it to the deck. So much blood – as though an animal had torn him open.

They buried the captain at sea, George reading a few appropriate words from the prayer book. The men were grief stricken, but they kept staring at George and muttering among themselves. George himself felt a pang of regret for the loss of the captain who had befriended and tutored him. That night, the first mate took the first watch and George hammered a bar across the door to his brother's cabin.

'Is that for my protection?' Jacob called out. He didn't sound remotely concerned. His voice was tranquil, as though he were speaking from miles away. And finally George retired to his cabin. For once, sleep overcame him, a deep, black trough without dreams. When he woke, the day was well advanced, and the wind had picked up. The ship was moving again, lifting and falling on a generous swell.

But the sails were flapping. Why wasn't anyone standing at the helm? George was alarmed. Had the monster struck again? He ran around the ship, looking for the crew, clambering below deck and into the hold. No one. He found no one. The ship was deserted. Back on deck, he realised both lifeboats had disappeared. Under cover of night, the entire crew had abandoned ship. Rather than spend another day on the *Dove*, they had entrusted themselves to the icy perils of the North Sea.

George was stunned. Why had they done it? What was he to do now, alone on the ship? He couldn't sail it on his own. But of course he wasn't alone. Not entirely. Where was Jacob? The crew wouldn't have taken Jacob, surely. George ran to his brother's cabin. The bar was still in place but George tore it away in a panic.

'Jacob. Jacob!' he called out, kicking the door open and storming inside.

Jacob was lying on the bed, looking much as he had two days before. The all-pervading gin-and-tobacco reek was overlaid with the smell coming from a chamber pot beside the bunk. But Jacob's eyes widened when George stepped into the room. He struggled to sit upright.

'The crew's gone,' George said. 'We're on our own now.'

This didn't serve to calm Jacob. His back was pressed to the wall.

'Gone,' he whispered.

'Gone. Abandoned ship. They've taken the boats.'

'Why?' Jacob struggled. 'What did you do?'

'I didn't do anything!' George shouted. 'The captain was murdered – by this monster they say was haunting the ship. Murdered by you, Jacob! And now we're on our own, and the ship is drifting.'

Quickly Jacob glanced at the porthole. Was he looking for a way out? George was aware of the listing of the ship, its rudderless drifting on the ocean, pushed by the wind and tides.

'We have to change plan,' George said. 'You must help me master the ship. Perhaps we can do it, between the two of us. If we can make our way west. Perhaps we'll strike Norway. Then we can make our way home, overland.'

'What about the lily?' Jacob whispered, staring at his brother. 'We have to hide it – get rid of it.'

George shook his head. 'No,' he said. 'You were right all along. We'll take it back – keep it safe. We needn't tell the council. No one shall know of its existence, except you and I. This voyage is a disaster. I should have listened to you.'

But Jacob was shaking his head.

'No,' he said, struggling to get the words out. 'No, no. We have to be rid of it. We have to carry on, just like the council said. It is dangerous. Too dangerous.'

'You don't trust yourself,' George mused. 'You killed the captain. I can watch over you, Jacob. We can live quietly, so it doesn't happen again.' Even as he spoke, George's mind was running ahead of his words. He had no intention of either trusting Jacob or watching over him. As soon as they were safe on dry land, he would put a bullet in his brother's head. He couldn't allow the murderous lunatic to live. He would take care of the lily by himself.

'George,' Jacob said. His breathing was laboured, sweat springing out on his face. 'George, I didn't kill the captain. For God's sake, man, look at yourself.'

George frowned. 'What are you talking about?'

'Look at your hands. I didn't kill anyone. It was you. You!'

George frowned. His brother was raving. Perhaps it would be best to kill him now. He shook his head. It was no good. He needed Jacob to help sail the ship. Without a word he turned away from his brother and wandered blindly around the *Dove*'s empty deck. He made his way, unthinking, to the captain's cabin. A mirror in a golden frame hung above the desk. A crack wormed its way across the glass surface, but the reflection was good enough. Cold inside, George lifted his eyes to consider the image offered back.

Long sable hair, in a sailor's plait. Dark eyes, a black beard. And bloodstains, splattered across his face. George couldn't breathe. He lifted his shaking hands, covered with dried blood, right up to his elbows. His clothes were black with it, and his throat, the hair on his chest. Why hadn't he noticed before? Suddenly the events of the past few days slotted into place. He remembered how the crew had looked at him when the captain's body was discovered. He must have been a terrible sight, covered in sticky gore, and ordering them around as though nothing were wrong. And dimly, as though in a dream, he remembered the nights he had peeled off his clothes and loped around the ship, clambering over the rigging like a monkey, glorying in the feel of the sea air, the power of the sea. And he remembered his father, and the premonitions of violence he had ignored.

The strength drained from his body. He struggled to keep on his feet and stumbled onto the deck, into the chilly sunshine. The ship leaned in the water, at the mercy of every gust of wind. The sails flapped over his head. George felt hollow, as though his heart and guts had turned to dust. He couldn't think, couldn't feel. His mind went black.

'George.' Jacob stood behind him, holding out a hand.

George opened his mouth to speak, but he couldn't find a word to say. He drew out the pistol from his belt and lifted it towards his brother.

'It is the lily that's done this,' Jacob said. 'We must be rid of it.'

'Take it,' George whispered. 'Kill me, Jacob. Before I kill you.'

Slowly Jacob stepped forward. He took the gun – and flung it over the side of the ship into the ocean.

'I can't kill you,' he said softly. 'You're my brother.'

A storm of images and urges rose up in George's mind, crowding out the voice of his sanity. A hunger to destroy, a lust for power, a deep yearning to hold the lily to his breast and soak up its radiance and warmth. What wouldn't he do to keep it, to enjoy its nurturing strength? He clapped his hands to the side of his head in anguish and cried out in despair. It shouldn't be like this. Grief overwhelmed him, for the loss of his life and peace. He yearned for honour. He had wanted to be good and kind. In one last moment of clarity he ran across the deck and dived overboard, plunging headlong into the cold, salt embrace of the sea.

The ship drifted for weeks. Jacob had no idea where he was heading. All alone on the ship, he fell into a fever. Dimly he was aware of the sun rising and sinking. He assumed he would die, when the stores ran out and hunger or thirst got the better of him. He thought of throwing the lily overboard, after his brother, but he couldn't bring himself to do it. The orders were, he remembered, to hide it away – not to lose it. In the meantime, he stared at the ocean, and at night, lay on the deck and gazed at the maze of stars, till vertigo got the better of him and instead he hid away in his cabin. Without any rein to guide her, the *Dove* alternately lazed and frolicked. Her course was haphazard and fanciful. Then one night a storm blew up, and with no one to steer her, the ship was smashed against rocks, breaching the hull so tons of seawater flooded her belly and stole the sealed bottles of olive oil and the crates of spices. As the deck tilted, with waves breaking over his head, Jacob took the lily in its glass case and half jumped, half fell into the water.

8

The Rose
London, 1890

A filthy London night, choked with fog and smoke. Above the pall, the sky burned red and sulphurous yellow, like the coal furnaces of a thousand city manufactories. Miranda and her aunt Mary were travelling in a cab to St James Theatre to see a play. The grandparents were allowing Miranda to stay overnight with her aunt at the hotel. Thus an evening of adventure lay ahead, moving among the crowd of actors, artists and writers who had attended parties at her mother's flat. How many had concerned themselves with her mother's illness? she wondered. Perhaps the outing wasn't such a good idea – it would stir up too many thoughts of the one person she most longed to see.

As though sensing Miranda's doubts, her aunt stretched out a hand and patted her arm.

'It's a vile night,' she said. 'But we'll soon be out of the weather.'

Miranda nodded. The tainted air caught in the throat. She stared through the window, seeing street lamps loom in the fog.

Mary had tickets for a new play. The audience was a mixed bunch, respectable couples rubbing shoulders with raffish young men in cheap suits. Miranda was thrilled by the play and for an hour or more, all worries about her mother were mercifully pushed from her mind. Applause and cheering at the end, and then a trip to a café where several actors from the play joined Mary and some of her friends for drinks. It was a homecoming for Miranda, a return to the free and easy ways of her previous life, before the rules and formalities imposed at her grandparents' house. Here people joked and laughed, and there was no subject beyond the pale when it came to discussion and debate. She sipped coffee, watched the goings-on, and eavesdropped on conversations. Several of her mother's friends asked after her, expressed their concern, and Miranda felt bad once again for assuming they didn't care. Why had she fallen into this habit, expecting the worst of people? It was warm and comforting inside the café. The tall glass windows afforded a view of the night, and the pavements where passers-by ambled. The street was busy with revellers, people spilling from the theatres and public houses, heated with excitement and drink. A tall, elegant woman strolled by, a neat felt hat perched on her blonde hair. She caught Miranda's eye, and smiled. Miranda smiled in return, wondering why the woman looked familiar. The woman stopped outside of the café, apparently considering the menu board, but she glanced at Miranda again. A memory fell into place in Miranda's mind. Wasn't this the woman who stood under the lamp post, in the rain, outside her grandparents' house? Who was she?

'Would you like more coffee, Miranda?' Her view of the blonde woman was obstructed by Mary, who sat herself in the chair on the other side of the table.

'No I'm fine,' Miranda said. Then, uneasy to be broaching the subject, she blurted: 'Mary, what really happened to my father?'

The subject had preoccupied Miranda all day – almost displacing her mother for a time. David Kingsley had disappeared from her life three years ago, and her memories of him were patchy because he had often been away. She remembered her mother and father laughing and embracing in the summer garden of her aunt's house. And she recalled the many letters he sent from cities all over Europe, Egypt and North Africa.

That very morning, in the parlour of her grandparents' house, she had found three photographs of him, among the collection arranged on the back of the piano. She hadn't dared investigate them before, but Mrs Kingsley was out making calls on her friends, Mr Kingsley was taking a walk and, for a time, Miranda had the house to herself.

The first was a picture of David as a fat baby in a white gown, with curls of dark hair and big round eyes. His name and the date of the picture were written on the back of the picture, though Miranda was certain she would have recognised him in any case. The second photograph depicted the teenage schoolboy – perhaps the same age as she was now – brandishing a tennis racquet, while other sporting paraphernalia lay at his feet. These careful props attested to his athletic prowess, no doubt. Miranda picked up the picture and stared at it. Something about his face sent a curious electric thrill through her body. Despite the different colouring, David looked uncannily like she did. His face was echoed in her own – the set of the eyes, the curve of cheekbones. Didn't her grandparents see this resemblance? Had they chosen not to? Slowly she replaced the picture and picked up the third – showing David as a bright young man. The pose was stiff and formal, but that did not disguise the good looks and the energy of the sitter. Luminous with youth and health, he gazed from the picture right into the eyes of his daughter. This was the father she remembered, the precious, fleeting memories of the laughing man with his arms around her mother, holding her hand as they wandered in the sunny garden in the countryside.

'He was a splendid-looking young man,' said a gruff voice. Miranda spun around with a gasp. Hurriedly she replaced the picture on the piano, shuffling them all back into place. Mr Kingsley was standing in the doorway, his face red from the cold outside. There was an awkward silence for a few moments – Miranda waiting for him to leave, the grandfather struggling for words to say. But the old man surprised her. He stepped into the room and picked up the picture himself.

'I miss him so much,' Mr Kingsley said. Then he looked at Miranda. 'You know, you do look a little like him. My wife would never admit it, of course, but I can see it. It's very hard for her, having you here. Too many memories.'

Miranda cleared her throat nervously, thrown off balance by her grandfather's sudden admission. She plunged in.

'What exactly happened to him?'

'What did your mother tell you?'

Miranda remembered the day, when she was eleven, and a letter in a strange hand arrived from Algiers. It contained the news, official and starkly written, that David Kingsley had been drowned in an accident at sea. She told Mr Kingsley what she knew.

'What was he doing there?' she asked. 'My mother just told me he was travelling – that he was an explorer. But I could never understand why he wanted to spend so much time away from us.'

'I don't know much more,' Mr Kingsley admitted. 'He didn't confide in me. He had some burning quest and nothing would stand in his way. But it was such a waste. Such a terrible waste. It destroyed us both. My wife has never recovered.' Miranda glanced at her grandfather, and saw his eyes were filled with tears. Without thinking, she stretched out her hand and touched him gently on the arm. They were silent, sharing a moment of their hurt and loss. Then, abruptly, it was over. The old man shook his head, as though banishing his tears. He stood up straight, replaced the photograph and wandered out of the room.

In the café, Aunt Mary frowned. 'Your father?' she repeated. 'What do you want to know?'

'Why didn't they marry?'

'Julia didn't agree with it. She didn't want to be a man's possession.' Mary wrinkled her nose. 'I wouldn't marry either, on principle.'

'So it wasn't that my father didn't want to marry her?'

Mary laughed. 'Not a bit of it. He pleaded with her to marry him. He never gave up.'

'She should have,' Miranda said. 'For my sake. For me.'

Mary shook her head, lighting up another cigarette. 'Julia is a free spirit, Miranda. You should be proud of her. We have both defied convention. It is an unjust world, and women bear the brunt of its injustices. She was prepared to step beyond the boundaries of acceptable behaviour, because of her beliefs. Did you ever lack for anything? Did you ever feel unloved or unwanted?'

'I do now,' Miranda said painfully. 'My grandparents don't want me. If my mother had married – that would be different.'

Mary placed her hand over Miranda's. 'It is a difficult time,' she conceded. 'Not just for you – for all of us. There's so much happening. Your father wasn't on a pleasure trip. He was engaged on a project for your mother and me – a project I've been pursuing since his death. My trip to Greece – that was a part of it too.'

Miranda shook her head. 'What are you talking about? What project?'

Mary sighed. 'There's a great deal you don't know – that you have never needed to know. Perhaps now is the time to share it – but I won't talk about family matters here. Tonight, when we get back to the hotel, I'll explain what I can. It could be of critical importance to us all.' Mary looked nervous for a moment, glancing around the room, touching her handbag. For some reason, Miranda remembered the glamorous blonde woman peering into the café. Picking up Mary's unease, she shivered, and wrapped her arms around herself. Then someone called out to Mary – a handsome young actor from the play – and everyone began to laugh at something he said, which Miranda didn't catch. Her anxiety passed, but all of a sudden she felt very tired. She tugged Mary's sleeve.

'Can we go now, please?' she said. 'It's late – nearly midnight.'

Mary nodded. 'I'll call you a cab,' she said. 'I have one or two things to sort out first, but I won't be long. Here's the key for the hotel. Make yourself at home and order some hot chocolate.'

Hansom cabs were lined up in the street outside, horses and drivers weighed down with blankets as they waited for trade in the bitter cold and fog. Mary instructed the driver as Miranda stepped inside the cab, and they were off, clopping through the streets to the hotel. The cab smelled of pipe smoke and old perfume. The seat was badly stuffed and uncomfortable. Miranda ached to be in bed. The cab drew up at a crossing – and without warning the door opened. The blonde woman stepped inside, smiled a greeting and, uninvited, sat down opposite Miranda.

'Good evening,' she said smoothly. 'My name is Blanche. And you are Miranda Maysfield.' She held out a neat, gloved hand which Miranda was too stunned to refuse. It was hard to see clearly in the gloom of a cab, but Blanche looked very young and very pretty. Her hat was plumed with handsome feathers and a silver pin.

'Who are you?' Miranda said. She shifted uneasily on her seat. What did the woman want? Should she call out for help? Make a getaway?

'Oh, don't worry,' Blanche said. 'We're relatives – of a sort. Distant relatives.'

'You know my mother?'

'Julia. I haven't met her, but I know of her. And your father, David Kingsley, and your aunt Mary. You see, we have a great deal in common. That is why I wanted to meet you.'

'Then why didn't you come into the café and speak to me there?'

Blanche took a deep breath. She touched her hair.

'I've come to help you,' she said. 'You don't know it, but you're in danger, Miranda. I want to protect you.'

Miranda shook her head. 'Why am I in danger?'

'Will you trust me on this, Miranda? Will you come with me? I will tell you everything as soon as I can.' She leaned forward, and stared into Miranda's eyes. 'Please,' she said. 'Your life could depend on it. And your mother's.'

Miranda struggled with a rising sense of panic. 'What about her?' she said. 'What do you mean?' She rose to her feet and banged on the roof of the cab with her fist. Like a shot, Blanche grabbed her, pulling her down to the seat. The cabbie stopped the vehicle, but Blanche pressed a handkerchief to Miranda's face, covering her nose and mouth. She called out through the door: 'Carry on, driver. We're fine!' A ripe, chemical stink imbued the hanky – causing Miranda to choke. She struggled violently against Blanche but the woman possessed surprising reserves of strength. Miranda punched wildly, trying not to breathe, but the substance soaking the hanky was getting the better of her now, sending tendrils of poison through her veins and brain. Her mind was clouded, her limbs grew heavier every moment, as though she were fighting to stay afloat in a marsh. She heard Blanche say something, from far away, but she couldn't make out the words. The world receded – and the light went out.

An indistinguishable mass of time passed, in darkness and disorder. Miranda was dimly aware of movement and voices. Like a dream, a stream of disconnected images flowed through her brain – Blanche leaning over her, the concerned voice of a man, and then a vague struggle as she was lifted and placed in a confined space. She couldn't see, couldn't move at all. For a time her mind struggled with the weight of her body, aware she should get out, but her thoughts seemed entirely disconnected from nerves and muscles. Blanche again, and more of the anaesthetising chemical that had sent her into a stupor. Miranda sank deeper into a mire of unconsciousness.

When she woke, she was slumped on the seat of a carriage, and Blanche was sitting opposite. Miranda's mind reeled. Was she still in the cab? What had happened? Was it a dream? But her head ached and she felt sick to death. She was also desperate to pee. Aching all over, she pushed herself upright. Spruce, smiling, Blanche looked her over.

'How are we feeling?' she asked. 'I expect you need a drink. I apologise for my tactics – but not for my intention. There was no time to persuade you.'

Miranda didn't answer. It wasn't a cab, but a larger carriage, and outside the window a vista of autumnal fields flew past. They were travelling at speed.

'Where are we? Where are we going?' she croaked. Speaking made her head ache worse. Her throat was dry as dust. Never had she felt so bad.

'To the coast,' Blanche said brightly. 'A boat is waiting for us, and then we are heading across France to meet friends in Prague. You will be safe there. We can protect you.'

Miranda struggled to process this information but the pain battering her head made thinking near impossible. Blanche handed her a bottle of water.

'Have a drink,' she said.

'I need to pee,' Miranda said weakly, taking the water and tipping it into her dry mouth.

'I'm afraid you'll just have to hold on. We simply can't stop.'

Miranda crossed her legs, and glowered at Blanche. She eyed the carriage doors.

'They're locked,' Blanche said. 'Don't think about it, Miranda. Just sit tight. We won't be long.'

Miranda leaned back, into the corner of the carriage, and slowly sipped the water. The rolling motion of the carriage

106

didn't help her sickness, but bit by bit her headache subsided into a dull throb. A sense of panic was rising. She couldn't understand why this woman had taken her. What was going to happen? How would her relatives find her? Somehow, she had to escape before they smuggled her out of the country. She ignored Blanche's attempts at making conversation and winning her over. Instead she had to think – and think quickly.

They stopped at a coaching inn but Miranda wasn't allowed out of the carriage. Blanche disappeared briefly, locking the door behind her, and returned with a basket of food and drink. Then the journey resumed. At one point, out in the middle of nowhere, Blanche called on the driver to stop the carriage so Miranda could pee behind a bush, but even then, the blonde woman was close beside her allowing Miranda no opportunity to make a getaway.

By nightfall they had reached the coast. Miranda's headache was getting worse again. She was exhausted and strung out with fear. She could hear the cry of gulls, and in the gloom, spied the moonlight glittering on the expanse of ocean, beneath the cliffs.

'Nearly there,' Blanche said. 'Not long to wait now. There is a boat waiting for us, something small and discreet to get us over the channel. We'll be in France in a few hours. Will you behave yourself, or do I have to get the chloroform again?'

Miranda shook her head. 'No,' she said. 'Not that.' She peered out of the window. She was running out of time. The carriage turned from the cliff-top road down a narrow, cobbled lane to a small village at the edge of the sea. It was a dark place, poor-looking and closed up. No one was about. The horses slithered on the precarious road to a tiny harbour, and pulled up outside an inn called The Mermaid. Miranda could see the sign swinging in the wind, and the friendly yellow glow of candles in the windows. Blanche unlocked the door.

'Come along,' she said, grasping Miranda by the arm. 'Any nonsense now and you know what'll happen.'

Miranda stepped out, into a cold, buffeting wind. The sea roared, crashing giant waves over the harbour wall. The air tasted of salt and seaweed. The door of the inn swung open and a man strode out, huddled in a long coat. The wind tore at his fair hair.

'Blanche!' he called, holding out his arm. They embraced and kissed, Blanche still keeping a grip upon Miranda. When they separated, the blond man glanced at Miranda.

'Come inside,' he said. 'Out of this filthy weather. They can't take us tonight. In the morning – first light – the storm will have blown itself out then.'

They hurried Miranda into the inn. She hoped for crowds of friendly-looking people inside she could appeal to for help, but despite the fierce fire in the hearth, the inn was virtually deserted. A rough-looking man with a barking dog stood behind the bar, and a toothless elderly man, doubtless some ancient mariner, was sat on a bench close to the hearth. They stared at Miranda when she stepped into the room but neither looked in the slightest bit warm or helpful. Indeed, their expressions seemed hostile and resentful.

'We'll go straight to our rooms,' Blanche said. 'We're both exhausted.' Her companion nodded.

'Bring us some hot water and food,' he ordered. The man behind the bar nodded. His dog was still barking, on and on. The sound hammered into Miranda's head. The pub was filthy and full of shadows, and the whole dismal scene was like a bad dream. Nothing made sense. What was happening? Why had they taken her?

Blanche bundled Miranda up the stairs to a bedroom at the front of the pub. This was a large room, relatively clean though hopelessly old-fashioned, with a chamber pot under the bed. Blanche and the man sat down. They stared at Miranda.

'This is my husband, Edmund Tremayne,' Blanche said. Edmund didn't say anything at first. He continued to look at Miranda.

'Sit down,' he said at last, gesturing to a chair.

There was a bang, and a girl pushed the door open with her foot. She had a dingy dress and dark ratty hair under a white cap. She stepped in with a tray of food in one hand and, precariously, a jug of steaming water in the other. Hurriedly she dumped the tray and jug on a table, so shy she hardly dared raise her eyes to the occupants in the room, though Miranda inwardly pleaded for her to do so, to make a connection. Maybe this would be the person to turn to for help. With a brief curtsy, eyes still downcast, the girl scuttled out of the room.

'We'll leave you alone to wash and eat,' Blanche said. 'But don't go to bed yet. We want to talk to you first, and explain why we've taken you. Perhaps then you will understand why we resorted to such dramatic measures. I want you to trust me, Miranda. I will lock you in, but we have the room next to this one, so call if you need me.'

This was an unspoken warning of course. Call out for help, make any fuss, and we shall hear that too.

Miranda nodded. Mr and Mrs Tremayne left the room, and Miranda heard the sound of the key turning in the lock. At last she was alone. Cold, afraid, and weary to the bone, she tipped the hot water into a bowl and washed away the dirt of a day and a night's travel, brushed her hair, and ravenously consumed the stewed beef and potatoes provided by the maid. There was good, hot tea as well, laced with sugar and heartening to drink. Then she waited for Blanche to return, and for an explanation. Her aunt and grandparents must be frantic with worry. They would have called the police, maybe tracked down the cab driver who saw Blanche steal her away. Miranda might feel on her own, but, she reassured herself, there were people who must be searching for her right now.

Miranda lay on the bed, and she must have drifted into sleep because when she opened her eyes again, Blanche and Edmund were standing over her, looking down.

'Wake up,' Blanche said. 'I have a present for you.' She was blocking out the light from the candle, so it was hard for Miranda to see what Blanche was holding in her hand.

'What is it?' Miranda said.

'Have a look.' Blanche dropped the package into Miranda's hands. Brown wrapping paper tied with string, which fell away under her fingers to reveal a pack of tarot cards. Miranda gasped. She scrambled off the bed to hold them in the light. She forgot everything else for a moment, caught up in admiration. Beautiful they were – so finely made. Her own cards were crude in comparison, the card soft, the pictures clumsy. These were miniature works of art, glittering with gold and scarlet, weighty in her hand, smooth as silk.

'You like them,' Edmund said, with satisfaction. 'They're the best money can buy. I ordered them from Italy, especially for you. Call it a welcome home gift.'

Miranda heard him only distantly. She was studying the cards, one after the other, marvelling.

'How about reading them for us,' Blanche said softly. 'You have a gift, I understand. You can see the future.'

Miranda closed her hands over the deck. This was what they wanted, the Tremaynes? Her fortune-telling talent? For some reason, which she could not quite put a finger on, Miranda felt more confident. Perhaps it was simply the presence of the cards in her hand. Perhaps it was because they believed she had a special power.

'How do you know that?' Miranda said.

'We've found out a lot about you, Miranda. We were first introduced to you by another girl who has a talent comparable to yours. Then we carried out further investigations and learned a great deal more,' Edmund said. His voice possessed no warmth, but some kind of passion seemed to burn in his face. Miranda was wary, sensing intelligence, and a lust for violence he had constantly to check.

'Your mother's friends are not the most discreet people,' Blanche continued. 'There were several all too keen to share the nature of your family circumstances with us. About your mother and aunt, about your father too.'

Miranda swallowed, still gripping the cards. She could imagine it all too well, when the drink was flowing, her mother's crowd sharing the exciting details. It was the downside of their easy-going, permissive lifestyle. The uptight Kingsleys would never pass on such details to strangers, however friendly and keen to buy champagne those strangers might be.

'Once we knew so much, we could fill in the details,' Edmund said. 'It is possible we are relatives, Miranda. And if we are not directly blood relatives, our ancestors shared a close bond, an oath of loyalty. In one way or another, we are family.'

'I don't know what you're talking about,' she said crisply. 'And if I am such a valuable soothsayer, why did I have no idea you were going to kidnap me?'

Blanche murmured. 'No,' she said. 'We haven't kidnapped you. We want to protect you.'

'From whom? Why do I need protecting?' Miranda began to shuffle the cards. They slid easily and gracefully between her fingers.

Blanche sighed. 'Where do we start?' she said to Edmund.

He shook his head impatiently. 'I haven't time for all this. You talk to her. I need a drink.' He stomped out of the room and downstairs, leaving Blanche with Miranda, who stared at her, waiting for an explanation.

'I'll tell you a story,' Blanche began, sitting herself on the side of the bed. 'You probably won't believe it, but that doesn't stop the story being true. At the time of the Crusades, in the middle of a desert, twelve knights faced an insurmountable force. They were cut off from their fellows, stranded in a network of caves, and the Mohammedans were closing in. The knights, pious Christians, prayed for deliverance. These appeals were heard.

111

An angel descended and gave the men a holy lily which conferred upon them a host of magical powers. They were blessed with supernatural physical strength. They could see into the future, and across vast distances. Of course they won the battle against great odds and went on to set up a powerful army, the Order of the Lily.'

Miranda smiled to herself. The story appealed, despite its improbability.

'These knights – the order – what happened?' she said.

'They grew in wealth and power, all over Europe, and their descendants inherited the powers of their fathers. Eventually they grew too strong. The Catholic church joined forces with various rulers to bring them down. There were accusations of witchcraft, devil worship and heresy. The leaders were hunted down, tortured and executed.'

'But that wasn't the end of it?' Miranda said.

'No. Not at all. The order went underground. A new council of twelve was appointed from the descendants of the original knights, to guard the lily and continue their work. The Council of the Lily continued in secret for hundreds of years, until 1790 when they finally decided to disband and the lily was hidden away.'

Miranda chewed her lip, lost in thought. 'But its influence continues?' she said. 'You think you are descended from the knights, and because I can read cards, you think I am too. So what is your gift, Mrs Tremayne? What can you do?'

Blanche smiled coldly. 'I'm not blessed with any special power,' she said. 'But I wish to be – it is my right – my inheritance. We have been much diminished, but the time has come for the order to be re-established. A new council will be elected and the lily restored to the light.' She leaned towards Miranda confidentially, and placed her hand on Miranda's arm.

'Are you a religious person, Miranda? The lily was a gift from God, and using its powers the order did good work in his name. That is what we wish to do again. Why should this light be hidden? Think of what we could achieve, how we could turn the world around before it is entirely covered with darkness.'

Blanche's face possessed a luminous intensity. She was caught up in her own feverish vision of future glory. Miranda stared, still sliding the cards from hand to hand. Knights and angels, secret orders, a holy lily. The images glowed in her mind.

It was a fantastic story – but she didn't believe a word of it.

Miranda waited a few moments more, watching Blanche's rapt face. Her own thoughts slotted into place. The more she knew, the better her chance of escaping.

'So who are you protecting me from?' she said at last.

'There are others, who want to stop us.'

'More of these descendants?'

'Yes. They want to keep the lily hidden away, Miranda. They won't stop at anything to prevent its discovery.'

'Why would they do that? It doesn't make sense.'

'I don't know,' Blanche admitted. 'Why wouldn't you take a gift that is offered? I think they want to keep it for themselves, because they're selfish. But I know they'll deceive and kill to keep us in the dark. To keep you in the dark, Miranda. Think how much more potent your talent might become if the lily were uncovered.'

Blanche rose to her feet, leaving Miranda with this thought to chew on.

'Go to sleep,' she said. 'It's late, and we have an early start in the morning and another long journey. Don't be afraid. We'll protect you now. This is the beginning of something good – something marvellous.'

The door shut, and the lock turned. Miranda closed her eyes and emptied her mind, and laid out ten tarot cards in a circle on the bed. Then she looked at the arrangement. The Queen of Swords presided. The Nine of Swords, the Tower, the Fool, and the Knave of Rods. Webs of meaning rose up between them, connections one to another – and a host of images flashed into her mind.

A tower in a forest, a young man stretching out his hand, the corpse of an old man on a train thundering through the forest.

Miranda strained to see more, drawing back the curtain of the present to see what was to come. Who was the young man? She had seen him before, in another vision, at her grandparents' house.

She focused on the tower. The tower and the Queen of Swords. Who was the queen? Blanche? No use asking questions – no use thinking. She closed her eyes again and cleared her mind, waiting for the picture to come. The Queen of Swords. In the tower, surrounded by forest, the girl with long, tangled hair who always had her back to Miranda. Who was she? Who? Miranda pushed aside her thoughts and focused on the girl. Closer she came, and closer. She stretched out a hand to touch her and suddenly the girl turned around.

Miranda gasped. She saw a rose. The girl's face was as red as a rose.

Early the next morning, Miranda was bundled onto a small boat. The storm had blown out, and the sea was a glittering, silken blue in the sunshine. Blanche and Edmund Tremayne sat either side of her as they headed away from England.

9

All Roads Lead to Prague
En route to Prague, 1890

Pale, grey light crept through the blinds of the sleeping compartment, as the train powered through miles of gloomy forest. Jack lay awake for a moment, enjoying the warmth of his narrow bed, with its fine white sheets and woollen blankets. The marvel of his adventure still hadn't entirely sunk in.

Beneath Maslin's bunk, secured with a new padlock, lay the tin chest rescued from the embers of the fire.

How excited they had been, the two of them that early morning, desperate for the metal to cool so they could open it up and see what lay in side. Jack was agog. Could it be? Could it be the lily inside? What would it look like? What would happen? While Maslin didn't chatter and fret like Jack, there was no doubting the effect this discovery had on him. Despite the horrible welt across his face and the horror of the night attack, Maslin's eyes were shining. As soon as the tin box was barely touchable, Maslin struggled to open it up. He cursed when he burned his fingers, and used the tail of his jacket to protect them as he fiddled with the catch. But the heat had welded the lock tight shut. So Maslin picked up the chest, and with it tucked under his arm, they headed back to Jack's home.

The family were still asleep. Jack led Maslin to his father's workshop in the farmyard, where his farrier's tools were kept, and used a chisel to pry apart the metal latch, smeared by the heat. When the lock broke they waited for a moment, the two of them, in the gloom of the shed. Jack's mouth was dry. Everything was silent. All around them, hanging neatly from nails on the wall, the tools were covered with dust and cobwebs, after months without use.

'Do you think . . .' Jack started, swallowing hard. 'Do you think this is it?'

Maslin shrugged abruptly. 'I don't know,' he said. 'I doubt it.' But his hands were shaking when he stretched them out to flip open the lid. Jack could hardly breathe.

The lid fell back, with a creak. It was lined with torn, green fabric. They stepped forward, Jack and Maslin, to look inside. Lots of yellowed paper. Jack let out a long, disappointed sigh. Maslin stuck his hand inside, to root around. Some of the paper spilled, envelopes with foreign stamps, scrawled notes and diagrams. Then Maslin pulled something out and held it to the light. Jack tried to make out what it was, this small, dark something brandished in Maslin's hand.

'It's not the lily,' Jack said, in a small voice.

Maslin shook his head. 'I didn't expect it,' he answered, a tremor in his old voice. Colour suffused his face. 'It's a picture.' He wiped his eyes with his sleeve. 'It's a picture of my mother.'

Later that day Maslin paid Jack's mother handsomely for the boy's services as a groom, servant and companion and the two of them set off on horseback to the coast. Together they crossed the sea to France, and then began the long train journey across Europe, through the strange, unrolling landscape. They passed fields where peasants toiled in the rain, and huge cities where endless coils of smoke rose from blackened factories and mills. Mountains and forests were succeeded by the sprawl of coal mines, where columns of ill-dressed, coal-blackened men trudged past monstrous mounds of slag and cinder.

Jack was well-dressed now, kitted out for the journey and his new role with good, warm clothes. Maslin treated him as an equal, and Jack was eager to prove his worth. From time to time, Maslin was overcome by weakness and rending headaches, when he gulped laudanum and relied on Jack to take care of him. Often they talked, Maslin commenting on their journey and the places they passed. Jack had not got over the thrill of hearing people speak another language, their exotic fellow passengers and the train staff, the vendors with trays of coffee and bread rolls and newspapers in the stations where they stopped. The quality of light seemed different, even the scent of the air he breathed.

Jack sat up in bed, and peered through the blinds at the forest. It was a gloomy place, broken every now and then by barbarous rocks where streams tumbled. He glimpsed the antlered head of a deer, retreating from the noise of the train. It would be breakfast soon, so he slipped off the bunk to wake Maslin.

The old man was dead.

His mouth had dropped open, his eyes were sunken, the skin gone tight against his skull. Jack put his face close to Maslin's, to detect if he was breathing. He touched the side of his neck, to detect a pulse. Was he dead? Was he really dead? Or was this some kind of profound swoon, an imitation of death, like the time Jack had first found him in the old house. That must be it. Jack stood back, his own heart racing, as he prayed for his bene-factor to wake up. Maslin the corpse lay perfectly still, his white hair spread over the pillow, his hands by his sides. Jack was at a loss. What was best to do? He moistened a towel and wiped Maslin's face with water from the jug. He picked up one stiff, bony hand and rubbed it, in the hope of inducing the blood to flow. Finally he recovered the bottle of laudanum from Maslin's coat pocket, uncorked it, and dabbed a drop of the liquid onto Maslin's blue lips.

Nothing. Still nothing.

Maslin had to wake up soon. What if he stayed like this for days? Someone would see him. What kind of horror would follow then?

'Mr Maslin. Mr Maslin, sir,' Jack said, in desperation. 'Wake up. You have to come back to me. Please, sir. Please.'

Seconds passed, and minutes. Miles rolled by outside the window. In the train, the sounds of morning activity had commenced, people moving in the corridor. A waiter would soon deliver them breakfast. Jack waited in tight suspense.

At last, a shudder ran through the old man's body, a horrible convulsion that threw back his head and twisted his spine. Then Maslin fell back on the pillow and opened his eyes wide. His face was etched with horror.

'Mr Maslin!' Jack called out. 'It's all right, sir. It was a bad dream. You're safe now. It was only a dream!' At first he thought Maslin couldn't even see him. The old man was staring at something, perhaps an imaginary event still lingering in his mind, even though the reality of the train was all around him. Maslin gasped for air. He stretched out his hands in front of him.

'Jack!' he called hoarsely. 'Get me some water. Quickly now.'

Then, when he had gulped a mouthful or two, clumsily spilling water down the front of his shirt, Maslin began to speak.

'I have bad dreams,' he said. 'Ever since I was a child. Nightmares!' His face was ghastly. 'Sometimes I'd wake up screaming. I had to have a candle burning beside my bed, all night long, or I wouldn't sleep at all. Images of the past, Jack. That's what I dream. I didn't understand at first, where they came from. Nothing made much sense – no logic to them. No context. And when I was older, the dreams were stronger, and I fell into the stupor you've seen. I have to be careful. That's why I need you. People think I'm dead – as you did that first time in the house – and I have a horrible fear one day I will be buried alive.' Maslin sat up in his bed. The colour was returning to his face but his hands were still shaking. He looked very thin and frail.

'You were dreaming of the past?' Jack said.

Maslin nodded gravely. 'I dreamed about the lily,' he said. 'It's the first time I've done so, directly. Because we're on the trail, maybe. Or because we found my grandfather's box.'

'What did you dream? Does it help us?'

Maslin considered. 'Perhaps,' he said. 'It confirms the need to destroy it.' He glanced at Jack. 'I dreamed of two brothers on an island of Greece, and a journey on a ship. It was the time the council decided to bury the lily forever. There was a death on the ship, and one of the brothers drowned. The other, Jacob, was shipwrecked with the lily. He was my great-grandfather – and the one who hid the lily. He shared the secret of its location with no one – not even his children.

'I think the council had its secret headquarters on Kefalonia for many years, once the order had gone underground, but I don't know exactly where.'

'Was it Jacob who built the house in Ireland?'

'No. I know little about Jacob. He travelled a great deal, all over Europe, and then settled down on the coast of Scotland, miles from anywhere. It was his son – my grandfather – who built the house in Ireland. He was another George. Jacob named him after his dead brother.'

'So your grandfather – George – was the owner of the tin chest?'

Maslin nodded. 'Yes. Please – bring it here.'

Jack stooped down and pulled the chest from beneath Maslin's bed. Maslin flipped the lid open. Inside were the bundle of letters and a small oil painting of a pale woman with long, black hair. Maslin lifted out the picture with reverence and laid it on the bed.

'Your mother,' Jack said. 'Rachel Maslin.' Together they had pored over the contents of the box many times, since discovering it in the ashes of the house.

'Not Maslin then. Rachel Flynn. This was painted before she married.' The old man stared at the picture, suddenly vulnerable, tied by precious threads of memory to the face it depicted.

'But she was one of them too? The descendants of the knights?'

Maslin nodded. 'I believe so. Much of the genealogy of the original twelve has been lost, but I think she was. Perhaps I have a gift because both my parents were descendants. So many generations have come and gone, there must be hundreds, maybe thousands, of descendants by now. Very few of them will know anything about it.'

'Except the Tremaynes.'

'Yes. Except them.' Maslin took out the letters, about a dozen of them altogether, and read them all over again, perhaps hoping an umpteenth reading would open his eyes to some hitherto undetected clue.

The letters were written by Rachel Maslin to George, her father-in-law. She was in her thirties when she wrote them, already a widow with a son, James. Her husband, James's father, was called Felix Maslin. As Edmund Tremayne had so brutally revealed, he had killed himself in a riding accident. The coroner's report had recorded the event as an accident, but it was widely known James's father was losing his mind. He was afflicted by terrible nightmares and long, crushing depressions and one cloudy night he had ridden his horse at a gallop off the edge of a high cliff. The following morning the broken bodies of man and horse were found on the rocks, and the animal's deep hoofprints were identified in the turf high up.

It seemed the circumstances of her husband's death had prompted both Rachel and her devastated father-in-law to undertake some family research of their own. The lily was still blighting lives – they wanted to find it, and this time they had no thought of hiding it away. They wanted to try and destroy it.

Unfortunately Jacob had taken the secret of its location to his grave.

Rachel had sent the letters from Prague, the city where the last remaining archives on the Order of the Lily could be found. She carried out diligent research, which she wrote up and sent to her father-in-law in Ireland. James, about twelve or thirteen, had been despatched to boarding school. They spent only summers together now, at his grandparents' house in Ireland.

The letters referred to a painting of the twelve knights and the angel, and ancient records belonging to the order in its earliest days. Rachel found old books surviving from the order's library, and accounts detailing expenditure and revenues from the order's lands. But all these details merely filled in details of the past – they did not help her find the lily's final hiding place – and all of the time she was aware of pursuit. Others were watching. She wasn't the only one on the trail.

Finally, after months pursuing the truth, Maslin's mother had found something. The last letter was a hasty scrawl.

She wrote: *There is a strange man living in the Jewish quarter, an old man, who says he knew Jacob Maslin. He has dogged my steps for weeks. Now he wants to talk to me. Tomorrow I shall meet him in the church of St Mary of the Snows. He says he has documents and letters from Jacob. I will write again tomorrow.*

The letter was signed, simply, *Rachel.*

Maslin was staring at the letter. He folded it with reverence, put it back in the tin, and took out the picture again.

'She was beautiful,' he murmured, raising the picture to his lips. Once Jack had seen Maslin press one of the letters against his face, breathing in the scent of it. The spectacle of this ancient man yearning for his long-lost mother unsettled Jack. Their journey had been too exciting for him to have any feelings of homesickness yet, and he hardly gave his own mother a thought. His own new life had gobbled him up, body and soul.

'So what happened to her? What did she find out?' Jack hardly dared ask the question. He remembered Tremayne's cruel jeer, that Maslin's mother had been confined to an asylum.

Maslin sighed. 'I don't know what she found out,' he said. 'That's the last letter. I wasn't told anything of this, at the time. I was far away, at school. Some time later she became ill. My father's suicide preyed on her mind more and more, and when I came back to the house in Ireland for the summer my grandfather told me she was in hospital, and I wasn't allowed to see her. As it turned out, the hospital was an asylum. I would never see her again. Three years later, just sixteen, I came home for her funeral. She had died of a fever and inflammation of the brain.'

Maslin fell silent, and stared out of the window, lost in thoughts of the past. Jack ached to offer some reassurance or comfort, but he couldn't think of the right words to say.

It was night when the train drew up in the station at Prague. Snow was falling, and a light veil covered the city, churned to black slush by the hooves of horses on the roads. It was bitterly cold. Maslin and Jack wrapped scarves around their necks and faces. A porter, pink-faced, conveyed their luggage on a trolley to a cab outside.

'Where are we going?' Jack asked. They were sitting in the cab. Jack peered through the window, hungry for a glimpse of the city. But his view was obscured by the darkness and the snow.

'Sit still,' Maslin chided. A seasoned wanderer, he'd seen Prague before and was not apparently interested in the view. Instead he said he wanted a warm room with a fire, and a hot bath to wash away the grime of the journey. These comforts had no appeal for Jack. He wanted to jump from the cab and run through the streets. He yearned to drink it all up, the beauty and strangeness of the place, revealed in captivating moments when a street light illuminated a marble statue or moonlight pierced the snow clouds and glittered on a church dome.

They took up lodgings in a house Maslin had stayed in before. It was a comfortable place, just a street away from the Old Town Square. The landlady was prepared for their arrival and the fire in the large, tiled hearth was high, just as Maslin had wished. Jack had a smaller room, next door, but before retiring to bed, they dined together on a stew of meat and dumplings.

'What'll we do tomorrow, sir?' Jack asked. 'Where are we going? When shall I wake you?'

Maslin smiled. 'I wish I had your energy, Jack. Don't wake me up. I intend to lie late tomorrow. The journey's taken it out of me. But if you wish to explore on your own, be my guest. Find the church of St Mary of the Snows, if you can. See the painting.'

'You've seen it before,' Jack said.

'Yes. The portrait of my glorious ancestor,' Maslin said, with a smile that did not convey pleasure. He pushed his plate to one side. 'I can't eat anymore. Finish it off, Jack, if you're hungry.'

Maslin had eaten very little, but Jack readily wolfed the remainder of the stew and retired to his little bedroom next door. At first he was afraid he wouldn't get to sleep at all, strung out with excitement, but within minutes of lying down, he pitched into a deep, exhausted slumber.

It was broad daylight when he woke, past nine o'clock. Jack jumped out of bed and opened the window. Snow covered the city, but the sky was a clear, brilliant blue. Below him, in the street, two carters were arguing loudly and incomprehensibly. The air was laden with the cold perfume of snow, the tang of horse droppings, coal smoke, and cooking. The street was already busy, the white pavements marked with footprints. The carters' horses stood patiently, flakes of snow clinging to their shaggy manes. Jack dressed swiftly, sliding on his warm clothes, his long boots lined with fur, and a pair of snug sheepskin mittens. Compared to long-ago Ireland (a few days in time, long years of life) he was dressed like a prince. Above his bed was a small mirror in an elaborate plaster frame, and Jack gazed at his reflection, the narrow, gawky face above the fine winter coat. The good food suited him. His complexion had cleared and glowed with health. His eyes were shining. Pleased with himself, Jack ran his fingers through his short, springy hair, picked up his scarf and skipped downstairs to the front door.

The city took his breath away. He wandered to the Old Town Square and stared. A forest of spires broke the skyline. The houses were tall and elegant, festooned with arches, brightly coloured and painted with elaborate pictures and patterns. Some were decorated with gold, many were peopled with hundreds of glorious statues. At one end stood a mighty church with two huge black spires, and spires on the spires, branching out, each one tipped with a golden cross, glittering in the early sun.

Jack wandered in a daze, his head tipped back to take in the spectacle, dizzy with the splendour of it all. The square was busy, traders calling from stalls, shops opening their doors to the elegantly dressed tourists. The tempting aroma of fresh coffee and chocolate drifted from a café close to the church, and Jack dug his hand in his pocket to feel his coins, wondering if he dared go inside. But this was a new world, he reasoned. No one knew who his parents were, or the straitened circumstances of his upbringing. Indeed, he thought, standing up straight and holding his head high, he was as well dressed as anyone here.

So he took a deep breath, and headed for a table outside the café. As he approached, a waiter ran out and brushed off the snow with a cloth. Then they stared at each other, waiter and boy, and Jack wondered what to say. Would this man speak English? But clearly something about his appearance suggested English would be appropriate because the waiter said: 'Shall I bring a menu, sir?' His accent was impeccable. Jack, who had never been called sir before, opened his mouth to reply but found the words refused to come. He took his hands from his pockets.

'Chocolate,' he said awkwardly. 'A cup of chocolate. Please.'

With a quick nod, the waiter hurried back into the café and returned five minutes later with the steaming cup on a saucer. Jack leaned back in his chair, and smiled. The world was his oyster, his life one marvellous adventure. How satisfying it was to sit in the centre of one of Europe's most beautiful cities with a little money in his pocket, and a chocolate to drink, and a great mystery to unravel. Despite the stories of death and madness, despite the terrifying adventure with Tremayne and the burning of the house, Jack was neither afraid nor now entirely believing in this quest of ancient knights and magical flowers. He was entirely content to let Maslin's story carry him along. What else should he do, but grin, to have the city lying in wait before him and a pair of fur-lined boots on his feet?

He spent the entire morning wandering the streets of Prague's city centre. He wasn't the only tourist – wandering along the cobbled walkway of the Charles Bridge he encountered a party of smartly dressed English people, and others he guessed were French or German. The River Vltava flowed sluggishly beneath the bridge. Statues of the saints loomed on either side, and hawkers pestered constantly, with offerings of nuts and fruit, postcards of the city and offers of guidance through the city's historic places. And Jack, ostensibly looking for the church of St Mary of the Snows, declined them all.

He wasn't in any hurry, and it was lunchtime before he found what he was looking for. In the end he was obliged to ask for directions, turning to one of the English gentlemen tourists for help. Hearing his uncouth Irish accent, the gentleman was a little offhand and Jack realised it might not be as easy as he had expected to throw off his lowly origins – at least, not among the

English. St Mary of the Snows was ancient. Crushed between two tall new buildings, the church wasn't pretty. Quite the contrary, it was old and dark, a sooty crone crouched between two willowy maidens. An arched wooden doorway led inside, and Jack was a little uneasy, stepping in on his own. Was this allowed? He half expected someone to stop him.

Inside, the church was very dim. A huge stained-glass window filled most of the back wall, but the colours in this sea of glass were dense and dark. Above his head, vaults full of ribs and arches, and beneath his feet, huge flagstones covered with arcane inscriptions and carved with death's heads. Hundreds of yellow candles burned on iron stands on either side of the altar, filling the air with a miasma of smoke that made his eyes sting. At first Jack thought he was alone in the church, but as his eyes adjusted to the gloom he made out several hunched figures in the pews, old women bent over on their knees in prayer. Unwilling to disturb them, Jack tiptoed to the altar and stared at the huge altar piece. Here it was at last, the painting of the knights and the lily.

The altar piece was a triptych – a painting in three parts. It dated back to the fourteenth century, and the artist was an unknown Bohemian master of the Gothic style. Gold and more gold, on the heavy, ornate frame and in the background of the pictures. The central panel, the largest, showed a knight in armour mounted on a huge pale horse, and bearing in his right hand a huge white lily. Around him, another eleven knights, his fellows, talking amongst themselves, gesturing to the lily, while above in a cloud Jesus, his chest open to reveal his bleeding heart, raised his hand in benediction. His eyes were sad. The picture on the left showed the first knight, on his knees, receiving the lily from an angel with a bland, oval face. The one on the right showed the same knight with the fleur-de-lis banner in his hand, seated on a throne with his fellow knights all around him and golden haloes over the heads. The colours of this spectacle, even in the limited light, were very dark and rich. Midnight blue, blood red, a luminous moonstone white, amid the overpowering expanse of torrid gold. The frame was elaborately carved, punctuated with tiny rosettes of wood in which portraits of the principal characters were painted. Jack was impressed, and daunted. He had never seen a picture like this before. It was intimidating, encrusted with gold and jewels, so much to look at. He felt the urge to drop to his knees and cross himself. Another part of him was repelled by the picture, its gaudy display and the strange, cold faces of the characters acting out the ancient story of the lily.

'What do you make of it?' A ghostly voice loomed from the darkness behind him, and a white hand gripped his shoulder. Jack gasped.

'Mr Maslin,' he whispered. 'You startled me.' Maslin smiled, almost wolfish in the gloom with his narrow face and long, white teeth.

'I'm feeling better now,' Maslin said, his eyes glittering in the candlelight. 'In fact, I feel much better.'

'What would you like to do, sir?'

'The Jewish quarter,' Maslin said. 'My mother said that was where she met the man who knew Jacob Maslin. We have to follow the trail.'

'But that was decades ago,' Jack said. 'The man will be dead, and in any case he couldn't have known Jacob – the dates don't fit.'

'Perhaps,' Maslin murmured. 'The trail is old and cold, but it's all we have at the moment.' They turned away from the picture and walked out of the church. As Maslin opened the door, Jack looked back to see one of the bundled elderly women standing up in a pew and staring after them.

They headed for Josefov, the Jewish quarter, tenements and shops in a maze of tiny alleyways between the Old Town Square and the curve of the river. It was teeming with people, the alleyways awash with dark slush. There were new buildings too, construction underway, replacing the piled up, age-old slums, but to Jack, the Irish country boy, the quarter was utterly exotic and perfectly thrilling. He had not the slightest hope that Maslin would find any clues, so while trailing the old man dutifully his attention was drawn to the life of the streets, the perfume of alien cooking, the children coming out of school, chattering in yet another incomprehensible language. What did Maslin hope to find anyway? They had no name or address. Maslin strode up and down the streets and alleys, muttering to himself, turning his face from side to side as though waiting to recognise something. He walked very fast, so Jack had to trot to keep up. Now and then, Maslin would accost someone in the street, ask something in a foreign language, and when the man or woman inevitably shook their head or shrugged their shoulders, he glowered and walked on again. What did he ask? Jack wondered. Do you know a foreigner who lived here sixty years ago? What was the likelihood that anyone would say yes to that? So Jack jogged after him faithfully, waiting for the old man's energy to wane. It would be dark soon, night drawing in very early, and already over the snow-dusted rooftops, streamers of pink and gold extended. The chill in the air deepened.

'We'd better go back,' Jack said. Maslin shrugged him off. Then half an hour later, he tried again. 'They're lighting the street lamps. We'd better return to the lodgings.' He thought they'd wandered every street and alleyway in the quarter, which wasn't a large area, maybe twice or three times over. People were beginning to stare.

'Let's go,' Jack pleaded, pulling Maslin's arm. 'We'll try again tomorrow, in the light. We'll talk to some more people. What about the old records your mother talked about in the letter? Perhaps we'll find something looking at those.'

'The records? Hah. They're no help to us. Don't you think

I've tried?' And he strode away through the gathering dusk, while in the windows of shops and houses, lights were burning and people were hurrying home to be out of the cold.

'Mr Maslin,' Jack called out. 'I'm tired now. I want to go back.' He stopped in the middle of the pavement, letting the old man stride away without him. But Maslin didn't walk far. At last, he stopped. His back still to Jack, Maslin sighed deeply and his shoulders sagged. He turned around, and went back to the boy.

'You're right,' he said. 'I'm sorry, Jack. I was just so certain we would find something.' He gestured to the street around them. 'It's changed so much in the Jewish quarter since I last came, ten years ago. It was grim then, so many people crowded in, houses almost on top of each other. It's better now, but so much of the past has been swept away too.' They began to walk back to the Old Town Square, and Maslin put his arm on Jack's shoulders.

'We'll try the lawyers tomorrow, as you say. Perhaps they can point us in a new direction. But something has to come of my mother's letters. It has to.'

Maslin's lawyers in Prague were members of the coterie of men who administered his inheritance. He said the firm had cared for his family's legal and financial affairs for centuries, since the dissolution of the Order of the Lily. Clever legal minds had connived to ensure a proportion of the order's vast estates remained in the possession of the Maslin family, even though the majority was seized by the authorities.

Just as they turned into the square, Jack took one look back at the maze of Josefov, and caught a glimpse of a low, bulky figure scuttling along the path behind them. It – whether he or she, it was impossible to make out – ducked into an alleyway. Jack walked on. In the letters, Maslin's mother had mentioned pursuit. Who was following them, and why? Surely this elderly baggage was no threat. Jack said nothing to Maslin, but as they crossed the square together he felt a cold tingle down his spine. All at once it seemed that everyone was glancing at them, the carters loading and unloading, the boys selling hot chestnuts from braziers, the waiters standing with cigarettes in the door-ways of restaurants, taking a break before the inevitable evening rush. Jack stepped closer to Maslin. He was beginning to feel afraid. When at last they arrived at their lodgings, Jack felt a huge sense of relief. He was sure to lock the door behind them.

In the morning, a letter arrived for Maslin. The landlady slipped it on their breakfast tray, along with bowls of porridge, hot bread and slices of ham and cheese. The letter had no enve-lope. The paper was grimy and clumsily folded. Maslin snatched it up. Jack reached for the porridge. Maslin read it silently, and smiled.

'Well, well,' he said. 'I don't think we'll trouble my lawyer after all.'

'What is it?' Jack asked. But Maslin was already busy, retriev-ing the tin box and searching for one particular letter.

'Here it is,' he said, with a flourish. 'Some similarities here, after all.'

'What is it?' Jack repeated, his mouth full of hot porridge.

'Let me read you this, Jack. It says: *I live in the Jewish quar-ter. I have information concerning your great-grandfather, Jacob Maslin, which may be useful to you. Please meet me in the old cemetery this morning at eleven.* Well! What do you think of that?'

Jack shook his head. 'It doesn't make sense,' he wondered. 'It's just as your mother said. But it can't possibly be the same man because that was sixty years ago. Could someone else have seen your mother's letter? Are they setting out to trick us?'

'That's my first thought too,' Maslin brooded, staring at the letter. The handwriting was a dreadful, clumsy scrawl. 'But this doesn't smell of the Tremaynes, to my nose. They are perfectly prepared to resort to violence without the need for secret letters and mysterious assignations. This is someone else, Jack. Doubtless they want something from us, but then again, the link with my mother's letter is so strong I can not possibly ignore the request. We have to go.'

10

Gypsies
Bohemia, 1890

Cloud hung low above the forest, heavy with snow and occluding the stars. It was bitterly cold. Jacinth huddled by the fire, wrapped in a blanket, wishing she could escape the endless icy draught that spun through the tower. The forest was entirely silent under the snow's thick, white cloak, and Jacinth was achingly lonely. Tremayne hadn't visited for several days, busy on the trail of Maslin, and she longed for the sound of a human voice. Tremayne had ensured she was supplied with coal and wood, but even with the fire roaring all day and night, the tower was cold. The sun was late to rise, and darkness fell soon after four in the afternoon. Jacinth had virtually abandoned her studies. She just sat by the fire, as close as she could, longing for its heat to reach through to the chill in her bones. The cold, it seemed, didn't only come from the outside. Her heart was icy too. She was never comfortable, and sleep didn't bring any release or refreshment. Was this the curse of the villagers' doll? she wondered. Thorns had pierced the poppet's body through and through. But Jacinth had her doubts about the efficacy of the villagers' magic and suspected instead she was troubled by the needles of her own guilt. The photograph of Maslin lay on her desk, still mutilated with pins, and it troubled her constantly. While goodness required effort, it seemed evil needed application too. It didn't come naturally to her. Every day, every hour, she had to remind herself why she had wished trouble upon this stranger and what benefit might come to her as a result. Tremayne had promised power. Without power, what was she? A disfigured, shunned nobody without a family or friends. So she looked at the picture with a shudder, and resisted the near overwhelming temptation to pick it up and pull all the pins out.

Jacinth stared into the flames and pulled the shawl closer over her head. She had nailed blankets over the windows, in a bid to cut off the shrill winds that whined through holes in the wooden shutters. For a time, she drifted into a shallow, fitful sleep, troubled by dreams of the villagers crowding around the tower, pointing fingers and shouting out curses. Every curse hit her physically, like a dart, lodging in her body and impossible to remove. In the dream she shouted out, begging for mercy, but the villagers refused to leave and their curses grew louder and fiercer.

Then she flicked her eyes open. An unexpected sound – a real sound – had broken through her sleep. She waited a moment, straining her ears to hear. There it was – the jingle of a bell. Jacinth was instantly on the alert. Who was it? Had the villagers come again? The bells jingled, a clear, beautiful sound in the silent snowy forest, and faintly Jacinth heard the movement of a horse, the clink of a bit and a low voice murmuring. She got up from her seat by the fire and moved towards the window. She pulled the piece of cloth aside and peered down, through a chink in the shutter. The cloud had cleared away now, and a huge bone-white moon hovered above the treetops, spilling light across the glistening snow. White-sleeved, the trees cast exact blue shadows in the clearing around the tower, where a boy stood with a pony. Jacinth moved from side to side to see as much as she could through the narrow crack in the shutters. The boy was apparently alone. The jingling bells were fastened to the pony's bridle. Both boy and pony were highly decorated. The pony was a skewbald, naturally painted with uneven chestnut and white patches. Its mane was full of long plaits, adorned with beads and ribbons. Metal charms shone from its bridle and saddle. The boy looked about fifteen or sixteen, though it was quite hard to tell, with long, dark hair similarly interlaced with plaits and beads. His thick clothes were bright red. He spoke soothingly to the pony, and then looked up, unerringly, to the window where Jacinth was hidden.

'Witch girl!' he cried out, in rough French, with a smile and a wave. He wore a red woollen hat, stitched with ribbons. When he tipped his head back, the moon shone bright on his handsome, vital face. Jacinth sucked in a breath and stepped back from the window. Of course he couldn't see her. He was guessing. What did he want? The questions galloped through Jacinth's head. The boy didn't look hostile or afraid. In fact, he seemed entirely friendly, but was this a trap? He wasn't a villager, by the look of him. Probably a gypsy, one of the tribe of travelling people that passed like a tide through the forest every year.

'Witch girl!' he called out again. 'Come down. Open the door. I want to talk with you.'

Jacinth leaned back against the wall of the tower, in a storm of confusion. What should she do? He looked so lovely, and his smile was so warm. She yearned for some company, for a friend. Quickly she took up her veil, pulled on her long boots and hurried down the stairs to the ground floor. She turned the key in the lock and opened the door. Then she stood, in the doorway, the brilliance of the moonlit snow now dimmed by the veil across her face.

'Witch girl,' the gypsy said again. He was in front of her now, almost close enough to touch. The pony's rein was looped over his arm. The pony whinnied softly and nuzzled the boy's arm impatiently. He chided it, in some unfathomable foreign language, and stroked its whiskery muzzle with a gloved hand.

134

'My name's Jacinth,' she said, unable to quell entirely the tremor in her voice. She hadn't conversed with anyone but Tremayne for such a long time. The boy was possibly older than she thought. He had a man's way about him, an adult's assurance. And he was beautiful. There was no other word for it. Large, lustrous brown eyes, perfect olive skin, a shapely mouth, and all in perfect balance and harmony. The boy grinned again, a natural, impossible to resist smile, and Jacinth, feeling more hideous than ever, couldn't help but smile back.

'Luca,' he said, tugging off his glove and holding out his hand. Jacinth took his hand, which was very warm and alive to her own cold, stiff fingers. Then they stared at each other, Luca still grinning. The pony pushed him with its nose.

'Why aren't you afraid of me?' Jacinth said. Luca laughed.

'Why should I be afraid?' he said. 'Will you use magic on me?'

'What do you want?' Jacinth hardly dared ask. She didn't want him to leave.

'To talk,' Luca said. 'I was riding. I saw the tower and I was curious.' This with a shrug.

Jacinth glanced around the clearing. She longed to invite him inside, but still she suspected a trap. Perhaps Luca had bandit comrades lying in wait among the trees. 'Are you alone?' she asked, peering, shrewish, into the shadowed larches.

'Yes,' he said, looping the pony's reins on the post by the door. He was assuming he would come inside, and Jacinth didn't want to stop him. She turned around and led the way to the first floor, where the fire burned. Hurrying ahead, she covered up the photograph of Maslin on the desk. Then she lit half a dozen candles in crusted holders on the walls, and on the black iron candelabra hanging from the ceiling. While she was busy, Luca waited, good-mannered, until she invited him to take a seat by the fire. He tugged off the red hat and unbuttoned his jacket, which was lined with sheepskin. Close up, in

135

the candlelight, Jacinth saw his clothes were elaborately decorated with embroidery. They were not very clean, either.

'Why do you wear this?' He gestured to her veil, apparently not knowing the French word for it.

'My face,' she said, feeling herself blush. 'My face is – my face is spoiled.'

Luca, whose own face was more lovely than any woman's Jacinth had ever seen, shook his head abruptly.

'It doesn't matter,' he said. 'Let me see.'

Jacinth felt a rush of anger then. Who was he to barge in and say it didn't matter, to demand a chance to leer at her poor, damaged face? She stepped back and shook her head. Tears sprang to her eyes. Luca blinked, surprised at her reaction.

'I'm sorry,' he said more gently. 'My French is not good. I don't say what I mean. I want us to be friends, Jacinth. I want to be your friend, whatever your face looks like.'

'Why?'

The question hung in the air. Luca let it dangle for a moment or two. Then he inclined his head and said: 'We travel through Bohemia every year. We stay in the forest for a few days or weeks. And everywhere we go, the villagers despise us. Sometimes they are afraid of us – think we'll steal their children.' He laughed, a more painful sound this time, coming from centuries of persecution.

'And they hate you too,' he said. 'So I think, that means we should be friends.'

'How do you know about me?' Jacinth was not ready to relinquish her veil yet. She needed to know him better.

'We stopped at the village near here, to buy food. They all come out and stare at us. They wanted us to play at a wedding. My father is the best violin player. They want us for some things, you see, but they don't want us to stay. They don't want us close. So we played at the wedding, and an old woman warned us to keep away from the tower. She said you were a witch. At night she's seen you flying over the forest, in the sky, and she said you had no soul.'

Jacinth swallowed and dropped her face forwards, squeezing her hands open and closed. The old woman must have some psychic sensitivity, to see Jacinth using her far-sight. Of course she wasn't physically flying, it was only some immaterial aspect that left her body to travel and see, but the old woman had sensed her passing over. No wonder they were afraid. And no soul? She remembered the picture of Maslin, and his blank features. Was this soullessness a part of the lily's strange blessing? Is that why the camera hadn't registered his face?

'What she says is true,' Jacinth said. 'Are you afraid now?'

Luca held out his hand and took hold of Jacinth's. How long was it, since any other human being had touched her? Tremayne recoiled from her, insisted she wear the veil. He had, she realised, built up her self-image as a monster.

'I am afraid,' she said. 'I'm afraid you won't want to be my friend once you've seen my face. Villagers or no villagers. At least you're whole and beautiful.'

She said the last words in a rush, without thinking, and then she was embarrassed and drew away so his hand dropped from hers. But Luca said, 'Beauty isn't a . . .' He searched for the right word. 'It isn't a virtue. It's an accident. I deserve my face no more than you deserve yours. It isn't who I am, and it isn't who you are.' His voice was very grave. Again Jacinth found it hard to work out how old he was. He looked so young, but he had the gravity of someone very much older.

Jacinth nodded. Slowly she reached for the end of her veil and folded it back from her face. Then she looked directly at Luca. How long was it, since anyone had seen her exposed face so closely? She felt utterly vulnerable, as though she'd been peeled and all her nerves were exposed. But she held herself straight and tall, braced for rejection. She was a sorceress after all. She was no ordinary mortal.

'It's not so bad,' Luca said, almost offhand. 'Forget about it now. Do you have anything to eat?'

He stayed for hours, departing just as the sun was rising. They ate heartily, and talked even more. Luca spoke most, telling her about his travelling life and his huge extended family, famed for their music. He could trace his ancestors back hundreds of years. This was his inheritance, the colourful history of his family which was told and retold to each new generation of children.

'Will you come back?' Jacinth asked, as the first sunlight stole across the treetops. Of course the gypsies wouldn't stay long. Perhaps they would be moving on today. But Luca nodded. 'Of course,' he said. And riding away from the tower on his patchwork pony, he turned back to wave to Jacinth, at the window. He disappeared along the track through the trees, and Jacinth realised how quickly she'd forgotten to worry about her face.

Thrilled and buoyed up, Jacinth waited that night for the boy to return. She waited in vain. He didn't come the following day either. Her exhilaration melted away and depression replaced it. The gypsies must have moved on. The snow came down and obliterated the pony's hoofprints, and it was as though the whole encounter had been a blissful dream. Jacinth resumed her studies, and agonised over Maslin's pierced photograph. She tried to use her far-sight to locate Luca, but her talent was stubborn. She couldn't focus, couldn't reach the right frame of mind. Instead she mulled over everything Luca had told her. If she had no soul, what was there to lose? she wondered. No soul. If the lily were a gift from God, why should its followers have lost their souls?

Two days later, the silence of the tower was broken again, this time, in daylight, four riders in the snow, bringing noise and commotion. Jacinth recognised Tremayne's voice. There was another man with him, a woman and a girl, all swathed against the winter weather. Jacinth, veiled, opened the shuttered window to gaze down at them. She recognised the girl at once. She had spied on her in London, and then, having been complicit in her kidnapping, indulged in fantasies of friendship. The girl was Miranda Maysfield.

Tremayne hammered on the door. 'Open up, Jacinth,' he shouted in his execrable French. 'We're cold. I hope you have a good fire.'

They filled up the tower, the two big men and a pretty blonde woman dressed in furs. Tremayne introduced them – his brother Edmund, and Edmund's wife Blanche. Both stared at Jacinth's veiled face. Then Edmund pushed Miranda forward, rather more roughly than necessary. Jacinth stared. Miranda was very pale, her skin seemed almost translucent. Her hair was colourless, her face pinched with weariness and cold. Slowly Miranda raised her eyes to Jacinth. For a moment they regarded one another, these distant cousins. Miranda's eyes widened. There was a flash of recognition – an unspoken understanding. They knew each other – had been aware of the other's presence. Jacinth had spied on Miranda in London, had dreamed of her coming.

Then Jacinth looked away. She was conscious of the Tremaynes watching the meeting greedily, all three of them. Then Blanche spoke. Unlike her brother-in-law, she spoke French perfectly. Her accent was flawless.

'This is an historic meeting, quite the family reunion, all of us here together,' Blanche said. Then she repeated the sentence to Miranda in English.

Miranda scowled. The Tremaynes continued to stare. What were they expecting? Jacinth wondered. Fireworks? Certainly their faces were keen and hungry, as though the elements they had brought together would finally deliver their goal. But Blanche broke away. She placed a hand on Miranda's shoulder.

'She's cold and tired,' Blanche said to Jacinth. 'Can we build up the fire? We'll have a meal now.'

139

Nicholas Tremayne filled the coal bucket himself, and heaped fuel on the fire, cursing the cold all the while. Miranda waited in the background without saying a word. Jacinth longed to speak with her but didn't dare, in the company of the Tremaynes. She was stricken with shyness, to have so many people in her tower after so much isolation. Perhaps the meeting with Luca had prepared her a little – but the Tremaynes were something else.

Edmund and Blanche talked together in English about the long journey and the dingy inns they had stayed in on the long journey across Europe in the dire winter weather, the trains held up in the snow, the ridiculous price they paid for horses. Jacinth couldn't understand everything they said, but she gathered the gist of it. And despite the complaints, Jacinth sensed all three were fired up with their quest. The trail was hot. They had located Maslin again, in Prague. Some clue of the lily's whereabouts had come to light.

Finally Miranda was invited to sit by the hearth and Jacinth fetched her food to eat, broth she had cooking over the fire, and hunks of dry, dark bread, dropped off a week ago by Tremayne's servant. The new arrivals had brought food of their own besides, cheese and dried fruit and bottles of red wine. As they ate and drank and warmed by the fire, the Tremaynes relaxed and their voices grew louder. Only Jacinth and Miranda were quiet, each eying the other but not yet saying a word. Jacinth divined Maslin was staying in his usual lodgings with a servant boy he had brought along from Ireland. Maslin was in a hurry, if the speed of his journey was anything to go by. The Tremaynes had spies on his trail, keeping a record of his every move and conversation, and best of all, they had the two girls whose extraordinary powers derived from the lily. After years of search and study, they were closer than ever.

'It worked, you see,' Edmund said. 'He'd gone to ground. We burned down his house and set him loose. He knows where

140

it is. I'm certain of it. How could he have let the secret go? If we follow closely, he'll lead us to it, sooner or later.' Jacinth liked Edmund even less than she liked Nicholas Tremayne. He was blond, like his wife, with chilly blue eyes, and she sensed he could be brutal. His expressions were crude and when he spoke he banged the chair with his fist. Perhaps her knowledge of the brothers' disagreements, and Nicholas's concerns about his brother's impetuous nature and tendency to violence, had influenced her impression. But Edmund frightened her nonetheless. Why would any woman be attracted to him? she wondered. Blanche was young and good-looking, well educated judging by her voice and manners. Was she blind to Edmund's coarseness, his aggression? Jacinth was well aware that Blanche kept looking at her, that she was curious about the little freak her brother-in-law had rescued from the streets of Paris and locked up in a tower for three years. But Jacinth kept a discreet distance and didn't say a word. What would be expected of them? What plan had the Tremaynes dreamed up, to harness their abilities? Not even her far-sight had ever afforded a glimpse of the lily's whereabouts. And what exactly could Miranda do? She longed for a chance to speak with her, and finally the opportunity arose.

'We're travelling back to Prague tonight,' Blanche said, as the darkness descended. 'Miranda will stay with you, Jacinth. But you must keep her close. Lock the door. And you will get to know her better, you understand? She mustn't escape. Not,' she gestured to the forest outside, 'that there is anywhere for her to go. But take no chances.'

Jacinth nodded. So she was to be a jailor. 'And what is it, exactly, you wish from us? From Miranda and me?' Blanche's physical attractions repelled Jacinth. Unlike Luca, Blanche seemed proud and self-conscious. She wore her beauty like a badge of honour.

'We shall find out tomorrow,' Blanche said. 'Nicholas believes that if you use your abilities in tandem you might better sense where the lily can be found. Of course Mr Maslin could save us a great deal of trouble, if he simply revealed our inheritance. Ours, Jacinth. Yours and mine.' The woman lowered her face, so it almost touched Jacinth's veil. 'Think how much more you could do if the lily was brought to light – if you could touch it – hold it.

'It is our birthright. A gift from God. Miranda doesn't understand yet. She doesn't have faith, which is why you have to keep her safe. In the end she will be glad of what we've done.'

Blanche's eyes burned bright, fired up with her own conviction, her invincible sense of divine right. Jacinth watched her coldly. Inspired by the dream of their shared destiny, Blanche impulsively hugged Jacinth, a most surprising turn of events. Jacinth did not hug her back, conscious Miranda was watching this demonstration of affection and loyalty. And who exactly was Jacinth loyal to? What did she truly want?

The Tremaynes cantered away from the tower and Jacinth locked the door behind them and slipped the key into her pocket. Then she climbed the stairs to the first floor, where Miranda had taken a seat close beside the fire. Alone now, just the two of them, the girls stared at each other. Miranda didn't look welcoming. Her face was stiff and cold. Jacinth felt a little intimidated. Her earlier fantasies of friendship seemed utterly foolish and melted away. Why should Miranda be her friend? Jacinth was one of her kidnappers, after all. She sat on a second chair on the other side of the fireplace and for a long time neither girl said anything. At last, in competent French, Miranda said coldly:

'What happened to your face?'

'You speak French?' Jacinth said, foolishly.

'My mother taught me French and Italian. I've been learning all my life.'

'Do the Tremaynes know?'

'The Tremaynes,' Miranda sneered. 'I don't tell them anything.'

'But you've told me. I could tell them.' This was a question, a tentative exploration of where loyalties might lie. Did Miranda have any understanding of Jacinth's ambiguous relationship with her host and captor, Nicholas Tremayne?

Miranda gazed at Jacinth. 'I've seen you before,' she said, her voice still chilly. 'You have a face like a rose. I've seen you, with your long hair and a mirror. 'What happened?'

With a deep sigh, Jacinth took off the veil and exposed herself to Miranda.

'I've seen you too,' Jacinth said. 'I flew to London, looking for you. You shone out, like a bright light.'

'And you guided the Tremaynes to my doorstep.' Miranda was still studying Jacinth's face. 'Tell me,' she said. 'What happened to your face?'

Jacinth wondered if this icy, self-contained girl could ever be anyone's friend. But like her or not, they were in the same boat now. They would have to accommodate one another somehow.

'My family lived in Paris,' Jacinth said. 'My parents were unconventional people. My father was an artist, and my mother was a dancer in a theatre in Montmartre. They married, and rented an attic apartment close to the river, and later I was born. We didn't have much money, but it was a marvellous life. So many people around all the time, so much music and dancing. I grew up in the theatre, and the actors were my friends, and once I even took part in a show. It was like a little world all to itself, the theatre and its company. We didn't care what anyone else thought of us. The only problem was, my father started drinking heavily. He was jolly to start with, the drink made him happy. But as the months and years went by, he became depressed and angry, and of course then my mother was unhappy too and spent more and more time away from him. There was never any peace.'

Jacinth broke off, and looked at Miranda. 'Do you understand me?' she said.

Miranda nodded. 'Continue,' she said.

'There is not much more to tell. Once, about four years ago, when my mother was at the theatre, I was lying in bed at home, while my father was working on a huge painting. It was a commission – a real commission – from the owner of the theatre where my mother worked. He had a huge canvas, and it was painted with dancers and actors, so many bright colours, so much vigour and movement and life. He was a very good painter. The picture was almost finished, but my father was in a bad mood. I was supposed to be asleep, but he had woken me, with his shouting and cursing and knocking furniture. I was afraid, lying there. I wondered if I should go and help him, but I was worried he would be angry with me. That he might hit me. He hit my mother once, but only once, and afterwards he cried – cried like a little boy.

'In the end I crept to the door of the bedroom and peeped out to watch him. He was drinking absinthe, pouring glass after glass. And he stared at the painting. He couldn't see how good it was, because he started cursing and swearing at it, and cursing himself, and weeping and holding his head, and drinking again.' Jacinth stopped for breath. She had almost forgotten Miranda was present, caught up in the painful recollection. The scene rose up in her memory, bright and vivid. Her heart contracted and her eyes blurred with tears. She ploughed on:

'It happened so fast, in the end. My mother came home and found him in this terrible state. He tried to destroy the picture, and she fought with him, to stop him. My father fell onto her, and knocked over his easel, and the table where his paints were, and the candle in its tin saucer. Then fire was everywhere – it took hold so quickly. Within moments it seemed the attic was a mass of flames. I ran to the window and screamed for help. Banners of black smoke were pouring from the windows, and all the people from the apartments below us ran out into the street. I could see them in the alley below, and they were waving and shouting, but what could they do? I called for my mother, but she was trapped in the room with the fire, I couldn't see her anymore.

'Then the fire was on me. It was so hot, it burned my clothes. A beam fell on me, on my face and neck, and there was nothing else I could do. I didn't think – I just threw myself out of the window.' Jacinth balled her fists and squeezed her eyes shut, remembering the long fall, the terrible agony of her burned flesh, and smoke that stopped her throat so she couldn't breathe. But somehow she had survived the fall. Afterwards it seemed someone had caught her, prevented her smashing to pieces on the cobbled alleyway. Senseless, Jacinth was taken to the hospital, where she woke two days later with bandages wrapped around her face. Her parents were dead. She was utterly alone and terribly disfigured. The agony of her charred skin was equalled only by the unspeakable pain of her bereavement. Weeks passed, and dosed with obliterating morphia she sank into a dreamless sleep, as deep and dark as the fathomless depths of the ocean. Every time she resurfaced, reality was too terrible to bear. But finally, when the bandages were removed, she was declared well enough to leave the hospital. Just ten years old, fearfully scarred and without a soul in the world to turn to, Jacinth was taken into the care of an orphanage attached to a dingy Parisian nunnery. She endured the poor food, the cruelty of the other children and the indifference of the nuns for about a year before running off into the streets of Paris. And there Nicholas Tremayne discovered her, begging for food, sleeping rough, eking out a degraded and miserable existence, malnourished and dead in spirit.

These final details she did not reveal to Miranda, the depths she had sunk to.

The only sound in the tower was the crackle of fire in the hearth. Miranda pressed her lips together.

'Burns,' she said. 'Your face was burned.'

Jacinth nodded. She was tired now, wrung out by the recollection. Miranda didn't evince any kind of shock or sympathy, on hearing the tale. But neither did she seem repulsed or horrified by Jacinth's ruined face. She didn't avoid looking at her, or recoil in any way. Instead she said: 'Was it your father then? Was he – was he a descendant?'

'Yes.' Jacinth nodded. 'Tremayne studied genealogy. He found out my father was one of them. Then he followed the trail to find me. The hospital, and the orphanage.'

Miranda sighed. 'My mother's sick,' she said. 'She was admitted to an asylum. To Our Lady of Sorrows.'

'And your father?'

'He died – three years ago. In North Africa.'

Jacinth felt a flash of compassion for icy Miranda. She had lost her parents too. She must feel the same aching aloneness. But it was so hard to tell what she was thinking. On the surface she seemed so cool and distant. This admission about her parents – said so matter-of-factly – was this an expression of sympathy or simply an exchange of information? They had a lot in common. Both were orphans, effectively. Both were held in the custody of the Tremaynes, and perhaps most importantly, they each had a remarkable and powerful talent.

'So why do they want you?' Jacinth asked. 'What exactly can you do?'

Miranda gave a wry smile. She dug in her pocket and retrieved a pack of cards.

'I tell fortunes,' she said. 'You'll go on a long journey. You'll meet a handsome stranger. *Et voila*. Here I am.' She began to shuffle them, sliding the cards one over another. The fine colours glinted in the candlelight. 'Of course I know what you do. I've seen you. It seems a far better power than mine – your far-sight.'

Jacinth inclined her head. She found Miranda intimidating

but Jacinth, after all, was variously host, jailer and sorceress. She wanted to have the upper hand. She had anticipated Miranda would be afraid and needy. Instead she seemed remarkably calm and self-possessed. Was this an act? Surely it had to be.

'Will you show me?' Jacinth said. 'Will you read my fortune?'

'What? So you can tell them, the brothers Tremayne?'

'I won't tell them,' Jacinth jumped in. 'I promise. I won't tell them anything.'

Miranda shrugged. The cards were still moving in her hands but she did look tired. In fact, she looked deathly tired.

'Tomorrow,' Jacinth said. 'Go to bed now.'

Miranda didn't undress, she simply collapsed on Jacinth's big old bed on the second floor. Within seconds she was fast asleep. Carefully Jacinth took off Miranda's boots, still damp from the snow, and pulled the pile of blankets over her. Then she lay down on the other side of the bed. Miranda looked different, asleep. She looked very much younger and more vulnerable. So exhausted, so deeply asleep, Miranda did not wake up an hour later when Jacinth was roused by the familiar sound of bells and the whinny of a pony.

Jacinth was so delighted she could hardly breathe. Was she dreaming? Was it really Luca, come back to see her? For a moment she lay perfectly still, her heart beating against her ribs, as she strained to hear. Then she heard a low whistle, and a voice called out her name. Jacinth jumped out of bed and peered through the crack in the shutters. Yes – there he was, at the foot of the tower, waving.

'Come down,' he called out. 'Put your warm clothes on.'

Jacinth glanced at Miranda, then swiftly dressed. She helped herself to Miranda's warm woollen mittens. She ran down the stairs, unlocked the door, and stepped outside with a huge smile on her face.

'Plait your hair,' he said. 'You're coming with me.'

'Going where? I can't go. This is my home.'

Luca held his finger to his lips. 'Shush. We won't be long. I'll bring you back, I promise.' Jacinth looked anxiously at the tower, where Miranda lay sleeping, and she locked the door behind her, so her English visitor wouldn't escape. Then she nodded eagerly at Luca. How could she resist?

Luca helped her onto his pony's back, and then jumped up behind her. They set off into the forest.

'Where are we going?' Jacinth asked. But Luca shushed her again, with a smile. 'Wait and see,' he said.

The night was perfectly still. The moon was full and radiant, filling the forest with light, inking long, blue shadows under the trees. Frost had crisped and powdered the deep snow. Beautiful it was, and to Jacinth, charged with ancient magic. This was old forest, potent with the memories of a thousand winters.

But it was dangerous too. Alone in the frozen forest you would die of cold. As the pony stepped eagerly through the snow, Jacinth began to worry. Where was Luca taking her? Hadn't she been foolish and impetuous, entrusting herself to this stranger? Everywhere moonlight glittered on ice, and in the countless snow crystals kicked up by the pony's hooves. Jacinth lost track of time. Perhaps it was a mile they travelled. Maybe five miles. She had no idea where they were. Once she tried to ask the boy but he shook his head and refused to answer. He just lifted his hand and gestured vaguely to the forest.

Then, in the distance, she heard music and saw the hot red and gold of a fire in a clearing. Someone was playing the violin, a brisk, discordant rather raucous tune, to which a male voice was singing. Several dogs were barking too, and as they drew nearer, Jacinth heard children shouting out. Without thinking, she put her hand to her face. She realised she had forgotten her veil.

'Luca,' she said. 'I don't want to. Take me home. I don't have my veil.'

148

Luca shook his head and clicked his tongue, urging the pony forward.

'Come,' he said. 'Don't worry.' It was too late in any case. Luca had been spotted. A host of children ran out from the clearing towards them, calling out greetings and waving. Luca waved back. He swung his leg over the pony's quarters and dropped easily to the ground, scooping up one of the smaller children in his arms. Then he took hold of the reins and led his pony, Jacinth still on top, to the gathering of people by the fire in the trees.

Jacinth suffered an agony of self consciousness. She fought off the temptation to cover her face with her hands, forcing herself to hold her head high. She was a sorceress after all – the descendant of holy knights and magicians. She had powers beyond these ordinary people, no matter how much they might stare. And they did stare. Jacinth felt their eyes like needles sticking into her. About twenty adults, about a dozen children, all dressed like Luca in bright, decorated clothes. Without any evident fear or embarrassment they studied her damaged face. One of the children pointed and his mother didn't shush him, instead nodding and saying something to him in a language Jacinth did not understand.

Finally the pony came to a halt near the fire and Luca helped her dismount. A tall man, with strands of wintery white in his long black hair and a brown, weathered face, came up to them, and held out his hand to Jacinth. He said something unintelligible, but it seemed to be a greeting.

'This is my father,' Luca said. 'He's head man. He welcomes you, Jacinth. You're our guest now.'

The man gestured to one of the women, who hurried forward with a steaming cup. They seemed welcoming, but Jacinth could not shift her sense of unease. What did they want? How should she behave among them?

'Take it,' Luca encouraged. He took off her mittens and

cradled the warm cup in her hands. She sipped the welcome concoction of spiced, sugary tea. The man nodded and smiled, backing away, gesturing to the arrangement of tents and barrel-top caravans arranged in a circle around the clearing. Luca led her to the largest of the caravans. A lantern depended from its front. He called out, and then pushed open the door. 'Go inside,' he said. 'Take your boots off.' Jacinth climbed up the short wooden ladder, left her snowy boots propped on the ledge beside the door, and stepped inside. Luca was close behind her.

It was very warm, and after the dazzle of snow and moon-light, it seemed gloomy. An iron barrel stove threw out heat at the back, and beside it, perched on a bench covered with rugs, Jacinth saw a tiny, elderly woman with a scarf tied around her head. Luca pushed Jacinth forward.

'Sit down,' he urged, pointing to a stool. He squatted on the floor beside her. The only illumination came from a dim lantern hanging over the stove but as Jacinth's eyes adjusted, she saw the interior of the caravan elaborately decorated with painted flowers and swirls and patterns. From numerous hooks and ledges hung icons of saints, prophets, the Christ child and the Virgin Mary, all painted with brazen gold. There were other pictures too, which Jacinth recognised as Egyptian, men with the heads of animals.

The old lady crept forward. She smiled, teeth missing, her face a web of wrinkles. Then she stretched out her hand and touched Jacinth's face, running her fingertips over the scars. It was almost intolerable for Jacinth. She burned with a sense of shame and humiliation. She wanted to strike the old woman's hand away, to hit her and knock her down. Then the hand was gone. Jacinth sighed and opened her eyes. Suddenly her rage drained away. She let it go.

'This is my great-grandmother,' Luca said. 'She wanted to meet you. She knows all about you.'

The old woman nodded, and taking both Jacinth's hands in

her own, she began to talk. Every now and then she stopped, so Luca could translate.

'You belong to the Order of the Lily,' Luca said. 'The lily has poisoned generations of your family, but after seven hundred years its time is nearly finished.'

Jacinth looked from one to the other. How did the old woman know about this?

'Finished?' Jacinth broke in. 'It can't be finished. We want to find it again – bring it to light. Restore the order!'

Luca translated, and the old woman shook her head, and gabbled on, her voice now louder and more strident.

'My great-grandmother is a wise woman. Her ancestors have known about the lily since its beginning, Jacinth. They know its nature. For centuries they've followed its fortunes. She wants it given back to the angel. We have bided our time this long while, waiting for the story to be played out as it was foretold. We witnessed the consequences of its theft by the knights. Now the story is near its end and you are part of it. That's why she wanted to meet you.'

Jacinth's thoughts tumbled over themselves. Did the old woman know where the lily was hidden? Was this the lead she and the Tremaynes had been longing for? How great would her authority be, she thought, if she uncovered its whereabouts? As though sensing her thoughts, the elderly woman shook her head and began to speak again. She gesticulated, and pointed to Jacinth, raising her voice.

'You must return it,' Luca said. 'You must give it back. It is the prophecy, Jacinth.'

'What is the prophecy? What do you mean theft? The knights were given the lily – by an angel! By God himself.'

'The lily cannot be destroyed. Crushed, or thrown into a furnace, it would still survive. The lily is not of this world – the matter making it up belongs elsewhere,' Luca translated.

'The prophecy says that three are needed to return it. They

151

will be able to open a door to the other world, because they will see at once into the past and into the future. You are one of those. You are the rose, Jacinth, you have the gift of far-sight.'

'Who are the others? And how can I give back the lily if I don't know where it is?'

Luca relayed the question. The old woman nodded and spoke again.

'The white girl, from England. She is one,' Luca said. 'The third is an old man, the last of them, the Maslins. His forefather stole the lily. It's right he is the one to take it back.

'But we don't know where the lily is. We followed it for years, but it disappeared from sight. You will have to find it.'

Jacinth took another sip from the spiced tea and licked her lips. Strands of hair from her plait fell forward. She thought fast.

'How do you know all this?' she said.

'It is part of our history,' Luca said, without referring to his great-grandmother.

Afterwards, he took her on the pony back through the snow to the tower. Jacinth felt cheated and betrayed. Luca was not a friend after all. Like the Tremaynes, he had sought her out in order to use her. He and his family were plotters in the endless and convoluted conspiracy of the lily. He hadn't come to the tower at random. All along, he'd had a motive, and the motive related to the source of her one power. She shook her head.

When they reached the tower he helped her down from the pony. She turned away from him, unable to look into his face.

'You're angry with me,' he said. 'What's the matter, Jacinth?'

But Jacinth couldn't speak. She looked down at her feet, all choked up.

'What is it?' he repeated. 'Talk to me.' He stretched out his hand and touched her arm. Some impediment broke inside her. She knocked his hand away in a rage.

'You're not my friend,' she said. 'You want to use me – just like Nicholas Tremayne.' Her face burned, and tears filled her eyes. Luca stared. He said something quickly, in his own language. He turned away, throwing out his arms in an arc, startling the pony.

'That's why you came to see me,' she said. 'That's why you're kind to me. Because of the lily. Because of that!' She was crying properly now, the accumulation of days boiling over, the villagers' poppet, and the photograph of Maslin with the pins, the Tremayne brothers descending with the captive she had helped to trap. All alone. She was entirely and utterly adrift.

'No,' Luca said. 'No, no, no.' His face was also contorted with feeling. He reached out his hand but again she knocked it away.

'Get away from me,' she shouted. 'I'll curse you. I'll stick pins in you. I'll hurt you.'

But Luca wasn't deterred. He approached her again, and resisted when she tried to push him off.

'Jacinth,' he said. 'Listen! Let me speak!' They faced each other, standing in the snow, moving from side to side like wrestlers waiting for an opportunity to strike. Jacinth could hardly think straight. Her outburst had loosened a hundred violent feelings, and now, like huge birds, they flapped around inside her, blundering and snapping and hurting. She couldn't see properly, couldn't control what she was saying.

Luca edged around her. 'Jacinth,' he said more gently. 'I am your friend. Truly I am.'

She shook her head, half blind with tears. 'No you're not. I'm a tool. Something to be used.'

'No,' he said. 'When this is done – when the lily's gone – I shall still be your friend. You can trust me, always. Whenever you want me, I shall be there to help you.'

Jacinth stood still for a moment, wrapping her arms around herself.

'Why would you do that? You're just saying this, to win me over, so I'll help do what you want, you and your grandmother.'

'Jacinth.' His voice dropped. Some of his self-assurance seemed to fall away. 'I knew one day I would meet you. I had a dream — a very long time ago — about a girl hiding in a tower with hair that reached the ground.

'But you're not a dream. You're more than that. Jacinth — all that you have endured — on your own. How strong you are, and resourceful and patient. Anything you want from me — whatever I can do to help — I will do it.'

Jacinth raised her eyes to his face. She longed to trust him. But one small part still curled up, protective, a piece held in reserve. Words were easy, after all. Let him prove himself.

'You can help me now,' she said, taking the tower key from her pocket.

'Miranda is asleep. I'll wake her up and she can write a letter to her family, to tell them where she is. You can take it to Prague.'

'I'll send a telegram — if she gives me the address. It'll be quicker.'

'And then tomorrow night you must come back,' she said. 'I need to talk with Miranda — we have to work out what to do next.'

11

Bohemia, 1480

Midsummer's eve, and the feast of St John. The sun was late descending, a fiery chariot burning over the treetops of the faraway forest, the sky a fathomless vault of blue. Along a narrow paved road, two dozen riders made their way. Tiny, like ants, between the plunge of sky and the wide plain, fringed with trees, the party rode in silence. Two carried banners, displaying the symbols of the Roman church. Behind them, three church officials dressed in silk and fur, and then a captain and twelve soldiers. Despite their finery, all were covered in a layer of dust from the journey. The only sound was the patter of hooves and the clinking of the horses' bits. The animals tossed their heads and swished their tails wearily against the ubiquitous insects. Ahead of them, massive in its robes of hewn granite, rose the monastery-fortress, the headquarters of the Order of the Lily.

Standing on the battlements, high above the plain, Grandmaster Stephen Maslin gripped the hilt of his sword. How brave they were, he thought as he watched the party's progress to the huge oak doors, so few against the might of the order with its fortress and hundreds of soldiers. Then again, a man might be more than the sum of his own parts. The inquisitor general represented the strength and authority of the Roman church. The size of his company was a statement in itself. He needed no army.

'So they have come at last,' Maslin said, as the fortress-monastery swallowed up the inquisitor and his company. Beside him on the battlements, his fellow members of the council, knights all, made no reply.

'They have come to destroy the order,' Maslin said gently. 'We knew the time would come. The church has turned against us.'

Just before he turned, a flash of colour caught his eye in the forest hem, far away. He shifted his gaze, trying to see better. Next to him, a knight murmured:

'Travelling people. We sent men out to move them on, but they keep coming back. Shall I despatch soldiers?'

Maslin pondered. An ancient link existed between the gypsy tribe and the Order of the Lily. The origins of this connection were unknown, but the knights had persecuted them over the years. Nothing deterred, the travellers continued to dog the order.

'No,' he said. 'We have other priorities. Let them be.'

The inquisitor dined with them at the high table in the long hall. His papal banner hung down the wall behind him. To left and right, long banners of the order, dark blue with the white fleur-de-lis. The inquisitor was not a young man. About fifty perhaps, but lean still, his muscles honed by riding and fighting. His hair was iron grey, short-cropped, his eyes a cold, icy blue. His face was weathered, all spare flesh honed away by years so the skull was evident beneath the skin. He ate little – some fruit and bread. His movements were neat and scrupulous. His assistants, two administrator priests, were also seated at the high table, to the right of the inquisitor. The captain and his soldiers dined beneath them, at the long benches among the rank and file of the order's soldier-monks. Of course, this assembly in the great hall represented only the most important of the monastery's vast population. These were the order's aristocrats. Elsewhere in this world within a world, there were junior scholars and novice monks, not yet sworn into the order. Then again, the walls contained foot soldiers, blacksmiths, wheelwrights, cooks, grooms, armourers, servants, labourers, carpenters, herbalists, scribes, barbers. Hundreds of people, tiny cogs within the efficient machinery of the order's mighty headquarters. Maslin filled his cup with wine from a golden jug. He regarded the assembly with pride and misgiving. The order had monasteries all over Christian Europe, but this one, in Bohemia, was the hub at the centre of the wheel – the headquarters, the home of the council and the resting place of their most sacred relic, the lily gifted to his forefather by an angel of the lord.

The inquisitor was biding his time – this again an exercise of his strength. He could make them wait. The Order of the Lily was wealthy and powerful, but at last the might of the Roman church and an alliance of Europe's kings had joined together in a single demand for the order's destruction. It owned too much – wielded too much political power. Tolerated for its strength and usefulness for three centuries, the order had become a liability. Both pope and king feared it was too strong. The order had become a threat to their authority, and consequently, the pope had made his opening gambit. A charge of heresy. At the end of the meal the inquisitor announced he would begin questioning the council at dawn.

Maslin didn't sleep that night. He dismissed his servant and headed for the chapel at the heart of the monastery. He was sixty now, tall and gaunt, grizzled by war and time, with three long scars on his face and a gnawing rheumatic pain in his jaw, broken in battle decades before. Thirty years ago he had travelled to Rome and knelt before Pope Nicolas V to swear his lifelong allegiance. He had devoted so much of his life to the order. As a child and young man he had lived in England. He had loved and married, fathered three sons. But when his own

father died, he put his family behind him. They were well provided for, of course, his wife and children. It had been his
duty – and his fulfilment – to leave them. But he missed her
still, his wife. Not a day passed when he didn't think of her. She
would be an old lady by now, their sons middle-aged. The
youngest was a novice in the English monastery, soon to take
holy orders. Maslin knelt before the altar in the chapel, made
the sign of the cross, and sighed. His body felt very heavy,
requiring an effort to keep it upright, to be straight. A life
passed very quickly, and the body seemed to age so fast. One
moment he had been a slim, smooth-faced boy burning with
energy. The next he was a weary old man, troubled with aches
and pains, irritated by old wounds that wouldn't heal. There
was never any peace.

He cleared his mind to pray, but other thoughts bubbled up.
Scenes of battles rose before him, the long campaigns against
the Turkish armies of the Ottoman emperor in the east, the
months living under canvas – sleeping, eating and fighting in
searing heat and bitter cold, in rain and mud and dust. Always
leading from the front – inspiring the men – and he recalled the
joyous, exhilarating moment when fear dissolved and his army
charged towards the enemy. For that instant, past and future
disappeared and there existed only pride and anger and a lust to
kill the heathens coming against them. And in all those years,
the lily had protected him – granted him a strength beyond that
of ordinary men. He had been injured, yes, but in truth he
should have died many times over. The lily had granted him
countless victories – charged his sword arm with power and
inspired his courage. Now, finally, that time was over.

His head bent, eyes closed, he heard the doors at the back of
the chapel open and the susurrus of gowns as his eleven fellow
councillors entered. Maslin rose heavily to his feet to confront
them. The leader nodded, and Maslin led them past the altar.
He unlocked a door behind a curtain and they stepped through,

in silent single file, into a large circular room. The floor was tiled in black and white, banners dangled from the wall. Tall wooden chairs stood at intervals around the circle, and each man took his place. Right at the centre, locked in an ornate wrought-iron cage, was the lily in its casement of occluded glass. It cast a faint radiance into the room.

Maslin stood before the tallest chair and regarded his eleven fellows. These men were the descendants of the twelve knights who received the lily in the desert. They made up the Council of the Order the Lily and they governed it. The eldest, Matthias, wore a mask across half his face and white silk gloves on his hands. Maslin made the sign of the cross and said a prayer, asking for God's blessing, for wisdom and courage, for the safety of the relic and the order. The councillors joined him in the final Amen, and then, as one, sat down upon their seats.

Maslin sighed. This would be their last meeting, here in the monastery-fortress of Bohemia. Tomorrow, inevitably, the inquisitor would find them guilty of heresy and all over Europe the order would be outlawed and disbanded. Its wealth would be stolen, its monasteries, farms and hospitals confiscated. The reputation of the knights would be cast into shadow – into dirt.

'After long nights of debate, we have reached an agreement,' Maslin said. 'We have the strength to fight them – the armies of all the kings of Europe. Armed with the lily we could take them on. We have powers to destroy, we have talents beyond ordinary men. But we couldn't be certain of victory and the war would destroy the Christian world. Too much would be lost – too many lives, too many cities. The cost would be high. Besides which, the order has sworn an oath of loyalty to the Roman church and we must submit to its authority.'

Several of the councillors shifted in their seats and murmured. The argument had been well rehearsed. And besides, they did not have the legendary gifts of the order's first knights, who could kill from a distance, shattering skulls and stopping hearts through God-given powers of the mind. Perhaps they were less worthy than those first men, less pure of heart. And in any case, they were loyal to Rome. But was this oath still binding when the church was treacherous? Maslin held up his hand, bidding them be silent.

'We must be loyal,' he said. 'Tomorrow the inquisitor will begin his examination. We shall not meet again, but the council will endure in secret. We have, each of us, appointed a successor. My son in England will take the Maslin seat. You have all instructed an heir – a son or nephew – who will take the oath of allegiance and continue the line of the first twelve holy knights who received the lily from the Angel of the Lord in the desert.

'Matthias,' he said, looking to the councillor with the mask. 'You alone will escape. You will lead the new council, at its first meeting, and assist my son until the day he is fit to be leader of the order. You understand what is to be done? You are fit for it?'

Matthias nodded. The others turned to him. Pity and envy mingled in their faces. They knew what fate lay in wait for them, but Matthias walked a dark path of his own.

'Then we are agreed,' Maslin said. 'This is the night our own seers have foretold. Our enemies are among us, but we understand more than they do. We can see further, and we know the council will endure. We are well prepared and everything is in place.' He rose to his feet, took a huge black key from his belt and strode across the circle to the lily's cage. The lock turned, and he opened the heavy lid to withdraw the lily in its glass case. Maslin felt the pulse and heat in his hands, and the holy radiance beamed through the glass in response as he lifted it aloft and turned around, so the light should fall on each of his men. Maslin embraced the lily, held it to his chest, pressed his cheek against it, euphoric, to feel the white light pulse through his body, among the pathways of his brain, in his heart and bones and bowels.

The other councillors rose to their feet and walked towards him. They closed in to the centre of the circle and each held out a trembling hand to touch the box with its shining cargo. For the last time they stood, these twelve, each in contact with the sacred lily, infusing them all with its other-worldly light and power. Maslin closed his eyes, to savour the last moments of the bliss that pulsed through his body. He felt the white light filling the chambers of his mind, cleansing and purifying, charging him with the strength and courage he would need to endure the next days and weeks.

Then the light died away. The knights stepped back, each replenished by the lily's powers. They stared at one another, the light still shining in their eyes, their bodies still possessing a faint luminescence. Maslin replaced the lily, but did not lock the cage. Then the men dropped to their knees in a circle about the relic, and all began to pray.

The inquisitor set up a court in the great hall. To left and right, his administrators sat with books and papers, preparing to take notes. The inquisitor summoned Maslin and the knights of the council. They were lined up before him, like schoolboys. The inquisitor was polite and direct, but suggested by his tone of voice he would brook no dissent. Confident of his authority, he didn't need to raise his voice. He simply expected to be obeyed.

'Stephen Maslin – Grandmaster of the Order of the Lily,' he called, gesturing to a seat the other side of his table. 'You are under arrest and charged with five counts of blasphemy and heresy. We have obtained evidence to substantiate each of the charges, which are as follows: firstly that you worship a false idol, namely the so-called lily. Secondly, that you deny Christ and any knight sworn into the inner circle of the order has to spit upon the crucifix; third, the order worships the devil and receives from him supernatural powers of prophecy and conjuring; fourth, that you abjure the sacred ritual of the mass,

161

replacing it with your own blasphemous ceremonies, and finally, that you have stolen and murdered infants, sacrificing them to the devil during diabolic rituals.'

Maslin heard a suppressed laugh from one of his companions, still standing in line behind him, facing the high table. The charges were, of course, totally absurd. Where had such ludicrous stories come from? Who had they paid, questioned, threatened or tortured to extract such risible charges? Of course it could have been any one of the thousands of servants connected with the order across Bohemia and the rest of Europe. Doubtless the inquisitor's own servants had been busy, pressing whatever stories they required from the mass of innocent and ignorant people who served them. These charges were ridiculous – they were also terrifying. What would a man admit to if he were stretched upon a rack?

The inquisitor glanced at the knights, trying to ascertain who had laughed. Maslin thought fast. How to deal with this? He would speak the truth, as long as he was able – deny all the charges. How long would he hold out, when his body was broken? How long would his comrades endure? In the end, of course, many would admit to the charges. He would die under torture, or else, convicted by false testimony, be burned at the stake. There was no way out for him now – nor for his comrades.

'Wait,' the inquisitor said sharply. 'There should be twelve knights, and I see only eleven. Where is the other?' He looked at Maslin, his face as hard and stern as the granite making up the monastery walls.

'The twelfth – Matthias – he's confined to a cell in the sanatorium,' Maslin said. 'He is very sick.'

The inquisitor shook his head in irritation. 'No matter. Bring him here. There is no avoiding the charges.'

'My lord,' Maslin said, 'Matthias is a leper.' He pronounced the last word slowly and deliberately. He studied the inquisitor's stony face and detected the faintest tremor of distaste. Then the cold blue eyes fixed on him again.

'A leper,' the inquisitor said bluntly. 'A punishment from God. An affliction for his sins. The body belongs to the world, Grandmaster. It is a weak vessel, prey to sinful urges, and to suffering, which we must endure for Christ's sake, as he endured agony for ours.' He turned to one of the administrators.

'Go with the Grandmaster to the sanatorium. See for yourself if this story is true. Do not be deceived.'

The administrator, chubby and sleek beside his lean and wolfish superior, nodded nervously and hurried to his feet. Maslin rose from his chair and led them through the rooms and corridors of the monastery to the hospital. They descended a flight of narrow stone stairs to a rank of three dark cells. The air was hot and confined, stinking of sickness, old straw and human excrement. The administrator covered his nose and mouth with his sleeve. Maslin nodded as he unlocked a cell door.

'Be prepared,' he said. The door swung open, and the stench intensified as the vile perfume of the cell flooded out. The administrator let out a faint, horrified moan.

'Matthias,' Maslin called out. 'Matthias, step out into the light. We need to speak with you.' After a moment, they heard a rustle of straw, and from the darkness emerged a bent human shape, cloaked and hooded in filthy sackcloth. In the doorway, the creature tipped his head to one side and the administrator gasped. The man's face was partly eaten away on the right side. The skin was tight and dry, like old white leather. Across the right cheek, right down to the jaw, the skin was entirely gone, exposing the man's cheekbone and teeth.

The administrator struggled to speak, his voice trembling. 'Tell me,' he said. 'Tell me, what is your name? Can you speak?'

The disfigured man nodded his head and stretched out a parched hand, from which three fingers were missing. 'I can speak,' he said, gesturing to the golden pendant still hanging from his neck. 'I am Matthias, knight of the Order of the Lily.'

The administrator took from his pocket a bible, leather bound and tooled in gold. 'Will you swear to this?' he said. Then, in a panic: 'Do not touch it – do not – contaminate – it. Hold up your hand, and take an oath.'

Matthias gave a ghastly smile. He raised his right hand, and swore before God and the Virgin Mary he had given his rightful name. The administrator nodded. 'Then pray,' he said. 'Pray to the Lord your sufferings will appease him for the sins you have committed. Pray for mercy.'

Matthias turned away, and shuffled back to his stinking prison. Maslin locked the door behind them, and with an audible sigh of relief from the administrator, they left the hospital cells behind and returned to the great hall and the inquisitor general.

Five days later, after hours of questioning and many reams of notes taken, the inquisitor decided the Grandmaster and ten knights should be escorted to Prague for further interrogation. State officials and soldiers had arrived to take over the running of the monastery and estates. Already the council had the reins taken from their hands.

'Before we leave,' the inquisitor said, 'you must take me to your holy relic. We shall confiscate it, and send it to Rome where the pope will decide what is to be done with it.'

Maslin nodded, heavy-hearted. 'Can it not stay? This is its resting place – its home. The lily was entrusted to my forefather by an Angel of the Lord – entrusted to the keeping of the knights of the order. Why not wait until the trial before deciding if the relic is forfeit?'

The inquisitor shook his head. 'We take it with us,' he said. 'If you are cleared of the charges – then the lily remains in your keeping.'

Maslin took him to the chapel, and released the glass box

from its iron cage. The inquisitor's assistants murmured to see the secret circular chamber, and their eyes widened to see, at last, the casket of the lily, an angel's gift, and a key to the Christian victories over the hordes of Ottoman Turks for decades. Even the inquisitor looked impressed. Perhaps he had doubted its existence.

Maslin held out the glass casket to the inquisitor. 'Do you wish to take it?' he said. For a moment the inquisitor was undecided.

'Wrap it up,' he said. 'Wrap it well. My servants shall carry it.'

The following morning, Maslin and his ten companions were fastened in irons and mounted on horses for the journey to the city, for trial, torment and execution. The casket was bound up in woollen cloth and bulky hides and loaded onto a mule. The travelling people watched from the shelter of the trees as the knights rode away through the forest.

Three months later, the eleven men were dead. Many had signed confessions admitting to the trumped up charges. All over Europe the secular authorities took over the property and estates owned by the Order of the Lily and arrested its leaders. Monasteries were converted or razed to the ground. Monks were turned out to fend for themselves as best they could. In Rome, the pope ordered the glass casket to be smashed open, and discovered inside the shrivelled, desiccated remains of a lily. He declared the relic a heretical fake, a proof, if more were needed, that the knights were liars and blasphemers.

The following winter, when snow lay deep on the ground, the new administrators of the Bohemian monastery-fortress decided they could no longer provide for the patients in the hospital. They turned out three senile old men, half naked, into the bitter winter. They also ejected a deformed leper, kept in a locked cell underground. Before he was cast into the snow, this leper secretly fished out from his soiled straw a glass casket, which glowed with a dim radiance. He disguised it with his own dirty rags and took it with him into the freezing night. Armed with a staff and bell, he survived the cold and followed highway and byway for many weeks and months until he reached the sea, where a boat was waiting to take him across the Mediterranean, to Greece, and then to Kefalonia, and the new council.

12

The Cemetery
Prague, 1890

Snow had fallen during the night, another brief disguise for the city, covering the mud and muck. Coils of smoke rose from a thousand chimneys.

It was half past ten. Jack was hurrying after Maslin, who took long, loping strides through the snow towards Josefov, the Jewish quarter, for their assignation with the mysterious letter writer. Maslin had been crotchety all morning, complaining of headaches and dosing himself rather too liberally with laudanum. He had brooded over the tatty letter, lost in thought, trying to make sense of the nonsensical. How could this be? More than sixty years ago, Maslin's mother had received a similar letter. Possibly, if the sender had been twenty then, he might be in his eighties now. It was conceivable, Jack thought. Then again, it might be some kind of trap – a ploy by the Tremaynes to draw them out, into the open.

'Mr Maslin! Mr Maslin, sir!' Jack had to run to keep up with his master. His skinny shoulders hunched, white hair pouring over his back, Maslin didn't respond to Jack's calling. Lost in thought, wrapped up in memories, he strode on entirely oblivious and Jack was left to jog along behind him.

The streets were busy, despite the snow. A cold wind nipped, although the sun was bright. Long icicles glittered on gable ends and beneath gutters. A horse pulling a trader's van had threads of ice hanging from its whiskers and snow clogged its mane. Just before eleven, Maslin stopped at an iron gate in a high wall. He turned to Jack, and gave him the briefest of nods.

'Be careful,' he said. Then he opened the gate and they stepped inside the old cemetery.

Jack's eyes widened. He had never seen anything like this. He was accustomed to his humble village churchyard, a green space on the hillside sparsely sown with wooden crosses. The Jewish Cemetery was a dense forest of stone, shadowed and hemmed in by the city. A narrow path wound between ranks of headstones, hundreds of them, with barely a space between them. Muted amber, dull brown, heavy grey – with the years' painting of lichen and green moss – the stones were elaborately carved with names and symbols. Some had rows of little pebbles balanced along the top. And all of it, the walls, the stones, the narrow spaces between them, covered in the glistening veil of snow.

Maslin stood on the path and scanned the cemetery, looking, possibly, for the Tremaynes. At first they could see no one. They were alone, among the countless graves of generations of Prague's Jewish people. Jack shaded his eyes. The graveyard possessed a profound air of melancholy, but he liked it all the same. He felt no unease – no sense of menace. In the absence of any meeting, enchanted by the cemetery, he wandered away from Maslin and tried to read the names inscribed on the headstones. The stone forest closed around him. The path weaved away from the iron gate. It was very peaceful, this snowy bottle of space in the hustle and bustle of the city. Here and there, impenetrable dark green trees rose up among the graves. Jack squatted among the stones, and wiped away the snow from a name with his gloved hand.

'Jack,' said a hoarse voice, just behind him. He turned swiftly, hemmed in, trying to see who had spoken.

'Over here, Jack.' An old dry voice. Jack turned again and stood up. Was it Maslin, calling him? For a moment he could see no one. Then – beyond an impassable sea of jostling, leaning stones – he saw the gaunt, black shape of his master.

'Mr Maslin!' he called out. 'Over here!' But Maslin didn't seem to hear. Jack was about to shout again when someone grabbed his arm and pulled him down. A bundle of rags, and the smell – what was it? A dry, graveyard smell, of dust and old bones. Jack didn't have time to think any further. A hand wrapped in strips of cloth had a tight grip of his elbow. He was about to cry out but the stooped, ragged figure raised a finger to his lips – except that Jack couldn't see his face, lost in the shadow of a deep hood.

'Don't be afraid,' the man said. 'We'll go to him.'

'How do you know my name?' Jack said.

A sound that may have been a laugh stole from the hooded man. 'Jack, it's my business to know,' he said. 'Come along. Introduce me to your master. I've waited a long time to see him.'

'You were following us,' Jack said. 'Yesterday – I saw you. And in the church – was that you?' He shivered. It was easy to believe this man was at least a hundred years old. He held out his arm, but the offer of help was declined with a hiss. Instead the old man pushed Jack out of the way, checked the coast was clear, and then shuffled along the path through the stones. Maslin saw him – he stood and stared. Jack glanced at Maslin's face, trying to fathom his expression. Dread, certainly, but compassion too. Did Maslin know who this ancient beggar might be? The two old men drew slowly together, in the snowy cemetery with its accumulated cargo of sadness, and the picture of the meeting branded itself on Jack's memory.

When they met, no words were spoken. They simply regarded each other. The moments ticked by, and it seemed to Jack the wind dropped, and a deeper hush descended on the cemetery. Then the stranger pushed back his hood. His head was wrapped in bands of cloth, like an Egyptian mummy.

Maslin took a deep breath, and held out his hand.

'I am James Maslin,' he said. 'As far as I know, the last of the line. Guardian of the fleur-de-lis, although it is lost.'

The old man took Maslin's hand in his own. Three of his fingers were missing.

'You know who I am,' he said, in his dry voice. 'My name is Matthias. The first. One of the first.' He withdrew his hand, and fumbled in the layers of his rags at his chest to draw out a golden fleur-de-lis, like the one Tremayne stole from Maslin. The gold glinted, in a stab of sunshine. With a clatter, two pigeons flew up from the cemetery wall, startling Jack. The gate opened, and two bearded young men in black hats stepped inside. Instantly the atmosphere changed and Jack was aware of the distant hum of the city beyond the walls, and the possibility there might be spies lurking, the ever-present eyes and ears of the Tremaynes. Jack stepped closer as Matthias pulled up his hood.

'We have to go,' Jack said.

Maslin glanced around them. 'We need to talk,' he said. 'Not here – somewhere private. Will you come to my rooms?'

Matthias shook his head. 'Like this?' he said. 'People think I am diseased – a leper. They won't let me in. They fear – contamination.' There was no self-pity in his voice. He was stating a fact.

'Where do you live?' Maslin asked.

'Close to here. The Jews – they have treated me more charitably. I have a shelter not far from the cemetery, where I have lived, on and off, for years. Soon it will be cleared away, with the rest of the slums, but it will last me long enough.' Matthias turned, gestured them to follow, and headed out of the cemetery through a narrow side gate. He walked awkwardly, using a stick, but he covered the ground with surprising speed, leading

170

Maslin and Jack through a series of stinking alleyways to a low hovel propped up against a wall. He opened a makeshift door and stepped inside. Maslin had to stoop to enter. Jack furtively scanned the alleyway before he too ducked inside, shutting the door behind him.

It was dark, a dismal fire smouldering on the floor. A bitter draft blew through cracks in the wall and a filthy mattress lay on the ground. Jack had never seen such a miserable place – could not imagine living in it. Matthias glanced up at him.

'I live here in winter,' he said. 'In the warmer weather I walk. It is my only relief – my consolation – to wander. People do not tolerate me for long. But here they are kind enough. They feed me, give me fuel for the fire.'

For the duration of this exchange, Maslin had stared at Matthias. He seemed to gobble up every single word he said.

'Are you truly Matthias? One of the first?' Maslin said. What did he mean? Who was Matthias?

'Do you want to see?'

Maslin shuddered. 'I'm afraid to see,' he said. 'How bad must it be, after seven hundred years? And the boy.' He nodded to Jack. 'Think of the boy.'

'Just a little then,' Matthias said. 'Enough to prove what you already know.'

He put back his hood again, in the safety offered by the hovel. Jack, prepared for the worst, was trying not to react. Matthias did not simply look old. It was much worse than that – so much worse. His face was partly covered with strips of cloth, but it was clear to see how much of the skin had disappeared from his skull. A few wisps of grey hair protruded from the remains of his scalp. His lips were creased and torn, but his eyes were very bright and white in the pits of his eye sockets.

'See,' Matthias said, folding back his sleeve. Slowly he began to unwind the fabric around his hand. The process took some time, but when the grimy bundle finally dropped to the floor,

Matthias revealed a hand that was utterly without flesh or skin. Only the complex web of bones remained, and the ligaments holding them together. Matthias raised his bone hand, and wriggled the fingers. Curiously, Jack did not find the spectacle entirely repulsive. The bones were so dry and clean, the hand resembled a piece of elaborate machinery.

'How?' he started. 'Why – how?'

But Maslin shushed him. 'You are Matthias,' he said, his eyes glittering. 'I heard the stories – that one of the knights – you – endured. But I confess, I didn't believe them. Now I see it is true. It must all be true.'

Matthias nodded. He began to cover his hand again, wrapping it in cloth.

'It is all true,' he said. 'I will live as long as the lily endures, James Maslin.'

'How can you live?' Jack broke in, burning with questions. 'The body – how can it work? For so long? Can't you take your own life? Drown yourself? Anything! Anything rather than endure like that. It is too bad. Too horrible.' The stream of questions surprised even Jack, as though shock were getting the better of him. Now the reality was sinking in, he couldn't believe it. Holy Mary and all the saints – he was talking to a corpse.

'Jack! Be quiet!' Maslin admonished. But Jack couldn't control himself. Tears sprang to his eyes. He made the sign of the cross without even thinking. This was the devil's work! What was he doing, with these terrible people so far away from home, from his parents and his own place? For the first time the distance between him and his own home seemed to yawn wide open. He scrabbled for the door, instinct taking over, wanting to be anywhere but here, cooped up in a hovel just an arm's length away from a corpse. But Maslin grabbed him and held him tight.

'Be still!' he hissed. 'Stop struggling, Jack. No one's going to hurt you. Keep still!'

Maslin, as Jack had discovered before, was much stronger than he looked. However much Jack fought and kicked, Maslin wouldn't let him go.

'How much does he know?' he heard Matthias say.

'As much as I do, in essence,' Maslin answered. 'We thought if the lily was hidden long enough its powers would fade. And certainly it seems those with its gifts are few and far between now. But its evil effects show no signs of dying away. I think they are more prevalent than ever.

'From time to time over the last century, other people, descendants of the knights, have wanted to uncover the lily with a thought to using it but no one has come close. Now, though, we have the Tremaynes, and they are more persistent and more violent than any of the others.'

Maslin relaxed his grip on Jack, who opened his eyes again, and rubbed his arm where Maslin's iron fingers had dug into his flesh. Matthias smiled at him, a ghastly smile.

'Do you think I haven't tried to take my own life, Jack?' he said gently. 'Whatever is done to me – whatever I do to myself – my body knits itself together again. Death by water, by poison, by the sword? I have tried them all, and each time my body repairs itself just enough to sustain me. Just enough. I'm invulnerable. That is the curse of it, my immortality. As long as the lily endures, then so do I. My fate is connected to it.'

'Then the lily is evil!' Jack burst out. 'God help me, why didn't you destroy it a long time ago, if it did this to you?'

'At first my long life seemed a blessing. Once I helped them save it, when the order was broken up. Even worn out and degraded as I became, nothing mattered to me except possession of the lily. When the order went underground, the council of twelve remained and eventually I begged them to spare me, to try and destroy it. But they wouldn't listen. They locked me up for a long time – for decades. Then they cast me out and disowned me. Then I heard the council of Kefalonia had also broken up and the lily was hidden away. There was nothing more I could do, except to wait.'

'My mother,' Maslin said in a low voice. 'You saw her – here in Prague.'

'Yes. I met her, in the cemetery, just as I met you. But it was too much. Too much.' He lowered his voice. 'When she saw me, like this, she became hysterical and ran away. I followed her afterwards, but she left Prague very quickly and I didn't see her again.'

'She lost her mind,' Maslin said softly. 'She lost her mind, Matthias. Seeing you must have tipped the balance.' His eyes burned. Did he blame Matthias? Maslin shook his head abruptly, banishing his memories.

'Why now?' he said. 'I've been to Prague before. Why speak to me now?'

'It is time,' Matthias said. 'I've seen you before but I had to be sure it was the right time.'

'Time for what?' Maslin said.

'Time to find the lily. Time to finish it. There was a prophecy, and now the elements of this prophecy are coming together. I have something to give you. Meet me tonight at the church of St Mary of the Snows. Come at ten, after the last service, when the church is quiet.'

Maslin sighed. He looked very tired. 'We'll come,' he said. 'I have a great deal to think about. And there is much more I want you to tell me,' he said. 'But we'll leave now. Do you need money? Supplies? Surely I can find you somewhere better to live – somewhere quiet.'

But Matthias laughed. 'Too late for me,' he said. 'You can better serve me another way.'

Outside the gloomy hovel, the snow was dazzling bright. Jack took two or three gulps of fresh air, trying to cleanse his lungs. Walking back to their rooms, across the Old Town Square, Jack was acutely aware of every pair of eyes turned in their direction – paranoid that every conversation was about them. He kept looking behind him, scanning the faces, certain they were being followed. Maslin was lost in thought, scarcely aware of his surroundings, but Jack couldn't help thinking something very bad was going to happen. Had anyone seen them in the cemetery? Were spies eavesdropping as they talked in the hovel with Matthias? It would have been easy enough – the walls were thin and full of holes. Perhaps the Tremaynes had followed them to Prague. Had they paid spies? Edmund Tremayne's face leered out of Jack's memory, along with the sound of his staff striking Maslin's head, and the blood rising to the skin. Uneasy, scared of his shadow, Jack kept close by his master's side.

At the lodgings, Maslin complained of another headache and retired to his bedroom with the curtains drawn. He wouldn't speak to Jack, waving him away abruptly. The landlady brought up a tray of stew and dumplings, but Jack was too anxious to eat and the stew congealed and grew cold on his plate. Instead he sat on his bed, hunched up, his mind going over and over the events of the morning. Maslin meeting Matthias on the path in the old cemetery. Matthias pushing back his hood, and holding up his skeletal hand. The story just didn't make sense. How could an angel's gift cause so much suffering? Why should they have to destroy something holy? This was the puzzle at the very heart of the story. If the knights of the lily had received a gift from God – why had it poisoned generations of lives?

Finally Jack gave up trying to find an answer. His thoughts trod round and round in the same circles, getting nowhere. He tried to think about something else – wondering about his mother and grandfather in Ireland, and his father in London. Now away from home himself, he wondered for the first time if his father ever felt homesick and lonely, away from his loved ones. He thought about the horses, and hoped his grandfather was tending to them properly. Eventually, worn out, he fell asleep, but even his dreams were polluted. He dreamed he was walking through the Old Town Square, and everyone was looking at him, and pointing. He ran after Maslin, but he got further and further away, leaving Jack all alone and at the mercy of the watchers, who pulled back their hoods to reveal they all wore the face of Matthias.

Jack woke up. For a moment the after-image of the dream floated in front of his eyes. The room was dark, the night drawn on. And it was cold, no fire in the hearth yet. On the tray, his uneaten stew was an unappetising clump. Jack jumped to his feet. He had no idea what time it was, but he sensed it was late. Had they missed their appointment? Without knocking, he hurried into Maslin's room. According to the clock on the wall it was gone nine and Maslin was still in bed. Jack went over, to wake him – but the death-like stupor had come upon him again.

This time it wasn't such a shock to Jack. He recognised the symptoms – the pale skin, the sunken eyes. He knew Maslin would wake, sooner or later. He didn't panic. The problem was, if Maslin didn't revive they would miss their appointment with Matthias. Jack sat beside Maslin, willing him to wake up. Apparently these fits were rare – but this one had followed hard on the heels of the last. Was the laudanum bringing them on? He picked up the little corked bottle on the bedside table. It was virtually empty now. Maslin had drunk the contents in just over two days.

Jack waited, watching the clock. Below the window, the street was still busy. A horse clopped by in the snow. Half a dozen male revellers went past, singing loudly. Now and then he heard the landlady coming up and down the stairs to attend to the other rooms. It was ten past nine, then half past. To reach the church by ten they would have to leave by a quarter to ten at the latest. Jack shook Maslin, determined to wake him up.

He splashed water on his face, shouted at him. These efforts were fruitless. Maslin lay as still and heavy as a corpse. Jack stared at the static face, wondering what scenes were replaying within the walls of Maslin's skull. The clocked ticked inexorably. Now it was a quarter to ten and Jack made a decision. He donned his coat and boots, told the landlady Maslin was ill and did not want to be disturbed, and then ran out on his own into the city and the night.

At least he knew where to find the church of St Mary of the Snows. It was very cold out, thick clouds obscuring the stars and snow beginning to fall. In the Old Town Square the street lamps burned yellow, haloed by the descending snow. In the café windows, Jack could see well-to-do diners drinking from crystal glasses. Out in the square horses and drivers waited patiently, the luckier horses covered with a rug, the drivers huddled in their coats, occasionally a red glow from a driver's pipe, and the perfume of tobacco smoke drifting through the falling snow. Running across the square, the sound of Jack's boots was muffled. The glamorous city seemed threatening now, the statues ugly and sinister. Two women and a man, all dressed up in smart furs, stood beside a brazier where a shivering boy sold roasted chestnuts. They turned when Jack hurried past, and one of the women said something in English, but he didn't stop to find out what she wanted. There was no time. He had to run.

The city was different at night. It took longer than he expected to find the church. The shadows played tricks. Once, not looking where he was going, he ran into a man walking in the other direction. The impact knocked the wind from him and the man cursed him, pushed him away. Further on, half a dozen urchins chased after him, throwing snowballs and laughing. Jack struggled on. It seemed the entire city was conspiring to stop him.

At last, there it was, St Mary of the Snows. Hot and out of

breath, Jack leaned on the door to recover. He had no idea how late he was. Would Matthias be waiting? He lifted the heavy latch and stepped inside.

The candles had not yet been extinguished but the pews stood empty, except for one figure praying on bent knees, lurking in the shadows at the back. It was Matthias. Jack went over, and knelt beside him.

'Matthias,' he whispered. 'I couldn't wake Mr Maslin. The fit came over him. It's not the first time. But he can't be woken, not till he's ready. So I've come instead, to tell you.'

Matthias pushed himself up and sat upon the wooden pew. He turned to Jack, his hideous face obscured by shadow.

'He must come,' Matthias whispered. 'I can't give the map to anyone but Maslin. Don't you understand?'

'Can't you give it to me? Or tomorrow. I'll bring Mr Maslin tomorrow – when he wakes up.'

'There is no one I can trust – no one but him. Tonight – it has to be tonight.' He looked around the church. 'After you came to the cemetery, there were others. They're following you.'

'The Tremaynes?' Jack blurted. 'They're in Prague?'

'Edmund Tremayne,' Matthias said, with a strange smile. 'How like his forefather he is. So much aggression and bluster.'

'Did he find you? Did he talk to you?' Jack interrupted. 'What do they know?'

'Jack! Jack, be quiet,' Matthias said. 'He didn't find me, though I saw him. He's looking for me – asking questions. He knows who I am, somehow, and knows I'm in Prague. I have to leave before he finds me. I have to go tonight, don't you see?'

Jack was burning with questions.

'Matthias,' he said. 'Tell me. Please tell me. If the lily is a gift from God, why has it caused so much suffering?'

Matthias stood still for a moment. The candlelight played upon his ravaged, bound up face. His eyes glittered. Slowly he extended a hand to Jack, and Jack took it, feeling the bones beneath the coverings of cloth. A sad, haunting smile passed across the old man's face. How many centuries of pain and persecution had he endured?

'We were bad men, Jack,' Matthias whispered. 'And I was the worst. I'm justly punished. The lily wasn't a gift, you see. The lily was stolen.' He released Jack's hand, but before he drew away he said: 'Tell Maslin a map is hidden in the central panel. Tell him I know this because I was present when the painting was commissioned. I'll see you again, Jack. Until then, keep safe. And may God go with you.'

Matthias opened the church door, peered outside, and then shuffled into the night. Before he closed the door a shower of snowflakes blew through, carried on a cold breath of wind, and settled on the floor. Then Jack was entirely alone in the church. For a time he stared at the stained-glass window, in the night an indecipherable pattern of silver and grey. Then he rose to his feet and walked across the church to the triptych. The central panel, Matthias had said – the picture of the knight in armour, bearing the lily. Should he do it now? Tear the picture apart to find the map hidden inside? But Jack wasn't quite brave enough. He would run back to Maslin and pass on the message. And he would tell him the truth about the lily.

Maslin didn't wake up until two in the morning. Jack lit a candle and sat beside the bed, waiting for him to revive. From time to time he dozed off, propped against the wall. When Maslin's eyes opened, he cried out in horror. Jack couldn't understand what he was saying – wasn't even certain the words were in English. The old man's voice was deafening. Beyond the door he heard footsteps, and the landlady knocking.

'What's going on?' she called out. And then something else in Czech that he couldn't understand. There were other footsteps pounding up the stairs, other disturbed guests doubtless fearing a murder had been perpetrated.

'Mr Maslin, Mr Maslin, be calm, sir. Please. Please!'

The landlady knocked again. Jack ran to the door and unlocked it.

'It's fine,' he assured them. 'Everything is fine. My master suffered a nightmare. Please – please don't worry.'

The landlady, in a billow of white nightie and sleeping cap, hurried into the room to reassure herself all was in order. Maslin was sitting up now, his face pale and his hands shaking, but indubitably not the victim of a murder.

'Please, accept my apologies for waking you,' he said. 'Be assured, I'm fine now. A bad dream – that's all.'

At last she was satisfied and left the room with reassurances for the other disturbed guests. Jack poured a drink of water for Maslin.

'What did you dream?' he asked. 'Did you go back? Did you see the past again?'

Maslin nodded. He took a sip of water. His whole body was trembling and a sweat had broken out on his lined face, and on his neck.

'Matthias,' Maslin said. 'I saw Matthias, and the breaking of the order. I saw the inquisitor general ride up a long road to the monastery and accuse the order of heresy. It was just as he said. Matthias tricked them. He took the lily away and carried it to Kefalonia, while the council surrendered a substitute to the church. An ordinary white lily in a glass casket.

'They arrested the council, and tortured them until they confessed to the charges. Tortured them to death. I was there, Jack. I was the other Maslin, the Grandmaster. I saw what they did to him. I felt it – felt his fear.' Maslin covered his face with his hands.

'I went to the church,' Jack said. 'You wouldn't wake up – so I went for you. I saw Matthias.'

An hour later, they set off again. The snow was whirling down, clouds of huge white flakes. Jack was deadly tired, his nerves strained to breaking point. Maslin had suggested Jack should stay behind, but Jack thought he could help and insisted on coming. The church of St Mary of the Snows was cold and dark, and the wooden doors were locked up, but this did not hinder Maslin, who had brought a narrow iron bar which he used to prise the doors open, while Jack kept a watch. Maslin seemed to feel no compunction in rending the door of the holy church. Once inside, he drew out a box of matches from his pocket and lit the row of candles in front of the golden picture.

'It's so old,' Jack said. 'It seems a pity to break it.' He took one long last look at the picture of the knight on his pale horse.

'I don't think so,' Maslin answered. 'In a sense it's mine anyway, by right of inheritance.' He jammed the end of his iron bar into the edge of the painting, through the joint of the frame with its golden rosettes. It wasn't easy. The frame was strongly built; the wood was deep and sturdy. Despite his strength, Maslin struggled to break it open. Finally, with a screech, the frame came away from the corner. The central panel fell apart. On the rear, unpainted side of the front piece, backing onto the painting of the knight, a thick piece of parchment had been pinned. Maslin pulled the parchment free, tearing the corners to do so. Then he inspected it in the candlelight.

'How will this help?' he murmured. 'Do you see, Jack? This doesn't tell us where the lily was hidden. How could it? The map was sealed up hundreds of years too early for that. No. The map tells us where the lily was discovered – where it was taken.

'So this is where we have to go next. To the lily's beginning.'

13

Tarot Cards
Bohemia, 1890

Miranda was lying awake in bed when Jacinth returned. She heard Jacinth talking, and the bells on the pony's harness. She strained to hear what was said, but even in the crystal silence of the winter night the voices were too far away. Perhaps she would find out later who the French girl's visitor was — and how he might be able to help her.

During the long journey to Prague, Miranda had spent the empty hours thinking and thinking, and her fear transformed into something more useful. The Tremaynes were too strong and too clever for any easy escape, and here in Europe Miranda was helpless. She was a child and she had no money. Abject terror wouldn't help. No, she had only her wits to rely on. She must be patient and canny. She had to gather whatever information and tools might come her way. Fear had to be put to one side. Escape and survival required cool thought, a readiness to use what opportunities might come her way. Sitting in the train, ignoring the Tremaynes, Miranda decided she would outwit them, sooner or later. She would get away.

Miranda heard Jacinth creeping up the stairs, so she closed her eyes, pretending to be asleep. Always she must be one step ahead. She must know more than her captors suspected, which is why she hadn't told the Tremaynes she could speak French.

And now she knew Jacinth had a secret friend. Lying in bed, Miranda thought of her mother in the asylum of Our Lady of Sorrows, and silently promised she would be home soon. She even thought of the Maysfields, and wondered if her grandfather was grieving for her, as he still grieved for his son. And she sent a prayer for her aunt who must be searching, without a clue to help her. She clung to the thought of these people, the unlikely foursome who cared for her, in their various ways. Even Marianne, her mother's old maid. Did she know Miranda was missing? They would all be waiting and worrying, but right now none of them could help her. She had only her own resources to rely on.

When Miranda opened her eyes again, it was morning and a pale light shone through an open window. Jacinth was already up and dressed. She had opened the shutters and pulled aside a makeshift curtain so the muted winter light, reflected from the snow, shone into the tower's upper room. Jacinth was wearing a dark red woollen dress and her cloak of hair was plaited into a coarse rope that reached her ankles. She was crouched before the fire, sweeping it out, so a fine white dust puffed in clouds. She dropped the ashes from a pan into an iron bucket, and then built up the fire with fresh wood that sparked and spat. Jacinth didn't have her veil on this morning. She turned to Miranda.

'Would you like some tea?' she said, in French. A kettle hung over the fire, steam jetting from the soot-blackened spout.

'Yes please.' Miranda propped her head on her elbow and studied Jacinth's face. Red blotches covered one side of her cheek and forehead, stretching down her neck and disappearing into the top of her dress. These scars caught the eye, as any difference does, but Miranda did not find Jacinth's appearance repulsive, as the second brother, Nicholas Tremayne, had warned her. Jacinth had otherwise pale olive skin, and beautiful grey eyes. But she looked uncared for – badly dressed, unwashed, and the astonishing hair was dirty. Probably her dress had not been cleaned for months. And why should she care, locked away in the forest? Miranda had tried very hard to get the measure of Jacinth, the previous evening, and Jacinth had proved a curious mix of childishness and hauteur. One minute she was proud, all high and mighty, and next she was like a little girl, much younger than her alleged thirteen years. But what kind of life had it been since her parents had died? At first Miranda thought Jacinth was cowed and slavish, a tool for the Tremaynes. Now knowing Jacinth had a secret friend, Miranda had to reassess. Maybe Jacinth could be useful after all – a help, rather than a hindrance.

Miranda climbed out of bed and sat beside the fire, the blanket still wrapped around her. She took the proffered tea.

'The Tremaynes will come back today,' she said. 'They'll expect something from us. You've served them already, finding me.' She took a sip of the burning drink, and waited for Jacinth's response.

'Do you want to help them?' Jacinth asked. 'Do you know how much more powerful our gifts might be, if we held the lily? If we possessed it?'

'I don't believe it,' Miranda said. 'How can you believe it? So much nonsense.'

'No,' Jacinth said, shaking her head. She was proud again, an adult talking down to a child. 'Downstairs, in my study, I've got a hundred books about the order. Some of them are hundreds of years old – I can show you. I've studied it for so long now. It's true. And you have a gift. Isn't that proof enough?'

'I have a gift, true. Why does that have to come from some magical lily of the Lord?'

'You have to believe it,' she said. 'The Tremaynes aren't the only ones involved. There are many others. The man James Maslin, he's in Prague now, trying to stop the Tremaynes. His family have kept it hidden for over a hundred years.'

Miranda remembered the Tremaynes whispering about Maslin. Their spies had discovered him in Prague.

'What do you know about him – about James Maslin?'

'He had a house in Ireland but Edmund Tremayne burned it to the ground. Now he's in Prague, with a boy he brought with him.'

'You spied on them too,' Miranda said carefully, narrowing her eyes. 'You reported back to Nicholas Tremayne.'

Jacinth blushed. She looked embarrassed and confused, uncomfortable in her role as the Tremaynes' accomplice.

'Nicholas Tremayne looks after me,' she said.

'Keeps you locked up in the middle of nowhere and convinced you no one else would want you – that you're a monster! That veil he makes you wear . . .' Miranda shuddered.

Jacinth's lip trembled but she glared at Miranda, the scars pulsing a fiercer red. She said something very quickly – too fast for Miranda to understand. Miranda watched carefully. Whose side was Jacinth really on? Jacinth didn't really like the Tremaynes any more than she did. How could she, considering what they had done to her?

'I hate the Tremaynes!' Jacinth said. 'Leave me alone! I hate them, of course I hate them! What else do I have? Nothing! Nothing at all. I have my talent – my power. You have people who care for you.'

A little tremor passed through Miranda. Sympathy for Jacinth – regret for wounding her – and an evil glow of triumph too, a sense of revenge. Wasn't it Jacinth's fault she had been kidnapped? It was Jacinth's fishing for supernatural talents that had guided the Tremaynes to her doorstep. It was her fault Miranda was here, trapped in a freezing tower in a Bohemian wood, hundreds of miles from home. Let her suffer a little.

A minute passed. Jacinth pressed her hands to her face, and tears leaked through her fingers. Miranda squeezed her own eyes shut but inside a column of stone seemed to collapse and fall to dust. She had endured so many endless days holding herself cold and tight, as the Tremaynes hauled her away, doped her, intimidated her, snatched away any last vestige of privacy. And Jacinth was another victim. Her suffering outweighed Miranda's few days many, many times. Miranda crept forward, and put her hands over Jacinth's. The girl's hot tears dripped onto Miranda's fingers.

'Jacinth,' she whispered. 'Jacinth, listen to me.' She prised Jacinth's hand from her face and looked into her eyes.

'I'm sorry,' she said. 'Please, hear what I'm saying. I don't want to hurt you. We should be friends, shouldn't we? We've got to help each other – we've got to escape. Leave the Tremaynes behind.'

Jacinth stared into Miranda's face.

'Without the lily – without the Tremaynes – who am I?' Jacinth said. Her voice was very low and quiet. Miranda realised Jacinth did not believe she was of any value at all – to herself or to anyone else. Miranda struggled for something to say – some reassurance.

'Are you happy here, as Nicholas Tremayne's captive monster? Is that what you want?' she said. 'Who you are – isn't that for you to choose? What you believe, what you feel is right?'

Jacinth looked into the distance.

'You're right,' she said, her voice flat. 'But we can't just run away. We have to stop them. If you want your mother to get better, we have to get rid of the lily – finish it. Then the Tremaynes will leave us alone.'

'What has this got to do with my mother?'

'There's a history of madness, among the descendants of the order. And over the years, it seems the gifts have diminished but the madness has increased. Like my father.'

Miranda considered. Her mother was ill, and she too was at risk. She remembered her walk in London, losing track of time and self. Madness could be her destiny too.

'Destroy the lily?' she echoed. 'How? Why?'

'Miranda, do you believe the story of the Order of the Lily?'

186

'Probably the order existed – but the story of the angel and the magical lily with its powers? That's hard to believe.'

'Far-sight is hard for most people to believe, but you know it's true,' Jacinth said. 'Perhaps we can try to see the lily. If we use foresight and far-sight together, maybe we could see further.'

'That's what the Tremaynes want us to do,' Miranda said, drawing away. She was suspicious again. Was Jacinth manipulating her more cleverly than she had expected? Perhaps Jacinth saw the doubt in Miranda's face, because she said:

'You don't trust me now. So – why don't you simply use your cards? Ask them. Ask them about the lily and what we should do.'

Miranda chewed her lip, thinking quickly. She hadn't consulted her cards under the constant surveillance of the Tremaynes, though they had asked her to often enough. Now, without making any conscious decision, she found the new cards were in her hands, running over each other as she shuffled. The time had come.

Jacinth backed away, giving her space. Miranda closed her eyes and cleared her mind.

Thoughts fell away, her surroundings, the noise of the fire, even the cold. The familiar dark space expanded in her head, beyond the limits of her body, to engulf her. Her fingers worked over the cards, shuffling, dividing, shuffling, until the moment was right and she dealt ten cards, laying them in a circle. Somewhere, within her, the question lingered. The lily. What was the lily?

Her eyes snapped open. The cards lay arranged in front of her. The Tower, again. The World. Justice. The Fool and the Hermit. The Ten of Staves and the Three of Pentacles. Eight and Seven of Cups, and the King of Swords. Like bright threads, the images wove together, rising up before her eyes. Like colours merging to create a new picture, or raw shapes fitting together to make up a new and complex design, the images rose in Miranda's mind.

A man in black in a crowded graveyard.

A boy running in the snow. (His gawky face rang a bell in her memory – she had seen him before, in a vision, riding across a pavement of stone.)

She saw a man in the desert, with a face burned brown by the sun. He stood on a sweep of dune, and the wind pulled at the hem of his robe. He called out her name, and waved.

A man wrapped in rags creeping away from the city, bent over a staff.

Julia, in the white room, her aunt Mary smoking and anxiously writing letters. Threads joined them all, weaving their lives together. Miranda sensed the connection, a path leading her on, to a single light, to the source. But what was the source?

In a glass box, in the darkness, a pure white light was shining. Buried underground, far away, it was the beacon she had always seen from afar whenever she read the cards. It was the flame burning in the darkness. Yes. Yes! It was the lily. Unknown, but longed for. Resonant, shining, even in the depths of its grave.

She reached for it – stretched out a hand. It was too far. Just a little too far. Reach further—

The lily was snatched away. Miranda opened her eyes and clutched her throat. She struggled to breathe. Jacinth was shaking her, staring down.

'Miranda! Come back!' Miranda sucked in a great, painful breath, filling her lungs.

'They're coming!' Jacinth was shaking Miranda, trying to pull her to her feet. 'The Tremaynes, I can hear the horses! Get up. Put the cards away.'

Miranda struggled to draw her thoughts together. She slid the cards into a pile and dropped them into her pocket. Jacinth ran across the room, picked up her veil, and went to the stairs.

Miranda put on her boots and tidied her hair. She found a jug and bowl, but the water, presumably from a stream or spring outside the tower, was covered in a thin film of ice. No wonder Jacinth didn't wash very often. Despite the cold, she broke the ice and splashed water over her face and hands. The accumulated weariness of the nightmare journey still weighed heavy. She shook her head. She would have to manage – had to keep her head clear.

'Miranda? How are you this morning?' Blanche Tremayne, looking spruce and fresh, had stuck her head through the hatch. 'Come down, will you? We need to talk.'

Both the brothers Tremayne had a gleam about them – an aura of excitement. Something had happened. They were like eager dogs on the trail of a fresh scent.

'Did you sleep well?' Blanche asked with a smile.

'Yes,' Miranda answered.

'Come and sit down then. Beside me. We have some astonishing news.'

Without looking at Jacinth, Miranda took the proffered place beside Blanche. Nicholas was sitting at the desk, staring at her. Edmund was pacing up and down by the window.

'Someone Nicholas knows has located a very important man in the city,' Blanche said. 'We have investigators working for us – following up information.'

'Spies,' Miranda interrupted, curling her lip. Blanche ignored the comment and proceeded smoothly.

'Someone we've heard of, but until now we doubted actually existed. It seemed too strange – too unlikely. A man who's lived for hundreds of years!'

'How can that be?' she asked slowly. 'Who is he?' They were speaking in English. Miranda was conscious of Jacinth fiddling with the fire, and wondered how much she could understand.

'In the beginning, in the desert, twelve knights received the lily,' Blanche said. 'One of those knights is still alive.

'We don't know why he was blessed with such long life, but there are records of his existence up to the time the lily was hidden and the council disbanded, about a hundred years ago. His name is Matthias.

'We were never certain if these stories were true. And we had no idea where he was, if he still survived,' Blanche said. 'But he was seen yesterday, in the Jewish Cemetery. He was talking to Maslin!'

Miranda looked from Blanche to Nicholas and then Edmund. The image flashed again into her mind – the old man in the cemetery. Was that Matthias?

'So what happens next?' she asked. Blanche glanced at her husband, perhaps seeking some confirmation.

'Everything is coming together.' Blanche's voice was urgent now. She gripped Miranda's arm. 'Maslin and Matthias are working together. They want to thwart us, but I think they will lead us to the lily. We have to follow Maslin. Matthias is the last surviving member of the council – he must know the lily's location. He must!'

'So why don't you let me go home, and kidnap Matthias instead?' Miranda said. 'He would be of more use to you than I am. I don't know where it is.'

Across the room, Edmund scowled and smacked his stick into the palm of his leather-gloved hand. Perhaps he wanted to hit her. But Blanche shook her head.

'We've already lost Matthias,' she said. 'In the night – he left Prague in the darkness. He melts away – like a rat – no trail to follow. But it doesn't matter. He's already communicated something to Maslin, and we have the old man in our sights.'

Miranda considered. 'So what do you want from me?' she said.

Blanche smiled at her, a co-conspirator. 'Work with Jacinth,' she said. 'Use your gifts together. Look for Matthias, and for Maslin. Jacinth can see over vast distances, and you have a window on the future. Try and find the lily. If we can reach it before Maslin does, so much the better. We need every clue we can find. And when we have the lily, your rewards will be great, Miranda. Think how your powers will develop. Think what our family – the family of the descendants of all the knights – could achieve. I know you hate us now, but I tell you truly, when all this comes to pass you'll be at the heart of it, and you'll be glad.'

Miranda glanced at Nicholas, who smiled. At the window Edmund was slapping his stick into his hand.

'We'll be back in the morning,' he said. 'And we'll want some answers. Don't disappoint us, Miranda. Jacinth will help you. She speaks a little English – enough for what you have to do.'

'And be ready for anything,' Nicholas broke in, standing up from his chair. 'It's possible we'll leave Bohemia tomorrow, depending on Maslin's next move. And if we go, the two of you will come with us.'

Blanche rose to her feet, with one last pat on the arm for Miranda.

'Be patient,' she whispered. 'Do this for us and you'll see in the end that I only want what's best for you – and for all of us. Our inheritance.'

The Tremaynes rode away from the tower. In the distance the brothers were talking together, but Miranda couldn't make out what they said. When they were gone, the room retained their aura of excitement. Miranda went to Jacinth and removed her veil.

'How much did you understand?' she said in French.

'Some. They said they'd take me from the tower.'

'Yes – if Maslin leaves Prague.'

'I'm afraid to leave.'

'You'll be leaving one way or another,' Miranda said. 'But I don't want to go with them – we mustn't help them.' She shared the details of her conversation with the Tremaynes, as well as the vision created by her tarot cards.

'I think it was him I saw – Matthias. He was – he was horrible,' she said with a shudder. 'And the lily – I saw that too. The strange thing is, it's always been there, every time I've read the cards. Like a bright light – illuminating things, sending me pictures from the present and the future. I didn't realise what it was before – didn't look at it closely.

'And it's beautiful, Jacinth. The most beautiful thing I've ever seen.' The recollected image rose in her mind, glowing with its pure white light, and Miranda yearned to see it again. How much more lovely would it be to hold it in her hands, to feel the light upon her?

'We have to find a way to give it back,' Jacinth said. 'And when we do, my gift will disappear.'

'It will be a sacrifice,' Miranda said, recalling the lily's allure. 'A sacrifice, yes. But it has to be done. I want my mother back.' She looked at Jacinth. 'Tell me – who were you speaking to last night, outside the tower? Will he help us?'

Jacinth looked surprised. Then she nodded slowly. 'Yes,' she said. 'I think he will. But where will we go?'

'To Prague first, to find Maslin,' Miranda said. 'I think he can help us – and we can help him. I have so many questions I want to ask him. And even if he can't help us, he wants to stop the Tremaynes. Doesn't that put him on our side?'

Jacinth shivered and pulled her shawl closer over her shoulders.

'I know you're afraid of leaving,' Miranda said. 'I understand it'll be hard for you. But you can't stay here any longer, and I'll be with you. I won't leave you, I promise.'

14

Prophecy
Bohemia, 1890

Jacinth was sitting at her desk, with the drawer pulled out. Inside rested the photograph of Maslin, the coronet of pins around his head. Miranda lay asleep on the chair by the fire. Jacinth had cooked her some porridge, bacon and toast, and as soon as Miranda had finished her breakfast, her eyes had grown heavy. Sleep had swallowed her up.

Jacinth stared at the photograph. It had been easy, in the end, to make a decision. How long had she screwed herself to the sticking point, twisting herself into a shape that didn't fit? Once it seemed she had no choice – no other path to follow – so she had forced herself to commit these acts that so offended her own sense of what was right and good. Survival, retaliation, self-preservation – these were her justifications for collaborating in the destruction of a man's home, in kidnap, and causing harm. Now she felt the distorting weight of this evil imperative taken away. She could say no.

Jacinth picked up the picture, and slowly drew out the pins. Then she smoothed the photograph, trying to press away the holes in the paper. I'm sorry, she thought to herself. I'm sorry, James Maslin. Whoever you are, whatever you've done, you didn't deserve this. I shouldn't have done it. She sat up straight, closed her eyes, and let out one long, profound sigh. Inside her, painful knots came loose. Of course she was still afraid. She was cutting herself off from the security Tremayne's protection had provided. She was stepping into the darkness, without a known way.

Jacinth opened her eyes and watched Miranda as she slept. The thin, pale body, usually so tense and watchful, was utterly relaxed. Her white hands lay open, the fingers gently curled. Her lips were parted; her body sprawled over the chair. Jacinth smiled, enjoying the sense of warmth the sight inspired. Already she was fond of Miranda, however cold and prickly her visitor had seemed at the outset. This friendship had not unravelled quite as Jacinth had fantasised. Miranda was difficult, unpredictable, even a little spiky. But she was clever too; resourceful in a way Jacinth was not. And while from time to time Miranda had stuck out her claws, Jacinth had still sensed her essential straightness and loyalty. She was brave. Very brave.

Jacinth stood up and began to prepare for their departure. She sorted out some spare clothes for herself and Miranda, as well as a day's supply of food and a couple of the more important books. In reality, there was little in the tower she needed or would miss. She just hoped Luca would abide by his promise and return to the tower that night. He would help them, wouldn't he?

Sunset came, flames of red and gold melting into the dark trees. The first star pricked out, low in the sky so it caught in the topmost branches, like a distant lantern. Miranda and Jacinth waited at the window, forlorn damsels from a fairy story. Frost bit the forest, turned the snow to powder. Far away were cities, trains, hospitals, factories. But this was hard to believe. Surely nowhere else existed, but the tower in the snow and its skirts of forest. The moon rose, almost round, glittering on the snow.

'There he is!' Miranda had spotted him first. Riding along the lane on his decorated pony, Luca waved a greeting, a huge smile on his face. Miranda waved back. Jacinth felt jealousy dig, a mean little knife in her ribs, at the prospect of her two precious friends maybe liking each other, but this had to be ignored. She turned from the window and ran down the stairs to unlock the door.

'Come in, come in!' she called, as Luca tied up the pony. The boy ran over to them, kicking up the snow. She ushered him indoors and up the stairs to her living room.

'Luca, this is Miranda. She's English.'

Luca took her hand, and bowed low.

'I am very pleased to meet you,' he said in French. Miranda blushed, clearly flattered and flustered. But quickly she drew herself together, motioned Luca to sit down, and asked him to help them escape to Prague.

Fifteen minutes later, the two girls were mounted on the pony, Luca walking beside its head. He had not questioned, argued or doubted.

'I'll take you to my family tonight, and in the morning, we'll go to Prague,' he said. 'We know where Maslin stays.' That was all. Jacinth left her veil behind, and after she had locked the tower door from the outside she threw the key away, into the forest.

The pony wended its way sure-footed through the forest and as the tower disappeared into the darkness, Jacinth felt a brew of terror and exhilaration. She was adrift now, without any anchor, cast upon the face of the unknown. She had only Luca and Miranda to rely on, and how much did she know about them?

A huge fire was burning at the heart of the camp. The gypsies called out greetings when they arrived. The gypsies were rowdy and familiar, slapping the boy on the back, shaking hands with the girls, pinching Miranda's cheek, tugging Jacinth's long plait. Several of the children ran up to hug her, firelight glinting on their faces. Miranda looked unsettled and distinctly uncomfortable amid the noisy mill of colourful people, but Jacinth squeezed her hand in reassurance.

Luca shooed the children away and led the girls to his great-grandmother's caravan. Miranda's face was whiter than ever, but she took off her boots as she was told and followed them inside. The old woman held out her hands in greeting and babbled to them. On the wooden walls, lantern light gleamed on the icons of the Virgin Mary and the curious pictures of Egyptian gods. Luca spoke with the old woman, gesturing to the girls. They sat on narrow couches running either side of the table, Jacinth and Miranda facing Luca and his great-grandmother. The old woman could hardly contain herself, touching her forehead and her heart, tears glistening in her eyes as she chattered on. Miranda was cool and still. Jacinth nodded and smiled from time to time, waiting for Luca to translate, to share what the old woman was saying. Eventually she stopped talking for a moment, and Luca turned to the girls.

'She's very happy to see you,' he said. 'We've waited a long time – our people have waited. She was afraid it wouldn't happen in her lifetime. Maybe wouldn't happen at all. Yet here you are, two of the three.'

Miranda poked Jacinth's arm. 'I find his French hard to understand. His accent,' she whispered. 'What did he say?' So Jacinth repeated the old woman's greeting.

'Two of the three,' Jacinth said. 'The third is James Maslin, who can see into the past.' She dug in her pocket and pulled out the photograph. She dropped it on the table. The old woman exclaimed – and picked it up. She made no comment on the holes in the picture, but she nodded.

'Of course you can't see his face,' Jacinth said. 'But it is him.'

Beside her, Miranda made a curious sound. She snatched up the photograph and stared intently. 'Why has he got no face?'

'I don't know, exactly.' Jacinth looked quickly at her friend. 'You have a photograph like this too? Did this happen to you?'

Miranda struggled to speak. 'Yes,' she said. 'When I was very young. No face – just like this. Why? Why does it happen?'

The old woman began to speak again, very animated, gesturing with her hands.

'She said the lily casts a shadow over the soul – poisons it,' Luca explained. 'That is why the face isn't seen.'

Miranda was silent but Jacinth sensed her tension and distress. Had the photograph, and the recollection of her own spoiled picture, convinced Miranda of the power of the lily? There was so much to learn. Jacinth assembled her thoughts, taking the lead.

'I want to know more about the prophecy,' she said. 'How do you know so much? What is your connection? Are your people descended from one of the knights too?'

Luca shook his head. 'No. We are closely connected to the order, standing in opposition to it. For hundreds of years we've followed the lily, and watched as its shadow spread. But we've never been strong enough to take it back. Our roots lie in North Africa, our ancestors lived in a great city in the desert, and they witnessed the theft of the lily. Since then, we have watched and waited, never letting it out of our sights, not until it was hidden away a hundred years ago. Now we wait for the three who will return it.'

So that was how the gypsies had found her, Jacinth thought. They had heard the tale of the flying witch from the villagers. How curious this must have made them. They had made enquiries, and calculated her ancestry. So, had other gypsy people spied on Miranda too, just as the Tremaynes had done? They were pawns, both Jacinth and Miranda, tiny pawns in a vast game covering hundreds of years. Other, more powerful forces dominated them, moved them and used them.

'And the prophecy?' Jacinth said. 'Where does it come from? What exactly does it say?'

The lantern dimmed for a moment. Outside the caravan,

Jacinth heard the voices of the gypsy children and the crackle of the fire. The scene was cosy, the warm yellow light on the old woman's face, the four of them very close in the caravan's bubble of stove-provided heat while outside all was clear and cold and white.

Luca and his great-grandmother exchanged a glance.

'Do you know the name Matthias?' he said. Miranda lifted her head, hearing the name. 'The ancient man,' she said. 'The last of the knights.'

'He came to us – told us something important,' Luca said. It took a long time to tell them the story. Luca told Jacinth, who often had to stop to explain to Miranda. The old woman frequently interrupted, breaking up the account with her own complicated interjections which Luca was then obliged to translate into French. And of course both girls had questions.

They learned that the council, secretive and hidden away, had apparently broken up in Kefalonia in 1755 when two brothers, Jacob and George Maslin, took the lily from the order's chapel to bury it away for good. But the hiding had not gone precisely to plan. Reports had reached the gypsies, from sailors who had abandoned the ship, that one of the brothers had lost his mind and committed a murder. Then the ship had drifted, who knows where.

Several years passed before the other brother, Jacob Maslin, reappeared in Spain, now a wealthy traveller embarking on the Grand Tour of Europe. He had hidden the lily – buried it deep, sharing the location with no one.

The gypsies waited, and watched as the lily's influence continued to poison the blood of the knights' descendants. Crime, murder, suicide, addiction and insanity. The gifts became fewer; the curse grew ever more virulent.

Then, fifty years ago, it seemed Matthias himself had gone to the gypsies. He was the old enemy – the worst of the knights, heavy with sin, oppressed by the curse of his immortality. Over the centuries he had fought the gypsies, accused them of heresy, used his power to persecute them. Now, after all this time, he asked for forgiveness.

It was midsummer, in the early 1840s. The gypsies were travelling across France, and had set up camp outside the walled city of Carcassonne. Europe was changing fast, the cities swelling, mines and factories spreading like a plague over the land. For the gypsies, however, life went on much as it had done for generations.

One day, a beggar wrapped in strips of cloth had come to the fire, begging for food. The children were afraid of him, but the gypsies were generous and offered him an equal portion, wine to drink, and a blanket for the night. Luca said his great-grandmother was among the company, already a mother with a brood of half a dozen children, and with the other adults she watched the beggar with curiosity. They sensed something about him – a breath of the supernatural. Was he an avatar from their gods? The gypsies had a host of gods – those carried from North Africa as well as the Christian God and a variable pantheon of his saints and martyrs. Vulnerable, relying always on good fortune and isolated from the settled community, they hedged their bets when it came to deities. Around this man, sitting by the fire, his face wrapped and shadowed, the more psychically sensitive could see the crackle of magic. Had the beggar come to test them? To ask their help? The head man approached him, bowed respectfully, and asked how they could best serve him. Then the beggar fished inside his rags and drew from his chest a heavy gold fleur-de-lis on a chain. A hush descended over the entire camp. Now they knew who he was.

At first they hadn't known what to do. Matthias had been the bane of their people, in the early days of the Order of the Lily. He had tried to drive them away from Europe – to stamp them out. He had the blood of their ancestors on his hands. The head man backed away, and as Matthias remained alone at the fireside, they consulted among each other. What did he want? How should they act? The younger men wanted to beat him, burn him, rend him to pieces. The older men were not so certain. Tempers rose, voices were raised, but they couldn't agree and did what they had always done. They waited.

When darkness fell, late in the midsummer evening, and the children had been sent to bed, Matthias rose to his feet and took off his robe. He unwrapped the bindings around his head and hands. Finally he stood before them, humiliated, entirely naked in the light of the fire, so they could see the walking corpse he had become.

'See me,' he said, holding out his bony hands. 'This is my punishment – the length of my own life. This, my decayed body, is the hell I carry with me.' The gypsies stared, their eyes glittering, seeing before them the architect of their suffering. Certainly he had suffered too – suffered justly! – so why had he come to them now?

The head man, Luca's great-grandfather, gestured to Matthias to dress himself again. 'What do you want?' he said gruffly. 'Why have you come?' Matthias had endured his terrible life for hundreds of years, and still served the lily despite his ordeal. He craved it. So why had it loosened its hold on him now? The head man was afraid Matthias had some ulterior motive. Did he now think he could use the gypsies in some way?

'I have something to tell you,' Matthias said. The assembly watched expectantly as Matthias, his broken face still exposed, looked to left and right, taking them all in.

'I have endured for over six hundred years,' he said. 'It isn't living. I do not have *life*. I was there, in the desert at the beginning. I was the perpetrator of this theft, as you know. But when I took it – when I held the lily in my hand for the first time – I sensed what it could give me. I felt it – the potency, the end of death.'

Matthias began to cough violently. One of the men offered him a cup of wine but Matthias waved it away.

'And I took it – greedily. I didn't understand then this long life would be so dark. It was a punishment for what I'd done. It is a long tunnel of suffering I walk every day and month and year. It has no ending. But still I craved it, the lily and all the powers it offered us, and the wealth and prestige the order conferred. Even when the truth about my long life dawned, when I understood my body would not endure in its wholeness, that I would become a monster, still I belonged to the lily. I would fight for it, kill for it. I was a slave to my own selfish hunger for what the lily seemed to offer.

'But in the end my torment outweighed my desire. The years wore me down. The council members had turned their backs on me and the lily disappeared. I looked back on the years of my own endurance and suffering, the fate that had befallen my friends and comrades, and their children and grandchildren. I longed for death but death wouldn't take me. I looked back over the centuries, and in an instant I saw it all as never before – the order in all its glory, the decline and hiding, my terrible punishment and suffering. I saw it all.

'So I went back to the beginning – to the place in the desert. I cast myself on the ground and begged for forgiveness. In the scalding sun I confessed my sins and called out for the angel to bless me. For three long years I stayed, enduring the ravages of cold and heat, the scouring storms of sand, and I surrendered my pride. I threw myself on the mercy of the angel.'

The gypsies began to murmur among themselves, intrigued now by the news Matthias had to tell them. Had he received forgiveness? If so, why was he still punished? The head man raised his hand, gesturing for silence. The hubbub was stilled.

'After three years, I had a vision,' Matthias said. 'The angel came, in a cloud of milky light. It bent over me, touched me gently on the forehead. The touch was light – but it burned like

201

fire. It told me my punishment wasn't over and the end could only come about when three children of the knights came together with one desire to send back the lily. They would be far-seers – able to look back and forward and beyond. And I saw their faces, the three who would come.

'And now I've seen the first in the flesh. He was staying in Prague. He is a young man and his name is James Maslin. I recognised him instantly! Yes – the last descendant of the order's Grandmaster. But I haven't spoken to him. We have to find the other two. That's why I've come to you now. I need your help.'

'Who are they, the others?' the head man asked, narrowing his eyes.

'They're not even born yet, but I've seen them. A girl with a face like a rose, and the other, cold and white. But I don't know them – their names, where they come from. I know you've watched them, the families. Our success isn't certain, you must understand. The end – the last days – are vague and full of shadows because others will try to stop us – nothing is certain.'

Luca, his great-grandmother and the girls discussed this story for hours. When finally they fell silent, the old woman took out a handkerchief and began to dab her eyes. Jacinth released a long, pent-up breath. Inside the stove the fire rumbled, but outside the snow world was silent. The other gypsies had retired to bed now. The night belonged to the trees and stars.

Jacinth and Miranda looked at one another. They were caught up in a dense, tangled web of lives and histories belonging to other people, which now lay heavy upon them – a great burden they didn't want and feared to take up. Jacinth laid her hands on the table, palms down, and gently stretched her fingers. She raised her eyes and addressed Luca in a low, serious voice.

'We are the two girls,' she said. 'No wonder you're so happy to take us to James Maslin. This is good fortune for you.'

Luca nodded. 'We will help you – any way we can.'

'And what if we don't want to do it? After all, no one knows where the lily is. What if we choose to walk away?'

Luca looked at Jacinth intently. 'I know you didn't choose this. But it does affect you. Already the lily's curse has blighted your family and it will go on to cause misery to many others. It lies in your power to change the future, Jacinth.'

Jacinth was tired and afraid. She had no wish for destiny and quest. She wanted to lie down in the warm and to sleep forever, for oblivion to close over her head. The days ahead were fraught with difficulty and danger and she didn't have the will to face it. The old woman muttered to her great-grandson.

'Go to bed now,' he said. 'You can stay here, in my grandmother's caravan, and in the morning I'll take you to Prague.'

The old woman gave them blankets and pillows, and the girls lay down on the couches at each side of the caravan, while their host clambered up to a bed at the top. It was much warmer than the draughty tower and Jacinth struggled to sleep despite her weariness. The story of Matthias and the gypsies turned over and over in her mind. If the Tremaynes knew about Matthias – and what he had suffered – how could they still insist they wanted to resurrect the lily? Were they so hypnotised by the prospect of supernatural power they could simply turn a blind eye to the evidence of its destructive nature?

The old woman woke them at dawn with cups of sweet tea. Jacinth had hardly closed her eyes, it seemed, and now the sun was shining. There was no time to lose. It was possible the Tremaynes were already on their way to the tower and the girls had to depart before the brothers came looking for them. Outside the caravan, Luca was already prepared for the journey. Two ponies were saddled outside, and as Jacinth and Miranda hastily consumed bread and burned bacon, he tucked the girls' meagre possessions into a saddlebag. Miranda was very quiet and self-contained, hardly speaking.

Before they left, the old woman held Jacinth's face in both her hands. Then she kissed her on both cheeks, talking all the while, tears leaking from her eyes. Miranda escaped this last embrace, tugging on her boots and slipping out of the caravan, breakfast still in hand. The camp was already busy, children collecting wood and feeding the ponies. Smoke drifted from half a dozen caravans. Luca helped Miranda onto a pony. Jacinth was to ride behind him. The entire gypsy assembly gathered all around them, a chorus of wishes for good fortune and success. Jacinth waved back uncertainly, feeling the weight of their expectation.

Despite the sunshine, the morning was bitterly cold. They couldn't travel fast through the thick snow, and Luca kept away from the forest tracks, to avoid them being seen. The forest was silent but Jacinth sensed pursuit, and a watching. When a clamour of rooks circled overhead, hoarse voices calling, she was acutely aware that somewhere else in the forest other riders might see and hear the birds, and wonder who had disturbed them.

Miranda trotted forward, to ride alongside Luca.

'Does he know? Does James Maslin know the prophecy?' she demanded. Miranda was fierce this morning, a note of antagonism in her voice.

Luca shook his head. 'No. We agreed with Matthias we would keep the prophecy secret among ourselves until we had found you two. It was too dangerous to share. Dangerous for you. If the story had leaked out, if the Tremaynes had learned you had the power to destroy what they have been looking for all this time, what might they have done? Your lives were at risk.' He reined in the pony, lifting his gloved finger to his lips.

'I can hear something,' he said. 'I think we'd better hurry.'

Both Luca and Miranda kicked their mounts into a canter. Jacinth clung on tight to the boy's waist. Snow flew up from the horses' hooves. A cold, black twig cut into her face when she didn't duck in time to miss it. Her fingers and toes grew numb.

At last they reached the fringes of the forest and the land opened up with snow-covered fields. Prague lay on the horizon, a dark blot on the pale blue sky.

'Hurry,' Luca nodded to Miranda. 'We haven't any time to lose. I've taken us on a longer route through the forest, so it's unlikely the Tremaynes would be on this road, but we can't be certain and they may have already discovered you've gone.'

The ponies alternately trotted and cantered along the narrow, rutted lane. They crunched through long black puddles of ice. Every now and then they had to stop when the snow balled in their hooves and Luca had to pick them out. Jacinth grew colder and colder. Her feet felt like icy stones in her boots, incapable of movement. She closed her eyes, her body hypnotised by the rhythm of the pony's motion.

Nearer the city, they joined a larger road and the traffic increased. They passed carriers with loads of hay and horse feed, firewood, timber, vegetables. Luca rode in the thick of it, hoping to hide in the mill of people. Then into the city itself, through narrow alleys and grand thoroughfares. So many people, bustling about their business, so many shops, rich women dressed in fur, a herd of noisy children running through the snow, and far away the shriek of a train whistle. It was too much to take in. Jacinth glanced across at Miranda. She looked cold too, sitting very upright on her pony, her eyes fixed straight ahead. The city was a spectacle, with its snow-robed statues, the grand buildings covered in bright paint and elaborate ornamentation, the endless spires and arches.

At last they stopped outside a house close to the huge town square. Luca dismounted and knocked at the door. The woman who opened the door was not impressed, eying him with obvious distaste. Jacinth could not understand what the servant said, but clearly something dismissive. But Luca stood his ground. He ushered Miranda forward.

'James Maslin,' Miranda said clearly in English. 'We have come to see James Maslin. It's very important.'

Clearly Miranda's appearance did not offend her so much. She closed the door for a minute, and then returned with another woman, perhaps the owner of the house.

'I've come to see James Maslin,' Miranda repeated stonily. The second woman shook her head. She said something in an English so accented that Jacinth could not understand. But Miranda looked aghast.

'What did she say?' Jacinth demanded.

'She said Maslin's leaving today. He's already gone to the train station to make arrangements for his departure. Only his servant is here, packing their bags.'

'Then we'll talk to the servant,' Jacinth said. 'We'll wait for Maslin to return for his luggage. We're not too late. He hasn't gone yet. Ask the woman if we can wait inside.'

Miranda relayed this information. The woman looked dubiously at Luca. He was holding the reins of Miranda's pony. 'Tell her I'm not staying,' he said. 'Tell her to bring the servant down.'

The mistress of the house and the servant disappeared again, and the door closed behind them. Jacinth stepped towards Luca. 'Aren't you coming with us?' she whispered. Luca took her hand. 'You need to travel with Maslin,' he said. 'Wherever you go, other members of our family will help you. And when everything is done, come and find me again. I've told you, I'll always be your friend, Jacinth.'

Luca looked from one girl to the other. 'Take care of each other,' he said, jumping onto his pony. 'Tell Maslin everything.'

Then, as the door opened again, he wheeled his pony round, and leading Miranda's mount he trotted away towards the city square, and disappeared into the busy streets.

When Jacinth turned back to the house, a gawky boy was standing in the doorway. He was well dressed, with bright blue eyes, rough dark hair and a crooked nose.

'We've come to see James Maslin. It's very important,' Miranda said for the third time. She seemed suddenly unsettled, looking strangely at the boy. 'I know he's preparing to leave but we have to wait for him. We have to.'

The boy looked from one girl to the other. His eyes lingered briefly on Jacinth's face but he didn't stare. Perhaps he sensed the desperation in Miranda's voice, because he nodded.

'Come in,' he said.

15

Orient Express
Egypt, 1890

They boarded a train at Prague that very day and headed for Vienna. Maslin booked for tickets on the Orient Express and they crossed Eastern Europe to ancient Constantinople, via Budapest and Belgrade. Jack, Maslin, Miranda and Jacinth shared a first class compartment. They were travelling fast – and in style. Once aboard, they had no need to disembark. Hundreds of miles flew past the window, unreal, like a dream. Forests, mountains, grimy towns, forgotten villages.

Two weeks later, Jack was riding on a camel across a sea of stone, sand and rubble. The sky was a dry, blue furnace. High up, almost too high to see, three black birds flew in circles over the desert.

Riding a camel was not so different to riding a horse. It came easily to him. Maslin was riding beside him; the two girls were together on a third camel. They had a guide, a toothless old man in a white turban called Muhammad who alone of them seemed impervious to the heat. It was winter, he told them. Why were they complaining? In the early mornings, while the Europeans soaked up the cool, he shivered in his blankets.

In teeming, stinking Cairo, Maslin had called in a favour from a wealthy Egyptian friend who lived in a white house with a tranquil garden surrounded by high walls. This friend had furnished them with the camel team, blankets and supplies and his best guide. From Cairo they rode out, into the desert. Every morning they rose early and rode all morning till the heat became too much to bear. Then they took shelter as best they could, until the late afternoon when they rode again till darkness fell. Then Muhammad and Jack set up the tents and lit a fire. They cooked flat bread and stews of goat's meat and lentils. During the day they snacked on figs and leathery dates, pieces of dry bread from the night before. On the third day Miranda was laid low with a debilitating stomach upset, though she suffered in silence. There was no time to stop for her recovery so they had to travel on, Miranda dosed with Maslin's ubiquitous laudanum to numb the discomfort. In the evenings, after the meal, Jack lay on his back and stared up at the stars. Never had they seemed so many nor so bright, as here in the desert. Beside the fire, Maslin and Muhammad argued over the map, and what landmarks the various scribbles might signify. Muhammad claimed the various marks were outposts of a desert realm guarded by a nomadic tribe, protectors of the lost city. He was afraid these marauders would slaughter them all before they could reach their destination.

They were all tired, after so much ceaseless travelling. The unaccustomed heat, the strange food and the nagging sense of pursuit wore them all down. The Tremaynes, and their agents, would be following of course. It wouldn't be difficult to trace their path. A bribe to a railway clerk would reveal their destination. A telegram travelled faster than a steam train, to prime an accomplice to follow them. Jacinth's far-sight revealed they had another pursuer – Matthias was also travelling south, stowed away on a freight train.

On the Orient Express they had shared their stories, but in the desert, after nightfall, they had little energy for chatter. Jacinth stayed close to Miranda, hoping to provide some comfort as she suffered. Still Jack couldn't help but love the desert.

It amazed him, that something so empty should be so beautiful. Mostly the landscape was rock and dust, but the sense of distance and purity stirred his heart.

On the seventh night, Jack stared at the stars feeling the cold night air upon his face, though his body was warm beneath the heavy quilt. Despite his weariness he wasn't sleeping well, waking at hourly intervals and observing the moon's transit in a smooth arc across the sky. He could hear the endless burble of the camels' noisy digestion, their grumbles and belches, and on the other side of the fire, Maslin's gentle snoring. He felt very strange, in this unknown land and amid these unknown people. He stretched out his legs, stimulating the circulation. Moonlight glittered on the endless fragments of broken rock littering the sand. Hard to tell what time it was – the moon was low on the horizon. Jack sat up. For a moment even the camels were quiet and he savoured the vast silence. The fire had diminished to a few glowing embers, there was not a breath of wind. He glanced at Maslin. Did he really know where they were going? Jack and the girls had no idea – they had blindly entrusted themselves to the old man and the even older guide – and here they were, isolated in the ocean of desert, far from anywhere.

Jack knew he wouldn't fall asleep again so he tugged on his trousers and boots and rolled up his blankets. It was bitterly cold, the converse of the day's brassy heat. Their resting place was a shallow valley, with several tall dunes to the east, over which the sun would rise. Eager to warm himself, Jack walked towards them. The sandy ground was littered with holes apparently home to scorpions, though Muhammad had reassured them they were not very lively in winter. Still Jack was cautious, picking a careful route. The moon cast long shadows behind the rocks. He reached the tallest dune and began to climb. Curiously, a natural path seemed to reveal itself, offering an easy ascent. Up he climbed, and up, growing warmer as he went.

Something compelled him now, this desire to reach the summit. He began to hurry, half running, jumping over stones. The dune twisted to the east, a skewed pyramid, and following the un-path Jack lost sight of the encampment. He saw something – at the peak – beside a tough, thorny tree. What was it? A pillar of some kind. Jack ran in earnest, forgetful of scorpions. The scene had significance, the tree and the post sticking up from the top of the sandy hill in the moonlight. A finger of stone, as tall as his shoulders, carved with signs and figures. Jack held out his hand to touch it, the stone icy cold beneath his fingers. What did it mean? Why had he found it, out here in the middle of the desert?

The sky paled and the sun shot its first hot arrow of light above the stony horizon. Jack felt it, the first blow of the day-long assault of heat. The flash of golden light glanced across the stone post, revealing its rust and sand colouring, the carvings blurred by wind and time. Dazed by the dream of the journey, by the lack of sleep and the constant aura of the supernatural that lingered around them, Jack wondered at the string of seemingly random events that had brought him to this place, by a sacred stone on a sandy hill deep in the burning desert. Had it all been laid out for him, this long path? Was it truly chance? He shaded his eyes, and a light wind blew, fingering his hair. A slight movement on the horizon beyond the hill caught his eye. He stared intently. There again, something shifted, a dark shape against battlements of weathered stone, far away. Jack felt his pulse quicken. Had he spied their pursuers? Were other riders hot on their trail? He strained his eyes to see. The movement was more distinct now. Horses, he decided, rather than camels. He could tell by the way they moved, by their agility and speed. Half a dozen maybe, heading towards them.

Jack took one last look, then he turned and ran as fast as he could down the hill and back to the encampment. He had to hurry and warn the others. What would they do? How could they defend themselves? He didn't want to fight – he wanted to keep well ahead, but perhaps the fight was coming, whether he wanted it or not. He ran on, arms flailing.

They were all awake, but only Muhammad had got up.

'Riders!' he shouted, out of breath. 'They're coming this way – men on horses! I think they're coming after us!'

Maslin glanced at the girls. 'Quickly – get ready.' Jacinth and Miranda scrambled out of bed and began to pack away the camp.

'What are we going to do?' Jack said in a panic. 'They're too fast, and too many. We can't outrun them. Where can we hide?' Just as elation had overcome him on finding the stone, now terror gobbled him up just as completely. Maslin stood up straight. The wind lifted his long, white hair. He looked very thin and brittle in the bright sunlight, very vulnerable. He was wearing a black belted robe, much like Muhammad's. He looked, to Jack, like a mad old prophet, a character from the Old Testament stories his mother had read so many years ago. But Jack was afraid they would all soon be dead in the desert, blood on the sand, the vultures circling. The vultures were huge. He'd seen one sitting on the corpse of a camel, as big as he was, with its hunched shoulders and glossy black feathers. Out here in the desert they were all alone. Edmund Tremayne could do what he liked – no one would help them.

'What are we going to do?' Jack repeated, his voice tight with anxiety. Why wasn't Maslin hurrying?

'We can't do anything,' Maslin said. 'Just be ready to leave. Help the others load the camels.' Maslin draped a dark cloth over his head and tied it round in a loose turban, long ends training over his shoulders. Out of habit, his hand went to his chest, feeling for the fleur-de-lis stolen by Edmund Tremayne.

A faint disturbance rippled the air before they actually heard the sound of hooves. Jack felt a prickle of fear run across his skin. He looked to Jacinth and Miranda. They were hiding behind a camel, faces white and scared. This was it then – this was it.

The drumming of hooves grew louder. Muhammad drew the old revolver from his belt and held it aloft. Maslin simply stood and stared. Seven riders, dressed in black robes, appeared from behind the dunes and hurtled towards them. The hooves threw up clouds of dust and sand. The riders' heads and faces were covered, leaving only their dark eyes exposed. The silken horses were caparisoned with tassels of black and gold that bounced as they moved. Their long manes flew over the hands and faces of the riders. Muhammad uttered a strangled prayer, calling on Allah, and clapped his hand to his brow. He brandished the gun and let off one wild shot but Maslin stepped towards him and knocked the gun from his hand, so it bounced on the ground.

Then the riders were all around them, the horses wheeling around in circles. Such noble horses – even in his terror Jack noticed how beautiful they were, how quick and strong. Sand and dust rose in a cloud all around them, catching at the back of Jack's throat, filling his eyes.

No one spoke at first. Gradually the horses calmed, and the seven riders drew them to a halt, spaced in a circle around their captives. All the men carried rifles, and heavy belts of bullets strung over their shoulders. One man dismounted and walked towards Maslin. Slowly he unwound the scarf covering his face. He was tall and powerfully built, with dark skin and a strong, square face. He stood confronting Maslin, and for a moment they were like reflections of one another, both tall and straight, both dressed in black. Neither man moved for several seconds, each assessing the other. If it came to a fight, Jack speculated, Maslin wouldn't stand a chance. The stranger was young and stern, his face smouldering with intelligence. A scholar, perhaps, as well as a warrior. He had a rifle across his back and a dagger in his belt. Maslin's hand, which Jack noticed was shaking, returned to the absent shape on his chest. He gestured to the stranger and shook his head. The stranger narrowed his eyes. He pulled down the front of his robe. There, embedded in the skin of his chest, was a tattoo of the fleur-de-lis. Miranda gasped. What did this mean? Was this man also a descendant of those first knights? If so, on whose side did he belong? Jacinth murmured urgently in French and tugged Miranda's sleeve.

'What did she say?' Jack whispered. Miranda frowned and shook her head. She was watching the encounter intently. Maslin extended his hand. For a moment it hovered between them. Maslin spoke in a language Jack couldn't understand, and the man responded, and laughed. In an instant the atmosphere altered. The threat evaporated. The other riders also dismounted, smiling and talking. The leader, his arm across Maslin's shoulder, guided him to meet his fellows. Everyone milled around. Except for Muhammad, Jack and the girls – who remained in a nervous huddle in the middle.

Miranda leaned towards him. 'Jacinth said – she thinks they look a bit like the gypsies from the forest near Prague.'

Jack absorbed this information. 'You mean, they might be the same tribe? The gypsies came from Egypt?'

'Isn't that where the name comes from?' Miranda said dryly. 'Egyptians – gypsies.'

'What do you think?' he said steadily. 'Is she right?'

Miranda shrugged. 'We'll soon find out.'

They were not formally introduced until an hour later, at the riders' encampment, some two miles away. Low awnings were pinned in the sand beside a deep stone well, and a solitary, stringy date palm casting a little shade. The dry, crumbled ruins of a village straggled beside it. Jack watered the camels from a long trough by the well and tied them up. Then Maslin gestured him to follow, and Jack ducked into the leader's tent.

Following Maslin's example he took off his boots and walked barefoot across the carpet, to sit with Jacinth and Miranda.

'This is Aashiq,' Maslin said. 'As Jacinth correctly surmised, they are part of a tribe of people as closely connected to the lily as we are. Over the centuries the tribe has changed and dispersed, all over the world, just like the children of the knights. But Aashiq and his men are the guardians of the cave where the angel appeared. They have protected it.

'It has been such a long time. I had heard of them – read about them. But I thought the legacy died out. I had no idea the guard still existed.'

'So how did you know where to find them?' Jack asked sharply.

'The map, of course,' Miranda said. 'Was there a sign? A warning?'

Maslin nodded. 'There are a series of way marks too. Old stone posts, marking their territory. Muhammad was certain our camp last night was close to one such place.'

'Yes,' Jack blurted. 'I found it – on the hill to the east. That's when I saw the riders.'

Aashiq was sitting cross-legged, listening to the conversation. He focused on Jack.

'So this is your servant, Jack,' he said in perfect English. And turning to the girls: 'Miranda, and Jacinth.'

Miranda stirred uneasily, hearing his voice. Perhaps she was surprised this desert nomad spoke English. Her pale face was sunburned now, her eyes were bright with illness and laudanum, and she had lost weight. But she held her head up.

'If I understand the story correctly, you should be our enemy,' she said, on her high horse. 'We are the children of the knights who stole the lily. Why do you welcome us as your guests?'

Aashiq smiled. His head was bare now, long, dense black hair falling over his shoulders.

'I know who you are,' he said. 'I also know the prophecy, and news of your coming travelled ahead.'

'So you will take us there – to the cave?' Miranda asked, still haughty. Was she afraid? Jack wondered. Is that why she was so chilly? It was hard not to admire her courage and pride, considering how ill she was, how much she must be suffering. And Jacinth – it was hard for him to get to know Jacinth, because he couldn't understand her. She was Miranda's strange, unsettling little shadow most of the time.

Aashiq gave a polite bow. 'I am your servant,' he said, apparently amused by Miranda's manner. 'Tomorrow morning, we shall take you directly. We shall escort you.'

The young people were dismissed and the rest of the day they spent at the campsite by the well. Maslin passed long hours talking with Aashiq in his tent. One of the other riders treated Miranda with a medicine he had in a stoppered clay bottle and bade her rest in the shade, to regain her strength for the onward journey the next day. Jacinth lay beside Miranda, mopping her brow, keeping her company. Even Muhammad was busy, taking the opportunity to drink sweet tea and smoke with the riders. So Jack mooched in the ruins of the old village, stooping inside broken rooms, wandering narrow lanes filled with sand. Then he visited the horses, tied up in the shade of another awning, dozing, switching their tails at flies. Jack, son of a long line of horse dealers, was filled with admiration. He had never seen animals like this before – so aristocratic and sleek, with their tapering muzzles and huge liquid eyes, delicacy and strength combined.

'You're a horseman.' The voice startled Jack. He hadn't heard Aashiq approach.

Jack nodded. 'At home,' he mumbled, 'in Ireland, we have horses.' Then he flushed, feeling like a fool. Aashiq was intimidating.

'Then tomorrow you must ride one,' Aashiq said, running

his hand along the crest of a horse's neck. He scrutinised Jack, getting the measure of him. 'Your master has told me a great deal about you today. He says you've protected him – that without you he wouldn't have reached us.'

Jack felt a surge of pride, to have earned Aashiq's respect. He turned to the glorious horses. 'I would be honoured to ride one,' he said.

They ate well that evening, pieces of lamb roasted over the fire and spicy bread. There was an atmosphere of celebration. Later the men were lively, almost frighteningly so, calling out in loud voices and letting off random shots from their rifles, startling the horses. For the first time since Prague, Jack wasn't afraid. He trusted Aashiq and his fierce companions to protect them. They were part of a company now.

Despite the noise, Jack fell asleep quickly and easily. The taunting moon was blocked by the tent; the carpet beneath him kept out the cold from the ground. His stomach was full of good food and Miranda seemed a little revived. Even the unsettling supernatural aura woven about the foretold threesome seemed diluted by the presence of Aashiq and his friends.

Just before he slept, Jack crossed himself and prayed. How many days since he'd remembered this lifetime's habit? He closed his eyes and thought of his mother in Ireland and his father working in London. He prayed for his grandfather's good health, and even for the horses he'd left behind. Would he ever return? It seemed far away now, another life. Perhaps it didn't even exist anymore. His heart contracted at the thought. Once that life had been everything – all he could conceive of. Now everything had changed.

16

Blood
Egypt, 1890

Miranda dreamed of a cool, luscious river. She was drifting in the water, down into its crystal depths. The healing liquid flowed into her body, washing away a tide of silt and filth. How soothing it was, how delightful, absorbing the accumulation of baking heat from her damaged body, leaving her cold and white as snow. She was very slightly awake, conscious of the dream, savouring it. She'd slipped the leash momentarily. Her body seemed far away; the tumult of the previous days did not intrude. The waters lapped over her, utterly delicious.

An explosion tore through the dream, jolting her awake. The world crowded in, a welter of unwelcome sensations. The roof of the tent was flapping loudly in the wind, and outside the tent a man cried out. Another shot was fired, and ricocheted on a piece of stone close by. Jacinth sat up suddenly, and Jack on the other side of the tent.

'What – what's happening?' Jack said. More shots, and a horse whinnied in terror, loud as a bugle. They heard men running.

'We're under attack,' Miranda said. 'My God, I thought we were safe at last.' She clambered out of bed. 'Hurry up,' she said to Jacinth. 'We've got to help.'

'Help?' Jack snapped. 'What can you do? You've got to hide.'

Miranda glared. He could be infuriating, this bossy boy who wanted to take charge.

'And what are you going to do?' she demanded. Then, to her immense surprise, Jack drew out from under his blanket a heavy black revolver.

'Where did you get that?' Another shot rang out; a bullet sliced through the fabric of the tent and embedded itself in the ground. Miranda and Jack stared at each other.

'Aashiq gave it to me – last night,' Jack retorted. He left unsaid the sentence floating in the air between them – his pride that Aashiq valued him, even if Miranda did not.

'Have you ever used one before? Do you even know how to?'

Jack didn't answer, replying instead with a grim smile. Exasperated, she turned away and grabbed Jacinth by the arm.

'Let's go,' she said, in English. 'We have to run away – hide somewhere.' They pushed their way out of the rear of the tent, and headed towards the ruined village. Let Jack play the big man if he wanted. As Miranda stepped out, even in the midst of the battle and its noise, she realised how much better she was feeling. Still weak, yes, still light-headed because she had been able to eat so little. But the long, miserable days of pain and sickness had passed away. The worst was over.

A huge moon beamed on the desert. The night was bitterly cold, and the wind cut like ice. Moonlight glinted on the stones of the broken buildings and the girls ran, as fast as they could. Miranda glanced back, trying to work out what was happening but it was hard to make out. She could hear the sound of horses, and shots were flying into the camp. The men were running around and letting off return fire but it was hard to see where their attackers were hiding. Cries rang out, calls of encouragement as well as the horrible shriek of a man wounded by a bullet. Jacinth pulled her. 'Come on,' she said. 'Leave them. We have to hide.'

Jack pushed his way out of the tent, revolver in hand.

Another bullet came past him, so close he felt the disturbance of the air. He flinched, and called out without thinking: 'Mr Maslin! Mr Maslin, where are you!' But a heavy arm was wrapped around his neck and he was dragged to the ground.

'Quiet, you fool! Do you want them all to know where you are?' It was Aashiq, swathed in black, only his eyes revealed. Jack was winded, humiliated and furious with himself. How stupid! Stupid! His heart was thundering.

He and Aashiq lay side by side on their bellies in the sand. Another burst of gunfire, and a shout. Then a tense moment of silence. Jack peered through the darkness.

'Who is it?' he whispered. 'Where are they? Where's Mr Maslin?'

Aashiq didn't get a chance to answer. With a terrifying cry, a dozen horsemen rode out of the night and into the camp. Aashiq fired his rifle once, then slung it over his back and drew out his dagger. As the first horse approached he jumped up at the rider and stuck the blade into his throat. Jack could hardly see what was happening, but the dagger flashed once in the moonlight, and the man fell from his horse with a horrible gurgling and blood was leaking everywhere, so much blood, as the dying man clutched at his neck and struggled madly. More shots – and the blade of a sword hissed past his ear. In a panic, Jack raised the revolver, pulled back the hammer till it locked and then squeezed the trigger. The gun fired, a wild shot causing no one danger except perhaps himself, and the revolver jumped from his hand. Jack fell to his knees, desperate to retrieve it, as hooves milled all around him, men fighting, the horrible sound of knives thumping into flesh and the cries of the wounded. He groped around in the sand, till at last his fingers closed over the stem of the revolver. He held it tight, and crept backwards, still on his hands and knees. His courage was faltering. Where was Maslin? The old man was his priority now. Still on his hands and knees, Jack hurried across the campsite through the fighting. He was kicked once, inadvertently, as one of Aashiq's men struggled to disarm one of their attackers. The blow knocked him over, but he didn't feel pain. A tide of adrenalin carried him on, senses quickened, as he scoured the camp for Maslin. Where was he? Had Maslin run off, like the girls?

A huge hand gripped the back of his neck, like a vice, and pulled him to his feet. Without thinking, Jack lashed out with his fists and feet. He struggled to draw back the hammer on the revolver but the man snatched it from him. An enormous man – a veritable giant – holding Jack painfully aloft so his feet didn't touch the ground. The man, his face glinting greasily in the moonlight, peered at Jack and his spare hand drew out a long, narrow knife. Everything began to move very slowly – each second drawn out impossibly long. Jack saw the blade was dark and sticky, already dirtied with the blood of his comrades. In a flash he sensed what would come next – the keenness of the blade, the impression it would make, carving into his throat, the parting of his skin, the sudden sense of cold – and in a blind panic he fought like a wildcat, kicking and hitting out and gnashing his teeth. In the face of death every atom of his body rallied, in a last desperate effort to avoid the fatal blow. He sensed it – the giant man drawing back his knife arm, readying himself to plunge the blade into his throat.

But the blow didn't fall. Instead the man's eyes widened. Something had surprised him. His knife arm remained suspended. A sudden sweat broke out on his face and his lips moved. Still he held Jack aloft, but Jack sensed the grip had weakened. The man opened his lips again, but this time a tiny ribbon of blood trickled out, and dripped on his beard. Jack kicked out again and the huge hand released him. The man rocked on his feet. His eyelids fluttered and he collapsed forwards onto the ground, his body twitching, and a dark lake of blood welling from a wound in the small of his back. Jack was stunned. He couldn't get his thoughts in any order. A tall, dark shape loomed out of the night.

'Jack,' a voice hissed in his ear. 'Come along now. That was a little close for comfort.'

Jack opened his mouth to speak but nothing would come out. A part of him was caught still, dangling from the giant's hand, contemplating the knife. He couldn't believe he had escaped.

'We have to move,' Maslin chivvied. 'Come along, Jack. You're out in the open.' He gave Jack a little push.

'My gun!' Jack exclaimed. 'It's here. I have to get it.'

'Forget the gun,' Maslin said, more urgently. 'We need cover. Hurry!'

Jack turned around and headed towards the broken walls of the old village, Maslin close behind him. Another shot came past them, very close, so Jack ducked to avoid it. To their left, a voice barked an order and another voice followed. It was hard to tell who was who, in the darkness. They hurried between the tents, Maslin's hand on Jack's shoulder, guiding him.

Where were the girls? Where was Aashiq? Jack didn't have the first idea who was gaining the upper hand; the battle was a horrible, messy confusion.

Another shot was fired from behind them, and Maslin jerked forwards. Jack turned towards him but Maslin pushed him onwards.

'Quick!' he said. 'Get behind the wall.'

Jack jumped over the mound of broken stones and curled up on the lee side. Maslin crouched down beside him. He had a revolver in his hand, and turned to fire from the shelter of the wall. He moved his left arm awkwardly, and Jack saw a dark trickle worming its way across the white skin on the back of his left hand.

'You were shot,' Jack exclaimed. 'Mr Maslin, you've been shot.'

'I know,' Maslin said dryly. 'Keep down, Jack. Keep your head down. We'll get out of here.' Maslin peered through the darkness and fired the revolver. Indistinct shapes moved about the camp. He fired again, cursing quietly.

Jacinth and Miranda moved among the broken walls and the low roofless houses. The ruined village was a maze of lanes and streets, slowing filling in with sand. Behind them the battle was a confusion of noise and movement. Jacinth tried to keep her mind clear, to quell the rising sense of panic.

'In here,' Miranda said. 'Go on. We'll hide in here.' They hurried through an old stone doorway. The moon cast long shadows, so the sand was striped black and bleached white alternately.

Jacinth pressed herself against a wall. She was shaking, whether through fear or the cold it was hard to tell. She felt as though she were hollow inside, her heart and marrow sucked out, and had a terrible sensation of falling, falling, as though she would never find any kind of firm footing again. But she had been falling for a long time – for years. Shouldn't she be accustomed to it now, the plunge into a terrible unknown?

'We should be safe here,' Miranda muttered, perhaps reassuring herself. She was speaking in English, without thinking, but Jacinth could understand this much.

The girls squatted in the darkness, side by side. Miranda was shaking too. Jacinth grasped her hand and they waited in silence. Beyond the village, they could hear gunfire and shouting.

'Who could they be? Tremayne's men?' Jacinth whispered.

Miranda frowned. 'I suppose so. I couldn't see them – couldn't see who they were.' She craned her neck, trying to see out through the doorway, back towards the battle.

A minute passed, a minute like a century. 'There must be something we can do,' Miranda muttered. 'Can we help, d'you think? Can't we do anything?'

'We don't have guns,' Jacinth answered. 'What can we do? Throw sand in their faces?'

Miranda shook her head impatiently. The moonlight glittered in her white hair.

'What was that?'

Jacinth strained her ears to hear. 'What?' she whispered. 'What did you hear?'

Miranda's eyes widened. She held up a finger to her lips, then she signalled back towards the camp. Had someone followed them? Were they being tracked? Instantly Jacinth looked across the sand, seeing with horror the telltale trail they had left. They hadn't hidden wisely. In an instant both girls were on their feet, running towards the one exit – but too late. A figure loomed in the doorway, filling the space.

'Come on!' Miranda shouted, and she charged, like a Valkyrie, her blonde hair streaming behind her, as she hurled herself against the man blocking their escape. But Jacinth was frozen to the spot. She couldn't move – couldn't lift a foot. Fear had frozen her joints, tied knots in her muscles. She watched, barely able to breathe, as Miranda slammed into the man with an angry cry. The man's large body seemed to absorb her momentum and swallow her up. His arm, swathed in black, wrapped around her head and neck and Miranda was plucked from the ground and slung over his shoulder. She was screaming now, a long, wild screech that knifed its way through Jacinth's eardrums and deep into her brain. Move, Jacinth told herself. Move. Help her. Help Miranda. But her body betrayed her; gripped by panic, her feet were rooted to the sand. Miranda screamed and kicked and flailed wildly with her fists, but the man did not loosen his grip. He glanced once at Jacinth, only his eyes visible, then ran out of the village.

Jacinth stood still as the sound of Miranda's long scream echoed off the broken walls, further and further away with each passing moment. It seemed the whole world must hear it, this cry of rage and fear and frustration. Even when the sound grew thin and died away, Jacinth could still sense it, like a ribbon floating on the air, as through she could reach out and touch it. She was alone now – totally alone. The ruins stretched around her like a broken maze. The cold sand heaped over her feet. The bald moon shone bleakly over her head, far away. Beyond the walls, men were engaged in battle. Heat, sweat, struggle. It was age-old, the war in the desert. The sand had soaked up so much blood. A curious sense of detachment washed over her. She felt ancient, like a cold goddess watching the meaningless process of living and dying from far away. Of course she had always been alone. Miranda had gone now. Her friendship had been a comforting illusion – a straw to cling to in the ocean – but Miranda had been snatched away.

'Miranda,' Jacinth bleated once, faintly. Her lips were cold and stiff. A wind blew among the fallen houses, picking at the sand. A few strands of hair blew across her face, brushing her cheek. The thoughtless sand settled over her boots. How long did she stand there? Perhaps no more than a minute or two, but the time stretched out, a vast space in which each man was a tiny mote, a blink, cast upon the face of the Earth only to be gobbled up again a moment later. The stones in the walls lasted longer. The grains of sand. What did it matter in the end? She would be dead soon, just like her parents. And so would Maslin, Jack and Miranda. Why did they struggle so hard to avoid it?

The wind blew again, its voice low and mournful through the ruined village.

Miranda screamed till her voice gave out. She was blind with rage and fury, kicking out wildly, using her nails and teeth and fists and feet against her assailant. But he was impervious to her, unflinching, as though his flesh were made of steel. She couldn't see where he was taking her, but suddenly she sensed other men around them, and she was dumped across the back of a camel. She smelled it, and heard its protests as the rider goaded it to its feet, the ungainly lurch forward and back as it rose to its feet, and then the swaying trot as the beast was urged to hurry, her face pressing against its rough blanket, the rider struggling to steer the camel and tie her hands together. She tried to scream again, but her voice wouldn't work. Her throat was raw, her body aching from its exertions. Where was Jacinth? Had she been taken too? Where were Maslin and Jack and Aashiq? Images of their faces flashed in her mind, a fear they had been captured or killed. She had to think – she had to turn on the faculty she had developed when she had been kidnapped before. Panic wouldn't help now her wrists were tied. Fear could make her mind keen, if she were clever.

The camel trotted out into the desert, and the sounds of gunfire and shouting diminished into the distance. Miranda took several slow, deep breaths and slowly the pounding of her heart subsided. They were alone, she was sure, the unknown rider and herself. Who was he? Where was he taking her? After a few minutes the rider slowed the camel, and gripping Miranda's shoulders, he tugged her upright so she could sit astride, in front of him. Miranda caught a glimpse of an unknown face, dark eyes that avoided looking into hers. The face was cold and implacable. She saw a rifle over his shoulder. He'd tied her wrists very tightly, so the blood throbbed painfully in her hands.

'Where are you taking me?' she whispered. The rider didn't answer. Perhaps he didn't understand English, or simply didn't care to reply.

'Please,' she said. Her voice was hoarse. 'Where are we going?'

Along the eastern horizon, light seeped across the desert and Miranda noticed the rider's hands were covered with dried blood – blood, presumably, that was not his own. It had congealed blackly in the creases of his skin. Miranda's head ached, and her hands passed through agony to numbness. The sun rose, burning away the night's cold, beating down on the face of the desert like a copper hammer. The camel began to pant and protest.

Then, in the lee side of a spur of rock, Miranda made out a camp much like the one Aashiq had set up by the ruined village. A meagre spring welled up in a basin of rock, and half a dozen low tents fluttered in the dawn breeze. Two camels were tethered close by, browsing on thorny bushes. The rider issued a command to his own tired beast, and it dropped gratefully to its knees so they could dismount. Miranda was hauled roughly from its back and dropped on the ground. Her hands tied, she couldn't save herself and her face fell painfully into the dirt. A pair of long, brown boots stepped into her field of vision. Miranda struggled and failed to get up, to see whose feet were contained within these elegant, well-polished boots.

'Well, well,' a voice said. 'We meet again. How lovely, Miranda. How helpful you've been.'

Jack heard Miranda scream. The sound tore through the night, impaled him. He jumped to his feet, forgetting about bullets, but Maslin pulled him down again.

'It's Miranda,' Jack shouted out. 'They've got her! They've got her!'

Then Maslin was beside him, and they weaved among the walls towards the source of the noise. Jack saw a man running away from the old village, Miranda's hair streaming behind him.

'There! There she is!' he cried, setting off in pursuit. But Maslin grabbed him again.

'No,' he said fiercely. 'Go and find Jacinth – I'll deal with this.'

Jack hesitated, loath to obey. But Miranda was already disappearing into the night and Maslin didn't waste any more time. He set off in pursuit and reluctantly Jack ran into the

227

warren of old streets and walls, following the disturbance in the sand to find the roofless room where the girls had ineffectively hidden themselves, two rats in a trap.

There he saw Jacinth, standing motionless. Jack hurried up to her.

'Are you hurt? Jacinth – did they hurt you?'

She didn't reply, didn't take her eyes from the doorway. Of course she couldn't understand him. Perhaps she was in shock. Her eyes possessed a frightening dark vacancy, as though she couldn't see him at all.

'Jacinth!' he shouted, grabbing her arm. Didn't she care about Miranda? Why was she just standing there, like a statue? 'We've got to go.'

He had to drag her, bodily, from the room. She stumbled clumsily behind him, without saying a word. Wary of the enemy, Jack kept them under cover but it was apparent the battle was over. Men were riding away from the camp, calling to comrades. Several bodies lay on the ground. Where was Maslin? And Aashiq?

Jack left Jacinth and ran about in the darkness, calling their names. Aashiq had a spray of blood across his face, but he appeared unhurt. He told Jack to look for Maslin while he attended to his own men. So Jack hurried hither and thither, calling Maslin's name, gripped by a horrifying certainty the old man was dead. What would he do without him?

But Maslin was not dead. He was lying face down in the sand, his wild white hair spread out all about him. Jack fell to his knees and turned the old man over. Maslin's eyelids fluttered and he gasped. Then in a panic Maslin clutched his chest, rummaging through the cloth of his robe. Jack stared.

'The map?' he whispered. 'Have they taken the map?'

Maslin swallowed, his head dropping back to the sand. His face was desolate.

'Miranda – where have they taken Miranda?' he asked.

'Jacinth's safe, but what will they do to Miranda?' The terror of the fight washed over him, now it was over. It caught him up. A series of images filled his mind – firing the gun, the giant man raising his knife to strike, the blood trickling over Maslin's hand. Jack's eyes blurred, filling with tears. It was too much – too much to bear.

The dead were buried under cairns of stone at sunset, while Aashiq recited prayers from a black book. The injured were bathed and bound up, and Aashiq briefed one of his comrades to take horses and accompany them back to a village where they could be properly tended. At last, duties done, as darkness descended, he came to talk with Maslin.

Aashiq's face was hollow with exhaustion, dark with grief. He bowed his head to the old man, and begged his forgiveness.

'We failed you,' he said. 'They surprised us. We didn't protect you, James Maslin. We didn't protect the young people.'

Maslin shook his head and stretched out his uninjured arm to grasp Aashiq by the shoulder.

'We were outnumbered!' he said. 'You didn't fail us, Aashiq. They've taken Miranda, but Jacinth and Jack are safe. This is only a setback. They would have killed us all if it weren't for the bravery of your men.'

Aashiq wasn't comforted, but he nodded curtly.

'What shall we do now?' Jack piped up. 'We have to go after them, don't we? We have to rescue Miranda.'

Aashiq and Maslin looked at one another. Aashiq waited for Maslin to speak. The old man pushed the hair from his face.

'It is safe to assume these were men hired by the Tremaynes,' he said. 'They must know where we are going, and with the map, they know how to find it. I think our best course of action is to proceed. We do not want them to get there before us.'

'What about Miranda?' Jack interjected.

Maslin wiped his face with the back of his hand. He glanced

at Aashiq, seeking some kind of confirmation, then turned again to Jack.

'Our destination is a city in a network of caves deep in the desert,' he said. 'They are hundreds of years old – maybe thousands. Aashiq and the guardians can take us to these caves, but it is the precise location of one particular place in the labyrinth that will cause our difficulty. We shall proceed, now, and I think we shall find Miranda ahead of us, Jack. I'm not abandoning her.'

Jack glanced at Jacinth. Was she listening to the discussion? It was hard to say. Her eyes were fixed on a distance Jack couldn't see. He felt like shaking her – shouting at her. Didn't she care about Miranda at all?

Nobody slept that night. After sundown, they broke up the camp and set off into the desert. Jacinth was set on a camel along with Jack. Aashiq and his remaining men saddled up their horses, and in the moonlight they headed across the desert to the west. They couldn't afford to waste any more time.

The day had passed Jacinth at a distance. Her mind was far away. Every now and then Miranda's scream echoed in her head, and she was back in the moonlit room watching helpless as her friend was snatched away. At other times her thoughts drifted, roaming over past and present, back to her childhood in Paris, the nightmare of her father's decline, the night of the fire, the days of despair in the orphanage and on the streets, and then the discovery of her powers and the years in the tower. Time was an illusion, because all the events of the past were as real – more real – than time present, in the desert. Her memories were so many doors she could open and step through. Realities shifted uneasily inside her head. The camel plodded, the night air bit her bare fingers, Jack cursed and fidgeted in front of her, but Jacinth was only partly aware of these present sensations. While one part of her mind kept a watch on the desert, another part was loosening its grip on her earthly body. For the first time, she was far-seeing while still conscious and awake. Her travelling mind, loosed like an arrow, flew up towards the stars.

The desert spread below her, glimmering in the moonlight, coils of exposed rock, the elegant rise of dunes, the plains of dust.

'Jack,' she whispered, still sitting on the camel's back. 'I'm looking for Miranda.' Her English was halting, and Jack didn't hear her the first time she spoke.

'Jack,' she repeated. 'Listen to me. I'm looking for Miranda.' This time he twisted round.

'What? What do you mean?'

'I'm flying over the desert. I can see further than you.' The words drifted. High up, her attention snagged on something – the bright jewel of a fire burning far away. She soared towards it, sensing the warm bodies of horses, the men moving around the fire, the guards nursing their rifles and peering uneasily into the night.

'Miranda,' she whispered. 'Where are you Miranda?' She floated around the campsite, darting among the men. In one tent she heard voices speaking in English, and peering inside, saw Miranda tied to a post, while Nicholas, Blanche and Edmund Tremayne sat at a low table and argued.

'Jacinth, what can you see?' The voice belonged to Maslin. Dimly her physical self saw him riding beside her, mounted on one of Aashiq's horses. It was difficult, maintaining her awareness in two places at once, like floating in and out of sleep.

'The camp,' she whispered. 'Ahead of us. The Tremaynes have Miranda.'

'Listen to them,' Maslin urged. 'Can you hear what they're saying?'

Jacinth focused on her astral self. She drifted towards Miranda and called out to her. She twined around her, brushing against her face. Miranda was half asleep, slumped against the post, but she shifted and her eyes flicked open. She lifted her head.

'Miranda,' she called again. In the background the Tremaynes were bickering still. Jacinth was dimly aware they were arguing about the route they should take.

'Where are they?' a voice broke in. 'Is Miranda safe? Find out where they are.' It was Jack, shaking her arm, wanting to know more. His nagging disturbed her concentration, interfered with her own desire to comfort Miranda. She flew up above the camp, hovered above it like a kite.

'There's a spur of rock, shaped like a camel's head,' she whispered. 'They're camped out beneath it. Men and horses and tents. Guards with rifles. It's not so far.'

Beside her Maslin kicked his horse into a canter, and rode up to Aashiq at the front of the column. The men spoke briefly, and the party increased its pace. Jacinth clung to the camel's saddle. Miranda's scream still trailed through her thoughts but her far-seeing self drifted for miles over the desert. How long could she stay like this, only half present? Had a lock in her mind snapped open, had a protective door blown off its hinges? Was this the reason for the epidemic of insanity among the children of the knights? She would not survive long in this state. She would lose her mind. She would be mad.

Dimly she was aware of Jack beside her. He was bright-eyed and feverish, and in his hand he held the revolver Aashiq had given him, which he rescued from the sand after the battle.

'Don't worry, Jacinth,' he whispered. 'We'll find her. I'll rescue her – I promise.'

17

Labyrinth
The desert, 1890

Red cliffs, and pillars carved by giants. The chasm was invisible from the desert plain, then a twist in the rocks, a sharp descent, and a long, narrow defile through broken stone. At every turn it seemed the path was blocked by blank columns of stone, but each time they switched to right or left through hidden passageways. Down, and down, they weaved one way and another – until, at the end of the descent, the chasm opened before them.

High up, above the vertical cliffs, was a ribbon of blue sky and the dizzying sun. Miranda shaded her eyes. Almost invisible in the heights, two birds circled slowly. She was mounted on a camel, her wrists tied loosely together. Ahead, Blanche and Edmund Tremayne pushed their camels into an awkward jog. Blanche let out a cry of excitement and waved her hat over her head. Behind her a murmur arose from Nicholas and the dozen armed men. Miranda glowered, but she could not quell her own sense of awe.

The chasm was perhaps half a mile long, a narrow rocky floor covered with a fine veil of sand. And halfway along, miraculous, two mighty columns were carved into the rock creating a grand archway over the dark mouth of a cave. The columns were huge, as though supporting the weight of the cliffs, and strove together, meeting in an elegant curved arch high up. Miranda drew a breath, marvelling. How had these monumental columns been shaped, on these sheer, vertiginous cliffs?

As they proceeded, Miranda noticed many other decorations on the face of the pale red stone. A succession of smaller caves, each adorned with columns and arches. Higher up, along narrow ledges, many more openings in the cliffs on either hand – more than Miranda could count; they had discovered the hidden city.

Blanche tossed her head and whooped. She pushed her camel into a shambling canter and Edmund slapped his mount with a crop, urging it to follow. Miranda scowled. Then she turned to see the men behind her. They were also impressed by the metropolis in the cliffs, but they did not evince enthusiasm. Instead, they hunched their shoulders and gave the caves quick, suspicious glances, as though expecting an ambush.

Miranda sniffed. Her face was covered with dust. Her skin smarted from exposure to the sun and her wrists itched from the coarse rope knotted around them. Her camel belched and snorted.

Outside the grandest of the pillared openings, the Tremaynes dismounted. Camels and horses milled around as the men found shade in which to tether them. Miranda was helped to the ground and escorted to the vast opening in the cliff.

'This is it, Miranda,' Blanche said with a cold smile. 'Our destination. The special place.' She gestured to the great doorway with her whip.

A breath of cool air drifted from the shadowed interior of the cavern, and a swift gust of wind spiralled along the chasm floor, raising dust into a tiny whirlwind. The wind sounded across the mouths in the cliff side, creating a low, uncanny moan. The men looked from one to another nervously but Miranda's attention was drawn elsewhere, to a movement high up, at the mouth of a cave. She saw a ragged man dressed in black, precarious on a ledge. He looked down, into her upturned face, and waved. She glanced away quickly – had anyone else noticed? When she looked back the man had disappeared. The image of him burned in her brain.

Blanche picked three men to accompany them, along with Miranda, while ordering the rest to remain on guard. Blanche had the stolen map in her hand; the men carried burning torches. Then, at Edmund's signal, they passed between the giant columns.

The cavern resembled a huge stone hall with a vaulted roof. Numerous mock pillars were carved into the walls, interspersed with complex geometric patterns that led the eye into curves and mazes. Doorways opened in three directions. While the men marvelled at the great hall, the Tremaynes brooded over the map. Its directions were not straightforward it seemed, but vague and unhelpful. Blanche and Edmund couldn't agree. Finally they proceeded into the room beyond the first, perhaps the second room referred to. Miranda kept her eyes open, alert to her surroundings, conscious of the men's anxiety. This place filled them with some kind of superstitious dread, and this she could easily understand. She felt something here. Her own psychic antennae stirred. What had happened here so many centuries ago?

They wandered vainly through a succession of corridors and caves for an hour or more, up carved stairways and into dusty cellars. The torches filled the dry air with acrid smoke. The encoded instructions proved difficult to interpret and the atmosphere between the Tremaynes grew tense. Miranda followed mutely, sinking into a strange daze. The place had an aura. She could sense it, seeping through her skin. The outside world had melted away and the caves swallowed her up, digested her, picked through her bones. The caves were exploring her.

This was a sacred place. For hundreds, perhaps thousands, of years, people had ornamented and inhabited the natural network. Surely they had worshipped their god or gods. They had linked the caves with man-made corridors and stairs, opened new paths between the dark spaces in the rock. So many centuries of dedication and prayer had impregnated the stone walls.

The men were growing more and more uneasy. They didn't speak to each other anymore, but huddled close together. The caves seemed to absorb the sound of their footsteps. Even the Tremaynes spoke more quietly, as they reconsidered, tried new paths, turned back. Which was the way? There were so many caves, how could they know which was the right one? What exactly were they looking for?

Miranda noticed a flicker of movement from the corner of her eye, but when she turned to look, no one was there. Was it the man who had waved from high up? But the movement happened again. And, again, when she turned her head, nothing to be seen. She wasn't alone, seeing these movements. The men were affected too. The leader went to Edmund Tremayne and warned him they were followed by ghosts. Tremayne was curt and dismissive – ordered the men to pull themselves together – but Miranda could see he was uneasy too. From time to time, his head twitched to right and left, straining to catch a glimpse of whatever it was that kept just out of sight. Miranda wasn't afraid. She felt detached, the strings of her mind coming loose, the peculiar spirit of the caves taking her into itself. There was no need to worry. Perhaps the caves would look after themselves. The Tremaynes could wander to their hearts' content and the place would keep its secrets folded away.

Once they emerged through a bottleneck of stone on a ledge high above the chasm. Another time, the Tremaynes led the party down a steep path into a hole in the ground, a deep dead end, like the oubliette in a medieval castle where prisoners were thrown to rot. They found nothing. The caves were entirely empty. From time to time Miranda would spy a discreet carving above a doorway – a fish, a star. Otherwise, once beyond the first hallway, the rooms were unadorned. They wandered at random, like thoughts in a huge stone brain. Miranda sensed night was drawing on. The darkness thickened. The air acquired a chill. Frustrated and tired, Blanche decided it was time to return to the first hallway. She was close, but still the prize was out of reach.

They camped out in the hall. The men set up a fire at the doorway and cooked up a filthy stew of salted goats' meat. Half the men remained on guard at all times, rifles in hand. Miranda refused to eat the stew so Edmund Tremayne struck her face and tied her hands again, in case she should try and escape. She had no idea if Maslin, Jack or Jacinth were still alive. But she nursed a hope. Surely the Tremaynes would not have posted so large a guard unless they feared others would come. Perhaps Aashiq and his men had not been entirely vanquished by Tremayne's hired band of thugs and criminals. She kept her hopes up, though she wouldn't allow them to get too high. Brooding over the possible fates of her companions wouldn't help her here and now. Best to keep her ears and eyes open, to wait for an opportunity to outwit the Tremaynes.

Blanche was sitting beside her, turning over the morsels on her tin plate with some distaste. Despite the heat, the journey and the bad food, Mrs Tremayne still looked impossibly neat and glamorous. She looked sideways at Miranda, as though she sensed her scrutiny.

'Why are you doing this?' Miranda was blunt. Blanche gave a cold half-smile.

'Doing what?' she replied.

'Why are you so desperate to find the lily? You must have heard the stories too.'

'Ah yes,' Blanche said graciously. 'The lily's curse. The legacy of death and lunacy.'

'You don't believe it?'

'Oh yes,' Blanche said. 'I know it's true. I think about your poor mother, for example. But what we must ask ourselves, Miranda, is why the bad things started to happen.

'It's my belief they began when descendants of the knights turned away from the lily – when they decided to hide it. The blight – the poison – came upon us as a punishment for rejecting it. Don't you see? It poisoned us – out of revenge.'

Understanding flashed in Miranda's mind. Of course. Blanche Tremayne was motivated by fear as well as a lust for power. Blanche believed that if she found the lily, it would protect her from madness. Miranda thought about her mother raving in the Hospital of Our Lady of Sorrows. Miranda knew it might be her fate too. Now though, the present held too many horrors for her to dwell upon the possible pitfalls of the future. She raised her head.

'But, Blanche,' she said calmly. 'Why don't we destroy the lily? Then we'll all be safe.'

Blanche shook her head. Her face, perpetually porcelain-cool, momentarily softened. 'I've known about the lily for as long as I can remember,' she said. 'My father knew about it. It devoured him – his whole life. He spent every waking hour, every penny the family possessed, trying to track it down. It was all he talked about – an obsession. My mother and I, we weren't as important. Except that as I grew older, I began to learn about the lily too. I inherited his passion. Probably it was to please him to start with.

'But he never got very far. Lots of stories, very little solid information. He travelled a lot, spent all our money, and built up enormous debts. He said there was a buried chapel in Greece full of gold, but he never found it. He said we would be powerful and wealthy beyond all our dreaming if he was successful.'

Blanche sighed. She traced a circle in the sand with her finger.

'He died of cancer in the end,' she said. 'He had amassed a

238

huge archive on the Order of the Lily by then, and there was little in it I hadn't read and absorbed. Tales about the crusaders, records, all sorts of bogus maps and books, complex genealogies, predictions by a medium he paid huge sums of money while my mother and I had barely enough to eat. But the cancer ate him up. He was riddled with tumours, in his chest and climbing his throat. It suffocated him.'

Blanche stopped short, lifted her face, and stared at the doorway where the men were playing some kind of game with counters of stone. Edmund was outside, checking on the animals.

'I want what you have, Miranda – to see further. I want to see beyond time. And there are many other powers the lily might confer.'

'So you followed up the genealogies and found the Tremaynes,' Miranda said. 'And you told them about the lily. You told them what it could do.'

'I couldn't find it on my own.' Blanche's impervious mask had snapped back into place. 'I needed them. And once they knew about the lily, they needed me.'

'How convenient to marry one of them. But why Edmund? Why not Nicholas?' The question was a sly dig, and Miranda didn't know how Blanche would respond. But Blanche was easily a match for her. They could see Edmund, talking to the men on guard, issuing brusque instructions.

'You know, Miranda,' she said, still staring at her husband, 'I fell in love with him. I admire him – his dedication. His sense of purpose and his courage to do whatever is needed.'

Miranda couldn't restrain herself. 'He's a brutal monster.' The ill-considered words spilled out and Miranda braced herself for an angry response. But Blanche gave a cold laugh.

'Well yes,' she said, climbing to her feet, the stew barely touched. Her face was haughty. 'But he's my monster. He's on my side.'

Late into the night the Tremaynes' men sang around the fire. The songs were low, sad and discordant, appropriate to the ancient, haunted chasm they occupied. One had a zither, and plucked out awkward tunes that echoed strangely in the cave-hall and disturbed Miranda's thoughts. She had been handed one meagre blanket, and in the night-time chill she shivered, curled up on the hard floor, using her forearm as a pillow. When she drifted into sleep, the ghosts from the labyrinth strayed from the stone corridors into the convoluted pathways of her mind. She saw them, dark shadows, cloaked and hooded. From time to time she caught a glimpse of a hand decorated with blue tattoos, or a face that reminded her of Luca or Aashiq. And she understood that alongside and in opposition to the clan of the twelve knights and their descendants was the tribe that had lived and worshipped in these caves so long ago, whose descendants were the gypsies roaming Europe and North Africa. On the chessboard of history, in a game lasting centuries, the ancestors of Aashiq and Luca had lined up on one side, while the Maslins, Tremaynes and their fellows had lined up on the other – the lily shining between them.

The game had altered now. The final pieces were in place. She and Jacinth had joined forces with the last Maslin, crossing the board to join the other side. Loyalties had changed.

But the picture was not complete. What, in truth, was the lily?

She was shaken awake in the darkness. A black shape loomed over her. A hand pressed into her shoulder – another lightly covered her mouth, indicating that she must be quiet. Quickly Miranda got to her feet and followed her rescuer deeper into the hall. They slipped through a side entrance and into the labyrinth. She couldn't see anything, relying entirely on her guide to take her hand and lead her through the maze of stone. Presumably the guards had their eyes focused outwards, into the chasm. The hall itself was dark in any case and they could not have seen her slip away. She was safe – at least until daylight, she hoped, when the Tremaynes woke up.

But who was he, the rescuer? The man who had waved – presumably another of Aashiq's clan, haunting the caves like the insubstantial ghosts she had glimpsed from the corner of her eye. She would find out soon enough.

Eventually, coiled tight in a ravelling of pathways, the guide halted. A light flared, from a match, and an oil lamp came to life. Warm yellow light filled the cave. Miranda stared at her rescuer and he drew back his hood. He turned to her, bareheaded, and smiled.

'Hello, Miranda,' he said.

Her breath stopped in her chest, all choked up. Memories fluttered in her head, tumbling over each other, flashes of sunlight and colour. The man stared at her intently, studying her face. He was burned and aged by the sun, his skin parched, premature wrinkles in webs at his eyes. But she knew him still. Yes, she knew him. Despite the three years of absence, the time that had changed them both, she recognised David Kingsley, the father she thought had died.

For a few moments neither moved. Instead they gazed at one another intently. Painful recognition, grief, hope and anger tumbled over each other. Could she believe her eyes? Was this a dream? Had the spirit of the caves plucked a memory from her mind to torment her? She stretched out her hand.

'Are you – are you real?' she said. Her voice trembled. Gently she touched his face.

'Do I feel real?' He put his own hand over hers, pressing it against his cheek.

'Where have you been? All this time! We thought you were dead. And my mother – she's in an asylum. Where were you?' The questions gushed.

David Kingsley took her hand between both of his and held it tight.

241

'I've been looking for the lily,' he said. 'They told me about it, your mother and Mary. Do you remember the photographs, where your face was blurred? There were always stories in their family, tales from the past, but no one really believed them. Then the pictures were taken, and Julia noticed that you had an uncanny sixth sense. We tried to find out more. And Julia had moments of sickness, even then. I wanted to help her. I wanted to save you. That's why I left.'

Miranda struggled to absorb his words, emotions in a tumult.

'But – but why have you taken so long? Why didn't you contact us? Where have you been? There was a letter – it said you'd drowned at sea.'

David sighed. His sunburned face wrinkled in a frown. 'It's a very long story, Miranda. I wasn't the only one trying to find out about the lily – there are many others. Those who want it for themselves, those who want it kept hidden or destroyed. There's been a hidden battle ever since the lily disappeared.'

'Yes,' she nodded. 'Yes I know. Was it the Tremaynes? Were they hunting you? This accident at sea – that wasn't an accident?'

'Edmund Tremayne – yes. My boat was attacked. I fell into the sea.' His eyes dropped, perhaps recalling the terrifying plunge into the arms of the ocean, the long, deathly drift to the coast. 'I was washed up, and when I discovered I was recorded among the dead it seemed easier to stay so, in order to hide from Tremayne, and to travel freely again. I changed my name.'

'But couldn't you have told us? Told Julia? Don't you understand what she went through?' Miranda was angry on her own account, recalling the long ache of his absence.

David grasped her shoulders. 'I couldn't take the chance of being found out. I didn't want to alert Tremayne, and I didn't want to draw more attention to you and your mother. Don't you understand how important this is? If we succeed, perhaps we can save your mother. And perhaps we can make sure the same thing doesn't happen to you. Isn't that worth it?'

'If we succeed?' she echoed.

'The promise,' he whispered. 'The prophecy made to Matthias. I've heard about it. Yes! I searched for years, here in the desert, and I found this place, Miranda. And then the guardians took care of me.'

'Aashiq? He knows you're here? Why didn't he tell me?'

'I had no idea you were one of the three, until Matthias came here too and he told me the prophecy was about to be fulfilled. That's why I waited. Then yesterday I saw your white hair – and I remembered the gift you had as a child. Of course it was you.'

She looked around the cave. Her father had made it comfortable enough. A rolled up mattress, blankets, cooking utensils, books and paper. Still, how lonely it must have been. Presumably the guardians had returned at intervals with supplies, but in between times, how had he survived on his own, in this eerie, haunted place?

For a few moments they stood and gazed at each other. Miranda remembered her visions of the man in the desert. It had been her father of course. She hadn't seen him clearly – hadn't recognised him – but deep down she had known he was waiting.

'We have to go,' David said.

'Where are we going?' She followed him out of the cave. David carried the lantern before him, casting long, sliding shadows on the walls.

'To the place,' he said. 'The place where it started.'

Jack lay on his belly in the rubble and sand, peering into the darkness. It was just before dawn. The night was cold, but excitement and trepidation kept him warm. Soon light would seep over the horizon and they would make a move. Aashiq and his men knew the geography of the desert fastness – every rock and dip, every cave and tunnel. They were few in number, but this knowledge would hold them in good stead. The attack would not come from the front, as the Tremaynes would expect. Instead, like monkeys, they would crawl down the narrow, invisible ravines and creep up from behind, via cave openings high up and beyond the chasm, following obscure pathways. It was a dangerous undertaking.

Maslin was a part of the raiding party, his injured arm bound in a sling. Jack was fired up, keen to be at the forefront, but Aashiq had ordered him to take care of Jacinth. She was still in a kind of trance. Was it shock? Jack wondered. Sometimes she didn't seem to hear what was said. Her eyes were focused far away. Jack was annoyed Aashiq had made her his responsibility. Instead of taking on the Tremaynes' bodyguards he was told to follow Aashiq and take Jacinth into the labyrinth as soon as a way had been cleared. They were relying on stealth and surprise.

A huge full moon dipped below the horizon in a last silver blaze and pale light leaked over the stony desert. A chilly breeze, the last before the assault of the day's heat, brushed Jack's face. Beside him, Jacinth was resting on her knees. She had not spoken for ages. Ahead of them Aashiq dropped over a rocky ledge and slipped behind a rough, red boulder.

'Come on,' Jack said. 'Time to go.' He caught Jacinth's sleeve and tugged her to her feet. She stumbled after him like an automaton.

Behind the boulder a tiny window opened in the rock, just large enough for a man to squeeze through. Jack signalled to Jacinth to enter first. The valley itself opened just in front of him, a dizzying vertical drop. The opening zigzagged across the desert, almost imperceptible to the eye unless you came right to it. From a distance it looked like another depression in the desert floor – nothing remarkable. Riding at a gallop, unaware of the chasm, you would plummet into it. Had it ever happened? He imagined it, the horse clawing for ground that didn't exist and the long fall into the depths.

Jacinth had disappeared through the hole, so Jack followed close behind. Inside it was cool and dark. It was a tight squeeze. If Aashiq had not already gone ahead Jack would not have dared push his way through. The rough walls scraped against his body. Claustrophobia threatened – a fear he would be crushed to death, or trapped, unable to move forward or back. But Aashiq was larger than he was, and Aashiq had passed safely. Jack rallied his courage and pressed on. The choking tunnel stretched ahead. Jacinth was before him, Aashiq in front of her, but Jack could see nothing. The rocky walls closed in till Jack was afraid he would suffocate. How much further was it? The path inclined gently downwards so he was heading deeper under-ground. The tunnel twisted to right and left, and soon he was entirely disorientated, pushing his way blind like a mole. He yearned for space. It had to open soon, surely. How much fur-ther?

Once he banged his forehead on an unexpected jut of rock. His knees hurt, from crawling on the hard, uneven ground.

Then it was over. Suddenly the tunnel opened up. Dazed, he clambered to his feet. They stood in a bare room flooded with sunlight. Cautiously Jack peered through a window in the rock and saw below them, closer now, the narrow floor of the chasm. Maslin and the others would also be worming their way to useful vantage points, waiting for an opportunity to pick off the Tremaynes' men one by one.

'Where now?' Jack whispered. But Aashiq was staring at Jacinth. She was murmuring to herself.

'It's here,' she said. 'It's close now. The angel, I almost see it. So many here – so many people, Aashiq, going back and back.

'And Miranda. I can see Miranda! She's not on her own. I can follow her. I can lead you.' And she set off through the laby-rinth, her eyes blank, apparently seeing by some other means.

Jack glanced at Aashiq. 'Shall I follow her?' he said. 'Where's she going?'

'Yes – quickly. Go with her. I shall be close behind you. I have to find the others first.' He handed Jack his lantern.

'I don't think Jacinth will need this – but you might,' he said.

Jacinth moved with surprising speed. She didn't hesitate, following an unerring path, down and down, through the mesh of tunnels and caves. The place unsettled Jack. He imagined whispered voices all around them. Shadows from the lantern didn't move as they should. He suspected they were being followed, but every time he turned around the tunnel was empty. And ahead of him, Jacinth walked without any regard for him, caught in a trance he could not break into.

Then she stopped. A sound like a long, slow sigh passed through the rock. Jack's skin prickled and his hand strayed to the gun tucked inside his shirt. He raised the lantern and saw Jacinth stretch out her hands to touch the rock face.

'Here,' she whispered. 'This is the place.' She stepped forwards, through a narrow doorway in the wall of stone.

'Jacinth!' he shouted out, oblivious to the risk of alerting the Tremaynes. 'Jacinth!'

The doorway was narrow, and as he passed through, cold rinsed over him. Then he was standing in a large stone hall. Jacinth was just in front, and beyond her, Miranda and a weathered man in a black robe. For a few moments, none of them spoke. At the far end of the underground cavern stood an alabaster angel, twice as tall as a man, with huge white wings arching over its shoulders. In the dim, torch-lit cavern it seemed to glow.

Miranda called his name.

'Miranda – are you all right?' He glanced at the man beside her. Was this one of Tremayne's men?

'This is my father! David – this is Jack. He came with Maslin from Ireland.' Jack was puzzled. Her father? He couldn't question her further, because Miranda reached out for Jacinth and held her in a tense embrace.

'I felt you, looking for me,' Miranda said. 'What's happened to you, Jacinth?'

Jacinth's eyes were huge and hollow in her face. She whispered, from far away: 'I can see so much, Miranda. All the doors are blowing open. I can't hold it for much longer. I'm losing my mind.

'Help me,' she whispered. 'I shall be stronger if you're with me.'

Miranda nodded. She took Jacinth's hand and led her to the statue of the angel.

Behind him, Jack heard a clatter of footsteps. Four people emerged from the doorway in the wall. He recognised the man – Edmund Tremayne holding a knife to Maslin's throat, pressing the edge of the blade into his skin. Beside them stood Aashiq – disarmed – and Nicholas and Blanche brandishing revolvers. Jack's heart plummeted. Was there no way to win this? Was every effort doomed to fail? Why did the Tremaynes always get the upper hand? Aashiq looked furious – but what could he do? If he so much as made a move, Maslin would have his throat cut.

'Thank you,' Blanche said. 'For showing us the way. I knew you would be useful in the end, Jacinth. So here we all are – quite the family reunion.'

Edmund glanced at David. 'We meet again,' he said. 'You're looking remarkably well for a dead man.'

'The lily isn't here,' Miranda said. Her voice was cold and even. 'You're wasting your time.'

'Oh I don't think so,' Blanche said. 'We have the three of you now. Between you, and the angel, I have a feeling we might learn exactly where the lily is hidden, don't you? Isn't that why Mr Maslin brought you here?'

Jack glanced at Maslin. The old man could hardly breathe

because Edmund Tremayne had the blade so tight against his skin. Edmund glanced at Blanche and she nodded. Keeping the knife close, he manoeuvred Maslin along the hall till he stood at the feet of the angel, beside Jacinth and Miranda.

'What shall we do?' Miranda said. She looked very thin and young, a child appealing for help. 'We have to help Jacinth. I think she's losing her mind.'

'Take my hand,' Maslin said. Edmund stepped back from him, taking the knife from his throat, but Nicholas cocked his revolver and aimed it at Miranda. Maslin glanced at Aashiq and David.

'As before,' he said quietly to the girls. He looked up at the angel, gave a quick nod to Jack. 'Don't be afraid.'

They stood close together, white-haired Miranda, Jacinth with her patched red face, the tall old man, and the angel statue. Maslin drew a deep breath and closed his eyes. Miranda's head dropped forwards. The angel gleamed.

Jack waited. What would happen? He had watched them before, testing their psychic powers, trying to bring them together. The hairs of the back of his neck prickled. He sensed the charge of the atmosphere, subtle movements in the shadows, an alteration of perspective as the hall seemed to stretch away, and then to close in. The air shifted, bringing echoes of faraway noise, threads of perfume. Jack's mind drifted. For a moment he was back at home, with the horses, hearing the sound of the sea. Then he was back again, in the hall. He looked around him. The others, all of them – Blanche, Nicholas and Edmund, David and Aashiq – were standing in a daze, caught in the aura. Jack heard the sounds of battle, voices raised in prayer, the clash of swords and screams. He wasn't in the hall any longer. The desert stretched below him, where a desperate, bloody battle was taking place. Jacinth, Maslin and Miranda had created a window in time.

18

Egypt 1179

Only twelve knights remained. They had fought bravely, madly, and beaten off their attackers – but at great cost. Blood churned the ground. The stench of it – broken flesh and sweat and terror – pooled in a smoke all about them. They didn't speak, these last few, standing in a circle back to back, swords still in hands, surveying the circus of death.

The desert, a furnace where battle was wrought. The sun was merciless. Above the mire of men and weapons, three patient vultures circled, high up. The landscape scrolled into a hazy distance, unending variations on the same theme – sand and broken rock.

William Maslin stared at the horizon, hating the place. He longed for green, for the fat country he came from, luscious meadows in spring, ditches overflowing with water, trees glittering with leaves. He longed for the smell of it.

His eyes blurred and stung, so he dropped his sword and pushed off the helmet clamped to his head. He wiped a film of sweat and blood from his face with the back of his hand. As he moved, half a dozen injuries cried out. In the heat of the battle he hadn't felt them, but blood was flowing freely. Beside him, spell broken, his fellows also broke their rank, casting their weapons down, exclaiming over the loss of friends and comrades.

William sighed. He dropped to his knees, crossed himself and prayed thanks for his safe deliverance. They had been thirty at the beginning, this company travelled from Palestine. They had been despatched from Christian Jerusalem, and ridden south into Egypt, set on destroying bands of robbers who had hidden out in the desert and periodically preyed on European pilgrims travelling in the Holy Land. The mission had lasted for weeks and the men were tired and disheartened. They had singularly failed to find any of the purported thieves and cut-throats, until today when they were set upon by a group of some forty ferocious and desperate men. Only a handful had escaped and ridden away. The remainder lay dead or dying on the ground with the bodies of the crusader knights.

The ground was too hard for burial, not enough wood for a pyre. In the end they heaped the butchered remains as best they could, Christians and heathens separately, and piled rocks over them, a slight protection against eaters of carrion. The survivors were exhausted, several seriously injured. What should they do now? William was at a loss. Their guide was dead. He wasn't even certain where they were, how best to find succour. That night, they huddled together around a small fire and he asked his men how each thought they should proceed.

Hot-headed Matthias, his face scorched by long days in the sun, slammed his fist in the ground and insisted they set off in pursuit of the surviving attackers and avenge the death of their comrades. Fired with zeal, burning with religious fervour, Matthias had served the longest in the Holy Land. He had belonged to the Order of the Knights of the Temple but suffered an ignominious expulsion for breaching their strict code of conduct. William had never discovered the true reason for his casting out. Rumours circulated, of course. Mention was made of a murder, and certainly Matthias was a terrifying fighter with an energetic hatred of their Moslem enemies.

The French knight, Gerard, a wiry, earnest young man, advised a return to Jerusalem and an end to the mission. Joseph, the pale, cool Englishman, suggested they find a new guide. The other eight were divided. A few wished to follow Matthias, some agreed a return to Jerusalem was the wisest course. The rest looked to William Maslin for his opinion, trusting his wisdom and judgement. Their supplies were low and the path was uncertain. Without their guide it would not be easy to find a way through the desert. William heard them all speak, and then bade them sleep. He would tell them his decision at dawn when they got up to pray.

He had bound up the worst of his wounds. The gash on his left thigh caused him the most trouble. Whenever he moved his leg, the jagged cut through skin and muscle burst open, spilling streams of blood. Lying back on the hard ground, wrapped in a blanket, his entire body pulsed with pain and exhaustion. He closed his eyes and tried to sleep, but dearly desired oblivion eluded him. He could not be comfortable. Beside him, to left and right, his fellows also struggled to sleep. From time to time he heard a grunt, or a moan. He was not the only one nursing painful injuries.

Beyond the aura of the dying campfire, a heavy silence oppressed the desert. It was a pitiless place – offering no illusion of comfort. But Christianity had its roots in the desert, and the faith of the Mohammedans too. The desert was the home of prophets and visionaries, a place of miracles. Hadn't Jesus met the devil in the desert, a time of testing, as he fasted and denied himself, for forty days and forty nights? No distractions, nothing to come between a man and the face of the Lord. William stared at the cold forest of stars glittering high above him. He was, by the grace of God, the leader of these men. Their fate lay in his hands. Which way would he take

251

them – deeper into the desert or on the long journey back to Jerusalem?

Just before sunrise the twelve men stood in a circle, and William prayed a blessing over their bowed heads. It was chilly still. They were a motley, unsightly collection, faces bruised, bandages soaked with dark blood, armour rent and broken. When the blessing was over, they raised their eyes to William and awaited his decision.

He looked in their faces, one man after another.

'There is nothing to be gained, pursuing the last of our enemies,' he said. Matthias cursed but William continued to talk, ignoring him.

'We are all tired and injured. It is best we head north and take the pilgrims' road back to the Holy Land, and to Jerusalem. If we can find another guide along the way, all the better.'

Gerard and Joseph nodded. They were profoundly weary, aching for peace and rest after long weeks of travelling, weeks on constant alert. Only Matthias had a heart for more killing.

Without a word they saddled up their horses. Struggling because of the wound in his thigh, William hauled himself onto his mount. Leaving behind the bodies of their fellows, the trampled ground of the battle, they set off north.

Two days passed, without sign of a village or any water. William's thigh troubled him constantly, veering between needles of agony and a terrifying numbness that spread through his leg. He was afraid the wound was poisoned.

They rode in silence, their mounts gasping and moving ever slower. On the third day two horses keeled over and couldn't get up, so their riders were obliged to leave them behind and walk. The third night, a cruel storm blundered through the desert, forcing them to take shelter behind a rough head of rock as sand and grit blew all around them. By the morning, another of the horses had died. It couldn't be far now, could it, till they found a village? Though who was to say a village would be helpful to them? Might they not meet more enemies, intent on their destruction? William rode in a stupor, thoughts dulled by heat and pain. The poison in his thigh was slowly seeping into his circulation, spreading the blight around his body. From time to time Matthias roused enough energy to rant about the path they had chosen. Sometimes he sang hymns and prayers in a loud, wild voice that sent the scorpions scuttling for cover.

On the fourth day, parched with thirst, the company passed a hill surmounted by smooth sandy dunes from which a finger of red stone jutted. Only William noticed the stone, so clearly man-made, and dimly he assumed it must be a signpost of some kind, a waymarker for those in the know. He reined in his horse and without speaking he pointed to the hill.

'Riders!' Matthias shouted, drawing his sword. 'Ahead! Coming towards us!' He kicked the sides of his protesting mount, eager to lead the charge.

But William Maslin shouted out: 'Put your sword away! Dismount, Matthias. All of you, dismount!'

Gerard, who had already lost his horse, stood on the ground beside William and murmured something in French. Then he said:

'Who are they?'

William screwed up his eyes. He didn't recognise them, the style of dress, the colours. Presumably they were another of the desert's various nomad tribes. It was possible they would be helpful.

'I don't know. I haven't seen men like this before. But we've no chance against them.'

It was a risk, he knew. As Christians, they were the enemy. The first Crusade had secured them Jerusalem, eighty years before. The Christians had massacred the inhabitants, and the

253

decades since had been fraught with intermittent warfare: skirmishes, executions, attacks and counter attacks. There was no knowing how this far-flung desert tribe might treat them.

The riders pulled up to a halt before the sorry company of knights. One man leaped from his saddle and stepped forward, to look at them better. He wore a white robe, a dark blue cloak and hood over it, a leather belt at which a dagger gleamed. He had a young, shrewd face, full of good humour, but he was strong too. All this William read as the two men eyed each other, cautious and taking measure. Finally the young man stepped forward, held out both hands, and greeted them.

William, who did not speak Arabic, gestured for Gerard to interpret.

'Tell him we wish for water and safe passage, and a place to rest,' William said. Gerard repeated the request and the young man smiled broadly. He gestured back the way he had come.

'He says his name is Raashid. We're his honoured guests, and he'll take care of us,' Gerard said. 'We have to follow him.'

William felt a profound sense of relief. The shadow of death had come upon them. Thank God for rescue at their time of need. If the tribe would offer them water, food, rest and direction the knights would be able to continue their journey. Perhaps they would have a healer too. The Mohammedans had skilled surgeons.

Their destination was astonishing – a revelation. Folded away in a deep chasm in the desert was a city carved in the cliffs. William, half delirious, saw towering rocky walls, mighty doorways framed by pillars, facades as grand as Europe's famed cathedrals. What was this place? Who were these people? They thronged from the caves to meet the newcomers. William passed in and out of consciousness, dimly aware he was carried into the cool caves and laid on a mattress. A woman's face loomed over him, and he felt her hands pass lightly over his body. She untied the stinking bandages from his thigh and dug her fingers into the corrupt flesh. William did not feel pain exactly. Instead her hands felt cold as ice, and as he lay, helpless under her ministrations, the cold spread out from his thigh and around his body, cleansing the blood, putting out the fire of poison. He had no idea how long he lay, floating in and out of wakefulness, as the woman tended to him. The long days' anguish in the desert receded into a distant past. From time to time he saw her face, the clear, brown eyes that sparkled when she noticed he was staring at her. She murmured to herself, words that William could not understand, and he closed his eyes again, sinking into blissful sleep.

He didn't move for several days. The fever receded quickly, but he was still very weak. Joseph came to visit him. The men had all been tended, he said, the horses fed and groomed, their supplies replenished.

Propped up in his bed, William gestured to the cave.

'Who are these people?' he said. 'Have you ever heard of a place like this before? Why does nobody know about it?'

Joseph frowned, lost in thought.

'They are very kind and generous people,' he said. 'They are also rich. They're craftsmen. They carve alabaster, they work gold to make jewellery. Raashid explained to me, how they can live in the desert. They have their own herds of animals, and water from a spring in the valley, but for wheat and fruit they trade with other tribes.'

'Then why have we never heard of them?' William repeated. 'Do the other tribes keep a silence, to protect them?'

William lay back upon his bed, lost in thought. He had seen evidence of the tribe's riches with his own eyes, the necklace with its plates of gold on the chest of the woman who tended him, the elegant alabaster cat glimmering white in a niche on the wall above the bed. Who were they, these accomplished, hospitable people? How long had they lived here, in the hidden city of caves?

The next day he was well enough to leave his bed and meet up with his comrades. At the lowest point in the chasm a spring bubbled up from the ground, and the clear water pooled in a basin hemmed with stone. A boy had filled a long trough so his goats could drink. He was dressed in red and blue, his face bright with excitement to meet the Christian knights. The men were sitting in the shade of a date palm, all looking much revived. They greeted him, and food was brought so they could eat together. The shade and the sound of the water soothed. The atmosphere was calm. Only Matthias was set apart from the others, unwilling to relax, suspicious of their hosts and their motives. After the meal he took William to one side.

'We shouldn't trust them,' he said. 'We don't know who they are or why they should be generous to us. I have a bad feeling about them. We have left ourselves too open.'

William regarded him. 'Why do you think so?'

'These people – they aren't Mohammedans. They are wor-shippers of demons. Haven't you seen them, the pictures on the walls? The statues of their gods? Who knows what they have planned? Perhaps to offer us as some kind of sacrifice. Why would they lay themselves open to us, otherwise?'

William frowned and shook his head. Matthias's voice was an irritant.

'What do you mean, demons?' he said. 'Why do you think they worship demons?'

Matthias looked around, then whispered to William: 'While you were sick, I haven't been idle. I've explored the caves. There is a complex labyrinth, heading back into the cliffs. They live in these shallow caves, where there is light, close to the water, but the tunnels go further back, and there, with a torch, I saw the paintings on the wall.'

Matthias was sweating, his fair hair caked to his scalp. His hand gripped the hilt of his sword. William was a devout Christian – why else would he leave his homeland to fight for the Crusaders in the Holy Land – and he believed implicitly in demons and evil spirits. What if Matthias were right? Did the tribe consort with demons? Was this the reason for their wealth and influence?

'Show me,' he said. But he insisted Gerard and Joseph should come too. He trusted their judgement. In another life, perhaps, Gerard would have been a scholar, in the library of a monastery, surrounded by books. He was educated and level-headed.

Matthias led them through the columned entrance into a great hall, and then into a maze of caves and tunnels. Many people milled around them, women tending children or milling grain, or weaving, craftsmen working gold. No one stopped or questioned them. Instead the men were greeted with smiles. William felt a growing unease. Did the tribe have nothing to hide – or nothing to fear?

In the darkness Matthias lit a torch. He took them to a tall room and raised the flaming torch high above his head.

'Look,' he said, his voice triumphant. 'Look at this!'

A huge alabaster statue rose above them. The white stone glimmered in the torchlight, giving the figure a semblance of life and movement. William stared. Beside him Gerard uttered something in French and crossed himself. This wasn't a demon! It was tall and graceful, more slender than a man, with long, elegant legs. Naked, its groin was smooth and sexless, the belly slightly hollow, hands by its sides, with tapered fingers. The face was simply carved and expressionless, two wide eyes, a tiny nose and mouth. And from the shoulders rose huge, silken wings, like a billowing cloak. William's mouth dropped open. Without thinking, he crossed himself as Gerard had done.

'Mikal,' said a voice behind them. William spun around, his hand on his sword. It was Raashid. In the poor light it was hard to read his expression. Had they betrayed a trust, entering the cave? They had come openly enough. No one had stopped them.

'We call him Mikal,' Raashid repeated, gesturing respectfully to the statue. He looked from one man to the other, William, Joseph, Gerard and Matthias. Then he shook his head and indicated that they follow him from the cave, leaving the statue alone in the darkness. He took them to his own rooms, high above the chasm floor. Sunlight beamed through the entrance, upon the mats he laid out for them to sit on. He spoke, and waited for Gerard to interpret.

'He asks if we want to know about his people,' Gerard said. William nodded. Beside him, Matthias shifted restlessly. Raashid spoke again.

'They have lived here for hundreds of years,' Gerard interpreted. 'He says their ancestors were princes of the ancient Egyptian kingdoms. When the kingdoms were destroyed, their ancestors were guided to the caves by Mikal, their god, who protects them and cares for them.'

Raashid looked closely at Matthias, before addressing Gerard again. A conversation started up between the two of them, perhaps an argument of some kind, which the others could not, of course, understand. Finally Gerard spoke in English again.

'He asked about our god,' Gerard said. 'I told him we fought for the one true God, for the Church of Rome. But he knows of the crusade and the wars in the Holy Land. He wants us to abandon our crusade and pledge our allegiance to his idol, to Mikal.'

Matthias sprang to his feet, roaring out curses. 'I would die first!' he shouted. 'This is the purpose of their false kindness – to tempt us to worship their idols!' He tugged out his sword and brandished it at Raashid, who continued to sit, unmoved and unafraid, as Matthias waved the blade in front of him.

William turned to Gerard. 'Why does he want this? Because we saw the statue?'

Gerard shook his head. 'We came to the city. He's afraid we'll tell the Christian armies about it, that we'll lead them here. So he wants us to change sides – to become servants of Mikal, so he can trust us and his people will be safe.'

William swallowed. 'And if we refuse?'

'He won't tell me what happens then. He says we won't refuse. Tonight, they will hold a ceremony to invoke him, their god. Then we shall see the truth with our own eyes, and we shall choose to be his servants,' Gerard said.

Matthias, still holding his sword, shook his head. 'Never,' he said. 'We shall not bow down before any false idol. They are devil worshippers! I should kill them all first!'

William's mind raced. Raashid looked very calm, despite the fact that Matthias was still ranting and threatening him with his sword. He looked as though he hadn't a single doubt – that he was utterly certain of the truth.

Thoughts galloped. Could they fight their way out? Could they make a furtive escape, under cover of darkness?

'Matthias, put down your sword,' William said. And then, to Gerard: 'Tell Raashid I shall attend the ceremony as he wishes, but I shall have to discuss it with the other men. They must each make their own decision.'

Beside him, Matthias was glaring at Raashid. Gerard and William ushered him from the room, keen to quench his temper before he tangled them in a fight they could not possibly win. They were so few, and the tribe so many. They had to think of a different way out. It was time to be subtle.

They talked it through, the twelve. It would sully them, to attend a heathen rite. A Christian could not bow down before a false idol. Matthias urged attack, but William and the others were reluctant to draw swords on their hosts, who had rescued them from certain death in the desert.

'Don't you see, that is how they trapped us,' Matthias argued. 'They wanted Christian spies. We gave them an opportunity. They were always ill-intentioned. We owe them nothing.'

'I think they helped us because we needed it,' Joseph said simply. 'And now they realise their generosity has put them in a difficult situation. They are looking for a way to resolve it.'

'Attack tonight,' Matthias urged. 'Attend to their devilry and then strike, when they least expect it. Put an end to their demon worship. Save their souls and gain our freedom. We could take their gold as a tribute to the church.'

But William was cautious. Raashid had hundreds of men, and they were only twelve. How could they take on so many and survive? Then again, what alternative did they have? Much better to die a Christian than endanger the immortal soul by tangling with heathen gods.

'We shall attend,' he said, heart heavy. 'But we shall be prepared to fight. Keep your mind alert, and pray for strength. But we shall be cautious. No one must draw their weapon until I give the order.'

But William's heart was heavy, his conscience uneasy. He didn't know what to do.

The moon rose over the desert, white as the face of the god in the cave. People filed from the caves, and processed along the floor of the chasm. The statue emerged from the dark, born on a cradle of wood by eight strong men. Moonlight slid over its blank face, the narrow body.

The people carried torches. They were dressed in their finest, linen robes, golden collars, beads of lapis lazuli and jasper. They carried offerings of milk in bowls, and a cage in which half a dozen white doves fluttered. Raashid walked before the statue of Mikal. In dishes of gold, burned mounds of frankincense and myrrh. The perfumes entwined, clouding the air.

William and Gerard walked side by side at the back of the procession, Matthias and the other men behind them. They were all afraid – of the heathen ritual and the possibility of a fight they couldn't win.

The procession wound its way through a narrow defile away from the chasm and up into the desert itself. The statue was placed on a plateau of rock, the dishes of incense placed about it, so the likeness of Mikal was occluded by fragrant smoke. The people gathered in a circle before it, and the sacrificial milk was spilled upon the statue's feet.

For several hours the company sang and danced around the statue, and then, as the moon reached its zenith, they began to move away. In ones and twos, in family groups, they all returned to the caves. Finally only twelve men and women remained, including Raashid, mirroring the number of the knights. William Maslin looked to his own men. Clearly another part of the ceremony was about to begin – perhaps some kind of initiation. At least, now, they were not outnumbered. Was this the chance they needed to escape?

Raashid called out, three times, in a high, fierce voice, the name of Mikal. Beside him, a woman opened the cage and six white doves flew out, straight up into the sky towards the cold, bare surface of the moon. William reached for the comforting hilt of his sword. He exchanged glances with Gerard, trying to reassure. Nothing will happen, he told himself. This is it, the ritual. Soon they will take the statue back into its cave.

A minute passed. Time stretched out, as they waited in the black and white night, only the smoke of the incense stirring. Raashid stood motionless, his face turned to the sky where the doves had disappeared.

Joseph grasped William's arm. 'Look!' he whispered. William strained to see. In the sky something shifted. A piece of the moon had detached itself – a white light, small at first, a dancing star. A collective sigh emerged from the twelve before the statue, and a murmur of sound, like the distant sea. The star grew swollen, soon as large as the moon itself, radiating an intense silver light. Gradually the shape became distinct, the long, slender figure, the smooth wings that seemed to flow like water from the god's shoulders.

'It's not a demon,' Gerard whispered, still clutching William's arm. 'It is an angel. An archangel – Mikal – it is St Michael who fought the devil and cast him out of heaven.' The Frenchman crossed himself several times, and as the angel's thin, bare feet alighted gently on the stony ground, Gerard dropped to his knees.

The angel lifted its cold, inhuman face. Its eyes were light, lacking pupil or white, as though the angel were illuminated from within. The wings rippled, a thousand colours moving over one another, and the angel took a slow step forwards, towards Raashid and his people.

William couldn't move, or think or breathe. He was held in the moment of the angel's presence. Everything else disappeared – his past, his future. Nothing existed, except for this precious moment, to be bathed in the icy white light flowing from the angel.

But Matthias interrupted him. Breathing heavily, sweating despite the cold, Matthias fought against the creature's spell. He bumped against William.

'It's the devil,' he hissed. 'Resist it. For hasn't evil the power to assume a pleasing shape? Cover your eyes and pray!'

But William pushed him aside. This creature could not be the devil. There was no sense of evil or corruption about it – only purity and beauty. His soul was not defiled in its presence. Indeed he felt exaltation, and rapture. The angel turned its face towards him and he felt the years of sin and death fall away. He fell to his knees and bowed his head.

Beside him Matthias let out a ferocious roar. He drew out his sword and charged towards the angel. In a blood-rage, massive like a bull, muscle and sinew bent on destruction, Matthias ran across the desert and swung his sword in a wide arc so the blade flashed once in the bright light pouring from the angel.

The angel opened its mouth and emitted a high, piercing scream. The sound resonated through the substance of the Earth itself, so the stones shivered and rattled on the ground. William clapped his hands to his ears. The gathering fell into disarray, struggling to defend their ears from the scream, trying to stand straight as the ground vibrated beneath their feet. What had he done? What had Matthias done to the angel?

Matthias bent down, and picked up the angel's severed forearm. As he grasped it, light exploded from the mutilated limb into Matthias's body, as though it would burst him into pieces. His body convulsed, jerking and twitching, but Matthias didn't let go.

Behind him, the angel screamed. The single note, containing the essence of its agony and shock and affront, didn't alter as the angel rose from the ground and slowly ascended the night sky, higher and higher. Then, in an instant, the angel was gone. It winked out, and the sound ceased.

Now Matthias stood in front of them, in place of the angel, clasping the forearm, the angel's hand unfurled in front of his face, like a flower. He still possessed some of the radiance that had surged into his body from the stolen limb. His face was ecstatic, and half mad. It was a horrifying spectacle. Matthias held up his hands, and brandished the angel's severed hand. The image blurred, Matthias still burning with the angel's radiance, so he appeared to have three hands.

'Trois mains,' Gerard whispered. He was standing beside William Maslin, tears shining on his face. 'Trois mains,' he repeated. 'Three hands!'

Raashid drew his dagger and charged at William. His face was contorted with rage and hate. He screamed as he ran. William drew his sword and shouted at his men to defend themselves as Raashid launched himself through the air, his honed blade pressing against William's chest. But Gerard knocked him aside before the dagger could strike, and William stabbed his sword into Raashid's throat.

Raashid's companions crowded around them, ferocious with anger, but the battle was swift. Matthias possessed the strength of a dozen men. He cut down their opponents like grass. The angel's hand, so evilly stolen, had invested him with power. Within a few minutes, Raashid and his eleven companions were dead.

Stunned and heavy-hearted, William and his knights made their way to the chasm and saddled up their horses. Matthias and some of the others took the time to plunder the closest caves, filling their hands with whatever gold they could find, killing willy-nilly. Then they rode off, out of the secret city, and north across the desert through the night.

They stopped, hours later, as the sun was rising. Matthias came to William, bearing the angel's hand before him.

'Take it,' he said. 'You're our leader. Take what it gives you.'

William stared at Matthias. The other men gathered around him in a circle, including Gerard.

'Go on,' Matthias said. 'It is a gift, to help us against our enemies. Think what we can do, against the Mohammedans. It will make us strong, in our crusade.'

William stared at the hand. There was no blood or flesh. It was as though the hand were made of moonstone, or alabaster like the statue. It still shone, even in daylight. And it tempted him. Lustrous as pearl, pleasing to the eye – he longed to hold it. Perhaps Matthias was right, he reasoned. We shouldn't cast such a gift away. We can use it in the service of the Lord. Part of him still resisted, appalled at what had happened, the mutilation of the angel and the killing of so many people of the desert tribe. But this voice was fading, because another part of him ached to take the gift. It was his destiny. The long journey of his life had taken him to this one point, to this choice. Should he seize this power, or throw it away? The angel had made a sacrifice, so they might benefit.

He reached out and took the hand. In that instant, a bolt of white light blasted his thoughts, and a sense of rapture flowed through his body. He felt a hundred doorways open in his mind, places he had never seen before, paths he might take, a new power falling into his lap. There was nothing he couldn't do. He opened his eyes, and smiled.

'This is for all of us,' he said. 'We are a brotherhood now. This is our gift and our secret. We shall seal up the hand in a casket, to protect it from the eyes of those who would not understand.'

And he passed the hand to Gerard.

19

Death
The desert, 1890

Jacinth stared across the stone hall.

'Trois mains,' she whispered. 'That was his name. Matthias Trois Mains. You see?'

They stood, stunned, in silence. The events of the past had unfolded before their eyes. They had borne witness. A window had opened, drawing on the power of James Maslin, Miranda and Jacinth, anchored by the presence of the alabaster angel, so many centuries old. Perhaps the story, cruel and potent, had embedded itself in the substance of the white statue and this, the three had tapped into. They had seen it – they were, all of them, *there*.

Jacinth drew a deep breath. Echoes of the past sounded in the hall. The casement had been drawn shut, but the air still spun with motes from the tumult, with the smoke of blood and incense. They had been caught up in the tempest, engaged in the broiling storm of rage and killing. Jacinth closed her eyes, trying to calm herself. The vision, the jolt of it, had plunged her back into her body. She was sane again, for the moment. Beside her, James Maslin dipped his head and gave a short, cold laugh.

'A lily,' he said. 'A lily from an Angel of the Lord.' She could see he was shaking. 'It wasn't a lily. It was an angel's *hand*.' He pressed the palms of his own hands against his face, hiding himself. He rubbed his eyes. Then he dropped his arms by his side and stood up straight.

'Aashiq – did you know the truth?' he said.

Aashiq shook his head slowly. 'No,' he said. 'No I did not.' His voice was abrupt and angry. 'The stories – stories we heard from the knights – said a lily.' He held up his own hand, in front of his face, spreading the fingers to resemble the cup of a flower. 'This is it. This is the lily.'

'Trois mains,' Blanche said. She was clutching Edmund's sleeve, her face drained. 'It's Tremayne. It's your name. Your name!'

Edmund regarded her. 'And your name too, Mrs Tremayne.'

Nicholas rounded on him. 'Don't you see what this means? If we carry his name, we are his descendants. Matthias is our connection to the Knights of the Order of the Lily. His blood runs in our veins!'

Edmund narrowed his eyes. 'So it does. I don't see what difference that makes. The lily is still what it is. It confers power. You saw for yourself.' He turned away from his brother, keeping his gun levelled at Miranda.

'There is still one vital detail,' he said. 'Where is the lily?'

Nicholas and Blanche stared at him, incredulous. 'For God's sake,' Blanche said. 'Didn't you see? Don't you understand? Your forefather mutilated the angel – he sliced off its hand! How can that not make a difference?'

Edmund glanced at his hostages. His eyes were cold and hard. He pressed his lips together and then he hissed: 'Must we argue about this now? You have known, known for a long time, that the lily was not honourably come by, Blanche. Isn't it a little late in the game for you to have moral qualms?'

Blanche paled. 'But this,' she whispered. 'This is not what I expected.'

'Nothing has changed,' Edmund persisted. 'We have to take it – take what is ours. Nicholas, take her gun.'

Nicholas did as he was told. He lifted the revolver from Blanche's hand. But Jacinth sensed he was shocked by what they had seen. Turmoil was visible in his face. Which way would he go?

'Where is the lily?' Edmund said to Maslin, stepping closer to Miranda so the barrel of the revolver was just inches from her head. 'I know you don't fear for your own life, but you wouldn't want me to take hers.'

Behind them, David stepped forward. 'Leave her!' he shouted. 'Leave her! Let her go.'

But Edmund shoved the revolver a few inches closer still.

'Get back,' he said, voice crisp. 'Get back and be quiet. Now – Maslin.'

'I – I don't know,' Maslin said. His voice trembled. He looked very gaunt and frail. 'Let her go, please. I don't know. Hasn't this gone on long enough? The greed, and the killing? Let her go. Let the lily go.'

'You can find it,' Edmund continued. 'We all saw it, this little show. It's amazing what the three of you can do. Just think how much more I will accomplish when the lily is in my possession – when I can hold it in my hand. I've spent a lifetime searching for the lily. It is my right – my inheritance.

'So try again. We are bound to it – all of us. It is already in our blood and together you can find it now.'

Jacinth stared at the gun, so close to Miranda's fragile head. She could hardly breathe, hardly move, in case Edmund should pull the trigger. Miranda was staring straight ahead, her hands clasped together tight and her face ice white. Jacinth looked to Maslin and he gave a tiny nod.

'Put the gun down,' he whispered. 'We'll do what you say. I don't know if we can find the lily but we shall try.' The moment stretched. Miranda's breath came in short, shallow gasps. She closed her eyes. They waited, all of them, as Edmund considered. Then, slowly, he drew the gun away.

'Leave her,' a voice said. 'There's no need for that. I know where the lily's hidden. I can tell you.'

A man had stepped into the stone hall. He was bowed, wrapped in rags so they couldn't see his face, but a ripple of recognition passed through the inhabitants of the room, like electricity.

'Matthias Trois Mains,' Jacinth whispered. Edmund spun round to see, still brandishing the pistol. Miranda made a choked sound, like a sob, and ran to her father. She threw her arms around his waist.

They stood confronting one another, Matthias and Edmund. Matthias pulled back his hood and let his cloak drop to the ground, revealing more clearly the condition of his body. Jacinth recoiled to see him, like a long-dead corpse, the bones showing through tears in his skin, the skull face and the bony fingers.

Edmund didn't speak. He stared at Matthias, his gun now levelled at the creature standing in front of him. What was he thinking?

'My son,' Matthias said at last. His voice resounded with a horrible amusement. 'Ah, my son. Hot-headed and greedy. So much like his forefather.' Then he stretched out his patched bone and sinew arms as though he wished to embrace his long-lost descendant. He took a step closer, hands held out to touch him, but Edmund retreated.

'You're nothing to do with me,' he said. 'Nothing. Keep back, or I'll shoot.'

But Matthias laughed again, wry and sad at the same time. 'Then shoot, if you must. It'll make no difference to me. I've been shot before.' He stepped towards Edmund again, and this time Edmund pulled the trigger. The deafening sound filled the stone hall, the initial explosion amplified by a host of crashing echoes. Jacinth clapped her hands to her ears. Matthias faltered under the impact of the bullet, but he didn't flinch or fall down.

His hideous face contorted into a kind of grin, and he shook his head slowly.

'You want to restore the lily to the light,' he said. 'You want to hold it and absorb its power. You want the gifts it would bring, the powers of the mind, the physical strength.

'Then see what the lily did to me, Edmund Tremayne. Because I was the one to strike the blow, because I seized the angel's hand first, I absorbed its life spirit, its energy. I soaked up the power of its immortality.'

'But that didn't happen to the others, only you, because of what you did,' Edmund said, still inching away from Matthias, gun levelled helplessly in front of him. 'It wouldn't happen to me, this.' He gestured towards the blackened, exposed ribs of the ancient knight, now seven centuries old.

'No,' Matthias conceded. 'It would not. But the lily is a curse on us, on all the knights. They all succumbed. They witnessed what I did, but they couldn't resist sharing the fruits of it. They were complicit in my crime, because they wanted the angel's power for themselves. And we have all been punished, time and again through the centuries. The gifts have grown fewer, but the curse continues to haunt every successive generation.

'Until now, Edmund. I've been punished enough. It's time to end it.'

'You know where it is?' Maslin spoke up. His face was shocked and incredulous. 'Why didn't you tell me? Why didn't you tell me the truth – what the lily is? We could have destroyed it!'

Matthias shook his head. 'The prophecy said three would be needed, to bring about an end. Three with gifts of sight. You had to come here to see for yourselves exactly what happened. You had to see the beginning.'

Jacinth glanced around at the others. They were staring at Matthias and Edmund, mesmerised. Miranda was clinging to her father, Aashiq stood beside them. Edmund slowly inched back, towards the alabaster angel. Jacinth moved out of his way, but not quick enough. Edmund grabbed her. Now she was the one with a cold gun pressed against her temple.

'Keep away from me!' Edmund barked. 'Or I'll shoot the girl. I'll blow her brains out. Then what'll you do, without your precious three? You'll have to live forever, you horrible ghoul! Keep away. Get back!'

Edmund wrapped her long hair around his free hand and pulled it tight. Jacinth gasped in pain. Panic surged. Every moment became distinct, the faces of Maslin and Edmund, the light glinting on the statue, the torchlight dancing on the black barrel of the revolver.

'Tell me where the lily is!' Edmund shouted. 'Or I'll kill her.' He cocked the hammer. The slide and click of the well-oiled mechanism slotting into place was loud against her skull. The seconds stretched out, each heartbeat lasted a lifetime. She prayed silently for Matthias to tell him, to rescue her. Forget the curse, the lily, Matthias's own longing to oblivion, she didn't want her bright, precious life to end. Even with her spoiled face, even carrying the burden of her parents' deaths and the years of despair on the streets of Paris, she did not want to die. Scenes flashed in her mind, full of sound and colour, walking in Paris with her father, the evenings in the forest, the night with the fox, the journey with Miranda and Jack. She longed for it, for more life. She didn't want to let it go. Tell him, Matthias, she willed. Tell him.

The shot rang out, filling the hall with its deafening stone-and-metal reverberation. Jacinth's mind blanked, the bullet's impact a violent thump against her body. She fell heavily. Hot blood soaked through her clothes, in a pulsing river.

'Jacinth!' Miranda's anguished voice echoed in the aftermath of the revolver's single shot. She drew away from her father and ran to them, Edmund lying over Jacinth, a lake of blood pooling over the stone floor. Maslin was beside her, pulling Edmund to one side, but Miranda looked beyond him. There, beside the statue, stood Jack with his own revolver still raised in his hand. The barrel breathed a tiny curl of smoke. His face was frozen.

'Jack,' she whispered. 'It was you.'

Maslin had lifted Tremayne from Jacinth, who lay in a faint on the floor. She was covered in Edmund's blood. Jack had shot him in the back.

Edmund's eyes rolled back in his head. Blood was leaking from his nose and the corners of his mouth, so much of it. Miranda tried to haul Jacinth out of the mess.

'She's all right, isn't she? She wasn't hit. She isn't hurt,' she appealed to Maslin. He wasn't listening. Maslin stood up before Jack, who still held the gun in front of him.

'Put the gun down Jack,' the old man said. 'It's done now. Let it go.'

The gun fell from Jack's hand with a jarring clatter. Maslin picked it up and passed it to Aashiq, who had come to help Jacinth. Jack still stood like a statue, his hand outstretched even though he had dropped the gun. His eyes were blank, still caught in the moment of firing the shot. Was he even aware of the man he had taken down, his life ebbing away on the ground?

'Jack, it's done,' Maslin repeated. His voice was low and calm, and he touched Jack gently on the shoulder. The contact sent a shudder through Jack's body, as though some arcane internal connection had been made, and he came back to life. His empty gun hand fell to his side.

Blanche ran to her husband and dropped to her knees beside him. She called out his name, brushed the hair from his face.

'You fool, you fool, why did you do this, why did you, why?' she repeated. Anger, shock and grief mingled, tears leaking over her cheeks as she cursed him for his stupidity and kissed him because she loved him.

Miranda cradled Jacinth's head upon her lap. Jacinth's eyelids fluttered, and then flicked open. Her eyes were bright. 'I'm not dead,' she said. 'I thought I was dying.'

Miranda pressed her hands against the sides of Jacinth's face. 'You're not dead,' she said fiercely, tears pricking her eyes. 'You've got to stay here, with me. I haven't got any other friends. Nobody else likes me. You stay, do you understand?'

She looked up at Jack, like a stranger, staring at her, his eyes dark.

'I saved her,' he said. 'And I saved you.' It sounded as though he were speaking from a distance. His voice was different. 'I might not have the blood of crusader knights in my veins, or any supernatural talent, but I saved you all the same,' he said.

Miranda nodded. 'Yes,' she said. 'Yes you did.'

The sun was low over the horizon, the sky awash with red and gold. They were gathered in a company around the fire, and Jack studied them, this unholy family. Matthias was humming gently to himself, staring into the flames. Jacinth and Miranda were sitting close together, Jacinth's arm looped around Miranda's. Beside Miranda, there was David, who was engaged in a heated conversation with Maslin and Aashiq. Beyond them, Blanche and Nicholas Tremayne a little distant from the fire but still a part of the circle. Blanche looked dreadful, her face puffy with tears, her face blotchy and grey. The grace and self-possession that had seemed so much a part of her had entirely melted away. Even her body seemed to have lost its shape, as though her muscles had grown soft and slack and she sagged beneath the weight of herself.

Jack tested his own feelings about this. He had killed a man. He had taken the life of Edmund Tremayne. He had shot him in the back. This fact would never alter. He couldn't take it back or rub it out. Every morning when he woke up, every night when he went to sleep, this knowledge would weigh on him. He was a different person now.

But what else could he have done? Edmund Tremayne had a gun to Jacinth's head and Jack had no doubt he would have pulled the trigger in order to get what he wanted. One or other would have died. Jacinth or Edmund? Jack had made his decision. He had seen – so long ago now – Edmund strike Maslin across the face with his stick and then burn his house to the ground. He had watched him hold a gun to Miranda's head, and then to Jacinth's. Edmund Tremayne was so fixed on the single idea of the lily and its powers, not even the revelation about its origins nor the spectacle of Matthias could dissuade him. Edmund had been beyond the reach of reason. He was cruel, greedy and single-minded. And so, Jack had killed him. He had pulled the trigger to save his friends. But a weight of guilt and horror oppressed him. Even if the killing had been justified, he was soiled by it. Edmund's evil had corrupted him too, because it had obliged him to commit a terrible act. Edmund's evil had tainted his own sense of what was right to do.

Jack sighed. He had run over the same arguments time and time again but no matter how many times he rehearsed it in his mind, his emotions refused to be calm. He felt a poisoning brew of guilt, shock and terrible shame. The scene was branded on his imagination – the recoil of the gun, the flower of blood opening on Edmund's back, the long moment's pause and then the man's heavy collapse on top of Jacinth, knocking her to the ground. He would never be free of it.

The others had been kind and considerate, reassuring him he had acted for the best, thanking him for saving them, but no one could take the burden from Jack. He had to carry it on his own.

They had buried Edmund Tremayne beneath a mound of rocks at the far end of the chasm. Maslin took back the gold fleur-de-lis Edmund had stolen from him and hung it around his neck. No one had felt inclined to make any kind of speech. When the burial was complete, only Nicholas and Blanche remained, standing one either side of it, Nicholas staring at the stones while Blanche continued to weep, her hair in long, untidy straggles blowing across her face.

Jack sighed. What else could he have done? The round of fruitless reasoning started up again inside his head, the justification to himself. Perhaps if he could find the right pattern of words, the deed wouldn't hurt so much.

'Jack!' Maslin's voice interrupted his thoughts. The old man came over and sat beside him.

'How are you?' Maslin said.

'Oh well. You know.' Jack shrugged. He found it hard to look the old man in the face so he picked at his fingernails. Maslin didn't say anything else, but he laid his arm across Jack's skinny shoulders.

'You know you saved us, Jack. All of us. We are all in your debt. Can you forgive me? For bringing you out here and putting you through so much? It wasn't even your battle. It was nothing to do with you.'

Jack shook his head, still fiddling with his fingers. He couldn't look at Maslin and his eyes blurred with tears. He cast his mind back to the afternoon he had set out blackberry picking. It seemed a long time ago. How could he go back? Did that place even exist anymore, now that he had travelled so far away from it? He felt such a pang, to think of his mother and father at home, and the horses and the farm. He ached with homesickness. But even if he returned, he would carry the burden with him. Life could not be undone. He would still have Edmund's blood on his hands.

Maslin didn't speak any further. Night covered the sky and a banner of stars unfurled along the top of the chasm. Silence fell over the company, except for the crackle of the fire. Exhausted, Jack's mind fell silent at last and Blanche curled up like a little girl beneath a blanket, her hand pressed against her mouth, her eyes fixed on the flames. At last Maslin turned to Matthias Trois Mains.

'How do you know where the lily is?' he said.

Matthias raised his head. He had his hood on, and in the firelight the horror of his face was softened.

'I have always known where it was.' His voice was quiet. 'Every day of every year of every century I have felt it. The fibres of my body yearn for it. The lily is like a magnet tugging at me all the time and wherever I am.'

'Where?' Maslin repeated. 'Tell me, so we can finish it.'

Matthias regarded the circle, Blanche and Nicholas, David and Aashiq, Jacinth, Miranda and Jack. Then he looked directly at Maslin and said: 'It's in Ireland. It is buried under a cairn on an island you can see from your family home on the west coast.'

Maslin's lips parted. Jack stared at Matthias: 'That's Elliott Island,' he said. 'Mr Maslin, that's Elliott Island he's talking about.'

Maslin's face was clouded with darkness. He dipped his head and pushed his hands through his hair.

'Elliott Island,' he said, in a choked voice. 'It has been there, all this time, and I never knew? It was so close to me – so close to my parents and grandparents? Why didn't they know?'

Matthias shook his head. 'Remember what I said – that I could feel the lily wherever I was. Don't you think your grand-parents could feel it too? They might not have been aware of it consciously, but they were drawn to the place. It felt like home. They wanted to live there, close to the lily without even know-ing that's why the place felt special to them. That's why they built a house there.'

Maslin looked at his companions. 'We have another long journey ahead of us,' he said at last. 'And Jack – I'm taking you home.'

The journey began the next morning, for all except Matthias. He would wait in the desert, he said. He would end where he had begun. As they said goodbye, Maslin and Matthias stood and studied one another. So many centuries of history lay between them, the bond between the line of the Maslins and the ancient knight who had severed the hand of an angel. The long road of their history had come to a final crossroads.

They parted from Aashiq when they reached the post on the hill so he could return to his people. He had friends to mourn, and families to console and support. But at last he could tell them the truth about the past and the heritage that was stolen from them by the crusaders hundreds of years before. Perhaps one day they would return to live in the city of caves in the heart of the desert.

Aashiq embraced Maslin and David, bowed to Jacinth and Miranda, and finally stood before Jack, man to man.

'I had faith in you, Jack,' Aashiq said gravely. 'And my faith was justified. You will always have a place here.'

Jack looked down, unable to find the words to respond. He felt grief, relief, guilt and regret. The feelings tumbled over each other. He banged his fist against his chest in confusion and looked up at Aashiq.

'But,' he said helplessly. 'But what have I done?'

Aashiq didn't speak but he stepped towards him and enveloped him in a tight embrace. 'Be brave,' Aashiq said. 'Take care of the others. Look after James Maslin. And come back one day, come back to the desert and stay with us.'

Aashiq mounted his horse, and the white mare wheeled on her hindquarters, kicking up the sand, eager to be away. He waved once, a sweeping gesture of farewell, and then the horse was off, hooves pounding across the desert.

Miranda stared at Blanche Tremayne. She felt no pity for her, only contempt for her collapse. Blanche, after all, had tricked and kidnapped her, snatched her from her loved ones and opposed her at every step of the long, difficult journey. Seeing this enemy inconsolably snivelling, Miranda felt a chilly satisfaction. What would happen to her now? she wondered. And what about Nicholas Tremayne? Without Edmund, the two of them seemed to lack the vital force that had compelled them to act with such ruthless determination. Nicholas, after all, had kept poor Jacinth a prisoner in the tower for years, treating her like a slave. Now he rode beside Blanche like a shadow, as though all the substance had been sucked from him.

The return seemed to last forever. There was no sense of compulsion, no fear of pursuit, only a longing to be out of the heat and dust, to be home again. The only benefit of this weary trek was the time she had to talk with her father, to tell him all about her life over the last three years, and about her mother. She told him how she had come to live with his parents and how they mourned and missed him. And David soaked up every word she had to say, asking questions, insisting she repeat stories over again so he could hear them again. He grew more lively and jolly as the days passed, telling her tales from his own childhood, and looking forward to a rosy future where he and Julia and Miranda were living together again, in a house in the country, and all would be well. How glorious the picture he painted, with Julia happy, blossom crowding the fruit trees, the grass lush and green, the trees huge and leafy, the perfume of rich, moist soil. But sometimes, at night, darker moods overcame him and instead of these rhapsodies on a perfect future, he shared his anguish from the past, the long years covering his name, the loneliness of his quest, the sojourn in the desert waiting for his daughter to rescue him. Then Miranda didn't know what to say to him, so she simply held his hand and waited for the shadow to pass. When he slept, he looked so much older than her mother. His hair was quite grey, his face jaded by the heat and struggle. His life had been very hard, and he had suffered it so she and her mother might be well. Softened by compassion, Miranda stretched out her hand and gently stroked his face with the tips of her fingers. Then she would sit next to Jacinth and Jack by the fire and instead of talking about the terrors of the past or hopes for the future, they taught one another songs they knew, French songs, Irish folk songs and popular English tunes from the music halls. Jack knew dozens of ballads, and he had a beautiful voice. They told each other jokes and made up stories and nonsense poems, and laughed a lot, laughed until their sides ached.

Just outside Cairo, Nicholas Tremayne announced they would be leaving. He and Blanche, he said, were travelling to Kefalonia in search of the chapel of gold still rumoured to be hidden on the island. They had no further interest in pursuing the lily. Miranda looked at Maslin. Would he let them leave? Shouldn't he call in the police and have them arrested for kidnapping? Then again, they might report Jack's role in the killing of Edmund Tremayne. There were too many secrets involved, too much they should not reveal about events of recent weeks.

It was not an affectionate parting. Nicholas hardly glanced at Jacinth or Miranda. He nodded a curt goodbye to Maslin and turned away. Blanche didn't speak to them at all, but meekly followed Nicholas. How would they fare? Miranda tipped her head to one side, watching them ride away. Well, she could hardly wish them joy in their grubby quest for ancient gold. Let it eat them up, Miranda wished. Let the hunt gnaw them and consume them. Let it be fruitless. She did not feel in the slightest bit forgiving. She had no room for pity.

The journey continued. They took a boat from Alexandria across the Mediterranean to Naples and then the train through Rome and Florence, and through the Alps to Geneva. David and Miranda sent a telegram and a long, enigmatic letter to Miranda's aunt Mary to tell her where they were, and as much as they could about what had happened. David abjured her not to tell his parents, not yet.

They stopped off in Paris. The city seemed like a dream to Jacinth, this place where she had lived a lifetime ago. Maslin invited her to walk with him around the city, and shy though she was to be alone with him, Jacinth smiled graciously and accepted. It was the beginning of spring, the first frail wisps of blossom appearing on the branches of ornamental trees in the parks and along the wide boulevards. The streets thronged with traffic, and rearing above them all, the dark, iron spike of the Eiffel Tower. The wind was chilly, nipping at her face, and she shivered, so they went to a shabby café where the sun shone through a banner of stained glass at the top of the window, depicting a bouquet of leaves and berries in moss green and scarlet. In the corner three rakish young men were drinking absinthe and talking about poetry in loud, inebriated voices. It was a joy to hear her native language again, to understand effortlessly the conversations of others.

Maslin ordered a cup of hot chocolate for her to drink, and coffee for himself. They waited in silence for the drinks to arrive, and then, as Maslin spooned sugar into his cup he said: 'What is it like, to be back?'

Jacinth smiled. 'Like a dream.' She struggled to find the right English words to explain how she felt. 'It is my city, but the girl who lived here was a different girl.'

Maslin nodded. 'You are different,' he said. 'I thought we were losing you, in the desert.'

'That I was mad? Yes. Nearly mad,' she said. 'But everything changed. When Tremayne held the gun to my head I realised I didn't want to die. All these years, since my parents died, and my face was burned, my life was pain and struggle and loneliness. Now I know I don't want to give up. I want my life.'

A thorn of guilt still pricked. She shifted uncomfortably on her chair and forced herself to look Maslin in the face. He had been so kind to her, and over the days of their voyage home she had grown fond of him. She had found a new family, who loved

280

her despite the scars on her face, and she feared, now, that her confession would destroy their friendship. But Maslin was looking at her steadily, his blue eyes bright in his face, waiting for her to speak.

'I have something to tell you,' she said. 'When I was living in the tower, Nicholas Tremayne asked me to stick pins in a photograph of you – to use my powers to hurt you.' She hesitated, but Maslin's expression had not changed.

'I did what he told me,' she said. 'I knew it was bad, but I did it. I am very sorry. Please forgive me.' She bowed her head as her eyes filled with tears. But Maslin nodded. 'I know what you did,' he said. 'And it did hurt me. You have a remarkable gift and it laid me low for a time. But I also know the situation you were in, and the choice you made to run away from the Tremaynes with Miranda. So of course I forgive you, Jacinth.

'My life hasn't been entirely admirable either, but it isn't too late for either of us to resolve to be better.'

Jacinth raised her head and sniffed. Her nose had started to run, so Maslin reached into his pocket for a handkerchief and handed it over.

'Finish off your drink,' he said. 'We have to join the others. We have another train to catch.'

20

The Island
Ireland, 1890

A grey-green gem in a sea of glittering blue, the island was a haphazard pile of rock rising from the waves. Shallow soil lined scoops in the rough stone where coarse, salty grass grew. Tiny beaches, decorated with broken shell and blue-striped pebbles, stretched from its flanks to the hungry waves. Gulls flew overhead, white-winged demons with amber eyes and angry voices. And around it, the vast Atlantic Ocean endlessly churned.

They stood at its summit, Maslin, Jacinth and Miranda, David and Jack. The sky was an endless clear blue above their heads. The wind was cold and brisk. Their clothes fluttered. Waves crashed below them, throwing tall, white plumes over the beach. The scent of salt and seaweed filled the air.

The old cairn, three heavy stones in a pile, rose from the island's apex. Years of storms had scoured the slabs of granite clean, except for a few coins of the toughest lichen. The boatman had left them on the little beach, and would return before sunset to collect them again. After weeks of travelling, they had found their way to the last place, to a tiny island off the west coast of Ireland.

Behind them, across the water, rose the cliffs of the mainland. Upon the summit, very distantly, Miranda could see the remains of Maslin's family home. They had driven past it in the carriage, the blackened stumps of walls and sodden mounds of ash visible through the locked iron gates.

Now they stood, the five of them, in a circle about the cairn. Bonds of history and loyalty bound them together, but for a time they were silent, each locked in their own private thoughts.

Miranda's mind flew to her mother, in the asylum in London. Over the last few days Miranda's longing to see her had swelled into a constant ache, a physical pressure beneath her ribs. When this was done – when the journey was over – surely her mother would be well again. She glanced at her father, catching his eye. Was he thinking about Julia too?

Finally Maslin stepped forward. They had brought tools for the job – a long crowbar, ropes and shovels. He signalled to David and Jack and together they began to lever the stones apart.

It took a long time. The cairn resisted their efforts. The stones were heavy, and gripped one another tight. At times it seemed they were impossible to move, impregnable parts of the indomitable island, but eventually, using strength and calculation, they breached the cairn and took the pile of slabs apart. Then, beneath them, level in the ground, lay one final slab, smooth and square as a fallen tombstone. Using the shovels, Maslin and David carved away the grass and soil from its edges. Then Maslin slipped the flattened end of the crowbar underneath it. He glanced up at David.

'Help me,' he said. 'It'll be heavy – very heavy.'

Together they pressed down on the crowbar, bringing their weight to bear. At first the stone held against them, but they pushed again. The slab growled and groaned, as slowly, slowly, it shifted to one side to reveal a black space gaping in the island's crown.

Jack dropped to his belly and peered inside. He stuck his arm down into the darkness.

'It's here! There something here!' Maslin crouched beside

him, and the girls crowded together, peering over his shoulder. Miranda couldn't see anything, except a puff of dust clouding the air above the opening. She was anxious – they all were. Was this the right place? And if it was, what exactly would they find? It wasn't a supernatural lily after all, but a grisly severed hand. What would it look like? How would she feel when she beheld it?

Maslin lay on his front and reached down into the opening. 'I have it,' he said, and he drew out an oblong parcel, the length of his arm, swathed in layers of cloth and leather, bound up with rope. He laid the parcel on the ground and drew out a pocket knife. He glanced at the others, but didn't say a word. Instead he dug the knife into the coverings and made one long cut from top to bottom. Then he pulled the package open and drew out from inside a case of glass pieces held together in a web of gold.

Some of the pieces were coloured blue and red and amber, and the glass was thick and cloudy. Even so, after all this time, a pure white radiance shone out. Years of darkness had not extinguished it.

Maslin held up the case. Dimly, through the glass, Miranda could see five white petals, the cup of the flower and the stout white stalk. A hand or a flower? So disguised, it was easy to understand how the first knights had sustained their deception. The glass blurred and distorted the form of the hand, but didn't prevent the white light shining out. Like a lantern it glowed, or a stained-glass window with sunlight blasting through. Even as Maslin elevated the fruit of their long search, the lily emitted a greater radiance and the light shone in almost tangible straight bright rays, like sunbeams piercing clouds.

Miranda's eyes filled with tears. How lovely it was – how rare and astonishing. The sight of it seemed to pierce her, the rays of light passing into her heart and mind, filling her with ecstasy and a yearning desire to take the case and hold it to her, to

284

possess it and consume the light and energy it contained. Her sense of the island and her companions receded, because the lily, surely, was the heart and meaning of everything, the centre of the world, the goal she had striven for all her life. No wonder the knights had longed for the lily. No wonder they could not destroy it. She stretched out her hands.

'No,' Maslin barked. The sound of his voice, his shout over the wind, broke her dream into ugly fragments. She glanced at the others. Jacinth's face was clouded and hard to read but her eyes were bright. Jack and David were not so affected. David stepped forward.

'Do you want me to take it? Perhaps it would be better,' he said. They were standing face to face, David and Maslin. Maslin was profoundly affected by the lily. She could read the conflict in his face, the power the lily wielded over him as it did over Jacinth and herself. A quick calculation ran through her mind. Could the three of them, Maslin, Jacinth and Miranda, overpower David and Jack? Could they take the lily off the island and keep it for themselves? Perhaps the same thought passed through Jacinth's mind, because she looked over at Miranda. They stared at each other for a moment.

'Will you give it to me?' David asked, his voice very calm and level. 'Think, James. Think clearly.'

Maslin held the glass case tight. His white hair was blown around his head in a cloud. His eyes glittered, his face full of fire. He lowered the lily, and hugged it to himself with both arms. He bowed his head. Then he moved the case away from his body. 'Take it,' he said. 'Take it now.'

David gently lifted the case from Maslin's hands, and as he did so, the tide of yearning seemed to ebb away from Miranda.

'Jacinth?' she whispered. And Jacinth nodded sadly. They were safe now. Maslin had passed the test, and the spell had been broken.

'What do we do now?' David said. He was nervous, holding the glittering box.

'Break the box,' Maslin said. 'Smash it up, so we can get the lily out.'

David's face was grim. He put the case on the rock and stamped upon it with his booted foot. But the glass case was tough, built to protect and endure. It didn't even crack or buckle.

'Try the shovel,' Maslin said. So David picked up the shovel, raised it high, and smashed it down on the surface of the case. Beneath the metal blade, the glass splintered and a web of fractures riddled one large piece of occluded glass. David brought the shovel down again, and the pane began to cave in. He tried a third and a fourth time. The sound was appalling. Even over the waves and the wind the shovel's pounding seemed to hammer through Miranda's skull. The violent destruction, even as necessary as this, filled her with fury. She clenched her teeth together and balled her hands. Let it be over soon. Let it be done.

At last, David put the shovel down. The case was broken open at one end; a spray of splinters and thick jewels of coloured glass littered the rock.

David stood up straight. He was out of breath, a film of sweat on his forehead.

'Shall I take it out?' he said. Maslin nodded. David swallowed nervously and dropped to a squat. Gingerly he reached into the case, fingers outstretched and tense, wary of the jagged glass and doubtless afraid of what his hand would come into contact with. They stood in silence, breath held . . .

'I have it,' David whispered. 'It feels – hard and cold, like marble.'

Then he drew his hand out again, and clutched between his fingers were the stiff white fingers of the angel. It looked, perversely, as though he were shaking hands with it. Miranda gave a sudden laugh, tension dispelled. It all seemed so silly and absurd. There was her long-lost father on his knees shaking hands with a disembodied angel. She clapped her hand to her mouth, to control her merriment. Maslin gave her a curious glance.

'It's like the hand of a statue,' David said, marvelling. 'It isn't flesh and bone at all. It hasn't corrupted.' He sniffed it. 'And it smells clean, and sweet. What is it made of?'

Although the hand was purely white, the substance of it seemed to flow. Wrapped in the whiteness was a spectrum of colour, which could be sensed but moved too fast to see. It did not belong. It was not a part of the material of the world.

They had all moved closer, to see the angel's hand with its halo of light.

'What now?' David whispered. 'What shall I do?'

'Give it to me,' Maslin said. 'Let me take it. Jacinth, Miranda – stand close. You know what we have to do. Remember the times before – by the statue and in the Orient Express. We have to connect with the past and the future. We have to reach into the distance to find the angel again.'

Miranda looked at Maslin and then at Jacinth. Her long hair was bound up in a thick plait to her knees but stray strands had been tugged loose by the wind and blew against her face. Her red scar was bright in the chilly air, but her expression was confident and controlled. Jacinth gave a nod.

'Yes,' she said. 'I am ready.'

Miranda didn't feel as sure, but she nodded in turn. She had come this far. What else could she do now but see it through? Over Jacinth's shoulder, she could see Jack looking at her. He gave a smile of encouragement.

'Me too,' Miranda said, with a deep breath. 'Let's see what we can do.'

She closed her eyes.

*

Jacinth cleared her mind. She was long practised now, and it wasn't hard to put her thoughts to one side, to let awareness of the island recede. Miranda looked uneasy but Jacinth felt strangely calm. She didn't know what would happen, but she wasn't afraid. If they were successful she would sacrifice her gift, but at last she was prepared for the loss. Let it go. What happiness had it brought her, truly? Exhilaration, yes. Escape from the trap of her life. But her life had changed now. She wanted it, and all it had to offer.

Darkness filled the space of her mind. The envelope of the earthly world fell away. She sensed the proximity of the angel's hand, the power of it coursing through her blood, the dubious gift of her ancestors connecting her to it like a shining thread. The hand lay at the root of her power, and now, so close, it filled her head with light. She was aware of the others, Maslin to one side, Miranda on the other, both moving into the same place, the tunnel of light radiating from the angel. Pictures of the past flickered through her mind from Maslin, the scenes they had witnessed before in the desert, the angel descending and Matthias reaching out with his sword. Through Miranda, she saw a hundred windows opened on a host of possible futures – the ascent of the angel, a summer in a country house with Miranda and her family. The scenes flashed before her like innumerable cards, too fast to seize on. Past and future, and the long road joining them together. But it was Jacinth, the third, who needed to reach out into the distance, further than she had ever gone before. She summoned all her strength, and linked to Miranda and Maslin she threw her astral self into the vault of the heavens. Where did the angel come from? She passed through the atmosphere, the veil covering the face of the Earth. Then – silence and darkness. Beneath her, she saw the curve of the planet, a swirl of blue and green, an island itself in the oceanic deeps of space. Far away, embroideries of stars glittered. For a moment she faltered, afraid of the distance between her astral self and her limited, earthly body. An invisible connection held her to it, the finest silver thread. But might that thread snap if she stretched it too far? Fear rose up like black water in the throat, threatening to choke and drown. But she wasn't alone. She heard Miranda's voice, and Maslin's.

'Don't be afraid,' Miranda said. 'We're with you, Jacinth. The angel's hand will show the way.'

'The hand is alive,' Maslin said. 'The substance of it. I think when the angel fled, it left an echo of itself, a disturbance, that we can follow. Focus on the hand, the very quality of it, so you can identify the echoes of the angel's passing.'

Jacinth let her fear fall away. Sensitive, receptive, she waited.

The darkness wasn't empty. It was a web of energy, an infinite sea full of endless, restless tides, stretching back to the beginning of time and reaching out to the end of all things. The stars and planets were jewels spun from intricate coils of energy, adorning the dark sea like a coronet, and bound together across the immensities of space in a tapestry of relation and belonging.

And Jacinth understood. Here the angel had begun. Like a pearl, created around a chafing grain of sand in an oyster, a wish or dream had coiled up, drawing energy to itself, generating a form and a mind. Here the angel had come to be. It was new and eternal. It was a piece of the universe. And the angel had passed through the heavens, bright as a sword. It had traversed the plains of space and finally alighted in the desert, where it was worshipped.

Until the brutal attack. The angel wasn't impervious after all. It experienced agony and assault. Horrible mutilation. Never before had the angel endured any kind of pain. It fled from the Earth, leaving a part of itself behind. Blank with shock, it hid away in a dark pocket of space, still linked to the missing hand as Jacinth herself was held to her physical body. Over hundreds of years it had ached to be whole again. Caught in a tumult of anger and burning with the agony of the amputation it had brooded and boiled in evil dreams of murder and death, causing the inheritors of the so-called lily to be poisoned in turn.

'It is here,' Jacinth said simply. 'It's here, in a fold of the dark.'

She couldn't see it, but she sensed its presence. Although her astral self couldn't smell, still it was something like perfume she detected, motes of it drifting from the knot of space, all closed up on itself, a tangle the angel had weaved for protection and now could not escape.

Jacinth drifted forwards and placed her ethereal hands on the cold outer casing. How could she set the angel free? Inside, she sensed it shift. It was aware of her. Gingerly the angel's thoughts reached out to her, still hurting after so many centuries, still wary of injury. And Jacinth felt ashamed, because searching her memories the angel would not find much to comfort. Her life had been a long catalogue of suffering, and her own record was not unblemished.

But it was no use wallowing in this. Her life had changed. She had forged connections with Miranda and Jack and James Maslin.

The angel stirred again, soaking up her thoughts of her friends and her hopes. Slowly the knot of darkness unravelled. The winding folds of it fell away, piece by piece. Inside, the luminous white form of the angel began to show, dimly at first, and then as the layers unwound it grew ever brighter.

When the final shreds of darkness were extinguished the angel rose up before her, like a great burning torch. Its face was a blaze of light, beautiful and terrible. Its face was full of hurt and it raised its unfinished arm to show them. Beneath the alabaster surface, just like the hand, a thousand colours seemed to flow too fast to properly perceive. Jacinth fell back. She reached out to her partners, Miranda and Maslin, and she tumbled away from the angel. She had never reached so far, and now she was plunging back, fast, too fast, tugged by the astral cord back to her small, vulnerable body. It was a precipitous flight. The presences of Miranda and Maslin were snatched away and still she descended. Miles and miles, till her sense of self was nearly obliterated. She fell like a meteor – she would be torn to pieces. Down and down, the sea rising up, and tiny as a pinhead in the ocean, the island where the five were waiting. Miranda, Maslin, Jack, David – and Jacinth.

Jacinth slammed into her own body so hard she thought her bones would shatter and the flesh burst open. She fell to the ground in a fit, losing consciousness for a few moments while her body twitched and convulsed on the rocky ground. The roar of the waves and the cries of the seagulls were loud in her ears. She sucked in great gulps of air, scrabbled about with her hands, trying to hold on tight to the ground so she shouldn't fall any further . . .

'Jacinth. Jacinth.' She opened her eyes. Miranda's face was looming over her own, vaguely shadowed because she was blocking the sun. Maslin was holding her shoulders, cradling her head. For a few moments Jacinth just stared. She couldn't make herself speak. The connections in her mind were loose. Her body felt heavy and lumpish.

Maslin looked at Miranda's worried face. 'Don't worry,' he said. 'Give her a moment. Just be patient. She's been a long way.' Maslin looked down at Jacinth again and smiled, gently brushing a strand of hair from her face.

Jack and David exchanged anxious glances. They had no idea what had happened. Maslin, Miranda and Jacinth had joined hands and the angel's hand had glowed with an intense white light that encompassed them all. A few minutes passed, when the three were entirely motionless and focused on some other place Jack could not see. And then, all of a sudden, Maslin and Miranda had fallen away and then Jacinth collapsed to the ground in a horrible convulsion.

What had they seen? Had they succeeded? He was bursting

with questions, but David put out his hand, restraining him, and put a finger to his lips. They must wait and be patient. But Jack found it hard to be patient. He hopped from one foot to another.

'Look!' David pointed to the sky. The wind was rising, whipping his black and grey hair around his face. His coat flapped loudly. Around the island the waves lashed and fretted. Jack tilted his head back. A black spiral had opened directly above them in the sky's blue dome. Slowly it reached down towards them, widening as it drew near, becoming a long black corridor that sealed itself over the island. Darkness swallowed them. Instantly the wind dropped, and sound of the waves was cut off. It was utterly uncanny, to look up and see faraway stars at the end of the tunnel. Jack stepped away, to the edge of the dark circle, and discovered he could move out of it. On the fringes of the island it was light again, the stars obliterated by the day's blue sky. But he stepped back into the dark, beneath the disc of stars. Miranda was helping Jacinth to her feet. Then they stood close together, all five, and looked up.

The angel descended. It was as tall as two men, with long wings like a cascade of white water from its shoulders. Its limbs were elegant and slender, its narrow body naked and sexless, and all the same colour-flowing white as the stolen hand. The five stood back, in a circle, and the angel's bare feet landed gently on the ground. Without thinking, Jack dropped to his knees and found himself muttering the prayers taught him by his mother. The others stood motionless, staring at the angel, stunned into silence. Jack could hardly breathe. This was the culminating moment of his life. All the paths he had taken, every thought in his head, every idle dream, every choice, had led him to this one single time and place – to the angel.

Miranda stepped forward. In the unnatural darkness, she was illuminated only by the angel's holy light. Miranda, so pale and colourless, was imbued with beauty. Her hair glimmered, her face was radiant and her eyes shone with the blue of the sea in summer. She held the severed hand aloft. The scene was like a painting in a grand church, burning with significance, as though it were charged with so much meaning Jack would never understand it all. Except that with his heart he understood. Scenes passed through his mind from the past months, the journey across Europe, the painting of the knights in Prague, Matthias bent and destroyed by time, the massacre in the desert and the shooting of Edmund Tremayne. Life was small and petty and grubby, hemmed in with hungers and doubts. But it was shot through with light and love and the arching aspiration to reach beyond narrow limits to an infinite reality, embodied in the angel before him. The image branded itself on his brain. Slowly, slowly, the angel reached out its mutilated arm. The substance of the hand flowed into it, like mercury moving. Hand and arm joined together, melting into one continuous whole. The angel, entire again, raised both hands before its face and regarded them. Then it lowered its arms to its sides and looked at the assembly. Miranda, Jacinth, Maslin, Jack and David. One by one it gazed into their faces, considering them, perhaps expressing some kind of rightness and completion. Then it stretched its arms upwards, over its head, and with a sweep of the drapes of wings it lifted from the ground and began a swift, powerful ascent through the column of darkness and out into the heavens.

The patch of night winked out, and glorious sunshine crashed over their heads. Waves and wheeling seagulls, the scent of salt and dried seaweed. Across the water rose the cliffs, and beyond them, his home and family. It had never seemed so precious or beautiful before. Jack sighed and smiled, and wiped the tears from his eyes. Maslin held his arms out, as though to embrace them all.

'It is done,' he said. 'It's over.'

21

Beginnings
Ireland, and London, 1891

The boatman took them back across the water at the end of the day and then in a cart up the road to Jack's farm. They were all worn out and Jack was in a daze. He could hardly believe he was going home again. The place was so familiar and at the same time so strange to him now.

'Are you all right, Jack?' Maslin was watching him. The old man was chipper, more colour in his face than usual. He had been humming too, a jaunty little tune that Jack didn't recognise.

'Nearly there,' Maslin said. 'It'll surprise them, won't it?'

Jack nodded. No doubt about that. How would his mother react, receiving a cart full of guests unannounced? What would be it like to see her again? And how much should he tell her about what had happened? He sensed it would be better for them both if he kept parts of his remarkable story to himself, even though he had never had a secret from his family before. It was an uncomfortable prospect, but one way and another he had to learn to accommodate some discomforts.

Miranda was sitting between her father and Jacinth. David had his arm around her and Miranda was leaning her head against his shoulder. Jacinth was quiet, a curious look of disintegration in her eyes as though she had not yet fully recovered from her experience on the island.

The light was fading, the spring air nippy as the sun disappeared over the sea. At home Jack's mother would be building up the fire and preparing the dinner. He could see her in his mind's eye, bending over the hearth and then peeling potatoes, while his little sister fed the chickens and his grandfather filled up his clay pipe in his chair by the fire.

The sky was full of colour, torn sheets of lavender and gold billowing over the sea. The darkness bore down on them, the first stars blinking. Down the road the Elliotts' farm hove into view, the road winding to meet it. Jack sat up straight, straining to see. Yes, there she was, his sister in the yard settling the chickens for the night, rounding up the geese and locking them into the shed. In the field outside he could see Tam, the bay horse, grazing the new grass, and the mare with a tiny new foal. He felt such a pang to think she'd given birth without him there to help. The horses whinnied and cantered up to the gate as the cart drew near. The foal galloped after its mother on long, awkward legs. Jack jumped down before the cart had even stopped and ran over to the gate to greet his horses. The foal was a fine creature, a chestnut colt, straight and well made. Perhaps it would race at Limerick one day. He ran his expert hands over its legs and down its neck.

'Just like his father,' a voice said, in a soft, familiar Irish accent. He didn't turn around right away, just savouring the sound of it.

'Always has to check upon his horses first – even before saying hello to his old mother. I know where I stand in the pecking order!'

Jack smiled. He gave the foal one last pat and slowly turned to his mother. There she was, just the same as ever, her apron a little smutty from the fire, wiping potato peelings from her hands. Jack couldn't stop grinning. For a few moments he just stood there, helpless, aware everyone was looking at him.

'How you've grown,' his mother said, her voice warm and caressing. 'How you've grown, Jack. I can't believe me eyes.'

'Hello, Ma.' He was sheepish and awkward, not knowing what to say.

'Oh for goodness sake,' she said, stepping towards him with her arms out. 'Haven't you got a hug for your old ma after all these months?'

Jack stepped forward into her embrace and hugged her so tight she squeaked and laughed. Then his sister ran up and hugged him too, and walking from the house Jack saw someone he hadn't seen for a year or more. The man looked smaller than he remembered, a little more stooped at the shoulder, a little more bowed at the knee, but still possessing that limber, wiry energy Jack had himself inherited.

'Da!' Jack shouted, disentangling himself from his sister. 'You've come home, Da!' He ran towards his father and clapped his arms around him, half knocking him off his feet. It was such a delight to be with his father again, the feel of him, the smell of him.

'When did you come home?' Jack asked. He was an inch taller than his father. It was an unsettling discovery, because his father had always seemed such a tower of strength.

'Just before Christmas. Your ma told me you'd got a job, and Grandpa wasn't well, so she needed another man about the place.'

'You looked after the mare,' Jack said. 'It's a fine foal.'

His father nodded. 'The best,' he said. Then he turned to the others, who had alighted from the cart.

'You'll be needing somewhere to stay tonight,' he said. 'Well, we haven't a lot of room but I'm sure we can accommodate you if you're not too particular.'

Maslin stepped forward, extending his hand. 'Mr Elliott,' he said. 'My name is James Maslin. I'm sure the name is familiar to you.'

'The house by the sea.' Jack's father nodded. 'I know it well enough. Not much left of it now though.'

'No there isn't,' Maslin said. 'I intend to rebuild it, however. I want to make my home in Ireland again. It is where I grew up. It's our place.'

Jack's father nodded. 'So did my son behave himself? Did he do us proud?'

Jack glanced quickly at Maslin. What would the old man say? His old face crinkled into a smile.

'Oh yes,' Maslin said, with a subtle wink for Jack. 'He did you proud. He was clever, brave and loyal and I'd entrust him with my life, Mr Elliott. A man couldn't have a better son.'

Jack looked down at the ground, his face burning with pride and embarrassment. His father shook Maslin by the hand for a second time.

'Yes,' he said. 'He's the best of sons. The very best.'

Jacinth woke up first in the morning. She was sharing a bed with Miranda and Jack's little sister, who was thrilled to have two young ladies from France and England to take care of. The little girl had stared at Jacinth's scars and even put her hand out to touch them, while Jacinth prickled with self-consciousness. But once the question was answered, Jack's sister was satisfied and treated Jacinth, simply, as Jacinth.

The birds were singing outside the low window, and distantly she could hear the bleating of sheep. She felt better this morning. The shock of her journey was fading. Already it had taken on the quality of a dream. Ordinary, everyday reality was asserting itself again. She did feel different. The angel's influence had drained out of her. There would be no more far-sight. Inside her mind, pathways had closed forever. She did not feel diminished by the loss. It had been a dubious gift, always walking a knife-edge, always at risk of losing her mind. Riding in the desert she had come so close to insanity. Now she was safe. Yes, she was safe.

Ah, who was she fooling? In truth she felt a sharp pang of

regret for what she had lost – even though she knew it was for the best. For so long she had planted all her faith in herself in the possession of the gift, and it would take a little while for her heart to catch up with what her head knew to be right. She wasn't a sorceress anymore.

They ate a fine breakfast together, fried eggs and brown bread with the finest butter, pale gold and fresh from dairy, with strips of savoury bacon and numerous cups of tea. It had rained in the night but now the sun shone from a clear, washed blue. The windows of the cottage were open, the air smelled clean and sweet.

In a few days' time Maslin would visit his lawyers in Prague to sort out his family affairs and raise the money to rebuild his house, so he could settle down at last. He wanted Jack and his father to work for him, to help build up the finest stables in all of Ireland. Today Miranda and her father would begin the journey to London, to their family. And what would Jacinth do? She still hadn't decided.

After breakfast she and Miranda took a walk in the breezy sunshine. They headed towards the sea, crossing the broken, rocky landscape where innumerable tiny spring flowers clung to the thin soil.

'Will you come with us?' Miranda asked again. Alone together, they spoke in French. All the previous evening she had cajoled and pleaded. 'Please, Jacinth. My father wants you to come. We both do. But I do mostly. I need you.'

Jacinth sighed. Maslin had offered her a home too, in the house-to-be overlooking the sea. By chance, or unconscious design, she and Miranda had reached the grounds of the old house and Jacinth pushed through the broken iron gates to survey the black, ruinous walls. Compared with the rocky landscape outside, the garden was lush and overgrown. Doubtless, in its heyday earlier generations of Maslins had imported soil so they might grow fruit trees and exotic flowers. Now it was hedged with rampant brambles. She could be happy here, certainly, with a view across the Atlantic and Jack close at hand. Not too many people either, unlike teeming London. On the other hand, could she bear to be parted from Miranda? Her friend was sometimes tetchy and domineering, but she was also clever and quirky and brave. The journey they had undertaken together had forged a connection between them, a friendship without pretence. They were two oddballs, yet with Miranda she felt entirely at home. Even now, being nagged, she smiled.

'Oh Miranda,' she said. 'Give me space to think!'

'Why do you need to think? You have to come with us.'

They picked their way through the garden. Around the back of the house, the first buds of blossom were unfurling on the apple trees. With a sigh of exasperation, Miranda sat down on a broken wall, as Jacinth dreamily meandered among the trees. It was so peaceful here, only the wistful song of a robin and the faraway sound of the sea. But a sudden movement in the brambles disturbed her. What was it? A narrow red muzzle emerged from a tunnel in the tough, thorny tendrils. Ears alert, nose savouring the air, a gaunt old dog fox stepped from the depths of the bush and stood before Jacinth. He was suspicious, his body tensed to flee, but he waited for a moment, to see what she would do. Slowly, slowly, holding her breath, Jacinth sank to her knees, making herself small. The dog fox, with his scarred, grizzled face, looked at her for a moment and then stepped closer. Jacinth raised her hand, and the fox sniffed it politely. She could smell him too, the sour, burned scent of fox. He was an old warrior, this one, solitary and wise. She didn't hold his interest for long. He turned away, cocked a leg and sprayed the brambles close by, and then vanished into the bramble tunnel from which he had emerged.

Jacinth laughed. She lifted her head so the sun shone on her face. She rose to her feet and looked across the garden to where Miranda was sitting on the wall. She walked towards her.

'Did you see that?' Jacinth said.

Miranda nodded slowly. 'It was amazing,' she said. 'How did you do it?'

Jacinth shrugged and laughed again. 'I've no idea,' she said. 'It has happened before, when I was younger. In the tower wild animals came to me. Foxes, deer. Even a bear once. But I thought it was part of my gift.'

'No,' said Miranda. 'It wasn't your gift at all. That bit was you, Jacinth. It's who you are.'

They were walking back to the farm when Jacinth finally made up her mind. She cleared her throat nervously, before she said: 'Miranda I'm going to stay in Ireland.'

Miranda stopped walking. Her mouth opened and shut. 'Why?' she said.

Jacinth sighed. 'It feels like home,' she said. 'It's peaceful and beautiful, and Maslin has become like a father to me now. And I need a father.'

Miranda looked disappointed, and she scowled.

'Don't you need a sister too? Anyway, Maslin's going to Prague.'

'He'll only be a couple of weeks. I'll stay with the Elliotts till he gets back, and then I'll help him plan the house, and plant his garden, and I'll make this my home. I can't go to London, Miranda. Too many people.'

'And you'll come back to see me, won't you? I'll write to you,' Jacinth said.

Miranda stepped towards her, and Jacinth realised she was crying too. The girls put their arms around each other.

'Don't forget me,' Miranda said fiercely.

Miranda and her father left in the afternoon. Jack was driving them into town in the pony trap. Maslin came out to say goodbye.

'Once the house is rebuilt, you will always be welcome here,' the old man said, giving her a hug. 'Bring your mother, Miranda. It would do her good – the sea air.'

She and Jacinth had already said their farewells, and Jacinth was inside the house, unwilling to watch Miranda ride away. Maslin and David embraced.

The town was an hour's drive away. Miranda and Jack sat in awkward silence. She sensed he wanted to talk with her, but for once she didn't know what to say, how to start the conversation. David fell asleep, his head tipped on his shoulder. Miranda stared at the horse in front of them, and Jack's strong, clever hands on the reins. Whenever she thought of something to say to him, her mouth seemed to dry up. It was annoying! Why was he getting to her like this? He was only an ignorant farm boy. As if he sensed her thoughts, Jack glanced across with a smile.

'What's on your mind?' he said.

'Nothing. Well, going home. Seeing my mother.'

'Really? And there was me thinking you were wondering how you would be managing without me.' His voice was gently teasing, and Miranda scowled.

'Don't be ridiculous.' Her voice was sharp. They drove on in silence for another ten minutes, before Jack said quietly:

'Well I shall miss you.'

Miranda's face burned. She pressed her lips together.

'No you won't,' she said.

Jack smiled. 'Yes I will. You're a pain in the neck, but I shall miss you. I hope you'll be coming back one day.'

Miranda sighed. She looked away from Jack to the rocky landscape, punctuated with stunted trees.

'Of course I'll come back,' she said. 'I have to see Jacinth.' Then, more gently: 'How do you feel now, about what happened with Edmund?'

Jack considered. 'It's something I shall have to get used to,' he said. 'It's not like I could be undoing it.' He fastened his eyes on the horizon.

'Do you regret it?' she persisted.

Jack sighed. 'No,' he said. 'It was Edmund or Jacinth. He would have killed her – and you too. I wish I hadn't had to do it. But that was the situation and I made a choice.'

'You made the right choice,' she said.

He dropped them at the railway station. As David negotiated at the little ticket office, Jack said:

'I'll be saying goodbye, then.'

They stood for a moment or two, and Miranda understood he wanted to embrace her. She stepped from one foot to another, studiously avoiding eye contact. One part of her yearned to be embraced – but another, larger part recoiled from the idea. It was too much – too embarrassing. She felt a forest of psychic prickles stand on end all over her body to ward him off. Clearly Jack sensed her, like a hedgehog, warning him to draw no closer. And in any case, David returned to them.

'Goodbye,' Jack said. 'Have a safe journey.'

'Goodbye, Jack,' said David, shaking his hand. 'Thanks for everything.'

And then Jack was off. Miranda watched him weaving through the crowd and back to the trap. He untied the reins, turned the pony away down the main road, and was lost among the traffic.

The hansom cab wove through the London streets from the heart of the old city, from the black river, the docks and the accumulated centuries of stone. It rumbled over cobbled, airless soil. The evening was light, spring stretching out the days and bringing a promise of warmth. In the city gardens, daffodils bloomed and fragile blossom opened on the trees.

The cab pulled up outside the Hospital of Our Lady of Sorrows. A man, a woman and a girl stepped out.

'This is the place,' Aunt Mary said.

David took Miranda's hand.

'Are you nervous?' he said.

Miranda shook her head. 'No.' Then she looked up at him. 'Actually, yes. I am nervous. What if she isn't better?'

They were admitted through a tall wooden door into the hospital and Mary gave her name. The building's religious past was evident. A stone cross adorned the wall, and the nurses even dressed a little like nuns. They were escorted by one nun-nurse to a plainly furnished living room and told to wait. Distantly Miranda heard someone crying and wailing. She interlocked her fingers and squeezed her hands hard.

'Miranda?' A gaunt woman in a long, white gown stood in the doorway, a nurse beside her.

For a moment nobody moved. Miranda and her father stared. Julia's long, black hair was thin and dull. Her pale face was hollow, her forehead etched with lines. She stretched out bony hands.

'Miranda?' she repeated, stepping into the room.

'Mother?' Miranda whispered. 'Are you – are you better?' Slowly she walked towards her, searching her face. There were no signs of madness, no distracted glances or compulsive tugging of hair. Julia swept up her daughter in her arms and held her tight.

'Yes,' she whispered. 'Yes, I'm well again. And I'll never let you down again, Miranda, never. I am so sorry.'

Miranda drew back so she was face to face with her mother, their noses touching. 'You didn't let me down,' she said. 'It wasn't your fault. I'm just so glad you're better – so glad!'

Suddenly Julia's body stiffened. Her eyes fixed on David at the back of the room. She released Miranda and stood up straight. They stared at each other, Julia and her long-dead husband. Except, of course, that he wasn't dead. Perhaps Julia didn't trust her senses, and feared this was another delusion. She would see how much he had altered, how weathered and aged he was by the heat and the desert and the lost years. Julia's lips moved nervously.

303

'Julia,' David said. Her face wrinkled, and she wrung her hands. 'Julia, it's me,' he said. 'It's David. I've come back.'

Julia's eyes widened. She made a sound like a sob, and put her hand over her mouth. David stepped towards her, and enveloped her in his arms.

Mary signed the release papers. Together they climbed into the waiting cab outside the hospital and made their way through the darkening streets towards the suburbs. They exchanged a few quiet words as they travelled, Julia leaning against David, and clinging to her daughter's hand. At last the cab drew up outside a villa with a powder blue door and a fanlight bordered with red stained glass. The name, carved on the stone gatepost, was Avondale.

'They have no idea we're coming?' Mary's voice was gleeful.

'None,' David said.

Mary paid the cab driver as David walked ahead of them up the garden path and knocked on the front door. Miranda couldn't see what happened, but she heard a gasp from the housekeeper when the door opened, frantic voices calling, and then cries from Eliza and John Kingsley as they saw their lost son's face for the first time in more than three years. He had come home.

Epilogue

North Africa 1891

Halls of stone. Endless days in the desert's furnace, long nights of aching cold.

The journey is almost over. The knot has been untied.

My crime can not be undone, but it has been redeemed. I sense the angel moving over the face of the Earth, searching for me. There is a connection between us. It will never be what it once was. Whole again, the angel is tainted with the knowledge of violence and pain – though it has been touched, also, by love and sacrifice. I lie in the desert at night and gaze at the stars, waiting.

Then it comes, descending from the heavens like a huge, ivory bird. Its eyes burn bright white, its wings curl around its back and it stoops over me as I lie, so much tired, broken human rubbish among the rocks and the stones.

Death is its gift. Slowly my thoughts unwind and drift apart. Blissful oblivion washes over me. The desert and the stars disappear. I dissipate and dissolve, finding peace, and I am, at last –

– nothing.

The First Knights of the Order of the Lily

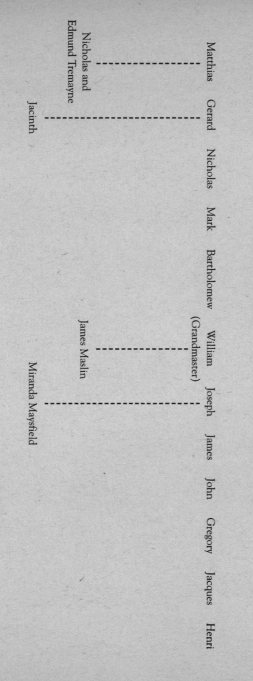

Matthias   Gerard   Nicholas   Mark   Bartholomew   William   Joseph   James   John   Gregory   Jacques   Henri

(Grandmaster)

Nicholas and
Edmund Tremayne

Jacinth

James Maslin

Miranda Maysfield

The Maslins

William Maslin – First Grandmaster of the Order of the Lily
(b. 1150, d.1241)

Stephen Maslin – Last Grandmaster of the Order of the Lily
(b. 1430, d.1481 – executed)

George Maslin ——————— Jacob Maslin (hid the lily and
(b. 1720, d. 1755)   kept the location secret)
half-brother of Jacob   (b. 1725, d. 1795)

George Maslin (built the house in Ireland in 1796
(b. 1760, d.1812)

Rachel Flynn m. Felix Maslin
(b. 1789, d. 1826   (b. 1785, d. 1818
of a fever in an asylum)   in a riding accident)

James Maslin
(b. 1810 ——)

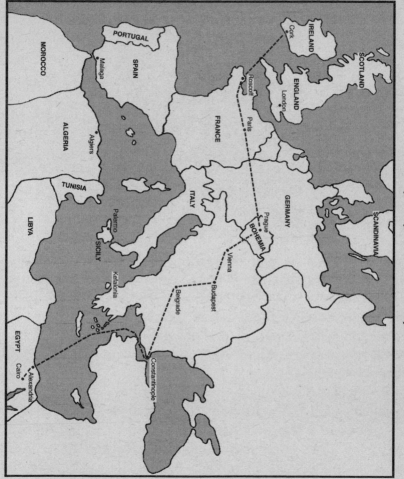

Maslin's journey in search of the lily

CENTURY BY SARAH SINGLETON

Mercy and her sister Charity live in a twilight world, going to bed just as the sun rises. Their house remains shrouded in perpetual winter, each day unfolding exactly the same as the last. Mercy has never questioned her widowed father about the way they live, until one day she wakes to find a snowdrop on her pillow: a first sign of spring – and a nod towards a new future.

A meeting with the mysterious Claudius unsettles Mercy and starts her on a winding path through the family's history, unearthing clues about her mother's death and their house frozen in time. But as each piece of the past slots into place, the world Mercy has known begins to unravel… Can she discover the truth without destroying her home, her father and all she has ever known?

ISBN-13: 9781416901358
ISBN-10: 1416901353

HERETIC BY SARAH SINGLETON

When Elizabeth finds a green-tinged creature in the woods she's amazed to discover that it's actually a girl of her own age. Isabella has spent the last 300 years deep in the faery world, hiding from persecutors who accused her of being the daughter of a witch.

But Elizabeth has her own persecutors to face. A Catholic priest is hiding with her family – an act of treason in 1585 – and the net is closing in. As they become friends, Elizabeth and Isabella must find a way to save the family from being torn apart…

ISBN-13: 9781416904038
ISBN-10: 1416904034